Gaslight Mysteries by Victoria Thompson

MURDER ON GRAMERCY PARK

Victoria Thompson

BERKLEY PRIME CRIME, NEW YORK

THE BERKLEY PUBLISHING GROUP
Published by the Penguin Group
Penguin Group (USA) Inc.
375 Hudson Street, New York, New York 10014, USA
Penguin Group (Canada), 90 Eglinton Avenue East, Suite 700, Toronto, Ontario M4P 2Y3, Canada
(a division of Pearson Penguin Canada Inc.)
Penguin Books Ltd., 80 Strand, London WC2R 0RL, England
Penguin Group Ireland, 25 St. Stephen's Green, Dublin 2, Ireland (a division of Penguin Books Ltd.)
Penguin Group (Australia), 250 Camberwell Road, Camberwell, Victoria 3124, Australia
(a division of Pearson Australia Group Pty. Ltd.)
Penguin Books India Pvt. Ltd., 11 Community Centre, Panchsheel Park, New Delhi—110 017, India
Penguin Group (NZ), 67 Apollo Drive, Rosedale, North Shore 0632, New Zealand
(a division of Pearson New Zealand Ltd.)
Penguin Books (South Africa) (Pty.) Ltd., 24 Sturdee Avenue, Rosebank, Johannesburg 2196,
South Africa

Penguin Books Ltd., Registered Offices: 80 Strand, London WC2R 0RL, England

This is a work of fiction. Names, characters, places, and incidents either are the product of the author's imagination or are used fictitiously, and any resemblance to actual persons, living or dead, business establishments, events, or locales is entirely coincidental. The publisher does not have any control over and does not assume any responsibility for author or third-party websites or their content.

MURDER ON GRAMERCY PARK

A Berkley Prime Crime Book / published by arrangement with Cornerstone Communications, Inc.

PRINTING HISTORY
Berkley Prime Crime mass-market edition / March 2001

ISBN: 978-0-425-17886-7

BERKLEY® PRIME CRIME
Berkley Prime Crime Books are published by The Berkley Publishing Group,
a division of Penguin Group (USA) Inc.,
375 Hudson Street, New York, New York 10014.
The name BERKLEY PRIME CRIME and the BERKLEY PRIME CRIME design
are trademarks belonging to Penguin Group (USA) Inc.

PRINTED IN THE UNITED STATES OF AMERICA

20   19   18   17   16   15   14   13   12   11

DEDICATION

With thanks to Julie and Georgia and all the members of the Vicious Circle, past and future, for helping me keep my head on straight, my feet on the ground, and my sanity intact (not to mention all the plotting, character analysis, and general advice you've provided through the years). Couldn't have made it without you!

PROLOGUE

She thought of the pain as a monster that dwelled inside of her. For long periods of time it slept, and then slowly it would begin to stir. It started with a dull ache as the beast came awake. Then it grew and grew as the monster dug his talons into her neck, squeezing and squeezing, the pain a living, breathing thing that consumed her, obliterating thought and light and even the air she breathed.

She welcomed the monster, greeted him like a beloved friend, because he gave her the only proof that she was still alive. For a few blissful moments, from the time the monster stirred until the pain became so great she had to cry out, she was awake and aware and alive, almost the way she'd been before.

She gritted her teeth, holding back the moan of agony that came rumbling up from the depths of her soul, stretching out those moments as long as she possibly could. Opening her eyes to see sunlight or lamplight or a human face. Drinking in every vision with the clarity only those who were denied even the most basic pleasures of life could experience.

But sooner or later the moan or the scream or the sigh

would escape, and they would know. Those who loved her. Those who could not bear to see her in pain. They would press the glass to her lips and force her to drink the bitter draft, the magic potion that would put the monster to sleep again. For a few more seconds she would revel in the beast's assault, counting each precious one of them until she felt the talons loosening their grip, slowly, slowly, ever so slowly, one by one by one, until the pain was gone and the monster slept again beneath the golden haze of the drug.

For long months she lay like this, watching each of the seasons pass by the window beside her bed. She had given up hope of ever tasting the outside air again, of ever walking down a gravel path or sitting a saddle or dancing a waltz or feeling the embrace of a lover. She had thought she would lie here forever, until at last the beast devoured her.

And then *he* came.

He was the only one who would put his hands on her. The only one who dared. He knew the name of the beast, and he put his hands on her and strangled it, choking it and killing it, and setting her free. Only one man could do that, one man in all the world.

Edmund Blackwell.

I

FRANK MALLOY FIGURED SOMEONE AT POLICE Headquarters must be mad at him. Why else would they send him out to investigate a suicide? Any drunken moron in the Detective Bureau could have handled this, and God knew, there were plenty of them to spare.

Of course, as soon as he'd heard the address, he knew why he'd been chosen. Gramercy Park. Some rich swell had blown his brains out, and the family would want the matter settled quietly. Frank knew how to handle the boys from Newspaper Row. He'd done it often enough. Give them just enough to keep them happy but not enough to cause the family any hardship. No hint of scandal could escape, and Frank could be trusted to be discreet.

As he approached the house, he glanced at the park surrounded by the high, gated fence that only residents of the streets around it could enter. The small patch of carefully tended grass and shrubbery would look like heaven to the urchins living on the Lower East Side who never saw anything green except rot. Here the swells had a fence to keep even their own kind from trampling on it.

When he checked the address, Frank realized with a start that he knew the house. He'd been there several months before, when the previous occupant had been found murdered. Found by Sarah Brandt, a lady of Frank's acquaintance. That's how his mother might have explained her, if his mother could have been forced to speak of her at all. Well, at least he didn't have to worry about Sarah Brandt getting involved in this case the way she had on previous ones. This wasn't really a case anyway. He was just here to tie up a few loose ends and see the body taken quietly away.

The beat cop stood guard at the front steps. He nodded at Frank and touched his round hat in a gesture of respect.

"What's going on here, Patrick?" Frank asked.

"The man what lives here shot hisself in the head. His poor wife found him, and she's in a state." He leaned closer, so that Frank could smell the whiskey on his breath, and added in a whisper, "She's breeding, too."

Frank managed not to flinch. "Breeding?"

"About to drop it right on the floor any minute, too, if you ask me," Officer Patrick offered, his round head nodding knowingly.

"Nobody asked you," Frank reminded him. "What's the dead fellow's name?"

"Edmund Blackwell. He's some kind of doctor."

Perfect. A pregnant woman about to give birth and a dead doctor.

Frank forced himself to mount the front steps, ruthlessly suppressing the visions of his own wife in her dying moments, her blood soaking the mattress beneath her as it ran unchecked from her body. This woman wasn't Kathleen. He had to remind himself of that twice before he could open the front door.

Inside, another beat cop was doing his best to keep several servants from entering the room to the left of the entrance hall. Frank figured this was probably the room the dead man had chosen for his own execution. The officer was visibly relieved to see Frank, who drew the servants' attention at once.

The tallest one, a man of middle years who held himself with an unmistakable air of authority, marched over to him. "Are you in charge here?" he demanded.

"Until Commissioner Roosevelt shows up," Frank replied sarcastically, referring to the infamous head of the New York City Police Department. Since the commissioner came from the monied upper class of the city and had managed to alienate practically everyone in that city with his puritanical reforms and his insistence on honesty in the police department, Roosevelt's was the one name certain to annoy if not frighten this snobby butler.

The butler stiffened but did not back down. "I must insist that you allow me to summon Mr. Potter. He is Dr. Blackwell's assistant. He will know what to do."

Frank gave him the grin that made hardened criminals sweat. "What makes you think I don't know what to do?"

A flush crawled up the man's neck, but to his credit, he held his ground. "I was referring to Mrs. Blackwell, sir. She came home earlier than expected today, and she was the one who found Dr. Blackwell. I should have been the one to—" His voice broke and his face lost a bit of its stiffness for a moment before he recalled his dignity again. "She is . . . very upset, and in her delicate condition . . ."

From the depths of the house, Frank could detect a pitiful moaning sound. He felt the cold sweat breaking out on his body, but he refused to so much as bat an eye. "You'd better send for a doctor, then."

The butler frowned his disapproval. "Dr. Blackwell doesn't hold with medical practitioners."

Frank pushed his hat back and stared up at the man. "Didn't you just say he was a doctor himself?"

The butler drew himself up defensively. "Dr. Blackwell is a healer," he explained with the utmost courtesy and unconsciously using the present tense. "A magnetic healer. He does not trust conventional medicine."

Who did? Frank wanted to ask, but he managed to restrain himself. For a second he was at a loss. A pregnant woman, obviously in labor or about to be from the shock of discovering her husband's brains spilled out on her carpet, and they wouldn't let him call a doctor. The irony was so great, he almost smiled. So much for his certainty that Sarah Brandt wouldn't be involved in this case.

Frank reached into his coat pocket and found his notebook and a pencil. He scribbled the Bank Street address on one of the pages and tore it out. He thrust it at the butler. "Send someone to this address and ask for Mrs. Brandt. She's a midwife."

The butler looked at the paper as if it were a snake.

The woman moaned again, and Frank's patience evaporated. "Who was supposed to help her if Dr. Blackwell doesn't believe in doctors?"

"He . . . he was going to deliver the child himself, I believe," the butler admitted.

Frank gave him another of his famous, bone-chilling glares. "Well, that's out of the question now, isn't it? So unless you want to leave her to the mercies of her maid—"

The butler snatched the paper from Frank's outstretched fingers and turned on his heel, summoning someone from the depths of the house.

Frank sighed. Sarah would find this very amusing. She'd probably never let him hear the end of it either. Well, at least this wasn't a murder case. If he let her help him with one more murder case, he'd never be able to show his face down at Police Headquarters again.

Sending the rest of the servants scurrying away with another of his glares, he turned to the officer guarding the door. "Let's see what we've got, Mahoney."

SARAH WASN'T SURPRISED to see an agitated young man at her front door. As a midwife, she frequently saw agitated men, young, old, and in between, who had been sent to summon her to an impending birth. This fellow looked unusually agitated, however, and his uniform marked him as the servant of a wealthy household. The instant she opened the door, he began to speak.

"Mrs. Brandt, you're needed right away. Mrs. Blackwell, she's in a bad way, and the policeman says for you to come at once." He spoke as if he'd been practicing the words all the way over from wherever he'd come.

"The policeman?" she asked, not quite believing she'd heard him correctly.

"Yes, ma'am. Dr. Blackwell, he's . . . well, he's dead, it seems like, and the police come, and when he found out Mrs. Blackwell was . . . well, he give me your address and told me to fetch you quick as I could."

"Was this policeman a detective sergeant?" she asked, managing to keep her expression suitably grave. She didn't want the boy to see her smiling smugly when he'd just told her someone was dead.

"I don't rightly know, ma'am. He's a big Irishman, and he said for you to come. Mrs. Blackwell, she needs you right now."

Many policemen could be called "big Irishmen," but only one of them was likely to have thought of summoning Sarah Brandt to the scene of a crime. "Of course," she said. "Just give me a moment to gather my things."

She left the young man on her front stoop as she went back into the house to change her clothes and get her medical bag. She changed quickly, with practiced ease, and she couldn't help thinking how it must have galled Malloy to send for her. Someone dead and the police called must mean another murder. He wouldn't want her involved in a murder, so he must be desperate indeed. A woman about to deliver a baby would have affected him that way, she assumed, considering how his wife had died.

Sarah must try to hide her satisfaction at his summons

and the surge of anticipation she felt at being involved in another murder investigation, however slightly. If she acted too delighted at being included, Malloy might be provoked into sending her from the house, impending birth or not.

When she stepped outside into the early autumn afternoon, she saw the young man was on the driver's seat of a carriage he had obviously brought to convey her. He hopped nimbly down to open the door for her.

"Where are we going?" she asked.

"Gramercy Park, ma'am."

She considered for only a moment. "I'll walk, then. It will take over an hour to drive there from here, and only a quarter of an hour on foot."

"But Mr. Granger said to fetch you in the carriage," the boy argued, alarmed by her refusal.

"Who's Mr. Granger?"

"The head butler, ma'am," the boy explained.

"Don't worry, I'll tell him I refused your offer and insisted on walking. If Mrs. Blackwell is really having her baby, it's important that I get there as quickly as possible. When Mr. Granger sees how long it takes for the carriage to get back, I'm sure he'll see reason."

His eyes widened with near panic. "Please, ma'am. You don't want to be carrying that heavy bag all the way uptown. At least let me take it for you."

"But I'll need my bag as soon as I get there. I promise it will be all right," Sarah said. "You won't get in any trouble."

The boy's face was a mask of despair, but he plainly had no choice. "I'd go with you, but I can't leave the carriage," he said.

"Of course not. I'll see you at the house. What is the address?"

When he gave it to her, she recognized it instantly. She'd known the previous occupant slightly. The house had an unhappy history, and it seemed as if the Blackwell family had just added to it.

Reluctantly, the boy climbed up onto the carriage seat and slapped his horses into motion. They slowly made their way into the crush of traffic.

Sarah took note of the carriage. It wasn't new, by any means, but had been refurbished quite expertly. She thought the gold leaf designs on the doors a bit much, however. New money, her mother would have scoffed. The team wasn't matched but seemed well cared for, a rarity in the heat of the city. Keeping a carriage and team of any kind here was expensive. Her new clients must have money, new or not. But she'd already guessed that from the Gramercy Park address.

Sarah set out at a brisk pace. Years of walking the city streets at all hours, hurrying to arrive before a baby did, had made her strong. And she'd been right about walking being the quickest way to get where she was going. The distance from her home on Bank Street to Gramercy Park was less than a mile, but a carriage would have to maneuver through streets choked with vehicles of every description, fighting for the right of way at every intersection. The boldest—or the most foolhardy—soul was the one who got through first, and no one gave way for anyone else voluntarily.

The only way to travel quickly through the city was on the elevated railway, but that only went north and south. Rumor said the city fathers were considering an underground railway that would take people all over the city. Sarah could hardly credit such a thing. If they dug tunnels beneath the streets, what would keep the streets from collapsing? For an instant she pictured the entire city sinking into a gigantic hole.

Banishing that disturbing thought, she realized she'd forgotten to ask the young man how her patient's husband had died. He must have died violently, or Frank Malloy would not have been involved.

Did the boy say the dead man was a doctor? Sarah thought the name was familiar, but she couldn't recall meeting a Dr. Blackwell. Someone new in town, perhaps. Or maybe he wasn't really a medical doctor. Many people called themselves "doctor" without any credentials at all.

Well, she'd find out soon enough, she thought as she darted between carriages and wagons and carts all stopped at the intersection of Bank and Hudson and Eighth Avenue, their drivers screaming curses at each other as they fought for the right of way.

"I ALREADY TOLD that other officer everything I know," the butler informed Frank, who'd summoned him to the front parlor to question him.

"Then it'll be fresh in your mind, won't it?" Frank said amiably. He was sitting in a comfortable chair, and he let the butler remain standing. "Your name is Granger?"

"That's right."

"Where were you this afternoon?"

"I was visiting my mother. She's quite elderly, and I visit her every Wednesday afternoon. That is my customary afternoon off."

"Are all the servants off on Wednesday?"

"Yes."

Frank noticed he wasn't saying "sir," but he chose to ignore the man's subtle insult. He was already uncooperative enough, and Frank had other ways of humbling him if he needed to. "Do the servants always leave the house on their afternoon off?"

"Usually, although sometimes one will stay. Today, however, Dr. Blackwell ordered me to make sure all the servants were out."

"And why was that?"

Granger straightened even more, although Frank would have thought that impossible. "He said he had an appointment, and he wanted to be sure no one else was in the house."

"Do you know who his appointment was with?"

"He did not confide in me."

Frank had no patience with this. "You're a good butler, aren't you, Granger?"

Granger seemed insulted by the question. "I pride myself in that."

"If you *are* a good butler, then, you must have known, or at least suspected, who he was seeing today."

The observation placated him somewhat. "Ordinarily, that would be true, but Dr. Blackwell was very mysterious about this meeting. He did not confide in anyone."

"And you're sure no one else was in the house?"

"You can question the other servants, but I'm certain they were all out. They understood this was Dr. Blackwell's wish. I made that very clear, and I remained until they had all gone," he added.

Frank was sure he had. "Was anyone else here when Mrs. Blackwell came home and found her husband?"

"Not that I am aware. I arrived shortly afterward. As I told you, she is usually gone much longer than she was today, and I try to arrive back before she does, in case she needs anything when she arrives."

"Where does Mrs. Blackwell go?"

Granger plainly thought this was none of Frank's business. "She visits the sick."

"What sick does she visit?"

"You will have to ask her that. I'm sure I don't know."

Frank figured he probably knew perfectly well, but he was going to make Frank work for the information. "Did you see the gun on the desk beside Dr. Blackwell?"

"Yes, I did."

"Have you ever seen it before?"

"Dr. Blackwell has a similar pistol. He keeps it in his right-hand desk drawer. It appeared to be the same one, but I couldn't be sure without examining it more closely and checking the drawer to see if it's missing."

"Don't trouble yourself, Granger, I'll do that," Frank said. He didn't like this butler, but then, he seldom liked butlers. They were all uppity and thought they were better than common policemen. "Did anyone else know Blackwell kept a pistol in his desk?"

"I'm sure everyone in the household did. I had warned them so they wouldn't come upon it by accident when they were cleaning."

"They clean inside the doctor's private desk drawers?" Frank asked mildly.

Granger pretended he didn't hear the question.

"So everyone on the staff knew about it," Frank continued. "What about visitors to the house?"

"I'm afraid I wouldn't know that. You would have to ask them."

"Did he have a lot of visitors?"

"Yes, he did."

Frank was beginning to feel the urge to commit a murder himself. "Who visited him?"

"His patients frequently came to consult with him."

"Thank you for your kind cooperation, Granger," he said, his sarcasm wasted. "If I need anything else, I'll be sure to let you know."

Granger did not look happy at that prospect.

Soon ENOUGH, SARAH arrived at the relative tranquillity of Gramercy Park. Traffic avoided the square, no street vendors hawked their wares here, and no streetcars clattered past. Residents of the Lower East Side who lived five to a room in squalor would probably imagine that such stately homes could house only happiness. Sarah knew better.

A policeman guarded the front door. He'd been slouching in the shade until he realized she was going to try to enter. He straightened, trying to look official.

"I'm Mrs. Brandt, the midwife," she said.

He visibly relaxed. "We've been looking for you, missus," he said, then glanced around. "Where's the carriage?"

"Still in traffic, I would imagine," she replied, climbing the front steps.

He pushed open the front door and stood aside for her to enter. "The midwife's here," he called to anyone inside.

Sarah knew a moment of reluctance when she remembered the last and only time she'd entered this house. Death had visited here again, but this time she wouldn't be the one to discover it.

She was surprised to see how much the place had changed in a few short months. Plainly, the new residents were anxious for people to recognize that they were comfortably fixed. The decor was lavish, bordering on ostentatious, with brocade wall coverings and heavy velvet drapes and Oriental carpets. She saw an elephant's-foot umbrella stand in the corner by the front door, and an enormous Oriental vase stood by the stairs to the second floor.

She glanced into the room to the right, where she'd found that other body, and almost expected to see it still lying there. But the room was entirely different now, and nothing untoward lay on the expensive Oriental carpet. Another policeman stood by the door to her left, the room where she guessed the new murder had been committed. The door behind him opened, and Malloy stepped out.

Sarah felt the odd sense of pleasure she always experienced upon seeing him, no matter how intimidating he might look. He certainly looked very intimidating at the moment, probably because he was so unhappy to have had to call for her.

"Mrs. Brandt," he said gruffly, by way of greeting. "I see you got my message."

"I'm glad I was available," she replied, equally formal. She glanced around. "This house has a sad history."

"It does," he agreed.

They were both conscious of the others listening to their every word. Sarah longed to ask him what had happened here, but that would have to wait.

"My patient?" she asked.

"She's upstairs. She was the one who found her husband. Looks like he committed suicide. She was pretty upset, and considering her condition . . ."

Sarah nodded her understanding, knowing she shouldn't be disappointed to learn Malloy wasn't investigating a murder. Her own life was exciting enough without sticking her nose into someone else's trouble. She'd already put herself in danger too many times from trying to assist Malloy in his business.

A butler had materialized from somewhere. "Mrs. Blackwell is upstairs in her room," he informed Sarah. "I will escort you."

Then the butler took her bag, and she glanced at Malloy, who nodded his approval. She gave him a look that warned him she'd want some more details later, then followed the butler upstairs.

"Mrs. Blackwell came home earlier than usual," the butler said gravely. "Ordinarily, I would have been here before her. I should have been the one to find him. If any harm comes to her because of that . . ." He caught himself and said no more.

Although he was managing to maintain his dignity, Sarah could see the man blamed himself for Mrs. Blackwell's horrible experience and was enduring the guilt of having caused her so much distress.

"You couldn't have known," she reassured him. "And although this is very tragic, it probably won't harm either mother or child if the baby was ready to be born anyway. It's really no one's fault."

The butler didn't look convinced. Sarah felt genuine pity for him and great respect for his devotion to his mistress.

Mrs. Blackwell's maid admitted her to a large bedroom furnished in white, French-style furniture. The walls were covered in paper that depicted a bucolic scene in the French countryside over and over again all around the room, and the windows were draped in a heavy, floral-patterned material that hung bunched on the floor in a style designed to show the occupant had money to buy fabric that wasn't even necessary.

The enormous four-poster bed sat high off the floor, and Sarah had to walk over closer to even see the occupant. Mrs. Blackwell was an attractive young woman, probably in her early twenties. She lay with her eyes closed, moaning softly, her face damp with perspiration, even though the room was comfortably cool.

"Mrs. Blackwell?" Sarah said softly, waiting until the woman opened her eyes. "I'm Sarah Brandt. I'm a midwife." Sarah was already rolling up her sleeves and assessing the situation.

"Does Edmund know you're here?" she asked in alarm. Her face was pale and her lovely blue eyes were dilated. Sarah realized she might well be in shock from discovering her husband's body.

"Yes," Sarah lied without regret. "He sent for me. He wants to make sure you're well cared for."

She seemed doubtful, but she didn't argue and even seemed to relax a bit. Sarah turned to the maid and began giving her instructions on what she was going to need.

Malloy WENT BACK into Blackwell's study swearing softly under his breath. He'd thought he was safe involving Sarah Brandt in this case. Clearly, Blackwell had shot himself, or so someone had taken great pains to make it appear. If Police Headquarters had sent someone else, perhaps that would have been the official report, too. Unfortunately, they'd sent Frank, and he'd discovered the truth.

He heard the front door open again, and this time Officer Patrick announced the medical examiner.

A moment later Dr. Haynes stepped into the study, a small room with heavily draped windows in which the smell of death was strong.

Dr. Haynes was a small man, well past middle age, who had seen too many dead bodies in his life. His eyes were sad behind his spectacles, and his clothes hung on him, as if he'd shrunk beneath them.

"A suicide, Malloy?" he said hopefully, assessing the situation at a glance.

"That's what it looks like from here, but I'm afraid it ain't going to be that easy."

Haynes frowned. "The neighbors won't like it. Another murder in this house. Are you sure?"

"Tell me what you think," Malloy invited.

The dead man had been sitting at his desk and was now slumped over it, his head a blasted wreck, his blood and brains spilling over the desktop and onto the floor. A pistol lay beside his right hand.

"Is that his gun?" Haynes asked.

"The butler says he had one just like it that he kept in his desk drawer there." He pointed. "It's not there now."

Haynes gave him an impatient glance. "Looks like a suicide to me, and it would to anybody else, too," he insisted.

"Look again." Malloy pointed to the piece of paper lying on the desk, beneath the blood and gore.

"A suicide note?"

"I doubt it." It wasn't possible to read all the words, but one thing was clear. "See there?"

He pointed at the last word on the page. It was just one letter that ended in a long, jagged line and a blotch, as if the writer had been startled or jarred, and the pen had fallen and made a blotch. "See the ink on his fingers? He was sitting here writing, and something surprised him. A man doesn't shoot himself in the head while he's in the middle of writing a letter, and if he does, he usually finishes it first. And even if he doesn't, he wouldn't surprise himself, would he?"

"Maybe somebody in the house startled him."

"He was alone in the house. It's Wednesday afternoon. The servants had the afternoon off, and he made sure they were all out. Told the butler he had a meeting with someone, and he didn't want to be interrupted."

"Who was he meeting?"

"Nobody knows. I don't like where the pistol is laying, either. It's all very neat, but a little far from his hand. If he'd dropped it, it might be anywhere, and if he didn't drop it, it would be in his grasp. Instead, it's right there, close to his hand, and placed just so, as if the killer wanted it to be there but couldn't bear to touch Blackwell to put the gun in his hand."

"Or didn't want to get all bloody."

"He risked it by moving the pen," Malloy said. "Remember I said Blackwell was writing when he was shot? The killer put the pen back in the holder after he shot Blackwell. It's got blood on it."

"Maybe it got splashed when this poor fellow's head went flying all over the room," Haynes suggested.

"The blood is on the wrong side of the pen for that. And it's a little smeared." He showed Haynes what he meant.

"Looks like the mark of a finger in the blood, too." Haynes sighed. "Frank, why can't you just go along? You know nobody wants this to be a murder."

"They'd rather let a killer go free, I guess," Frank said. "What if somebody snuck in here to rob the place and found Blackwell and got scared and killed him? The neighbors should be worried about that."

"If that's what happened, the killer wouldn't have gone to so much trouble to make it look like a suicide," Haynes pointed out.

"So you agree with me? It's a murder."

Haynes sighed again. "Frank—" he began, but he was interrupted by a commotion in the hallway.

The door to the study burst open and a man burst in. He was short and round and balding, with muttonchop whiskers, his face red with outrage. "What's going on here?" he demanded, and then he saw the body. "Edmund!" he cried. "My God, what happened?"

"Who are you?" Frank demanded as Mahoney made a belated effort to restrain the gentleman.

"What have you done to him?" the man was shouting.

"We haven't done nothing to him, yet," Malloy said, stepping in front of the man to block his view of the body. "Who are you?" he asked again.

"What?" the fellow asked, still looking with horror at the body.

"Your name?" Frank prodded. "And your reason for being here."

At last he looked at Frank and seemed to recover himself. "Oh, yes, of course. My name is Potter. Amos Potter. I'm Dr. Blackwell's assistant." He glanced at the body again. His face had visibly paled.

"Let's go sit down someplace, Mr. Potter," Frank suggested gently, and took him by the arm.

He offered no resistance as Frank led him from the room.

"I tried to stop him," Mahoney offered as he closed the office door behind them, but Frank just glared at him. He'd settle with him later.

"Have a seat, Mr. Potter," Frank said when they'd reached the formal parlor across the hall. Frank pulled the doors shut behind him.

Potter sank down gratefully onto the ornately carved sofa and pulled a handkerchief from his pocket to wipe his face. "Good heavens. How horrible." Then he seemed to remember something. "Mrs. Blackwell will be coming home from her visits soon. She ministers to the poor every afternoon, you know, and she should return any moment. She's in a . . . a delicate condition. The sight of all these policemen will frighten her. Her health is very fragile, and the shock—"

"Mrs. Blackwell is already here," Malloy interrupted him. "She was the one who found her husband's body."

Malloy had only thought Potter was pale before. Now even his lips lost their color. "Good heavens," he said again. "She . . . I must go to her. She must be hysterical." He started struggling to his feet.

"There's no need. Mrs. Blackwell is being attended to."

"By whom?" he asked indignantly.

"By a midwife."

Potter sank back on the sofa. "Oh, dear." He mopped his face again. "How is she doing?"

"I'm sure she's fine. Now, what can you tell me about this Dr. Blackwell?"

"What do you mean? Don't you know who he is?"

"I know he's some kind of phony doctor."

Potter was incensed. "He's a *great healer*!"

"He *was* a healer. Now he's just dead. What I need to know is who might have killed him."

"Killed?" Potter echoed incredulously.

"You did notice he was dead, didn't you?"

"Yes, but . . ."

"But what?"

"I just didn't . . . You think someone *murdered* him?"

"Would he have had a reason to kill himself?" Frank asked with interest.

Potter seemed surprised. "Well, I . . . I'm sure I don't know how to answer a question like that."

"You're Blackwell's assistant, you said."

"Yes, that's correct."

"What exactly do you assist him with?"

Potter seemed taken aback by the change of subject. "I . . . I assisted him in his cures. And I plan his schedule and make his bookings and manage his lectures."

"Lectures?"

"Yes, Dr. Blackwell gives . . . gave lectures to explain his method of healing. Many prominent citizens attend them. Many prominent citizens were his patients. He was very successful."

"Did he have any patients that he couldn't help? Someone who might be angry enough to murder him?"

"No! Certainly not! I can't believe you think anyone

would take Edmund's life! Besides, I thought . . ."

"What did you think?"

Potter applied his handkerchief to his forehead again. "I saw the gun on the desk. It looked like . . ."

"Like he'd shot himself?" Frank supplied.

Potter swallowed. "Yes."

"I'm sure that's what the killer wanted people to think, but I believe Blackwell was murdered."

"By whom?" Potter's voice was hoarse.

"That's my job, to find out. I was hoping you could give me some ideas, since you knew Blackwell so well."

Potter blinked a few times as he considered Frank's proposal. "I . . . I really don't . . ."

"The servants said he had a meeting with someone this afternoon. Do you know who it was?"

Potter seemed to be thinking, trying to figure something out. Frank waited. Some of his most valuable time was spent waiting for people to decide to tell him something.

"I . . . there was someone . . ." Potter began tentatively.

"Someone he was going to meet this afternoon?"

"I'm sure I don't know about that," Potter insisted, "but there was something, something that happened just last week . . ."

Frank took a seat in the chair opposite Potter. "Tell me all about it."

"Well, it's a rather ugly story. It does Dr. Blackwell no credit, and it's . . . Well, it could hurt Mrs. Blackwell."

"Would it give Mrs. Blackwell a reason to kill her husband?"

Potter's small eyes widened as he considered this apparently unthinkable possibility. "Good heavens, no! She knows nothing about it!" Potter's face had grown a dangerous shade of red again.

"Who does, then?"

"Well, I knew," he reluctantly admitted. "Edmund

confided in me, because he needed my counsel."

"Why don't you confide in me, then. Let's see if we can figure out who might have killed Dr. Blackwell."

Potter glanced at the door, as if he suspected someone might be listening. "It's quite a scandal, or it could be if anyone—"

"Potter," Frank warned in the tone he used to reduce hardened criminals to quivering terror.

Potter gulped audibly. "Well, you see, Dr. Blackwell . . . That is, a young man came to see him last week. A young man who had come all the way from Virginia."

"Who was he?"

"He was . . . is Dr. Blackwell's son."

"Blackwell had a son in Virginia?"

"Yes, he . . . from his first marriage."

Frank nodded, believing he understood. "Blackwell thought the scandal of his divorce would ruin him?"

Potter shook his head. "Oh, no, it wasn't that. He . . . he was not divorced at all. He is . . . was still married to the boy's mother."

Finally, Frank was beginning to really understand. "And the lady who discovered his body today?" he prodded.

"Was not legally married to Edmund," Potter said softly. "Naturally, he wanted to protect her and their . . . their unborn child. He was going to meet with the boy today in an attempt to ward off any scandal. He had withdrawn a sum of money to give him in exchange for . . . for his silence."

"Would Blackwell have had the money here with him?"

Potter had to consider this. "I suppose he would if he intended to give it to the boy."

"We didn't find any money," Frank said, although he knew that if the killer hadn't taken it, one of the servants or even the beat cop Patrick might've done so when nobody was looking. It wouldn't be the first time a cop had helped himself in a situation like this.

"Then that proves the boy was here, doesn't it?" Potter asked. "Which means he must be the killer."

Malloy didn't bother to answer since there were so many other possibilities. "Do you think the boy would have accepted the money in exchange for his silence?"

Potter mopped his forehead again. "No, I don't. He was very angry and bitter over the way Edmund had abandoned him and his mother. If you're looking for someone who wanted Edmund dead, I think you should look for this boy."

"What's the boy's name?" Frank asked, pulling out his small notebook and a pencil.

"Uh, his name is Calvin Brown."

Frank looked up in surprise. "You said he was Blackwell's son."

"He is, of course. Dr. Blackwell changed his name when ... Well, his name originally was Edward Brown."

"I see." Frank did see. Blackwell had changed his name either to escape ties to his family and whatever else he'd left behind when he left Virginia, or else to give himself a more dignified name, most likely both. "Do you have any idea where I might find this Calvin Brown?"

Potter studied Frank for a moment, as if trying to decide something. Then he said, "I'm afraid not. I'd suggest a cheap lodging house, for a start. Locating him won't be an easy task, I'm sure, but perhaps if I told you that I am offering a five-hundred-dollar reward for finding Edmund's killer, it might increase your level of enthusiasm for the task."

Frank thought about the surgeon that Sarah Brandt had recommended to him, the man who might be able to cure his son's crippled foot. Five hundred dollars would go a long way toward pay for the surgery. "I'll do my best, Mr. Potter."

2

SARAH WAS CONCERNED ABOUT HER PATIENT. HER labor didn't seem to be progressing, and she still seemed to be in shock. Or at least that's what Sarah had been thinking at first, but she was beginning to suspect something else. While Mrs. Blackwell was resting between contractions, Sarah stepped into the woman's dressing room for a quick look around. Sure enough, just as she'd suspected, she found a drawer full of patent medicines, all of them for female complaints, and all of them containing some form of opiate. One of the bottles was empty, the cork out, the traces of liquid still visible. It hadn't been empty long.

Like many women of her class, Mrs. Blackwell had obviously discovered the relief to be found in those little glass bottles. One could hardly blame her for seeking it under the circumstances, either. Perhaps it was as well that her brain was clouded by the drug instead of the horrible vision of her husband's dead body. Still, if she took these remedies frequently, she might be an opium eater and the baby could be, too. In any case, the opiate could prolong her labor, and any of this could put the child's life in danger.

She heard Mrs. Blackwell moaning and hurried back into the bedroom. The woman's head was tossing back and forth on the pillow, as if she battled internal demons in addition to the forces of her own body. Sarah wiped her brow with a damp cloth, hoping to make her more comfortable.

She opened her eyes and tried to focus on Sarah's face. "Who are you?"

"I'm Sarah Brandt, the midwife," she replied, not mentioning that they'd had this conversation not long ago. Plainly Mrs. Blackwell didn't remember it. "I'm here to take care of you."

"Edmund won't approve," she said, her lovely blue eyes darkening with distress.

"I'm sure he would want you taken care of," Sarah said reasonably.

She frowned. "I remember something . . . Edmund is dead, isn't he?"

"I'm afraid so," Sarah said, knowing it would be foolish to deny it, since Mrs. Blackwell had been the one to discover her husband's body. She might want to deny it, but the image would be all too real.

Mrs. Blackwell closed her eyes and sighed, sinking back into the pillows. She murmured something that sounded like, "It's my fault."

Sarah wanted to reassure her. People often blamed themselves when a loved one committed suicide, and the generous thing to do was to tell the woman it wasn't her fault at all. Unfortunately, she couldn't be sure. For all Sarah knew, Dr. Blackwell's wife had driven him to it. At any rate, none of this was her concern. She had a far more pressing problem.

"Mrs. Blackwell, I need to know if you take patent medicines on a regular basis."

"What?" the woman asked, her eyes narrowing with confusion.

"I saw the bottles in your drawer. I know you must have taken something after you . . . after you had the shock. That's only natural, to want something to calm your nerves. But I need to know if you drink those remedies very often."

"Oh," she said, struggling to comprehend. "Oh, no. I only . . . only when I can't . . . not very often at all!"

Relieved, Sarah smiled and patted the woman's shoulder. "Thank you. That's what I needed to know. Now let's see what we can do about encouraging this baby to arrive. If you feel like doing some walking, I think that will help," she suggested. A woman in heavy labor had difficulty concentrating on anything else, and she wanted Mrs. Blackwell's mind free of unpleasant thoughts for the moment.

"Do you think it will help?" she asked.

"Oh, yes. Let me give you a hand down from the bed."

FRANK STOOD IN the hallway looking up the stairs, thinking he'd like to know what was going on with Mrs. Blackwell. Or perhaps he was just looking for an excuse to see Sarah Brandt again. Actually, he had no such excuse. Blackwell's body had been taken away, he'd questioned all the servants, he'd heard Amos Potter's theories on who might have killed Blackwell, and he'd gleaned all the information he could about Edmund Blackwell's mysterious son. He would need to question the neighbors, too, but that would certainly be a waste of time. They would never tell a common Irish policeman anything useful, even if they knew anything useful.

At any rate, he had no further excuse for staying there. The Blackwell baby would be born in its own sweet time, and Frank wasn't going to wait around until then just for a glimpse of Sarah Brandt. And if he didn't see her, he wouldn't be able to tell her that Blackwell had been murdered and give her a reason for wanting to become involved in the investigation. He didn't want her involved in another of his cases, so he'd best be on his way.

"Will you be needing anything else?" the butler asked, emerging from the depths of the house.

"No, I'm finished here, for the time being. Is Mr. Potter still here?"

"Yes. He wanted to wait to be sure everything is all right with Mrs. Blackwell. He is very devoted to the family."

Frank wondered what the motivation for that devotion might be. Potter had seemed awfully concerned about Mrs. Blackwell's welfare, almost more than he'd been concerned about Dr. Blackwell's death. Well, maybe that was a slight exaggeration. Frank was probably just too jaded, looking for ulterior motives where none existed. Or maybe Amos Potter had seduced Mrs. Blackwell, gotten her with child, and then killed her husband so they could live happily ever after.

Well, now Frank knew it was time to leave. The very thought of meek little Amos Potter seducing anyone was so preposterous Frank had to bite his lip to keep from smiling. He was just about to tell the butler he'd be back the next morning to see if Mrs. Blackwell was well enough to answer some questions when someone pounded on the front door.

Granger hurried to open it, and an imposing man in a tailor-made suit stepped into the foyer. Everything about him said power and "old money." Frank wondered what he'd done to deserve this.

"Good evening, Mr. Symington," the butler said gravely.

"What's going on here, Granger? Potter sent me the most mysterious message—" He broke off when he saw Frank. "Who are you?"

"Detective Sergeant Frank Malloy of the city police, Mr. Symington. I'm investigating Dr. Blackwell's death."

"His *death*? Good God! What happened?"

At that moment Amos Potter emerged from the front parlor. "Mr. Symington, it was so good of you to come."

"Good?" Symington boomed. "There's nothing good about this. This fellow says Edmund is dead."

"That's right, Mr. Symington, I'm sorry to say," Potter confirmed. "I wanted to break the news to you myself, but I see you've already learned the horrible truth. Even worse, the police believe he was murdered."

"Murdered? Who on earth would have a reason to murder Edmund?" He looked accusingly at Frank, as if he believed this was all his fault. "Where is my daughter? Does she know about this yet?"

"Mrs. Blackwell is your daughter?" Frank guessed.

"Of course she is," Symington said impatiently. "Where is she, Potter?"

"She's upstairs," Potter said uncomfortably. "A . . . a midwife is with her."

Frank saw the first genuine emotion cross Symington's face. "The baby?" he asked with a worried frown.

"Yes," Potter said. "The shock of finding Edmund's body—"

"She found his body?" Symington seemed to be experiencing some shock himself. He looked as if he needed to sit down.

"Perhaps we should step into the parlor," Potter suggested, nodding toward the butler, who stood nearby.

"Oh, yes, of course," Symington agreed, and allowed Potter to direct him into the other room.

Frank followed, even though he hadn't been specifically invited. He had a few questions to ask Mr. Symington. He closed the parlor doors behind them.

Symington had gone directly to a cabinet and opened it to reveal bottles of liquor. With the familiarity of a frequent visitor, he poured himself a drink and downed it in one gulp. Only then did he turn back to face Potter. He seemed a bit surprised to see Frank had joined them, but he didn't make an issue of it.

"This midwife," he said to Potter. "Is she someone Edmund approved?"

Before Potter could reply, Frank said, "I sent for her.

Her name is Sarah Brandt. She's Felix Decker's daughter." Frank figured Sarah's sterling family heritage would satisfy Symington, and it appeared he was right.

"Felix Decker, eh?" he said. "I'm sure Edmund wouldn't have approved, but I suppose, under the circumstances . . ."

"We really had no choice," Potter confirmed.

Symington nodded, then thought for a moment. "How did Edmund die?" he asked Frank. "And what makes you think he was murdered?"

"He was shot in the head."

Symington visibly winced. "And my daughter found his body?"

"That's right." Frank watched his face for any betraying emotions, but he saw only the expected ones.

"Who killed him?" Symington demanded when he had absorbed the information.

"Mr. Potter thinks his son killed him," Frank tried.

Symington seemed surprised, and he turned accusing eyes to Potter.

"Mr. Symington knows nothing about this," Potter assured Frank. "I hope you'll allow me to explain everything to him."

"Go right ahead," Frank said.

Potter turned to Symington, who was waiting with remarkable patience. "It seems that Edmund was married before, and his son from his first marriage came to see him several days ago."

"What did he want, and why would he have killed Edmund?"

Frank braced himself for the explosion that would come when Symington found out his daughter's marriage had been a sham.

"The boy believed Edmund had deserted his first family. He was very angry and bitter, and he threatened to spread all sorts of lies about Edmund unless he received a large sum of money."

"I assume Edmund refused to be blackmailed," Symington said, and Potter agreed enthusiastically.

This wasn't exactly the same story he had told Frank, but he was obviously trying to spare Symington any more pain. Sooner or later the man would have to find out the truth about his daughter and his grandchild, Frank supposed, but he'd let Potter worry about that.

"It's obvious that Edmund wasn't the man I thought he was. A man who deserts his family is beneath contempt. Had I known . . . But that's of no consequence now. I made a mistake, but when I make a mistake, I correct it." Symington turned to Frank, his eyes as hard as glass. "My daughter has suffered enough. I do not want her involved in a scandal. If you can find this boy and handle the matter quietly, you will be amply rewarded."

"Certainly," Frank said. He didn't want a scandal either.

"Here you are, Mrs. Blackwell," Sarah said as she tucked the swaddled bundle in next to the new mother. "A fine baby boy."

Mrs. Blackwell barely had the strength to open her eyes. Dawn was painting pink streaks in the sky, and she'd been laboring all night long. Both mother and baby were exhausted, but Sarah knew it was important for both of them to get the child to nurse immediately.

"I know you're tired," Sarah said as Mrs. Blackwell looked down uncertainly at the baby. "But if you can feed him even a little right now, it will help with your recovery, and I'm sure he could use the nourishment."

"Oh, I'm not going to feed him myself," Mrs. Blackwell said in surprise. "I've hired a wet nurse. Someone should send for her. Granger knows where to find her."

Sarah frowned. Many wealthy women hired nurses for their children, so she shouldn't have been surprised. Still, she couldn't stop herself from saying, "Even if you could just feed him for a few days, it would be so much better for both of you."

"Oh, no," she insisted, a little alarmed. "Edmund would never allow it. He said no gently bred woman should nurse her own children. Besides, I have to be free to travel for his lectures . . ." Her voice trailed off as she obviously remembered her husband would be giving no more lectures. "Oh, dear," she said very faintly and very sadly.

"I'm sure if you'd like to take care of the child yourself, there's no reason why you couldn't," Sarah suggested, tactfully not mentioning the fact that Dr. Blackwell's opinion no longer mattered. It was all she could do.

"Oh, no," Mrs. Blackwell said. "I wouldn't know where to start. I don't know anything about babies. Send for the nurse. She'll come right away. She said she would. Oh, and someone should notify my father. He'll want to know immediately." She looked down at the babe on the bed beside her, studying its tiny face. "He's awfully small, isn't he? I really . . . I don't know what to do with him."

"Just hold him for now," Sarah suggested. "You can learn the rest as you go. Look how sweet he is," she added, hoping to get Mrs. Blackwell interested in the child. "And where did he get that red hair? Does it run in your family?"

Unfortunately, her words seemed to have exactly the opposite effect. Instead of being enchanted with the child, as most mothers would be, Mrs. Blackwell looked down at him in horror. "Please, I don't . . ." Mrs. Blackwell said in despair, and Sarah had no choice but to take the poor child away.

An hour later Sarah had sent a servant to notify Mrs. Blackwell's father and met the wet nurse, a sturdy-looking woman who seemed, to Sarah's relief, both respectable and clean. Satisfied that her work was done, she left the baby in the nurse's care and Mrs. Blackwell sleeping on fresh sheets and made her way downstairs.

The house was quiet as she descended into the front

hallway. The servants would be engaged in their regular activities, and certainly no visitors would be lingering. Or so Sarah thought until a short, plump man emerged from the front parlor at the sound of her footsteps. He was well dressed, if a bit rumpled, and his rather homely features were twisted into a scowl. "Who are you?" he demanded.

"I'm the midwife," she replied. This usually had the effect of satisfying any such inquiry. People seldom cared what her name was once informed of her profession.

Instead of placating him, however, the information seemed to alarm him. "Mrs. Blackwell? How is she? Shouldn't you be with her?"

"She's perfectly fine, she and her new son. They're both resting comfortably now."

"Oh, thank heaven," the man said, placing a hand over his heart, as if trying to still it. "After the shock of finding poor Edmund, I didn't know . . . What a terrible, terrible thing." He shook his head for a moment and then looked up again, his small brown eyes anxious. "Do you think . . . Will there be any lasting effects? From the shock I mean. She's such a delicate creature."

"I'm sure she'll be fine," Sarah said. "She's young and healthy. She'll recover completely, once she's finished mourning her husband."

"Oh, she's healthy now, but it wasn't so very long ago . . ." For a moment he seemed lost in thought, absently fingering his watch fob. "Well, no matter."

"Does she have a condition that I should know about?" Sarah asked. "Something that might affect her recovery?"

"No, not now, at any rate. Thanks to Dr. Blackwell's skill. And of course if she should need any further treatments, I am fully trained in Dr. Blackwell's techniques."

He no longer seemed to be talking to Sarah at all, but rather ruminating to himself. He was fingering the watch fob again, and Sarah couldn't help but notice that it appeared to be a Phi Beta Kappa key. Perhaps he was more important than she had assumed at first glance. "Are you a family member?" she asked curiously, since this was a much nicer way of inquiring as to his identity than he had used on her.

"What? Oh, no, I'm Dr. Blackwell's assistant. Or, that is, I *was* his assistant. A terrible thing. Just terrible."

"Yes, it was, Mister . . . ?"

"Oh, yes! Potter. Amos Potter at your service, Missus . . . ?"

"Brandt," Sarah supplied. "I'm pleased to meet you, Mr. Potter. I'm sure Mrs. Blackwell will appreciate your concern."

"You may convey my best wishes to her, and assure her I will take care of all the details concerning poor Edmund. She need worry for nothing."

"That's very kind of you, Mr. Potter, but I believe someone has sent for Mrs. Blackwell's father."

"Oh, yes, of course, but I'll need to take care of Edmund's business affairs. Those are my responsibilities anyway. I'll do everything I can to ensure that no burden falls on Mrs. Blackwell."

Sarah wanted to ask him for some details about Dr. Blackwell's demise, but she felt that would be rude of her. Besides, she was more likely to get accurate information much more easily in the kitchen, which was where she had originally been headed. "It was so nice to have met you, Mr. Potter," she said, ready to take her leave, but Potter wasn't quite finished with her yet.

"That policeman," he said. "Malloy, I think his name was. You are acquainted with him?"

Sarah was surprised, but she didn't let it show. "Yes, we met a few months ago," she said, revealing nothing with her tone.

"Is he . . . Can he be trusted to be . . . discreet?"

"Oh, yes," Sarah said, quite honestly. "Detective Sergeant Malloy is very good at his job. He'll keep the news of Dr. Blackwell's unfortunate death out of the news-papers, if that's what his family wishes."

Potter nodded. "And will he be diligent about finding Edmund's killer?"

Sarah started. "Killer?" she repeated incredulously. "I thought Dr. Blackwell had committed suicide."

Potter pulled himself up to his full, if inconsequential, height. "Mr. Malloy believes he was murdered. While that is quite distressing to me, I am naturally concerned about his ability to find and dispose of the killer."

A thousand things were racing through Sarah's mind, but she took no time to consider any of them. "Mr. Malloy will certainly find the killer, Mr. Potter. You can rest assured of that."

She'd thought this news would comfort Potter, but instead he looked troubled. He would be thinking about the scandal, of course, and the effect it would have on Mrs. Blackwell. Or perhaps he simply didn't believe her assertion that Malloy could find the killer. Most of the police detectives were totally inept and corrupt, so that would be natural. "Thank you, Mrs. Brandt," was all he said, and then he took his leave.

Sarah's stomach rumbled, reminding her of her orig-inal destination. The cook was in the kitchen, preparing the noon meal, and instantly offered Sarah something to eat.

"Have a seat, miss," the cook said. "I'll fix you some-thing in no time. How's the Missus and the new babe doing?"

"They're both fine, but a little tired. It was a long night."

"That it was, and poor Missus, remembering how her poor husband looked when she found him. It's an awful thing, I tell you."

"It certainly is," Sarah agreed, taking a seat at the scrubbed oak table where the servants ate their meals. She wanted to plunge right in, asking questions, but she knew it was better to listen. She should also pretend she didn't know about the murder, since that was most likely a secret. The cook would relish the tale much more, thinking Sarah ignorant.

The cook was a buxom woman of middle years, plain of face and sharp of tongue, if Sarah was any judge. "Do you have any idea why Dr. Blackwell would have taken his life?" she asked, hoping she was right.

"Oh, law, he'd never do such a thing! Whatever for? He was famous, he was," she insisted as she struck a match to light the stove. "People—*rich* people—they come from all over, even other states, to see him, and they paid him all sorts of money to make them well. Like he did his wife."

"His wife?" Sarah asked, remembering what Potter had said about Mrs. Blackwell's health.

"Oh, law, yes, poor little thing. Crippled she was. A horseback-riding accident was what done it. She couldn't get up from her bed for nigh on a year, and she was in terrible pain. Mr. Symington—that's her father—he called in every kind of doctor you can imagine, and not a one of them could help her. She was wasting away until finally they found Dr. Blackwell. He cured her just like that!" She snapped her fingers, or tried to. Apparently, they were too greasy, though, and they only slid across each other. "Well, right quick like, anyways. Before you know it, she was right as rain. Been that way ever since."

Sarah waited until the woman had broken several eggs into the cast-iron skillet she was heating on the stove. "What kind of a doctor was Dr. Blackwell?"

"They called him a magnetic healer. How do you like your eggs, miss?"

"Sunny-side up, please. Do you know how he healed people?"

"I'm not rightly sure, but it had something to do with his hands. He had some power in them. He could put his hands on someone and use that power and make them well."

What a useful talent, Sarah thought, but of course she didn't want to show the cook her skepticism. "It's difficult to understand how a man with such a power would choose to take his own life, then," she remarked, taking the subject back to her original question.

"Oh, he didn't. I already told you that! I never believed it for a second, either, not a man like Dr. Blackwell, and then that police detective comes, and he says it, too. Says Dr. Blackwell was murdered, he did."

"He did?" Sarah echoed, managing to sound surprised.

"Oh, yes. Says somebody tried to make it look like Dr. Blackwell shot himself with his own pistol, but he didn't. He wouldn't have, and I told that detective so, too. He talked to all the servants, one by one. Asked all of us did we know anybody who'd want to shoot poor Dr. Blackwell."

"And did you?"

"Certainly not! Except maybe some of those doctors who was jealous of him, and there was a few, I can tell you."

The cook scooped up the perfectly cooked eggs and slid them onto a plate. When she'd set it down in front of Sarah, she produced a freshly baked loaf of bread and cut several thick slices from it. Then she served up some creamy butter and strawberry jam and a glass of milk. For a few moments Sarah forgot all about murders and murderers and just indulged herself in the delicious meal. But only for a few moments.

"I suppose no one else has any idea who might have killed Dr. Blackwell either, then," she surmised when she'd taken the edge off her hunger.

"No one I know of. Everybody on the staff says the same thing. He was such a good man, never a cross word to anyone."

"His marriage was happy, too?"

"Oh, yes, he doted on his wife, he did. Nothing was too good for her. I don't think she appreciated it like she should, though. She comes from money, you know, so she's used to fine things."

"And the doctor wasn't from a wealthy family?"

"Oh, law, no! He was common as dirt. His father was a farmer, he said. It was his talents that made him rise in the world. People was so grateful for his help, you see. They give him money and presents. It embarrassed him, I think, all the fuss. But he said it was his duty to help people, and he couldn't stop."

Sarah found it hard to believe that anyone would be embarrassed to be recompensed for his work, even if he were a charlatan. Or perhaps *especially* if he were a charlatan.

"This is a lovely house. How long have the Blackwells lived here?" Sarah asked between mouthfuls.

"About three months now, I guess. They lived in a flat uptown before that. Not that the doctor couldn't have afforded a nice home, but he was traveling so much. He didn't have time to find them a place. At least that's what I heard from her maid. She's the only one that's been with them since before they come to this house."

"So all the servants were hired just three months ago," Sarah said, wondering if this could possibly have any significance.

"Yes, that's right. It's a pity. They finally get a home of their own, and Dr. Blackwell only gets to live in it for a few months."

"What do you suppose Mrs. Blackwell will do now?"

"Law, I don't have no idea," the cook said with a frown. "I don't suppose she'll stay in the big house all by herself, now will she?" Plainly, she found the thought unsettling, since this would mean she and the other servants would be out of a job again.

Sarah was sorry she'd brought up the subject. She thanked the woman for the meal and prepared to take her leave.

"Do you want the carriage? It's raining outside, so you'd best take it. I can have Mr. Granger send around for it," the cook offered. "It'll only take a few minutes."

This time Sarah readily accepted. She was too tired to trudge back to her home, especially in the rain, and while the carriage ride would be long, she could at least doze on the way.

"You may wait in the front parlor," the butler instructed her when asked to make the arrangements. "You'll see the carriage pull up from the front window there."

"Thank you," Sarah said, sinking wearily into one of the chairs by the window that overlooked the street.

The butler cleared his throat, drawing her attention again. "Mrs. Blackwell, is she doing well?"

"Yes, she and the baby both are fine," Sarah said. She'd forgotten how involved the servants became in a family's life. They were, in many ways, more like relations than employees, albeit poor ones.

"Do you think . . . ? The shock of finding Dr. Blackwell, will that have any ill effects?" he asked with dignified concern.

"It was unfortunate, but I'm sure Mrs. Blackwell will recover fully." She'd have years of nightmares, but there was no use worrying the butler over something he couldn't help. "She is, as I said, doing very well already."

The butler nodded his thanks. "The carriage will be around in a few minutes," he said, and left her to wait alone.

With nothing else to do, she began to think about Dr. Blackwell's death and how she could get Malloy to confide in her what was going on with the investigation. He'd certainly balk at involving her in another murder case. She'd managed to put herself in danger twice before while assisting him, and he'd been particularly upset the last time. Maybe if she just expressed mild curiosity. Could she fool him? Somehow she doubted it.

However, she had already obtained a bit of information he might find useful. Probably he'd soon find out the same things she'd just learned, but she could at least save him some trouble by sharing what she already knew about how the dead man had cured his wife's injuries so miraculously when others had failed. She'd be doing him a favor, she reasoned. He couldn't object to that. Or so she told herself, knowing full well he'd object to anything he pleased.

Lost in thought, she'd been staring at the man who had just emerged from the house sitting catty-corner from the Blackwells' without realizing who it was. Malloy! He was no doubt going from house to house, questioning all the neighbors and their servants. Here was her chance.

Quickly gathering her things, Sarah hurried out, not waiting for the butler to open the front door for her. Fortunately, the rain had stopped for the moment, although it didn't look like the lull would last for long. Malloy was just starting up the front steps of the next house when she called his name.

He stopped and turned, recognizing her at once. She could tell by the way he stiffened in reaction. He didn't seem at all pleased to see her, but he turned and came back down the steps and began walking toward her.

Sarah resisted an urge to meet him halfway. It would hardly be seemly, but more important, she didn't want to appear as eager as she felt. She set her medical bag on the front step and waited with apparent patience.

"Good morning, Mrs. Brandt," he said when he reached her. His expression was resigned and a little reserved, but that did not deter her in the least. "I assume the Blackwell baby has been born."

"Good morning, Mr. Malloy," she replied. "Yes, baby and mother are doing as well as we could expect, considering Dr. Blackwell was murdered right in their home."

He sighed. "I should have known you'd find out all about it. But don't start thinking you're going to be involved. You won't have time anyway. I'll have the killer locked up by sunset."

"You know who it is, then?" she asked in surprise.

"Are you on your way home now?" he asked, ignoring her question. "I can get you a cab."

"They're bringing the carriage around for me," she said, undeterred. "I suppose you know that Dr. Blackwell was a magnetic healer and that he supposedly healed his wife after she was crippled in a riding accident."

If this was new information, he gave no indication. "What exactly does a magnetic healer do?" he asked instead.

"I'm not certain. It has something to do with laying his hands on people and curing them of whatever is wrong."

"How could he make someone well just by touching them?" Malloy asked.

"Oh, there must be more to it than that, but I'm sure they keep their actual techniques a secret. It's the only way to prevent others from doing the same thing they do and stealing their patients."

"But people really get well?" he asked doubtfully.

"Presumably, or these so-called doctors couldn't stay in business. The fact is that most people eventually get well from whatever is wrong with them if they believe strongly enough that they will, even with no treatment at all. These charlatans have the advantage of people wanting to believe their treatments will work, no matter how ridiculous they are. When someone gets well, they tell their friends, and people have even more confidence in the healer. So, who do you think killed Dr. Blackwell?"

Malloy's lips twitched, as if he were holding back a smile. "Nice try, Mrs. Brandt, but you're not getting involved in this. Go home, get some sleep, and forget all about Dr. Blackwell's death."

"Just exactly how do you propose I forget about it?" she asked, genuinely interested.

"Think about something else," he suggested. "I hear your carriage. It was nice to see you again, Mrs. Brandt. Good day."

He tipped his hat and turned away, even though Sarah was far from finished with him. She wanted to stamp her foot in protest, but such a gesture would only amuse him. "Thank you for sending for me, Malloy," she called after him.

He turned back, not bothering to hide his smile this time. "I needed a midwife, and you're the only midwife I know."

Sarah glared at him, but her effort was wasted. He was already walking away. She wasn't really angry, though. She enjoyed their sparring, and she knew he did, too. And she also knew she had a good reason to stay involved with the case. She'd be back tomorrow morning to check on Mrs. Blackwell and her baby. Then she'd find out if Malloy was as good as his word about finding the killer by sunset.

ALTHOUGH A FIERCE electrical storm woke Sarah several times during the night, the weather was fine the next morning, so she decided to walk back over to Gramercy Park. When the butler opened the front door, she immediately knew something was wrong.

"Mrs. Brandt, how good that you've come," he said, maintaining his dignity even though his pinched expression revealed his concern.

"Is Mrs. Blackwell ill? You should have sent for me at once!"

"Oh, no, Mrs. Blackwell is perfectly well. It's the child. He's ... well, he seems to be in some distress. The nurse has been up with him all night."

It could be simple colic, of course, but usually that didn't begin quite so soon. Her mind racing with possibilities—none of them pleasant—Sarah hurried upstairs. When she reached the landing, she could hear the faint sound of an infant crying. It was a hollow sound, one Sarah had heard before, but she knew she must be mistaken in what she was thinking. The cries came from farther down the hall than Mrs. Blackwell's room, which meant the child was probably in the nursery. When she reached the door, she didn't bother to knock.

She found the nurse walking the floor with the infant, vainly trying to comfort him. She looked exhausted and at her wit's end, and she seemed infinitely relieved to see Sarah.

"Oh, Mrs. Brandt, thank heaven you're here! I don't know what come over him," she exclaimed, absently patting the screaming child. "At first I thought he might be scared of the storm last night. It was so loud! Then I thought it was the colic, but don't nothing work for it. Seems like he don't even want to be touched, which ain't natural at all!"

It was true. Usually, a fretful baby could be stilled by a soothing touch or rocking or walking, even one with colic. Sarah reached out, and the nurse surrendered the child gratefully. As soon as she took the baby from the nurse, however, she understood what the woman meant. The child stiffened in her arms, resisting her embrace. She took him to the nurse's bed and laid him down, unwrapping his swaddling so she could examine him for possible injuries or defects she'd failed to notice yesterday.

His limbs were twitching, and his skin was pale and cool to the touch. He arched his little body as if in pain.

"Have you given him anything?" Sarah asked.

"Just my milk, and I never ate nothing that could upset him. I'm that careful with my milk, I am."

Sarah knew this was far more than an upset stomach, however. "I need to speak with Mrs. Blackwell," she said. "I'll be right back."

The nurse nodded, not really understanding, and took the baby when Sarah had wrapped him up again.

Sarah went to Mrs. Blackwell's room and knocked on the door.

"Come," she called weakly, and Sarah stepped into the room.

The drapes were drawn against the morning sunlight, but Mrs. Blackwell wasn't trying to sleep. She sat up in bed, propped by a stack of pillows, and she looked just as frazzled as the nurse. "Thank heaven you've come! Can you make him stop?" she asked Sarah. "He's been doing this all night. Between the crying and the storm, I haven't had a wink of sleep!"

Sarah didn't like the way Mrs. Blackwell seemed more concerned for her own welfare than for her child's, which may have put a little edge in her voice when she asked, "Do you have any idea what's wrong with your baby?"

Mrs. Blackwell's eyes grew large. "Certainly not! How could I?"

"I think you could. When you were in labor, I asked if you regularly took those patent medicines I found in your dressing room, and you said you didn't."

"I don't! Hardly ever! I just . . . After finding Edmund . . ." Her lovely blue eyes filled with tears. "I was so distressed! I needed something for my nerves, so I . . . I hardly ever use them. Only when I . . . when I get nervous."

A tear slid down her smooth cheek, and Sarah had the uneasy feeling the woman had practiced looking lovely when she wept. She didn't crinkle up her face or make unladylike sounds. She simply allowed her crystal tears to slip silently down her face in a most becoming manner.

"Mrs. Blackwell, your baby is very ill. He seems to be suffering from the effects of some narcotic substance, or rather from the lack of such a substance in his system. If his mother regularly used such a substance during her pregnancy, he would be just as dependent on it as she is, except he has no way to obtain it unless someone gives it to him."

"That's impossible!"

"Is it? Mrs. Blackwell, I've seen cases like this before. If this is indeed what's wrong with your baby, he will die unless he receives treatment, so unless you want your baby to die, you must be honest with me."

"Die?" she echoed incredulously. "He can't die, not from that! I've never heard of such a thing!"

"You may not have heard of it, but I assure you, it is *very* possible. Now you must tell me the truth. Tell me what medicines you take and how frequently."

"I . . . I tried to stop!" she exclaimed, forgetting to look attractive. Now she just looked frightened. "They said the baby would die if I *stopped*!"

"Who said that?"

"Mr. Fong. He's . . ." She caught herself and slapped one slender hand over her lips, knowing she had revealed too much.

"Mr. Fong?" Sarah repeated. This was worse than she'd even imagined. "A Chinese man? Why were you discussing this with a Chinese man?"

"I wasn't! I can't tell you!" she cried, contradicting herself. Her hands were fluttering around her face now, and her eyes were more than frightened. Unfortunately, Sarah had begun to put the clues together, and now she had a pretty good idea why.

"Mrs. Blackwell, have you been visiting an opium den?" she asked, trying to keep the horror out of her voice.

The woman looked as if she might faint. "I can't help myself! You don't know what it's like, the hunger and the craving! I thought I would die without it, and Edmund wouldn't . . . And then the baby . . . I could feel him fluttering inside me every time I started needing more. He was frantic for it, too, as frantic as I! They said the baby would die if I didn't take the morphine, so I had to do it! I didn't have any choice!"

Unfortunately, she was probably right. Sarah had a few unkind things to say to Mrs. Blackwell, but she would save them for later. Without another word, she went into Mrs. Blackwell's dressing room.

"What are you doing?" the woman demanded.

"I'm going to save your baby's life," Sarah said, yanking open the drawer she had discovered the day before. She noticed another bottle seemed to have been emptied. Since Mrs. Blackwell was unable to visit Mr. Fong, the opium content of the patent medicines would help ease her cravings until she was able to obtain a new supply of morphine. Sarah rummaged through the bottles until she found what she was looking for. Pure laudanum.

When Mrs. Blackwell saw her with the bottle, she cried out in protest. "They said the baby would be fine when he was born! They said he wouldn't need the drug anymore!"

"They lied," Sarah told her without apology.

She hurried down the hall, back toward the sound of the crying child. The nurse looked up hopefully when she entered. "Do you . . . ?" she began, and then she saw the bottle in Sarah's hand. "What on earth . . . ?"

Sarah didn't waste any time. She found her bag where she'd set it when she came in and rummaged inside until she located an eyedropper. Carefully, she drew a small amount of the amber liquid from the bottle and said, "Lay him on the bed, please."

"Oh, dear heaven," the nurse muttered, carefully laying the squalling child on the bed. "What is it? Can you give that to a tiny babe? Oh, dear, oh, dear, that's not the right thing to be doing! I never heard of such a thing!"

She stood wringing her hands as Sarah carefully dropped some of the liquid into the child's mouth. The baby started and made a face at the taste, and for a moment he was still. Then the crying started again.

"This should quiet him in a minute," Sarah said.

"Of course it should!" the nurse said indignantly. "That's what it's supposed to do. Does his mother know what poison you're giving him? I'm going to tell her if she doesn't! This ain't right!"

"Mrs. Blackwell is a regular user of morphine," Sarah told her. "The baby is accustomed to the drug, which passed from her to him when he was in the womb. That's why he's been crying. It must be past time for his regular dose, and without it, he will die. I've seen it happen far too many times."

"Oh, dear heaven!" the nurse cried again, this time in horror. "What's to become of the poor thing, then?"

"He won't need to take it forever," Sarah assured her. "We'll wait until he gets stronger, and then gradually wean him from it. I've done this before, and if the child is otherwise healthy, he should be fine." She didn't explain that the times she'd done this before had been with the children of prostitutes who habitually used morphine to dull the pain of their miserable existences. Why a woman like Mrs. Blackwell would feel the need for such oblivion, Sarah had no idea, and right now she was too angry even to care.

"He's twitching so," the nurse said, still wringing her hands.

"We'll wait a few minutes to see if what I gave him does the trick. If not, we'll try another drop and then another, until we get the dosage right."

Sarah sat down on the bed beside him to wait, her fury swelling inside of her as she watched the tiny body quivering in agony. Someone should pay for doing this to a helpless child, but she had no idea who that someone should be.

3

FRANK HAD BEEN RIGHT. THE NEIGHBORS HADN'T seen or heard a thing, and if they had, they weren't going to share the information with him. The neighboring servants had given him a bit of gossip here and there, of course. Apparently, no one thought it appropriate that Mrs. Blackwell kept going out every afternoon after her pregnancy became noticeable. It was said she visited poor and sick people, too, which only outraged her detractors even more. If she had no care for her own health, she should at least have been concerned for her unborn child and avoided the filthy poor and their unspeakable diseases.

To Frank's surprise, however, no one had a bad word to say about Dr. Blackwell, not even those who disapproved of his brand of medicine. He seemed to be a respectable gentleman who kept to himself and maintained the tone of the neighborhood. Until his unseemly death, of course. Maybe the neighbors were just happy to have someone more socially acceptable than an abortionist in residence. But whatever the reason, Frank could find no one with any idea of why the good doctor might have been murdered or who could have done it, and no one had so much as glimpsed the boy Amos Potter had told him was Blackwell's abandoned son. They hadn't seen anyone else coming or going from the house the previous afternoon, either.

So much for his boast to Sarah Brandt that he'd find the killer by nightfall.

The next morning, Frank returned to the Blackwell house to continue his investigation. The butler greeted him with the kind of condescending reserve to which Frank had become accustomed. Even servants felt superior to Irish policemen.

"How is Mrs. Blackwell today, Granger?" Frank asked.

"I'm sure I don't know. That midwife you sent over is with her now," Granger replied stiffly.

Frank fought down the instant anxiety he felt at the prospect of Mrs. Blackwell needing medical help so soon after her delivery. He had a momentary flash of his own wife with her life's blood draining away after giving birth to their son, but he ruthlessly banished it. "The midwife?" he echoed with as little expression as possible. "Is something wrong?"

"Not that I am aware."

Plainly, the butler thought it was none of his business, which was just too bad. He knew exactly where to get all the information about Mrs. Blackwell that he wanted. "When Mrs. Brandt is finished, tell her I want to see her."

The butler nodded curtly, conveying his disapproval with every ounce of his being without uttering a sound.

"Is anyone else here that you haven't seen fit to tell me about?" Frank asked with marked sarcasm.

The butler's lips paled as he squeezed the blood out of them in his impotent fury. "Mr. Potter is in the study," he said with obvious reluctance.

Good, Frank thought. Maybe Potter could give him some more information about Blackwell's son, who was rapidly becoming his prime suspect.

When Frank entered the study, he found Potter staring uncertainly at the desk where Blackwell's body had lain. The desk had been cleared, and all traces of the crime had been scrubbed away, except for an ugly stain in the carpet. Hearing Frank enter, Potter looked up with what Frank thought might have been alarm, but he quickly recovered himself.

"Detective, you startled me," he said, self-consciously straightening his vest. "Have you located young Calvin yet?"

Frank shook his head. "It would help if you had an idea where to begin looking. There are hundreds of cheap lodging houses in the city." He'd instructed some officers to begin making inquiries, but they weren't having much success.

"If he's even still here." Potter sighed. "In his place, I'd have fled immediately. And Edmund was going to give him some money, you know. He could be anywhere by now, of course, but you should probably check with his mother to see if she might know his whereabouts."

"Where can I find her?" Frank asked, annoyed that Potter hadn't suggested this yesterday.

Potter frowned, obviously trying to remember. "It's a small town in Virginia someplace. I'm not even certain I ever heard the name. Oh, dear, I guess I'm not being very much help to you."

Frank had to agree. If Calvin Brown had indeed fled the city, no one would ever find him. "Did you remember anything else about Brown that might help?"

"I'm afraid not. But surely you have informants who can assist you," Potter suggested hopefully.

"Only if I'm dealing with known criminals," Frank said, trying to be patient. "Someone like Calvin Brown probably wouldn't have been noticed by anyone in particular. He wasn't here that long, and he wouldn't have gotten into any trouble."

"Ah, yes, you're probably right. It's only been a week or so since he first contacted Edmund. It's my understanding that he saw an advertisement for one of Edmund's lectures and recognized his picture."

"You already told me about the lectures, but I'm not sure I understand why he had to give them. Couldn't he just advertise that he was a doctor? Hang up a sign or something?"

"He was a *healer*," Potter corrected him primly. "His treatments were quite revolutionary, not something the average person would easily understand, so he would give lectures explaining his successes in order to educate the public."

Educate and dupe them into coming to him for treatment, Frank thought, but he said, "Who came to these lectures?"

"All sorts of people. There was no admission charge, of course. Edmund didn't want fame or fortune for himself, but he felt it was selfish of him not to share his knowledge with those he could help."

"He helped his wife, I understand."

"Yes, Letitia was a complete invalid when her father called on Edmund for help. No doctor had been able to do a thing for her."

"She must have been very grateful," Frank suggested, not missing the fact that Potter had called Mrs. Blackwell by her given name.

"So grateful that she insisted on giving a personal testimonial at Edmund's lectures. Her story brought him to the public eye and convinced many people to try Edmund's services. Her family is quite socially prominent, you know."

"So I gathered from meeting Mr. Symington. What was wrong with Mrs. Blackwell in the first place?"

Potter seemed shocked at the question. "I told you, she was an invalid."

"You said it was a riding accident. Was she paralyzed? Crippled? Broken bones?"

"She was injured. She was in severe pain for almost a year, so severe she couldn't rise from her bed. With only a few treatments, Edmund was able to relieve that pain so she could live a normal life again."

Frank remembered what Sarah had said about most people getting well if they wanted to. Perhaps Blackwell's true gift was being able to make people want to get better. He noted that Potter hadn't told him exactly what Mrs. Blackwell's injuries had been. Probably he didn't know. For an instant Frank had an errant thought of asking Sarah Brandt to find out, but he quickly caught himself. If he truly wanted to keep her from getting involved in the investigation, that was exactly the wrong thing to do.

Outside Mrs. Blackwell's bedroom door, Sarah paused to take a deep breath. Venting the fury she felt at the woman would accomplish nothing. When she had mastered her feelings, she knocked on the door and entered without waiting for a reply.

Mrs. Blackwell appeared to be dozing, although still propped up on her mountain of pillows. She blinked uncertainly, obviously not recognizing Sarah at first.

"Oh, Mrs. Brandt," she finally realized. Then she listened for a moment. "The baby, he stopped crying. Is he . . . ?"

"He's sleeping," Sarah said. "The laudanum relieved him."

She sighed and closed her eyes. Sarah thought she probably didn't want to face her problems, and Sarah couldn't really blame her. They must seem overwhelming at the moment, especially to a person who needed morphine to deal with a normal day.

After a moment Mrs. Blackwell opened her eyes again. They were clouded and full of anguish. "I never meant to hurt the baby. You must believe me."

This was the opening Sarah had been waiting for. She stepped closer to the bed. "You were right not to stop taking the morphine. If you had, you most certainly would have lost the baby."

She seemed relieved to hear this. "They said he would be fine, though. They said once he was born, he wouldn't need it the way I do."

"I'm sure they told you what you wanted to hear. It wasn't in their best interests for you to stop using morphine, now was it?"

Her eyes filled with tears, but this time Sarah knew they were genuine and not an attempt to gain her sympathy. "I haven't been able to stop taking the morphine, no matter how hard I try. How will he be able to stop? He's so tiny . . ."

Her voice broke on a sob, and this time Sarah took one of her hands in both of hers. It was small and soft and icy cold. "I've seen this before," she said. "With a baby, it's possible to gradually decrease the amount you give him until he's not dependent on it anymore. We'll wait a few months, until he's stronger, and then we'll start weaning him off of it."

"But I've tried to stop so many times! The first time almost killed me, and I've never been able to do it again. The pain is unbearable." The tears were running down her cheeks unchecked now. Sarah felt her anger melting.

"We won't let your baby suffer, Mrs. Blackwell."

The younger woman looked at her with desperate eyes. "I know you're a midwife, but will you take care of him yourself? Will you come back and make sure he's all right and help wean him from that awful stuff?"

Sarah could not refuse. "Of course I will, if that's what you want. Tell me, though, how did you begin taking the morphine in the first place?"

She closed her eyes and seemed to shudder. "It was . . . when I was hurt. I fell off a horse when I . . . I hurt my back and my neck. The pain was horrible, and they gave me morphine. It was the only way I could bear it."

"Didn't you consult any physicians?"

Mrs. Blackwell stared at her in amazement. "Of course! My father called in every doctor he could find. There were dozens. None of them could do anything for me. They said I'd be an invalid for the rest of my life. I didn't leave my room for almost a year, and I hardly even left my bed. Walking was excruciating and I could only sit in a chair for a few minutes at a time. And then Edmund came."

"Your husband," Sarah said. "What did he do that the others didn't?"

Mrs. Blackwell's smooth brow furrowed as she struggled to explain. "He touched me. The others wouldn't touch me. It caused me too much pain. But Edmund told me he could make me well if he could just do some simple adjustments."

"What kind of adjustments?"

"To my spine. That's how he cures people. It's like a miracle. I felt better almost instantly. Within a few weeks my pain was completely gone."

"But you still needed the morphine," Sarah guessed.

Mrs. Blackwell closed her eyes again, and Sarah could only imagine the anguish these admissions cost her. "Edmund thought I shouldn't need the morphine anymore because my pain was gone. My father thought so, too. I didn't want to take it anymore, so I did what they told me and stopped taking it. I thought I was going to die."

"Stopping morphine is extremely difficult. Few people ever succeed," Sarah told her, not mentioning that some of the aids physicians sometimes used were even worse than the agony of withdrawal itself.

"But I *did* succeed!" she informed Sarah. "It was the hardest thing I ever did in my life, but I did it! I was finally free of both the pain and the morphine. I thought I could go back to my normal life again. That was all I wanted."

"But you didn't?"

Mrs. Blackwell sighed, and another tear slid down her cheek. "Edmund asked me to help him. He said he could cure many other people, just the way he'd cured me, but he couldn't unless those people knew his treatments worked. He was going to give a lecture in the city, explaining his techniques and how successful they were, but he needed someone to testify, someone he'd cured. He said . . . I mean, after what Edmund had done for me, how could I refuse?" she asked, her eyes pleading for Sarah to confirm her decision.

"Of course," Sarah said, knowing she could only imagine the pressure he must have put on her. "You must have been very grateful. But how did your father feel about it?" Sarah couldn't imagine her own father allowing her to do such a thing as speak about her health problems at a public lecture.

"He didn't really think it was proper, but he was so grateful to Edmund that he couldn't refuse. I think he felt some sort of debt of honor to him. Edmund told me what to say. He wrote it out for me. All I had to do was read it, but I was so frightened! There were hundreds of people, and they were all looking at me. I was so terrified, I almost fainted. I don't even remember giving the speech, but Edmund was very pleased, and many people came to him for his treatments after that. So of course he wanted me to speak again."

Sarah was beginning to understand what had happened. "You must have been very frightened," she guessed.

"I was so frightened, I knew I wouldn't be able to get up on that stage again, but my father felt we owed Edmund for what he had done. Edmund hadn't even accepted any payment for treating me, even though he'd been practically penniless. He only wanted my help. What could I do?"

"You could have told Edmund and your father how terrified you were," Sarah suggested kindly.

"I did, but they couldn't understand. They kept saying I'd get over it, that I'd be fine, just as I was the first time. But I hadn't been fine the first time, and I couldn't explain that to them! They made me do it, but the only way I could get through it was to take some morphine. Just a little," she hastened to explain, lest Sarah think badly of her. "Just enough so I didn't feel afraid. I wasn't going to take it anymore after that, but . . ."

"But you couldn't help yourself," Sarah guessed. She'd seen the power of the opiate to hold someone in its thrall.

"Once I started again, I couldn't seem to stop, especially when Edmund asked me to go to other cities for lectures. My father went with us, of course. It was all very proper, but I was still terrified of the crowds. I hid the morphine from them, so neither of them knew I was taking it. It was awful, lying to both of them and trying to buy the morphine when they didn't know. They would have been so angry . . . and so disappointed with me."

Sarah knew that morphine was readily available at any drugstore, but she also knew women of the upper classes had little freedom. An unmarried girl would have been chaperoned wherever she went. Mrs. Blackwell must have been clever indeed to manage to obtain her morphine without discovery.

"Then Edmund told me he'd fallen in love with me and asked me to marry him," she went on, so anxious to tell her story that she hardly seemed aware of Sarah's presence anymore. "I thought if he really loved me, he wouldn't make me do the lectures anymore, but I was wrong. Once we were married, he could take me anywhere he went without worrying about a chaperon anymore. I wanted to stop the morphine again, but I couldn't, not unless I told Edmund that I was taking it and unless he would let me stop doing the lectures. I tried telling him I didn't want to do the lectures anymore, but he wouldn't hear of it. He told me I had no choice, because without the lectures, he wouldn't get new patients and he wouldn't be able to make a living. He was my husband. I had to help him, didn't I?"

Sarah chose not to answer that question. "I can understand that you wanted to do the right thing."

"I don't know what the right thing is anymore," she said with a weary sigh.

"Well, one thing is for certain, with your husband gone, you won't have to attend those lectures anymore. So if you'd like to try stopping the morphine again, I can help you when you're stronger," Sarah offered.

"I can't think about that now," she said wearily. "I can't think about anything now. I just want to sleep."

"That's certainly a good idea. I'll make sure no one bothers you."

"Especially my father," Mrs. Blackwell said when Sarah started to leave. "He came yesterday, and he made me cry, talking about Edmund. I don't want to cry anymore. Please tell him I'm not able to see him."

"Of course," Sarah agreed, wondering how she would explain this to Mrs. Blackwell's father. She left to check on the baby.

MALLOY WAITED IN the parlor for Sarah Brandt. She didn't even say hello when she came in.

"So, Malloy, when do you plan to arrest the killer?" she asked instead, trying to nettle him.

He didn't let on that she had succeeded. She was the only woman he knew who could look appealing while being infuriating. "I need to ask Mrs. Blackwell some questions. When can I see her?"

"My guess would be a few weeks," she told him without a hint that she was teasing him. "She asked me a few moments ago to tell her own father she was too ill to receive him, so she's certainly too ill to see you."

"Is she?"

"If she says she is, then she is," she informed him. "Would you dare impose yourself on a woman during her lying-in?"

Frank tried not to feel the irritation he was feeling, mostly because it wasn't entirely unpleasant. He actually enjoyed arguing with Sarah Brandt, as difficult as that was to understand. "I need to find out what she knows about her husband's death, and the sooner I do that, the better chance I have of finding the killer."

"I would be happy to question her for you if you'll just tell me what you need to know," she said, taking a seat on the sofa and making herself comfortable.

"You are not a member of the police force, and you are not involved in this investigation," he reminded her.

"Well, then, I suppose you won't be interested in the fact that Mrs. Blackwell uses morphine."

"What?" Although he hadn't intended to, he sat down in the chair opposite her.

"Mrs. Blackwell has used morphine for several years, except for a brief period," she said. "It seems she began using it when she was injured in a riding accident."

"That's the accident her husband cured her of, isn't it?"

"Yes, it is."

"What was wrong with her exactly?"

"She said her back and neck were injured."

Frank frowned. "He cured her of a broken neck?"

"I doubt it. More likely, she sprained her back or pulled something. Such injuries can be extremely painful, and there is no effective treatment except bed rest and opiates for the pain. Sometimes they get better, and sometimes they don't."

"Except Blackwell knew of a treatment for it," Frank reminded her.

"So it appears. From what his wife told me, I think Blackwell must have been a bonesetter."

"A bone-setter? You mean he set broken bones?"

"Not exactly. I suppose in the old days, that's what bonesetters did, back before the science of medicine was so advanced and doctors began setting bones themselves," she said, and Frank managed not to snort in derision. His opinion of medicine wasn't quite as high as hers. "Nowadays," she continued, "bonesetters perform manipulations on bones that make people feel better."

"What do you mean 'manipulations'?"

"I mean they move the body around and somehow manage to make bones shift position, on the theory that they are somehow out of their proper position, which is what is causing the problems. I imagine that something in Mrs. Blackwell's spine or neck was somehow out of line from the accident, and Blackwell managed to realign it, thus relieving her pain."

"Is that possible?"

"Apparently. She said her pain was completely gone within a few weeks, after she'd been confined to her bed for almost a year."

"How did you find out she uses morphine?" Frank asked.

"Her baby became ill because he was no longer receiving the drug from his mother. I recognized the symptoms."

"You mean to tell me the woman gave her baby morphine?" Frank was horrified.

"Not directly," she explained patiently. "He would have gotten the effects of the morphine through the umbilical cord before he was born. Once he was born, he would no longer receive it. Sometimes, the baby receives enough of the drug through his mother's milk to satisfy the craving, but Mrs. Blackwell chose to use a wet nurse, so after about a day, he was desperate for the drug and showing all the signs of deprivation. He would have died without it, so I gave him a small dose of opium to ease his suffering."

"*You* let him have morphine?" Frank asked, horrified all over again.

She sighed with long-suffering. She always found Frank unreasonable, although he could never understand why. "My choice was to either give him the drug or watch him die in agony. What would you have done?"

Frank chose not to reply to that. "All right, so Mrs. Blackwell uses morphine. That's unusual for a woman of her social class, but—"

"It's not as unusual as you might suppose," she disagreed. "Many women of her social class use opiates of some sort."

"What on earth for?" He could understand why the poor used stimulants like alcohol and opiates to help them forget the grim realities of their existence, but what could a woman like Mrs. Blackwell need to forget?

"There are all kinds of pain, Malloy. Life can be hard even if you're rich."

He didn't bother arguing with her. It was usually a waste of time, even when he knew she was wrong. "All right, so she uses morphine. What does that have to do with her husband's death?"

"Her husband didn't know she was still using it. He knew she'd given it up after he cured her, even though it was very difficult for her. Have you ever seen anyone going through the process of weaning himself off an opiate? Few people ever manage to do it. But then he forced her to speak at his lectures. He gave lectures to promote—"

"I know all about his lectures," Frank said. "His assistant explained it to me, but he said Mrs. Blackwell was only too pleased to give her testimony of what the good doctor had done for her."

"Mrs. Blackwell tells a different story. She hated speaking in public. It terrified her, but her father and Blackwell forced her to do it."

"How could they force her if she didn't want to do it?"

"Really, Malloy, how do you force people to tell you things they don't want to tell you?" she asked, that gleam in her eyes that made her look so wicked he thought he should probably lock her away before she could cause any more trouble.

"Are you telling me they gave her the third degree?" he asked, giving her trouble right back.

"Of course not. You should know there are more effective ways of managing someone like Mrs. Blackwell.

Women of her class are taught from birth to be obedient and compliant and to please men."

"You're from her class," he pointed out, reminding her that she had been born into one of the oldest and wealthiest families in the city. "What happened to you?"

She gave him one of her looks, but she didn't dignify his words with a reply. "The important thing for you to know is that Mrs. Blackwell started using morphine again to help overcome her fear of appearing at those lectures. It was the only way she could do it. Her husband didn't approve of her using morphine, and she must have lived in constant fear that he would discover her secret. She also hated speaking at his lectures, which was why she needed the morphine in the first place. I imagine she was excused from doing them once her condition became apparent, but surely, he would have expected her to resume her appearances once the child was born. In fact, she told me he'd forbidden her to nurse the child herself because she had to be free to attend those lectures."

"Maybe you'll tell me why you think all this is important?" he tried, knowing it would annoy her to think he hadn't figured it out.

He was right. "Malloy, I'm surprised at you! Mrs. Blackwell might have thought the only way to avoid being discovered as a morphine user and having to speak at those lectures again was to murder her husband."

He almost hated to show her how weak her theory was. "You think a woman who was so frightened she'd take morphine to give her the courage to stand up in front of a crowd is going to have the courage to pick up her husband's pistol, put it to his head, and blow his brains all over her nice carpet?"

"Desperation can make people do strange things," she pointed out.

"Next I suppose you're going to argue that she wasn't in her right mind because of her delicate condition."

"I'm sure that's what she'd argue—if she's guilty, that is."

"I can't see any jury in the world convicting a woman with a baby in her arms. That's even if her father allowed it to get that far. I can't believe he would."

"Who is her father?"

"His name is Symington."

"Maurice Symington?" she asked with a frown.

"Probably. Do you know him?"

"I've heard of him, and my father knows him, I'm sure. I think he made his money in manufacturing."

"You mean he owns sweatshops?"

"That's exactly what I mean. I'm surprised he allowed his daughter to marry so far beneath her, unless Dr. Blackwell comes from money, too."

"He doesn't," Frank said.

"Well, then," she said, as if that proved everything. "Now I'm really surprised the father allowed her to appear at Dr. Blackwell's lectures. Such a public display would surely be offensive to him."

"I figured the same thing. Do you think Blackwell had something on the old man?"

"Looking for blackmail as a motive, Malloy?" she teased. "Sorry to disappoint you, but Mrs. Blackwell said they just felt they owed Blackwell a huge debt after what he did for her. He wouldn't even accept payment for treating her, and every other doctor had completely given up on helping her. It seems reasonable they would feel deeply grateful and obligated."

"Maybe," was all he would allow. Something about this case bothered him. Probably it was the idea that the man might have been done in by his own son. Frank found that very unsettling. He certainly didn't want to hear that the wife had done it instead, an even more unsettling idea.

"Or maybe she had a lover who took matters into his own hands," she suggested. "He would have the same motive as she, but he'd also have the will and the nerve to actually kill Dr. Blackwell."

"Do women of her class usually take lovers?" he asked, ashamed to admit that she might actually have come up with a good possibility. He hadn't yet seen Mrs. Blackwell, so he couldn't judge her character.

She considered this for a moment. "No, they don't. In fact, a woman from that class in society who is known to have taken a lover becomes a social outcast. It's simply too dangerous to risk."

Frank gave her a murderous frown for getting his hopes up, but she simply shrugged apologetically.

"All right, Malloy, you told me you'd have the killer locked up yesterday. If Mrs. Blackwell and her imaginary lover didn't do it, who did? That harmless little man, Mr. Potter?" she asked sarcastically.

"Never assume anyone is innocent, Mrs. Brandt. That's the best way to end up looking foolish."

She opened her mouth to say something that was probably outrageous, when someone knocked on the door, distracting them both.

"Yes?" Frank called.

The parlor doors opened, and Amos Potter stepped in. "Excuse me, but I was wondering how Mrs. Blackwell is doing."

Sarah Brandt smiled sweetly, probably thinking Potter was merely a concerned friend of the family. Frank had a feeling Potter's interest in Mrs. Blackwell was more than just friendly, however. He was just *too* solicitous.

"Mrs. Blackwell is just fine," Sarah said, "although she's very tired and has asked not to be disturbed anymore today."

"Oh, I wasn't planning on disturbing her," he hastily assured her. "I'm sure I wouldn't dream of . . . I mean, well, I did want to let her know the plans for Edmund's funeral, of course. We must have some sort of wake. He has many admirers, and his patients will want to pay tribute to him for all he's done."

"When were you planning to have the funeral?" Frank inquired, thinking this would be a good opportunity to look at all of Blackwell's acquaintances at once. The person who killed him would most likely be among them, unless his son really was the killer. In that case, Calvin Brown wouldn't very likely be in attendance since he would probably be a thousand miles away by now.

"I thought we'd have it tomorrow, since it's Saturday and . . . Well, that is, I already put it in the newspaper, so we will have it here tomorrow at ten o'clock. Just a small memorial service, you understand. There won't be a viewing, of course. I mean, under the circumstances, and with poor Edmund . . . Well, in any case, people need an opportunity to mourn. I know Mrs. Blackwell won't be able to attend, but I'm sure it will be a comfort to her knowing Edmund is being honored appropriately."

Not necessarily, Frank thought cynically, but he said, "Shouldn't you have checked with Mrs. Blackwell before making arrangements to have an event in her home?"

Potter seemed offended at the very suggestion. "Mr. Symington told me to proceed with the arrangements. I felt that was all the authority I needed. I assure you, Mrs. Blackwell will not be troubled in the slightest. Her well-being is my foremost concern, and I would never do anything that might cause her distress."

Frank could believe that. The man seemed *extraordinarily* concerned with Mrs. Blackwell's well-being. "I appreciate the opportunity to meet Dr. Blackwell's friends and associates," Frank said. "It should help me in my investigation."

Potter's round face grew red. "It would not be appropriate for you to question people during a funeral, Mr. Malloy. No one there will know anything anyway. You'd do better using your time to search for young Calvin."

"Who's Calvin?" Mrs. Brandt asked, and Frank winced. He'd been trying to keep her out of this, and now Potter had hooked her right in.

Frank considered trying to brush off her question, but she'd never allow that. He could tell by the expression on her face that she was like a hound on the scent now. In any case, Potter was already telling her everything she needed to know.

"Calvin Brown. He's a young man who had a . . . a certain grudge against Dr. Blackwell. I believe he is the one who killed Edmund," he added with more authority than he had any right to feel. At least he hadn't given her all the dirty gossip, Frank thought.

She turned to Frank expectantly. "If this man is the killer, why haven't you arrested him yet?"

"Because no one knows where he is," Frank replied, managing not to sound testy. It was a pure act of will.

"Oh, my, that is inconvenient, isn't it?" she asked without a hint of sympathy.

"Very," Frank agreed.

"If you could find him, you probably could have arrested him yesterday by, oh, I don't know, say by nightfall," she said.

Frank gave her a thin smile that she returned with a smirk.

"Oh, yes," Potter was saying, although no one was paying him any particular attention, "I'm sure this boy is the one who killed poor Edmund. He had an appointment with him that afternoon, and no one else was even in the house at that time. The servants had the afternoon off, and Mrs. Blackwell was out doing her visits. Who else could it have been? And now, of course, he's nowhere to be found. I'm sure that proves his guilt, the fact that he's vanished. Don't guilty men usually flee?" he asked Frank.

"If they can," Frank replied. At least Mrs. Brandt would think the killer was beyond their reach. Maybe she would lose interest in the case or maybe there wasn't really a case at all. Either possibility would keep her out of it.

This pleasant thought was interrupted by a commotion out in the hallway.

"What on earth?" Potter muttered, but Frank beat him to the door.

When he slid it open, he saw Granger confronting a roughly dressed boy of about sixteen who seemed determined to gain entry into the house over Granger's equally determined efforts to keep him out.

"There is a police officer here," Granger was saying with unmistakable warning. "Must I summon him?"

"Summon whoever you want, you old windbag," the boy said. "I come to see my father, and I ain't leaving until you tell him I'm here!"

"What's going on here?" Frank demanded, and Granger half turned to acknowledge him.

"This young man is obviously at the wrong house," he told Frank. "He insists on seeing his father, even though I have assured him there is no such person here. He was here the other day, too, and I had to run him off then as well."

Frank looked the boy over. "What's your name, son?"

The boy pulled himself up to his full height, making him still half a head shorter than Granger. "My name is Calvin Brown."

4

CALVIN BROWN! SARAH THOUGHT. HE'S THE ONE Potter thinks killed Dr. Blackwell! But he was just a boy, hardly more than sixteen or seventeen, and he certainly didn't look like a killer. Besides, if he'd killed Dr. Blackwell, he'd hardly be demanding admittance to his house today, would he?

Sarah heard Amos Potter gasp, and then he said, "That's him! The one I told you about. Arrest him, Malloy!"

The boy's face blanched, but he didn't look particularly intimidated. Quite the contrary, he looked even more defiant than he had before. "Arrest me for what?" he challenged. "Ain't no crime to come to see your old man!"

"Who is his father?" Sarah asked of anyone who would listen.

Young Calvin was the only one listening. "He's Eddie Brown, but that's not what he calls himself these days. Calls himself Edmund Blackwell, but that don't change who he is, does it?"

It took Sarah only a moment to judge that the woman upstairs, who was the current Mrs. Blackwell, could not possibly have given birth to this boy. She was no more than five years older than he, if that. Dr. Blackwell had a very interesting history, if Sarah was any judge, but she could tell from the look Malloy was giving her that she'd better not inquire too closely into the subject just now.

Malloy stepped forward, forcing Granger to stand aside so Malloy could confront the boy. "Dr. Blackwell is dead," he said baldly.

Sarah winced at the coldness of it. If the boy was truly Blackwell's son, this was needless cruelty.

The boy blinked in surprise, not yet comprehending what Malloy had said. "Dead? How could he be dead? Wasn't nothing wrong with him a couple days ago."

"There wasn't nothing wrong with him at all until somebody shot him on Tuesday," Malloy replied.

The boy's jaw dropped, but he still wasn't ready to believe. He glanced around wildly until his gaze settled with desperation on Sarah. "Is that true, ma'am?"

Sarah was touched. He'd chosen her as the most trustworthy person in sight. "I'm afraid it is, Mr. Brown," she told him as gently as she could.

They all watched as the emotions played across his young face—shock, confusion, despair, and finally anger. "Well, that's just something, ain't it?" he asked of no one in particular as he blinked back tears. "He's run out on us twice now, and this time it won't do no good to find him."

The story was coming clearer to her now. Dr. Blackwell—or whatever his real name was—had abandoned this son and the rest of whatever other family the boy had, changed his name, and made a new life for himself. Somehow the boy had found him, though, and . . . Oh, dear heaven! No wonder Potter thought Calvin might have killed his father. Potter had said the boy held a grudge against Dr. Blackwell, but this was far more than a grudge. Could such a young, innocent-looking boy have fired a bullet into his father's brain, no matter what that father had done to deserve it?

"Mr. Malloy, are you going to do your duty and arrest this boy?" Potter was asking, his tone outraged.

Malloy gave him a quelling look that silenced him, then turned back to the boy. "Why don't you come into the parlor with me, son. I've got some questions to ask you."

"You think *I* killed him?" the boy asked, even more outraged than Potter had been. "My own father?"

"I didn't say that," Malloy reminded him, taking his arm in his strong grip.

The boy instinctively tried to pull away, but the resistance lasted only a moment, until he saw the expression in Malloy's dark eyes. He seemed almost to shrink with his surrender to Malloy's superior strength and power. His bravado evaporated, and he was an uncertain boy again.

"Excuse us, please," Malloy said with uncharacteristic courtesy as he forced Sarah and Potter to give way and allow him and the boy to enter the parlor.

Sarah had a powerful urge to follow them in. Only her knowledge that Malloy would immediately—and not very politely—order her out prevented her from acting on it. She sighed as the parlor doors closed in her face.

"Will he arrest him?" Potter asked her anxiously.

Sarah glanced at the butler, who was listening to every word with the discretion to which he had been bred. His expression betrayed nothing, but Sarah imagined he was mentally recording every word and would repeat it belowstairs to all the servants as soon as he got the opportunity.

"Perhaps we should step into another room," she suggested. She could simply have brushed off his question and taken her leave—she had no real answer to give him, after all—but she felt certain he had a lot of answers to give her, if she simply asked the right questions.

She wasn't going to ask them in front of the butler, however.

"Oh, yes," Potter said, instantly realizing they needed some privacy for their discussion. "We could use the study, if you don't mind . . ."

The room where Dr. Blackwell had been murdered. Little did Potter know a woman had been murdered in the parlor they had just left, and Sarah had found the body. Sarah wasn't afraid of the dead. "Not at all," she said, and allowed him to precede her and open the door.

Sarah looked around with interest at the room which Edmund Blackwell/Eddie Brown had made his own. The furnishings were decidedly masculine: dark woods polished to a bright sheen, overstuffed chairs, several built-in bookshelves filled with leather-bound volumes, English hunting scenes hanging in heavy frames on the walls. Nowhere did she see any signs of the man himself, though. The desk had been cleared, of course, and it may have held some personal items that would have given her a clue as to his character. Nothing of him now remained except a dark stain that had been ineffectively scrubbed away from the carpet, so she was left to reconstruct his personality from what others said about him.

"Will Mr. Malloy arrest him?" Potter asked again when they were safely behind closed doors.

Sarah had an urge to check to make sure Granger wasn't eavesdropping, but she resisted it. "If he decides that the boy killed Dr. Blackwell, he will," she hedged.

"What makes you think he did? He's awfully young."

"A viper doesn't have to be large to be deadly, Mrs. Brandt," he said with some force. "I suppose you have surmised the relationship between the boy and Dr. Blackwell."

"Dr. Blackwell was his father," she said, confirming his suspicion. "And I gather Dr. Blackwell must have deserted the family."

"Yes, he . . . he left his first wife and children several years ago. It wasn't intentional," he assured her quickly.

Sarah raised her eyebrows, wondering how such a thing could be unintentional, but she didn't have to ask the question aloud. Mr. Potter anticipated her.

"He explained it all to me. You see, he was always a healer by profession, but he was doing very poorly in Virginia. That's where he lived then. He couldn't support his family, so he traveled to Boston to study with a well-known practitioner of the art of magnetic healing there. He thought if he could improve his talents, he could be more successful. He worked as much as he could and continued to send money home to his family. He never intended to leave them permanently."

"At some point he apparently changed his mind," Sarah pointed out. "Was it when he met Letitia Symington?"

"Oh, it wasn't like that at all! Letitia would never . . . She's much too . . . Oh, no, it had nothing to do with her at all!"

"Then what did it have to do with?" Sarah prodded, wondering why Potter felt he had to justify Blackwell to her but glad for his need nonetheless.

"He became quite proficient in the new art of magnetic healing, and so he came here to the city and began to build a following. He lived frugally, still sending money home when he could and depending on his satisfied patients to recommend him to their friends. One of those patients recommended him to Mr. Symington."

"For his daughter," Sarah said. "I understand she'd been severely injured in a riding accident."

"Yes, and her father was desperate to see her whole again. Letitia's mother had died years earlier, so she was all he had. He'd called in every doctor he could find, but nothing had made her any better. Edmund was the only one who was able to help her at all, and within days she was out of her bed for the first time in a year. It was like a miracle."

"I'm sure the Symingtons were very grateful to him," Sarah said, encouraging him in his tale.

"You can't know how grateful. Mr. Symington would have done anything to repay Edmund, but all Edmund wanted was for them to help spread word of what he had done for Letitia. Mr. Symington offered to rent a hall for Edmund so he could give a public lecture about his techniques, and when Edmund explained that he needed someone to speak who could personally testify to Edmund's abilities, Mr. Symington eagerly gave his permission for Letitia to do so."

"How did she feel about that?" Sarah asked, already knowing but wondering what Potter would say.

"Oh, she's very refined, and it was difficult for her, but she was so grateful to Edmund, she overcame her natural reserve. People openly wept when she told the story of how he had cured her. After that, Edmund's success was assured."

"I'm sure it was. He must have treated many wealthy people after that."

"Well, it's not so easy as it sounds. Many people were still skeptical, of course. His practice grew slowly at first."

"So he felt the need to do more lectures," Sarah guessed.

"It's important to educate people. You would be amazed at how many people distrust medical treatment of any kind."

"No, I wouldn't, Mr. Potter. I'm a nurse and a midwife by profession, remember."

"Oh, of course," he corrected himself quickly. "I did not mean any offense."

"You gave none. So I'm assuming that Blackwell didn't become an overnight sensation."

"It may have seemed like it to some, but he struggled for months before he could consider himself comfortable. By then he'd fallen in love with Letitia, and she with him. You may wonder that so young a girl was taken with a much older man, but Edmund is . . . *was* a very attractive and charming man, and women are often attracted to maturity. It was all very romantic, as you can imagine."

"I'm sure Edmund's first wife wouldn't agree," Sarah pointed out.

"Oh, you're right, I'm sure, but sometimes ... Well, while I cannot condone what Edmund did, forgetting about his first wife and family, I can certainly understand it. Letitia is like no other woman. Her beauty and charm are irresistible, and knowing how much she adored him, Edmund couldn't bring himself to disappoint her."

"Wasn't he afraid she'd be even more disappointed when she found out he was already married and she was living in sin with a man who had cruelly deceived her?" Sarah asked in amazement.

"I'm sure he intended that she never find out," Potter assured her defensively. "Edmund would have died rather than hurt her."

"He did die, and he still hurt her," Sarah pointed out.

For a moment Potter was nonplussed and stammered around for a reply. Sarah waited patiently, knowing there was virtually nothing he could say that would excuse Blackwell's behavior, and while she waited, a new thought occurred to her.

"Who else knew about Blackwell's other family?" she asked.

Potter stared at her stupidly. "No one. I am the only one in whom he confided."

"Are you sure? Did Letitia know? Or her father?"

"I can't imagine Edmund would have told anyone at all, particularly Letitia or her father," he sniffed. "A scandal like this would have ruined him. He intended to pay Calvin off and thus buy his silence. I'm sure he wouldn't have spoken of it to anyone else."

"Why did he tell you, then?"

Potter was beginning to dislike Sarah. She could see it in his tiny, mud-brown eyes. "I was Edmund's business associate and dearest friend. He needed advice from someone, and I was the only one he could trust."

Sarah was sure she now understood. "And you helped him get the money to bribe Calvin."

"Really," Potter huffed, so thoroughly offended that Sarah knew she had guessed the truth. "I'm sorry to have bothered you with this, Mrs. Brandt. You must think me terribly inconsiderate. A female must find this entire business extremely distressing."

Sarah wanted to tell him she'd seen birth and death and murder and murderers enough that hardly anything shocked her anymore, but she simply smiled sweetly, playing to Potter's prejudices. "You needn't worry that you have distressed me, Mr. Potter. I'm simply concerned for Mrs. Blackwell's health. A scandal could be very detrimental to her recovery."

"Oh, dear, of course. I should have thought of that. I was merely concerned with her mental state. I never thought . . . But you needn't worry, Mrs. Brandt. I am completely trained in the healing arts that Edmund practiced. If Letitia suffers a relapse, I am more than competent to attend her."

"I'm sure she'll find that a comfort, Mr. Potter," Sarah said, although she believed no such thing. "And speaking of comfort, I should check on Mrs. Blackwell. I want to make sure she wasn't disturbed by Calvin's arrival. The less she knows about this the better, as I'm sure you'll agree."

Potter did not protest her departure. He obviously had grown uncomfortable with the turn of the conversation. And clearly, she had gathered all the information he had to give her at the moment, although she doubted the accuracy of some of the details. Potter's version of events was colored by his loyalty to Blackwell—or his eagerness to whitewash Blackwell's reputation so he wouldn't be hurt too much by his association with him. At least she knew the bare facts now, however. Blackwell was a bigamist who had deceived a wealthy young woman from a powerful family. If that wasn't a motive for murder, Sarah would dance naked down Fifth Avenue.

CALVIN BROWN DID not resist when Frank pushed him down into one of the overstuffed chairs in the parlor. The boy's clear blue eyes were wide with fear, although he was doing his level best to pretend he wasn't afraid at all. Frank had to admire his spirit.

"Now, Calvin," Frank began, taking a seat opposite him, "tell me what you're doing here today."

"I come to see my father," he said defensively, suspicious of Frank's mildness. He blinked a few times as if trying to hold back tears.

"It was my understanding that you had an appointment with him two days ago. What kept you?"

Frank's sarcasm was wasted on the boy. "I did come two days ago, just like he'd said for me to. He said he'd . . . Well, never mind. I was to come then, in the afternoon. At two o'clock. I waited until I heard the big clock in the tower chiming, then I went up to the front door and knocked. But didn't nobody answer. I pounded for a long time, but nobody come. Houses like this, they got servants and such. I couldn't figure why nobody come, so I waited awhile and knocked again. Then some copper come and told me to be on my way, he didn't like my looks, and I was scared he'd arrest me. I figured I must've got the wrong day or something, so I left."

"Are you telling me you didn't come inside and you didn't see your father that day?"

"No, sir. I didn't see nobody in the house at all."

"If you had an appointment with your father, why did you wait two days to come back?" Frank asked, keeping his tone gently inquiring. He saw no sense in frightening the boy so long as he was talking freely, even if he didn't like his answers.

"I didn't. I come back yesterday, but I seen that copper again. He didn't see me, but he was walking around the park, acting like he wasn't going nowhere very soon.

I figured if he sees me, he'll give me his stick, so I kept going. Today I didn't see him, so I come up to the door and asked to see my father. That's when that snooty fellow tried to throw me out."

"I see. Now tell me, Calvin, how you came to be in the city in the first place."

The boy frowned. He wasn't eager to share this story, but he knew he had no choice. "I told you, I come to see my father."

"You came an awfully long way, and it's my understanding he'd been gone a long time. How did you even know he was here?"

Calvin shifted uncomfortably in his chair. "I seen his picture. It was a drawing. On a poster for one of his lectures. Someone sent it to my ma."

"Who?" Frank asked, perking up.

"Don't know. Whoever sent it didn't write no letter or anything. It was just the poster in an envelope addressed to my ma. We could see right off it was him. It was a good likeness, even though they said his name was Edmund Blackwell. Pa was named Edward Brown. Ma said it was like him to change his name to sound more uppity."

"Or so his family couldn't locate him," Frank suggested.

The boy snorted. "Likely he could've still called himself Eddie Brown and we couldn't've found him either. How could we? Last we heard he was in Boston. Boston's a big place. He could hide there forever without us finding him."

The boy was right. "You could have hired a detective to locate him," Frank suggested.

"You mean you can pay coppers to find somebody for you?" Calvin asked in amazement.

Frank forgot the boy was from the country. "No, there's private detectives you can hire to do things like this."

Calvin looked at him like he was crazy. "And how

could we pay somebody to do that? Pa used to send us some money from time to time, but he quit a couple years ago. Must've been about the time he come here. Even when he did send money, it was never enough, though. There's three of us kids. I've got two little sisters. Ma had to take in washing to put food on the table. I worked at whatever I could, selling newspapers and chopping firewood and whatever I could find until I got big enough to get steady work. Sometimes we didn't even have enough to eat, so how could we hire somebody to find Pa?"

"But you had enough money to come to New York from Virginia," Frank pointed out. "Exactly where do you live there?"

"A place called Lynchburg. I . . . well, there was something else in the envelope besides the poster. No letter or nothing, like I said, but there was a train ticket."

"Someone sent you a train ticket to New York?" Frank asked in amazement. This was growing more interesting by the moment.

"Yeah, and . . . and a little bit of money, too."

Frank stared at the boy. He'd been lied to by thousands of people in the course of his work, and he liked to think he could spot a lie a mile away. This boy was either telling the truth or he was the best liar Frank had ever encountered. "Sounds like someone wanted you to come to New York and find your father."

The boy shrugged. "I guess so. Ma, she thought someone was mad at Pa and wanted to get even or something."

"They must have wanted to get even very badly to go to all that trouble," Frank suggested. "How did you find your father when you got to the city?"

"I just went to the place where he was going to be, where it said on the poster he was going to be. There was lots of people there. I sat way in the back so he wouldn't see me, and then he come out on the stage. It was him, all right. I ain't seen him for almost five years, but I was eleven when he left, so I knew him right off."

"Did you confront him that night?"

"No. I didn't want to warn him off. And besides, there was this man who talked that night. He said Dr. Blackwell was married to his daughter. I didn't think that could be right. He's married to my ma! I was confused, and I needed to think about things some, so I waited around, after the lecture. I was gonna follow him home, but he got in one of them hansom cabs. I didn't know they was called that then, but I do now. Anyways, I heard him telling the driver where to take him. Gramercy Park. It was easy to find out where that was. I just asked somebody at the place where I'm staying."

"And so you called on your father. When was this?"

"I don't know. About five days ago, I guess."

"What was his reaction?"

Calvin frowned, his youthful face revealing every emotion. Plainly, he found the memory painful. "I don't know what I expected, but for certain it wasn't what happened. He pretended he was real happy to see me. Asked how everybody was doing and all. I thought he'd be mad or maybe act a little guilty, but he didn't. It was like he'd just forgot all about us, and I'd reminded him. Said he knew he'd been neglecting us, and he wanted to set things right. I thought he meant he'd bring all of us up here to live with him. That's what he should've done, and he's got plenty of room in this house, don't he? The reason he left was so he could do better and give us a better life. This was his chance."

"But he wasn't going to do that, was he?"

"He said the city wasn't the right place for us because it was so dangerous. He said we'd be better off to stay in Lynchburg. He was making money now, for the first time, and he'd start supporting us again. He'd even come to visit. But he had to stay here because that's where his business was." Calvin's tone clearly expressed his bitterness.

"What did you say?"

"I said I knew he had another wife now, and what would people think if they found out about us?"

"Did that scare him?"

"It made him real mad. He said if I did anything to hurt him, he wouldn't be able to make a living anymore, and we'd never get anything from him again. If I kept quiet, he'd send me back with some money, and he'd start sending us money regular again, too."

"Did you believe him?"

"I didn't know, but he was real mean. He scared me, like he might do something worse than not support us if I made any trouble for him."

"Did he threaten you?"

"Not right out, but he made it real clear he could make sure I didn't never get back to Lynchburg if I made trouble."

"So you didn't make any trouble," Frank guessed.

"I told him I wouldn't. He said to come back in a few days, and he'd have the money for me. I thought maybe if I had some money, I could do something. I didn't know what, but maybe Ma would know. At least it would make things easier for her if he started supporting us again. So I left."

"And you didn't come back again until day before yesterday."

"Yes, sir. And like I said, nobody answered the door. I thought maybe he had to go out or he forgot I was coming or something, but shouldn't somebody have answered the door anyway? That snooty fellow was here the other times I come and today. Seems like it's his job to answer the door."

"All the servants had the afternoon off that day," Frank told him. "Apparently, he didn't want anyone to know you were here or to see you again."

"No, I guess he wouldn't," Calvin said after he thought about it.

"And someone shot him while he was here alone."

Calvin's smooth face creased into a puzzled frown.

"Then he's really dead? But why would somebody shoot him?"

Frank leaned back in his chair, ostensibly unconcerned. "Perhaps because he'd deserted his family and then refused to pay the promised sum of money to them."

"But why—" he started, and then stopped when Frank's meaning sank in. "You think *I* shot him? Why would I do a thing like that? He was my father!"

"The father who deserted you and caused your family great hardship while he was living in luxury. The father who took another wife and now refused to acknowledge you."

Now Calvin was angry. "I might've hated him, but he was still my father! And besides, if he was dead, he couldn't help us none, now could he? Killing him would be stupid!"

"But what if he'd decided not to give you the money he'd promised? What if he told you to go back home and forget about him or some harm would come to all of you? I know that would make me mad enough to shoot somebody."

"But I didn't even see him that day! I wasn't even in the house. And I don't have a gun, either!"

Frank was inclined to believe him. Calvin didn't even know Blackwell was killed with his own gun, so the killer wouldn't have had one. The story about the policeman sending him on his way was easy enough to check, in any case. And his theory about Blackwell refusing to pay the boy seemed farfetched. Blackwell wouldn't dare take a chance on offending Calvin and having him spread his story. Paying him off was a simple solution to a very complicated problem, one that Blackwell would have been a fool not to accept. Frank didn't think Blackwell was a fool.

Besides, if Calvin *had* taken the money and killed his father, he'd be miles away by now, just as Amos Potter had suggested. He certainly wouldn't have come knocking on the door and drawing attention to himself.

Now the boy was looking really frightened. "Are you gonna put me in jail?"

It would be so easy. The boy was penniless and alone. No one except his mother would care what happened to him, and she was miles away and powerless to help him. Frank could stick the boy in jail, beat him until he confessed, close the case, and collect his reward from Potter and Symington. That's what most of the detectives on the force would do. Frank had done it a time or two himself, although never with an innocent boy. The people he usually dealt with were criminals, guilty of something or another, even if it wasn't the crime he was investigating. If they went to jail, they deserved it, and the world was a better place with them behind bars.

But Calvin Brown was guilty of nothing.

"Did you kill your father, Calvin?" he asked.

"No, sir! I already told you."

"If I don't arrest you, what will you do?"

His eyes widened. Frank could see the fear and the hope mingled in them. "I . . . I guess I can't do nothing much. I'm about out of money, so I've got to go back home soon. The ticket was just one way, so I'll have to hop a freight or something, but I got to get back home to help my ma." He thought a minute. "I sure would like to find out who killed my pa, though. I kinda feel like it's my duty or something."

Frank wanted him to stay, too. He might need to ask him more questions when he found out more about the case. And he did need to know who had sent the poster to Mrs. Brown. Someone, it seemed, was trying to cause Dr. Blackwell trouble. If he could find out who, he'd be a lot closer to finding the killer.

"If I pay your rent for another week, would you stay in town?" Frank asked. A few dollars was cheap enough for the help the boy might be able to give him. Besides, he wanted the boy close so he could keep an eye on him. "If you do, I'll even buy you a ticket back home when you're ready to leave."

Now the boy was thoroughly confused. "You ain't gonna arrest me?"

"I don't think you killed your father, Calvin, but you may be able to help me find out who did."

"How?"

"You can start by showing me the poster that was sent to your mother, if you still have it."

"I do. I even have the envelope, but it won't help you none."

"I'll be the judge of that. Let's go to your lodging house. I'll take care of your rent while we're there." The boy might be innocent, but Frank didn't trust him not to run if he had the means, so he wasn't going to give him money directly.

They went out into the hall to find Amos Potter waiting on a bench in the entrance hall. He jumped to his feet.

"Where are you taking him?" Potter demanded. "Are you arresting him?"

"Not yet, Mr. Potter," Frank said, noticing the boy's alarm.

"Why not?" Potter was outraged. "You know he's the one who killed Edmund! He's the only one who had a reason."

"I don't think we can be sure of that. But don't worry, Mr. Potter, Calvin will be in safekeeping in the meantime. Now if you'll excuse us, we have business to attend to."

Plainly unhappy, Potter reluctantly stepped aside and allowed them to leave. Frank was sure he'd have a few choice words to say later about the way Frank was handling the case, but he'd worry about that when it happened.

WHEN SARAH CAME downstairs after checking on her patients, she was furious to discover that Malloy had left with the boy. She'd intended to corner the detective and demand an account of what he'd learned. Now she'd have to find out later.

She collected her things, and Granger asked if he should summon the carriage for her.

"That won't be necessary. It's a lovely day, and I'd prefer to walk. I'll be back in the morning to see how the baby is doing," she told him.

"That wouldn't be a convenient time," Granger told her. "Dr. Blackwell's funeral is being held here at ten o'clock."

Why hadn't she expected this? Now she'd be *sure* to be here tomorrow. She wouldn't miss Blackwell's funeral for anything. "Thank you, Granger," she said, not telling him of her plans.

On the way home, Sarah mulled over the things she had learned from Amos Potter. She would have to share this information with Malloy, although she thought he probably knew most of it already. What he might not know was the difference in the versions of the truth that she had heard today. Potter insisted that Letitia had been happy to speak at Blackwell's lectures, and Sarah knew that Letitia had hated it so much she'd needed to use morphine just to get through them.

Did Potter know her true feelings? Was he trying to protect her, or did he honestly believe she was that devoted to her husband? Fortunately, it wasn't her job to find the answers. She could simply collect observations and pass them along to Malloy. He hadn't wanted her involved in this case, but here she was, in up to her eyebrows just the same. She hoped he'd be grateful for her help after all, but if he wasn't, it didn't matter. She was going to help him anyway.

A quarter of an hour later she reached Bank Street, and as she strolled toward her front steps, she saw her elderly next-door neighbor, Mrs. Ellsworth, come out with her broom and begin to sweep.

No dirt ever had a chance to collect on Mrs. Ellsworth's front steps because she was out there ten times a day sweeping. She used this activity as an excuse to encounter everyone who passed by. Sarah wondered when she had a chance to do her inside housework since she always seemed to be watching out her front window for any activity that required her attention in the neighborhood.

"Hello, Mrs. Brandt!" she called cheerfully.

"How are you today, Mrs. Ellsworth?" Sarah replied. Since Mrs. Ellsworth had once saved her life, Sarah would indulge her whenever she could.

"Oh, I'm feeling quite cheerful, Mrs. Brandt. My apron fell off this morning, and that gave me quite a laugh."

This didn't seem particularly funny to Sarah, but she knew Mrs. Ellsworth well enough to know there must be some hidden meaning in the event. Mrs. Ellsworth found hidden meaning in just about everything that happened. "And why did you find this so funny?"

"Because when an apron falls off, it means the wearer is going to have a baby within the year!"

Even Sarah had to laugh at this, too. Mrs. Ellsworth was in no danger of having a baby this or any year. "Perhaps someone is going to leave one on your doorstep," she suggested.

"Wouldn't that be something?" Mrs. Ellsworth said. "I don't think I'd even remember what to do with a baby, it's been so long. It's a nice thought, though."

"Or maybe it means you're going to be a grandmother," Sarah said, teasing her. "Has your son been keeping company with anyone special lately?"

"Lord, no," Mrs. Ellsworth said. "All Nelson does is work at the bank, day and night. I tell him it's making him old before his time, but does he listen? Of course not. He tells me he needs to get ahead. I tell him he needs to get a wife. I want some grandchildren to spoil before I die."

"I don't blame you. But sooner or later he'll meet a

nice girl and fall in love. Don't give up hope."

"And where have you been this lovely day? Delivering someone else's grandchild?"

"No, I was just visiting one of my patients who . . ." Suddenly Sarah realized Mrs. Ellsworth might know the deceased. She was always following the latest in medical cures. "Have you ever heard of Dr. Edmund Blackwell?"

"Blackwell? Yes, indeed. He's getting quite famous. I went to one of his lectures. Nelson always tells me I'm a fool for believing these charlatans, but how do you know that one of them might not have really discovered something that will help cure people?"

Sarah wasn't about to agree with something so outrageous. "What did you think of him?" she asked instead.

"A lovely man," she said, really meaning it. "Quite handsome and tall, and his voice was like velvet. Just looking at him made me feel better," she added with a sly grin, "so I imagine his treatments are quite effective."

Sarah couldn't help smiling back. "I had no idea he was so attractive," she said. This probably explained why Letitia had married him, in spite of the difference in their backgrounds and their ages.

"And I'm not the only one who noticed, either, as you can imagine. Ladies tend to get sick more frequently if their doctor is handsome and charming, so Dr. Blackwell was in great demand. I even heard . . . Well, that's of no matter."

Sarah glanced around to see if anyone else was in earshot and stepped closer to Mrs. Ellsworth's porch. "I guess you haven't heard about it yet, but Dr. Blackwell was murdered two days ago."

"Good heavens, no! I can hardly believe it!" She leaned her broom up against the house and came halfway down the steps so they could speak more quietly. "Did you say he was murdered? How on earth did it happen?"

"Someone went into his house and shot him. I understand the killer tried to make it look like suicide but—"

"But that nice Mr. Malloy wasn't fooled," she guessed. Mrs. Ellsworth thought very highly of Frank Malloy. "Does he know who did it?"

"Not yet. It seems Dr. Blackwell had a mysterious past that might have given someone a reason to kill him."

Mrs. Ellsworth snorted derisively. "I don't know what kind of a past he had, but I can assure you, if what I've heard about him is true, he has a present that might have given someone a reason to kill him, too."

"What do you mean?" Sarah asked eagerly.

"What I mean is that rumor has it Dr. Blackwell's treatments sometimes involved intimacies that other doctors would have considered . . . uh . . . unprofessional."

"Intimacies?" Sarah echoed.

Mrs. Ellsworth glanced around this time, making sure she would not be overheard. "It's said he sometimes seduces his patients, Mrs. Brandt. Not that the patients were unwilling. I'm sure they were actually quite eager. But some of them, I've heard, have jealous husbands who resented their wives' devotion to the good doctor, even if they didn't know how deep that devotion went. Perhaps one of them found out about his wife's involvement and decided to rid the world of his rival."

5

For the funeral the next morning, Sarah dressed in her best black serge and chose a hat that still looked moderately stylish. In the normal course of her life, she hardly ever needed to look stylish, but she'd been to far too many funerals since meeting Frank Malloy. She'd be forced to get a new hat if this kept up.

Although she was carrying her medical bag when Granger opened the front door to the Blackwell home, he could not miss the fact that she was here for the funeral, although she was a bit early. Her hat probably gave her away.

"I'm sure Mrs. Blackwell will be glad to see you, Mrs. Brandt," he said, although his tone belied the words.

Sarah, of course, didn't particularly care if Mrs. Blackwell wanted to see her or not. She was here, and they wouldn't dare cause a scene by trying to throw her out. She was, after all, Mrs. Blackwell's nurse, and who could fault her for paying her respects to the husband of her patient?

When she stepped into the foyer, she heard Amos Potter's voice coming from the parlor. He was instructing someone impatiently. Sarah peeked in and saw that Dr.

Blackwell's large, ornate casket had been brought in during her absence. It was closed, probably because after having his brains blown out, he wasn't in any condition for viewing. Several large flower arrangements stood around, their scent rather cloying in the confines of the room, and the furniture had been moved back to make space for half a dozen rows of chairs.

Potter was telling one of the maids to move the flowers closer to the casket when Sarah called, "Good morning, Mr. Potter. Is there anything I can do to help?"

Potter looked up in surprise, and for an instant couldn't seem to place her. "Oh, good morning, Mrs. Brandt," he said after a moment. "No, I'm sure we have everything taken care of. Is Mrs. Blackwell ill?" he added with some concern.

"Not that I am aware. I did think she might need some support today, however. This must be a terrible strain for her."

"Oh, not at all. I told her she didn't have to worry about anything. I've taken care of all the arrangements. And under the circumstances, no one expects her to attend the service, of course."

"Sometimes that's worse, knowing you can't do anything or take part in something of such importance," Sarah said. "And don't underestimate the importance of a funeral. One must be allowed to mourn a loss such as this, and being unable to attend her husband's funeral will make it difficult for her to come to terms with his death."

Potter didn't appreciate being instructed in such things. "I'm sure I will be able to give Mrs. Blackwell all the support she will need in the coming months, Mrs. Brandt. You need not concern yourself about her welfare."

Sarah simply smiled. She'd expected as much from Potter. He was certainly eager to offer every assistance to the lovely young widow. Maybe she hadn't been so far wrong in imagining Potter could have killed Blackwell because he wanted Mrs. Blackwell for himself. She was going to have to discard the theory that Potter had seduced Letitia, however. One preposterous solution to this case was quite enough. Malloy was going to tease her mercilessly if she couldn't come up with a more menacing suspect than Amos Potter.

"I'll leave you to your duties," Sarah said, and continued on her way upstairs, ignoring Granger's disapproving glare.

Sarah checked on the baby first. The boy appeared to be fine.

"I give him the drops, just like you told me," the nurse reported. "No more, no less. Then he's like an angel. Eats and sleeps just like he should."

Sarah listened to his heart and his lungs and thumped his tummy. His color was good and his eyes were clear. He turned his head toward the nurse when she spoke, and he followed Sarah's finger with his eyes. He wasn't deaf or blind, and he seemed sound of body. They wouldn't know about his mind for a while yet, but Sarah could hope he would be none the worse for the morphine his mother had taken.

"He seems perfectly healthy," Sarah judged with more than a little relief when she'd finished her examination.

"Except for that hair. Did the morphine turn it that color, do you think?" the nurse asked with obvious disapproval.

"Certainly not," Sarah assured her. "He simply has red hair."

"Never saw hair like that on a baby," the nurse insisted. "It ain't natural."

"Many people have red hair, and it's perfectly natural," Sarah assured her as patiently as she could. People had the oddest prejudices.

The nurse hmmphed her skepticism. "How long do you think we'll have to give him that horrible stuff?"

"A few months," Sarah said. "We'll wait until he's gained some weight, and we're certain he's healthy.

Then we'll gradually decrease his dosage. Have you heard how Mrs. Blackwell is doing?"

"Don't nobody tell me anything," the nurse said, a little disgusted. As a newcomer to the household she wouldn't have gained the confidence of the other staff members, and her job, of necessity, kept her from socializing with them. "I do know they're having the doctor's funeral this morning."

"So I gathered," Sarah said. "That's why I came today. I was afraid Mrs. Blackwell might be upset. I'd better go check on her."

The nurse made another rude noise. "If she's got some morphine, she probably don't even know what's going on in her own parlor."

Sarah gave her a quelling look which made her frown, but at least she didn't say any more. Sarah hoped she wasn't going to have to suggest that Mrs. Blackwell get another nurse, but if this one was going to be so disapproving of her employer, things could become very difficult.

Sarah learned from the maid lingering in the hallway that Mrs. Blackwell was awake and wanted to see her. The bedroom was dark when Sarah entered, the heavy drapes drawn against the morning sunlight. Mrs. Blackwell lay propped against her pillows, her face pale and her expression drawn.

"How is my baby?" she asked Sarah, who decided the woman might not be as selfish and spoiled as she had originally thought. At least she'd asked about the baby first.

"He's doing very well," Sarah said. "We have apparently determined the correct dose of morphine to give him, and he's thriving on the nurse's milk."

"Thank heaven," she breathed, closing her lovely eyes for a moment in apparent relief.

"What have you named him?" Sarah asked to be sociable.

Her eyes flew open, and Sarah was surprised to see

the alarm in them. "I . . . I haven't thought," she said. "Edmund wanted . . . but now . . . I don't know!"

"There's no hurry," Sarah assured her, disturbed by her reaction. The woman seemed incapable of making any decision without her husband's approval. If that were true, his death was going to hamper the decision-making process considerably. "It will be a while before he even knows he has a name," Sarah added in an attempt to lighten the moment.

Mrs. Blackwell didn't look reassured. "But other people will know," she pointed out. "My father . . . he'll expect me to . . ." She lifted the back of her hand to her forehead in a gesture of despair.

"Why don't you let me examine you," Sarah suggested, hoping to take her mind off of the terrible burden of selecting a name for her child. "Are you having any discomfort?"

FRANK HAD TIMED his arrival at the Blackwell home so he would be there to see the guests as they arrived. He wanted to get a look at the people who felt the need to honor Blackwell's memory or at least to assure themselves he was dead.

He found Amos Potter giving frantic orders to the servants, who scurried around trying to do his bidding. He didn't look at all happy to see Frank.

"Mr. Malloy," he said imperiously. "As I informed you yesterday, your presence here is completely unnecessary."

"Not unless you think it's unnecessary for me to find out who killed Dr. Blackwell," Frank replied.

Potter glared at him impatiently. "Surely you don't believe anyone coming here today could have killed him?"

"I won't know until I see them, now will I?" Frank said reasonably.

Potter didn't think this was reasonable at all. "I already told you who the killer is," he reminded him. "You had him in your power, and you let him get away."

"He hasn't gotten away," Frank said. "Besides, I don't have any reason to believe he's the killer."

"Who else could it have been? The boy is insane with grief and rage. His father deserted him and his family and left them penniless. He probably spent years trying to locate Edmund, and when he did, Edmund rejected him once again. Unable to control his fury, he shot poor Edmund and tried to cover up his crime. There, you see how simple it is? And I'm not even a policeman," Potter said smugly.

"Do you want me to accuse an innocent boy just so I can collect a reward?" Frank asked with as much genuine confusion as he could muster.

Potter barely controlled his impatience. "He isn't innocent!"

Frank waited until the maid who was straightening the chairs moved out of earshot. "I questioned him thoroughly, and he gave me all the right answers, Mr. Potter. I don't believe he killed his father."

"Then he is even more clever than I imagined," Potter informed him. "He's Edmund's son, all right. If he is at all like his father, he would have no trouble bending the truth to suit his needs, and he would have the advantage of his youth to lend him the appearance of innocence."

"Was Dr. Blackwell an accomplished liar?" Frank asked curiously.

The color rose in Potter's face, and he glanced uneasily at the casket standing nearby. "It's wrong to speak ill of the dead," he said.

"Then you believe that there is ill you could speak about," Frank surmised. "Tell me, who did the good doctor lie to? You? His patients? His wife? We certainly know he lied to the current Mrs. Blackwell by not telling her about the first Mrs. Brown."

"I refuse to discuss such a thing with Edmund lying dead just a few feet away," Potter sniffed.

"Then we can discuss it later," Frank said.

Plainly, Potter did not like being told what to do by a mere policeman. "You will excuse me now. I have many things to do before the guests arrive."

Frank let him go. He wasn't going to get anywhere with him right now anyway. He went to the kitchen to find a cup of coffee while he waited for the funeral guests to begin arriving.

"Do you know my husband's funeral is this morning?" Mrs. Blackwell asked Sarah as she finished her examination.

"Yes," Sarah said. "I noticed the preparations when I arrived. I'm sure you must be disappointed that you can't attend."

Mrs. Blackwell sighed. "Funerals frighten me. My mother died when I was quite young, and I remember how horrible it all was, everything draped in black. I can't stand the thought of it."

"Then I won't suggest that you try to go downstairs to at least pay your respects. I'm sure one of the servants could carry you if you really wanted to see your husband's . . . uh . . . casket."

Mrs. Blackwell shuddered. "Oh, no, I couldn't possibly . . . Edmund wouldn't want me to see him like that anyway. He'd want me to remember him as he was, I'm sure of it," she reasoned. She tried to reach over to the nightstand, but couldn't quite. "Could you . . . ?" she asked Sarah. "In the top drawer . . ."

Sarah opened the drawer in the bedside table, expecting to find a handkerchief or smelling salts, and was surprised to see a syringe lying there instead. "Do you inject the morphine?" she asked in horror. This was even worse than she'd imagined.

"Please," Mrs. Blackwell entreated, her lovely blue eyes filling with tears. "Don't judge me! I can't . . . You don't know what I've had to suffer."

Sarah had a good idea it wasn't so very much at all, compared with many who never turned to the oblivion of opiates, but she was a nurse, not a missionary. Reluctantly, she handed the materials to her patient.

"I can't bear to know what's going on downstairs. I must sleep so I won't hear it," she said, preparing the syringe with the ease of long practice.

Sarah could not watch this. "I'll be downstairs if you need me for anything," she said, quickly closing up her medical bag and taking her leave.

"Thank you, Mrs. Brandt," Mrs. Blackwell said with her best finishing-school manners. "You've been very kind."

Sarah didn't stop to wonder for what she was being thanked.

FRANK LOOKED UP from where he was sitting in the front hallway and saw Sarah Brandt descending the stairs. He didn't like to admit that his happiness at seeing her almost outweighed his annoyance. Whatever his personal feelings for her might be, she had no business being involved in this case.

"Malloy," she said, greeting him with her usual smile, as if she were as happy to see him as he was to see her. "Has anyone arrived for the funeral yet?"

"No," he said, rising to his feet as she reached the bottom of the stairs. "You can leave without anybody seeing you."

"Oh, but I intend to stay for the service," she replied confidently. "It's the least I can do, since Mrs. Blackwell herself can't attend."

"Are you her personal representative?" he asked sarcastically.

As usual, his sarcasm was wasted on her. "No, but I do feel a sense of obligation to my patient."

"You never even set eyes on the man," Frank reminded her.

"But I did bring his child into the world," she reminded him right back. "His legacy, born after his death to carry on his name—"

"That's enough," Frank said, raising his hands in surrender. "And Blackwell wasn't really his name."

"Oh, yes, I'd forgotten. I wonder what Mrs. Blackwell will do now. Did her father know about Blackwell's other family?"

"I don't think so. He didn't seem to know who Calvin Brown was, at any rate, but if he did, he'd certainly be a suspect in Blackwell's death."

"I suppose he would. I can't imagine what my father would do if a man did to me what Blackwell did to Letitia Symington."

"I can, and blowing his brains out would be the least of it," Frank said. "Symington couldn't know, now that I think of it, though. He's giving the eulogy this morning. He'd hardly do that for the man who ruined his daughter."

"Yes, that would pretty well prove he has no idea. Which would eliminate him as a suspect, too."

"Probably," was all Frank would allow, and Mrs. Brandt didn't miss his reluctance to exonerate Symington.

"You still think he might have done it?" she asked, her fine eyes brightening with interest.

"I don't know who did it," was all he would say. "I guess there's no way to get you to leave before the funeral starts."

"Short of throwing me bodily into the street, no," she replied cheerfully. "There's no telling what I might learn just from eavesdropping, and I already have some information for you."

"What?" he asked skeptically.

"I'm sure it would be better if we share our knowledge in a more private place," she said, glancing meaningfully over to where a maid was carrying a vase into the parlor.

Frank managed to refrain from saying he wasn't planning to share anything with her. She liked to think she was helping him, and he had to admit she sometimes did find out things that aided his investigations. But he certainly had no intention of telling her what he already knew in return She wasn't the detective on this case, so she had no need to know more than she already did.

Fortunately, he was saved from having to reply because someone knocked on the front door at that moment. "We'll talk later," was all he said.

Sarah nodded and took advantage of the butler's momentary distraction to slip into the parlor and take a seat. She chose one near the far end of the back row so no one would have to climb over her or even notice her. Being unobtrusive was an advantage, if one could manage it, and Sarah seemed to have done so.

She glanced around. The room was now perfectly in order, thanks to Potter's rigorous attention to detail. A spray of flowers stood at both the head and foot of the casket, which gleamed in the morning sunlight filtering through the lace-curtained windows. Flowers ringed the room as well. Sarah would have to check the cards later to see who had sent them. Perhaps that would be a clue to who had killed him. Or who hadn't.

She could hear Amos Potter welcoming the new arrivals. His tone struck her as particularly annoying. He was apparently trying to appear suave and sophisticated to Blackwell's well-heeled patients, but Sarah found him oily and toadying. Probably others did, too.

In a few moments Potter ushered the guests in, and Sarah kept her head bowed, as if she were praying. Even Amos Potter would think twice about disturbing a praying woman, or at least she hoped he would. Either her ploy worked or Potter failed to notice her at all, because he left without comment to her.

She looked up and saw that the first guests were a well-dressed couple who had taken seats near the front of the room. The lady was dabbing at her eyes with a lace-edged hankie and the man seemed to be merely resigned. Sarah based this judgment on the way his arms were crossed over his chest. The woman, probably his wife, whispered something to him, and he grumbled something back. Plainly, they were arguing.

She heard another knock at the front door, and checked the lapel watch she wore. Nearly ten o'clock. All the mourners should be arriving within the next few minutes.

Indeed, the room quickly filled with well-dressed, black-clad visitors. The women were in various stages of distress. Most were discreetly weeping, but a few sobbed openly. The husbands, the few who came, were as helpless and horrified as men usually are when confronted with a weeping female. Most of them sat looking uncomfortable, while a few were positively angry. Sarah couldn't help remembering what Mrs. Ellsworth had told her about Blackwell's reputation. If he indeed had seduced his female patients, their husbands would certainly be justified in being reluctant mourners at his funeral.

"Will you stop that caterwauling?" the man in front of her whispered to his wife, who was sniffling indelicately into her handkerchief.

"I'd think you'd be more sympathetic," the woman whispered back, "after all he did for you."

"I had a pain in my back, and he made it go away," the man said. "Does that mean I should throw myself on his grave and expire?"

"You could hardly move, and you know it," she snapped. "Dr. Blackwell performed a miracle on you!"

"And what did he do for you that you have cause to make a public spectacle of yourself?" he asked, forgetting to whisper.

"Attending his funeral is not making a public spectacle!"

"Carrying on like you've lost your best friend is," her husband countered.

"You know what he did for me," she said, her voice choking with tears.

"Sometimes I wonder if I do," he replied, earning a

sharp glance from his wife and an even sharper one from Sarah.

Just then, the room fell silent as Mr. Symington entered, followed by Amos Potter. Potter had chosen himself for the role of master of ceremonies. Sarah wondered why there was no minister present, but perhaps Dr. Blackwell was a freethinker and recognized no organized religion. Even if he hadn't belonged to a church in the city, many ministers would preach a funeral for someone as well known as Blackwell for the fee alone. If there was no minister, it was by design.

Potter welcomed everyone with the same unctuous tone he'd used earlier, and Sarah found herself embarrassed for him. He certainly didn't deserve her concern, but she believed no one should be allowed to make a total fool of himself in ignorance. She doubted Potter was the type to take constructive criticism well, however, so she knew she would never offer any.

"I know Dr. Blackwell would be gratified to see all of you here to honor him. His name will live long in the hearts of those whose pain and suffering he relieved, and as a pioneer in the healing arts."

A woman up front sobbed aloud, and Potter seemed to take that as an encouragement. He went on for several more minutes in the same vein, lauding Blackwell as a man ahead of his time who died unrecognized by a society who would someday revere him. Sarah thought it excessive for a man who had no legitimate claim even to call himself a doctor, but no one seemed to care about her opinion.

Potter was showing no sign of running out of steam when there was a slight disturbance out in the hall. After a moment the parlor door slid open a bit, and Calvin Brown stepped in. The boy recoiled when he saw all the well-dressed people turning to look at him, and Sarah's heart ached for him. No matter what Blackwell had done, he was still the boy's father. Sarah waved and caught his eye and motioned to the empty chair next to her. He scurried over and slipped in beside her grate-fully.

His eyes were wide and frightened, but his chin was set with determination. No one was going to shame him into missing his father's funeral. He clutched his battered cap in both hands and sat stiffly, aware that Potter had stopped his remarks to glare at him in disapproval. Sarah patted the boy's hand reassuringly, then nodded at Potter to continue, earning another glare for both of them.

She was aware of whispers around her. People would be wondering who Calvin was, and why someone so shabbily dressed was there at all. Good manners prevailed, however, and after a moment they all fell silent.

Potter cleared his throat, but he seemed to have forgotten where he was. After an awkward moment he turned his attention to introducing Maurice Symington, a man who had, according to Potter, more reason than anyone to be grateful to Blackwell.

Symington had been sitting in the front row, his head bowed as Sarah's had been when she was seeking to avoid notice. She couldn't help wondering what Symington's reason was. Perhaps he truly was overcome with grief at the death of his son-in-law, but she somehow doubted it. Symington was hardly the type of man to be overcome by anything.

Potter finished his introduction and took his seat, but Symington hadn't moved. In fact, another moment went by, and he still didn't move. Everyone waited patiently. They knew this must be difficult for him. Another moment passed, and the crowd sensed that too much time was passing. People shifted uncomfortably, no one quite certain if they should be concerned or annoyed that he hadn't gotten up to speak. Potter began to fidget nervously. Then, just when Sarah was beginning to think Symington might need her medical services, he finally rose to his feet.

The crowd's relief was palpable, and Sarah almost sighed aloud herself, but if Symington was aware of his faux pas, he gave no indication. He took his place behind the podium and cleared this throat.

"As most of you know, I had the greatest respect for Edmund Blackwell. I met Dr. Blackwell about two years ago. A business associate introduced us. My friend had suffered great pain for many years, and Dr. Blackwell had been able to help him when all traditional medicine had failed. My friend knew that I, too, faced a similar situation, although in my case, it was my beloved daughter whom traditional medicine had failed.

"Letitia is my only child and, since my wife died years ago, the only family I have left. I love her more than life itself, and when she was severely injured in a riding accident, I would have moved heaven and earth to heal her, if it had been in my power. To my great disappointment, however, moving heaven and earth was beyond my power, as was finding someone who could restore Letitia to health. She lay helpless and in pain for almost a year while a veritable parade of physicians of all kinds came and went, each of them pronouncing her case hopeless.

"My daughter would never know the joy of a husband and family and a home of her own. She would never know freedom or friendships. She would never dance or play the piano or attend a social gathering again. I had all but given up hope when I met Edmund."

The crowd murmured their understanding of how momentous this occasion must have been, but beside her, Calvin made a small sound in his throat, as if almost choking on his own bitterness.

"Edmund was most interested in Letitia's case," Symington continued. "He said he had often been able to help when other doctors had failed. His methods were new and revolutionary, and many in the medical profession did not accept them. He would, he said, do his very best to bring Letitia back to health.

"I could tell immediately that he was not like any other physician who had seen her. He spoke to her kindly, allaying her fears. He was more concerned about her than about his reputation. He only wanted to see her regain her strength. After only a few moments he had discovered the source of her pain. Then he told me he could, within a matter of weeks, have her well again.

"I was skeptical, as you can imagine. I'd seen many doctors who said they could cure her, only to be disappointed. But Letitia begged me to let him try. She believed in him, so could I do less? I granted him permission to treat her.

"I was a man without hope, so I did not expect much, but to my astonishment and joy, Letitia improved from the very first treatment. After a few weeks she was completely pain-free and able to leave her room for the first time in months. Soon my daughter was exactly as she had been before, and her ordeal was but a memory."

Again the crowd murmured its understanding. Sarah imagined that many of them had experienced equally miraculous cures. But when she glanced at Calvin, she saw the anger on his young face. This must be terribly difficult for him to hear his father lauded as a hero after what he had done to his wife and children.

"You will understand my gratitude to Dr. Blackwell. No amount of money could ever repay what he had done for Letitia, but all he asked was that I, like my friend, recommend his services to others. That hardly seemed enough to me. A man as gifted as Edmund should be known to the thousands whom he could help, so I proposed to him that I repay him by renting a hall so he could explain to the public what wonders his treatments could work.

"Since most of you discovered Edmund's talents through just such lectures, I don't have to describe them to you. And when he asked if I would tell Letitia's story at the lectures, Letitia herself insisted that she be allowed to speak instead. She is naturally reserved, but for this she overcame her shyness. She felt she could not do enough to make sure others were not suffering needlessly, as she had done for so long, when Edmund could cure them. Most of you already know the rest of the story, about how Letitia and Edmund fell in love."

This time Calvin made a noise that was almost a groan. Several heads turned to see who had made it, and everyone who looked saw a young man who was crimson with fury. Symington either didn't notice or didn't care.

"When Edmund asked me for her hand," he went on, "I could only remember that had it not been for his skill, Letitia would still be an invalid. Like a knight of old, he had earned the right to her, and I could not refuse him, nor did I want to. I was happy to give her to the man whose devotion had saved her."

Sarah could feel Calvin's misery radiating from him. She wondered that he could sit still and listen to this. This was the kind of anger that caused people to commit murder, she realized with growing unease.

Symington hadn't even paused. "Alas, their happiness was cut short when some fiend took Edmund's life. Who can explain such a senseless act? And how can we measure the loss of a man so gifted? How many will suffer because he no longer lives? How many will endure senseless pain because his talented hands are stilled? And the worst tragedy of all is that his son, born the day after his death, will never know him in this life."

There were a few gasps of surprise. Word of the baby's birth had obviously not yet spread. Calvin's gasp of pain was mercifully lost in the disturbance. Once again Sarah reached over and patted the boy's hand, but he didn't seem even to notice.

"Because my daughter cannot be here to mourn her husband, it falls to me to send him to his rest. I know I speak for all of you when I say he will be missed. Those whom he treated will, like my daughter, know lives free of pain and suffering because of his talents. That is his legacy. He could ask for none finer."

Women in the audience were weeping into their hand-

kerchiefs as Symington took his seat. Sarah could certainly understand why Blackwell had wanted Symington
to speak at his lectures. The man was spellbinding.

"That's the same speech he gives at the lectures," the
woman beside her murmured to her companion. "You'd
think he could have said something more."

"I'm sure he's too overcome with grief to make the
effort," her companion said. "That poor little baby. I had
no idea."

Beside her, Calvin was breathing hard, as if merely
sitting still were an effort of strength. Sarah could imagine that it was. He must long to stand up and tell everyone the truth about his father. Doing so in front of such
a group would be much too intimidating, however, so
he merely sat and waited for the ordeal to end.

Amos Potter was at the podium again, thanking everyone for coming and inviting them to partake of some
refreshments in the dining room. As soon as it was obvious the service was over, Calvin jumped up and fled,
ducking out the door even before Mr. Symington could
get there to greet the mourners as they filed out, and
accept their condolences.

Sarah wanted to go after Calvin, but he was surely
gone by now, so she stayed where she was, trying to
hear what each person said to Mr. Symington as he or
she left. Perhaps she'd pick up some useful information.
Most of what she heard were the usual clichés that people utter at such times, but a few of the women were
obviously distraught and couldn't seem to judge when
they'd said enough. One woman went on and on about
what a wonderful man Dr. Blackwell had been, until
another woman took her by the arm and forcibly led her
away.

Watching from under the brim of her hat, Sarah saw
Symington's face tighten. Either he was embarrassed by
the unseemly display or some other emotion had overcome him. Finally, the last couple reached him. They
were the ones who had been the first to arrive and who

had seemed to be arguing before the service started.

"Clarence Fitzgerald," the man said, sticking out his hand to Symington. He was a tall, spindly man of middle years. His thinning gray hair revealed a shiny pink scalp, and if his face had ever borne a smile, there was no indication. His wife was short and plump and wore a well-made suit that fit snugly enough over her rounded figure to suggest upholstery. Her pudgy face was splotched from weeping. "We've met several times at the club, I believe," he added to Symington.

"Oh, yes, of course," Mr. Symington said, although Sarah was sure he had no recollection of the man.

"I need to discuss some matters of business with you, Mr. Symington, concerning Dr. Blackwell's affairs."

"Not today, Clarence," the woman with him said in distress.

"Today's as good as any other, Martha," Clarence snapped, and turned back to Symington.

But Symington had no intention of dealing with the fellow. "I'm afraid I know nothing of my son-in-law's business. You'll have to take it up with Amos Potter. I'll be happy to introduce you if you'll join us in the dining room."

No longer having any reason to linger, Sarah rose from her place and made her way silently toward the door. She saw that Clarence Fitzgerald didn't like being put off.

"It's about this house," he told Symington, undeterred. "I own it."

"It's a fine property," Symington said. "I'm sure my daughter will want to continue living here for a while. Potter will discuss the arrangements with you. If you'll excuse me. . . ."

He turned to Sarah, silently dismissing them.

"I told you not to bring it up today," Mrs. Fitzgerald was saying.

He grumbled something in reply, but Sarah didn't catch it.

She put out her hand to Mr. Symington, whose expression told her he thought she looked familiar but could not recall her name.

"Mrs. Brandt. I'm the midwife who tended your daughter," she added. "I'm so sorry about Dr. Blackwell."

"My daughter, is she doing well?" Symington asked with all the concern Sarah could have wished.

"She was upset this morning," Sarah admitted, not mentioning the need for morphine to help her through it. "It must be difficult not being able to attend her husband's funeral."

"No one would expect that, under the circumstances," Symington said stiffly, as if he thought she was criticizing him in some way.

"Of course not. I meant it was difficult for her to mourn him properly. It must also be difficult for you to properly celebrate the birth of your grandson, too."

Another emotion flickered across his face. "Yes, I . . . I've been so busy, I've hardly had time to realize I even have a grandson. I trust he's doing well, too."

"Yes, he is," Sarah said, once again neglecting to mention the morphine that made this possible.

Symington looked at her and frowned. "Why are you here?" he asked, as if just realizing how inappropriate her presence was. "Did you know Edmund?"

"No, although I'm fascinated by his work. I felt I owed it to Mrs. Blackwell to attend, out of respect for her."

Symington didn't seem to agree, but he was too well-mannered to argue. "Well, if you'll excuse me, I have guests."

"Of course," Sarah agreed, and let him leave her standing there.

In a moment Frank Malloy was at her side. He'd been waiting discreetly in the hallway and also eavesdropping on Symington's conversations.

"Did you find out who the killer is?" he asked her.

She glared at him. "That isn't funny, Malloy."

"It wasn't meant to be. I was hoping you had. I'd like to settle this and be done with it. I don't like these people very much."

"That just makes you a good judge of character. I was a little surprised to see Calvin here," she added.

"I guess I should've warned him not to come. That snooty butler wasn't going to let him in," Malloy reported.

"But you intervened," she guessed. "I'm sure everyone was wondering who he is. He hardly looks like one of Blackwell's patients."

"If they were wondering, they can ask him," Malloy said. "I sent him to the dining room for some food."

"Oh, my! We should probably go rescue him. What if Potter starts in on him? Or what if one of the other guests finds out who he is?"

"Potter won't want to cause a scene, and I doubt these people will give him the time of day, much less start a conversation with him."

"Nobody ever wants to cause a scene. That's probably what started this whole mess in the first place."

"What do you mean?

"I mean everyone always insists that Letitia Blackwell voluntarily spoke at Blackwell's lectures when she says she hated doing it so much she had to take morphine to get through them. She didn't want to make a scene, so she put herself through torture! And why didn't anyone see that and help her?"

"That's simple," Malloy assured her. "The men didn't see it because they probably don't think they forced her into it at all. They just told her what to do, and she did it. They didn't particularly care what she had to do to get through it."

Sarah had to admit he was probably right.

"I suppose you know that Blackwell was still married to Calvin's mother," she said.

"Yeah, the boy told me the whole ugly story. Poor kid, he's got two younger sisters, too."

"How awful. I suppose Blackwell deserted the family."

"Brown did, anyway," he corrected her. "He sent them money at first, but then he stopped. They had a hard time of it, according to Calvin."

"I'm sure they did," Sarah said. "Who do you think knew about this other wife? That would certainly be a motive for murdering him, if it was someone who cared about Letitia and her reputation."

"You think Symington might've done it? Or hired it done?"

"Mr. Potter said no one else knew about it but him and Dr. Blackwell," Sarah said. "Of course, he might not know who else Blackwell had told."

"Blackwell wasn't likely to confide in his father-in-law that his marriage was a sham," Malloy pointed out.

"Could someone else have told him?" Sarah asked.

"Who else knew?"

"Calvin did," Sarah reminded him.

"How would Calvin meet Symington? And Symington didn't seem to know who the boy was the other night when Potter and I told him about him."

"That's too bad. I don't like him very much, and I'd like for him to be the killer," she said.

"Not me. A man that rich and powerful would never spend a day in prison, no matter who he killed."

"Do you think Calvin did it?" she asked.

"No, but that doesn't mean he didn't," Malloy cautioned her. "I'd better get to the dining room to see what's going on."

"We'll probably need to rescue Calvin, too. I hope Potter isn't rude to him."

"Potter will probably pretend he doesn't see him," Malloy said. "He won't want to make a scene."

Sarah ignored his sarcasm. "Maybe I can strike up a conversation with someone. You'd be surprised what you can learn from funeral gossip." She pretended not to notice the way Malloy rolled his eyes.

They started down the hallway toward the dining room, but they stopped when they heard Amos Potter apparently arguing with someone just outside the doorway.

"This is hardly the time or the place to discuss such things, Mr. Fitzgerald. I'd be happy to make an appointment with you—"

"You don't need an appointment. You just need to know that I own this house, and Blackwell was living here rent-free. Now that he's dead, I don't see any reason I shouldn't rent it out to someone who can pay, so you can tell Mrs. Blackwell she's got until the end of the month to get out."

6

POTTER LOOKED THUNDERSTRUCK, AND WHEN HE saw that Malloy and Sarah had overheard, he blanched. "I'm sure I have no idea what you're talking about, Mr. Fitzgerald," he stammered. "Please allow me to make an appointment to speak with you privately about this matter."

"What could that hurt?" Mrs. Fitzgerald asked her husband pleadingly. "And you can't throw Mrs. Blackwell out onto the street! She just had a new baby."

"I'm sure her father will take them both in," Fitzgerald said coldly.

"Then at least let me meet with you to make the arrangements," Potter pleaded, glancing nervously at Sarah and Malloy, who were waiting patiently instead of scurrying away, as most people would have done to save themselves the embarrassment of overhearing such an unpleasant conversation.

"Fine. Monday morning at nine at my place of business," Fitzgerald said, reaching into his inside pocket and pulling out his card.

Potter took it gingerly and quickly tucked it away. "I'm sure we can make arrangements that will suit everyone concerned," he said with forced heartiness.

Fitzgerald grunted noncommittally and turned away, but to Sarah's surprise, he entered the dining room, followed by his wife. The man was going to evict a newborn babe and his mother, but he didn't think twice about enjoying their hospitality. She glanced at Malloy, who apparently shared her thoughts.

"Who is that fellow?" he asked Potter.

"Clarence Fitzgerald," Potter said, after pulling the man's card out and examining it. "His wife was a patient of Dr. Blackwell's. He helped her tremendously. Sciatica, if I recall correctly."

"And she was so grateful she let Blackwell live in this house rent-free?" Malloy asked with a frown.

"I'm sure I know nothing of any such arrangement. Edmund did not confide in me to that extent."

"The Fitzgeralds are very generous," Sarah noted. "The rent for a house like this would be considerable."

"Oh, no, there was a scandal here, I understand. The Fitzgeralds owned it, but they were having trouble finding a tenant. Edmund said he cared nothing for such things, and he would take the house. He felt Letitia deserved a residence that matched her station in life, and of course he didn't tell her about the scandal."

"I guess it also helped that he was getting it for free," Sarah said.

"If that is indeed the case," Potter replied stiffly. "I believe Mr. Fitzgerald may be exaggerating his generosity. I haven't had time to put Edmund's affairs in order, but when I do, I'm sure I'll discover the facts of it. Now, if you'll excuse me, I must see to the comfort of our guests."

Potter entered the dining room and insinuated himself into the nearest group, rudely interrupting their conversation, while Sarah and Malloy stood watching in amazement.

"What do you think?" Sarah asked Malloy.

He shrugged one of his beefy shoulders. "I think Mrs.

Fitzgerald was way too grateful if she gave Blackwell this house to live in."

"That depends on what services he performed for her," Sarah said with a smug smile, and was gratified to see Malloy's jaw drop in surprise. She loved to shock him. "Why don't you take care of Calvin? I think I'll go make Mrs. Fitzgerald's acquaintance and see what I can learn."

Without waiting for Malloy's reply, she moved into the room, carefully stepping around the small groups that had formed for conversational purposes and looking for the Fitzgeralds. To her alarm, she found her quarry engaged in conversation with Calvin Brown!

Or at least Mrs. Fitzgerald was. Her husband was merely standing by, glaring in disapproval. Sarah slowly made her way through the crush of the crowd to the corner where they were standing.

"I knew you must be some relation to Dr. Blackwell," Mrs. Fitzgerald was saying. "The resemblance is striking. How long have you been in the city?"

"A week or so," Calvin mumbled, plainly awed by people of their social status and unsure whether to answer their questions or not.

"You must have been impressed to find your father living in such a grand house," Mrs. Fitzgerald said. "Which room have you been staying in?"

"I . . . I ain't been staying here," he said, looking more and more uncomfortable.

Sarah excused herself and elbowed her way around the last person separating her from them.

"You weren't staying with your father? Where on earth have you been staying, then?" Mrs. Fitzgerald asked, a little shocked.

"A lodging house on Essex Street," he said.

"And Edmund allowed that?" Mrs. Fitzgerald couldn't believe such a thing.

At last Sarah was close enough to intervene. "Calvin, there you are," she said with a smile.

The look he gave her showed desperation. She offered him hope.

"I believe Mr. Malloy was looking for you," she said, gesturing vaguely toward the dining-room door.

"Thank you, ma'am," he said, and made his escape with unseemly haste.

"Hello," Sarah said to Mrs. Fitzgerald when he was safely away. "It was a lovely service, wasn't it?"

Mrs. Fitzgerald looked surprised and a little annoyed that Sarah had sent the boy away, but she was too well-bred to be rude. "Oh, yes. I do wish they'd had a minister, though. It doesn't seem like a funeral without a minister." Sarah noticed that her eyes were red-rimmed and bloodshot and her nose was red on the tip, as if she'd cried quite a bit today.

"I know," Sarah replied. "I wondered at that myself. Perhaps Dr. Blackwell didn't hold with organized religion."

As she'd hoped, Mr. Fitzgerald finally started drifting away, bored by what promised to be nothing more than female chitchat and looking for something more interesting to amuse himself.

"Oh, Dr. Blackwell was a deeply spiritual man, I know," Mrs. Fitzgerald assured Sarah, apparently not caring where her husband went.

"I'm sure he was," Sarah replied. "Were you one of his patients?"

"Yes, although he didn't like to call us that. He preferred to call us clients. You see, he treated more than aches and pains. He wasn't like an ordinary physician at all. Didn't you know the doctor?" she asked, suddenly growing suspicious.

"Not very well," Sarah said, stretching the truth a bit. "I'm a friend of Mrs. Blackwell's, and I felt it was my duty to attend the service, since she couldn't."

"I see," Mrs. Fitzgerald said, suddenly cold. Sarah wondered if it was the mention of Mrs. Blackwell or the fact that she, Sarah, didn't know the doctor that the woman had found offensive. The first was the far more intriguing possibility, but Sarah didn't want to waste precious time finding out. She decided to win Mrs. Fitzgerald back immediately.

"My name is Sarah Brandt. My father is Felix Decker," she said, knowing both that it would gain her instant respect with Mrs. Fitzgerald and how annoyed her father would be to have his name used to gather clues in a murder investigation. Fortunately, he would most likely never learn of it.

The Decker name had the desired effect on Mrs. Fitzgerald. The Deckers were one of the oldest and wealthiest families in the city. Mrs. Fitzgerald need not know that Sarah had long ago turned her back on their way of life to become a common midwife.

"I'm very pleased to meet you, Mrs. Brandt," the woman said, so obviously impressed at meeting her that Sarah was almost ashamed. Almost. "I'm Martha Fitzgerald. That's my husband, Clarence," she added, gesturing vaguely to where Clarence had formerly stood.

"Could you tell me more about Dr. Blackwell's form of treatment and how it worked? I'm fascinated by what I've heard, but I can hardly credit the successes that are attributed to him."

"You may believe whatever you have heard, Mrs. Brandt. Dr. Blackwell could perform veritable miracles. Surely you know what he was able to do for his own wife."

"Yes, Letitia shared with me how he cured her, but I can't help believing that was some sort of fluke. Perhaps she was ready to get well and would have recovered without any treatment at all."

"I'm sure I can't speak for Mrs. Blackwell's case," she said with just a hint of disapproval, "but I know about my own. I had suffered for many years and was growing worse. I had such pain I could sometimes hardly move from my bed. Most days I couldn't walk more than a few steps at a time. Some of the physicians who had treated me had the nerve to hint that my suffering was imaginary! Can you believe it?"

"Unfortunately I can," Sarah said, knowing that many people's pain and suffering were brought on by their own determination to be miserable. She didn't dare suggest that she also believed this to be true of her companion, however, not if she wanted to hear what Mrs. Fitzgerald had to say.

"I think I would know the difference between real pain and imaginary pain, don't you?" she asked indignantly.

"Absolutely," Sarah agreed, less than truthfully.

"In any case, Dr. Blackwell took my case very seriously. He spent a long time discussing it with me, determining when the pain had started and exactly when and how often it occurred. None of the other doctors had cared to even ask such questions!"

Sarah was beginning to understand some of Blackwell's appeal. He took time to listen to his patients. Or rather, his clients. And, most likely, to humor them as well. This must have been a form of therapy in and of itself. Remembering Dr. Blackwell's tender care was bringing fresh tears to Mrs. Fitzgerald's eyes.

"He sounds like a wonderful man," Sarah tried.

"Oh, he was!" Mrs. Fitzgerald said. "And so gentle . . ." She quickly pulled a handkerchief from her sleeve and dabbed at her cheeks.

"I'm sure he would be touched by your grief," Sarah went on. "You must have been very grateful to him. I couldn't help overhearing your husband say that he owns this house and allowed Dr. Blackwell to live here rent-free."

"Well, actually," she said, lowering her voice to a whisper and glancing around to see if anyone was listening, "*I* own the house. My father willed it to me. We had no need of it, of course, and it wasn't grand enough for Clarence, in any case, so I let it out. It would provide a nice income for me, but I really don't need the money, so when I learned that Dr. Blackwell was in need of a home . . ."

She let Sarah guess the rest. It wasn't difficult. Her only real question was why Mr. Fitzgerald had allowed it. Perhaps he hadn't known until Blackwell died. "That was extremely generous of you. Dr. Blackwell must have been remarkably talented. Could you explain to me exactly what he did in his treatments that was different from other physicians? I can't seem to understand it."

"Oh, my, I can't understand it either. In fact, I hardly remember most of it myself. The doctor speaks to you until you drift into a sort of sleep. Then he does things that feel absolutely wonderful, and when you come back to yourself, you feel like a new person. The pain is gone, and you can forget you ever had it!"

"Oh," was all Sarah could think to say. Mrs. Fitzgerald was hardly enlightening, but Sarah had learned something valuable just the same: the true secret to Blackwell's success! She couldn't let on how excited she was without alarming Mrs. Fitzgerald, though. She had to change the subject. "Would your husband really put poor Letitia and the baby out at the end of the month?"

Mrs. Fitzgerald blinked in surprise at the abruptness of the topic change, and then her expression hardened. She didn't like discussing Letitia. "Well, we'd heard nothing about a baby, of course," she said, not quite answering the question. "Dear heavens, when did she have it?"

"The morning after Dr. Blackwell was killed."

"I see. The shock must have brought it on, I suppose. I know I was prostrate myself when I heard the news. And then to learn today that Dr. Blackwell had not one but *two* sons! I had no idea he had been married before, either." This fact did not please her at all. "There must be some unpleasantness between them or else why wasn't the older boy staying here with his father?"

She was obviously hoping that Sarah would give her some answers, but she had no intention of filling Mrs.

Fitzgerald in on the doctor's scandalous past.

"I'm sure Dr. Blackwell would have confided in you if he'd felt the need," Sarah said tactfully.

"Oh, my," Mrs. Fitzgerald said, considering this, and her eyes filled with tears again. "He was such a dear, dear man. However shall I go on without him?"

That seemed an odd thing to say about one's physician, no matter what wonders of healing he might have worked, but Sarah wasn't going to question her about it. Besides, she still hadn't answered the question about throwing Letitia and the baby out of the house. "Did you say you hadn't heard that Dr. Blackwell's son had been born?"

"Not only that, I hadn't known he was even expected! Dr. Blackwell hadn't mentioned it to me, and we were very close. He always said I was one of his favorite clients."

Sarah thought that an odd statement, but she let it pass.

"Of course," Mrs. Fitzgerald continued, "we knew she'd stopped appearing at his lectures, but no one thought anything of it. It was obvious she was desperately afraid of speaking before a crowd, so I'm sure we all assumed that was why. She certainly was never very effective. If you ask me, Mr. Symington does much better."

This woman had no sympathy at all for poor Letitia, and her spite sounded remarkably like jealousy to Sarah. "I heard someone say that the speech he gave this morning is the same one he uses at the lectures," Sarah said.

"Hmm, I suppose it was very similar," Mrs. Fitzgerald allowed, "but it certainly applied, didn't it? I mean, all the things he said about Edmund were true, regardless of when or where he said them."

Sarah hadn't missed the fact that Mrs. Fitzgerald had called Blackwell by his given name, an obviously unintentional slip. No matron of her position would call her physician by his given name unless she'd known him from childhood, and even then she probably wouldn't do so to a stranger. "How long were you under Dr. Blackwell's care?" she asked.

"Almost a year, I believe." She sighed. "I suppose all of the good he did will be undone now, with no one to carry on his work."

"I believe his assistant, Mr. Potter, was trained in the techniques Dr. Blackwell used," Sarah said.

"Pshaw, who could trust a man like that with their health?" Mrs. Fitzgerald scoffed. "He isn't even a physician. And those eyes . . . I just don't trust him. How could he possibly duplicate Dr. Blackwell's successes?"

Or Dr. Blackwell's charm, Sarah thought. The man must have been a wonder. She was almost sorry she'd never met him in person. And if homely little Amos Potter thought he could take over where Blackwell had left off, he was going to have a rude shock.

"Martha," someone said sharply right behind Sarah, making her start.

She turned to see Clarence Fitzgerald frowning down at his wife. "We should go now," he said.

"Yes, dear," she responded absently. "I'm afraid I must leave," she said unnecessarily to Sarah. "It was a pleasure meeting you, Mrs. Brandt."

"Thank you," Sarah said, unable to return the compliment. "I hope all goes well for you."

Mrs. Fitzgerald gave her a sad smile that said she couldn't imagine that this was even possible.

As soon as the Fitzgeralds had left, Sarah looked around for Calvin Brown. To her relief, he seemed to have gone, so she started looking for someone else who seemed to have been unusually affected by Dr. Blackwell's death.

WHEN THE LAST of the guests had left, Frank caught Sarah Brandt when she would have gone back upstairs to check on her patient.

"What did you find out?" he demanded, stopping her as she was about to start up the stairs.

"It's a good thing for you that I'm not sensitive, Malloy. I might take offense at your abruptness," she told him.

"I'm not being abrupt. I just asked you a question."

She sighed, as if she were being put upon, when Malloy knew perfectly well that if she had any information at all, she'd be dying to tell him. "Mrs. Fitzgerald is the one who actually owns this house, and her husband may not have known she was letting Blackwell live here rent-free. She also didn't know Mrs. Blackwell was expecting a child. I think Blackwell may have hidden that from his clients."

"Clients?" Frank echoed.

"He preferred to call them clients instead of patients."

"To each his own," Frank muttered. "And it isn't strange that he didn't tell his *clients* about his wife's condition. It's none of their business."

"True, but news like that gets out just the same. Mrs. Fitzgerald was actually shocked that he hadn't confided in her. She even seemed a bit jealous, too. She claims she was one of his *favorite* clients."

"Favorite? What does that mean?"

"You'll have to ask Mrs. Fitzgerald," she said. "I wouldn't even want to guess. She was also shocked to find out Calvin was Blackwell's son."

"How did she find *that* out?" Malloy asked in annoyance.

"He told her. Oh, she asked him who he was, I suppose, and he's too naive to lie," she added when Malloy would have expressed his exasperation. "By the time I got there, she knew his life story, or just about. I hope you got him out of here before he talked to anyone else."

"He was glad to leave. I never should've let him come in the first place, but Blackwell was his father, and he had a right to be here, I guess."

"It was still awkward, and hearing Symington talk

about Letitia was very difficult for him, I'm sure. I hope he'll be all right."

"He'll be fine," Malloy said, dismissing her concerns. "Did you learn anything else that might be useful?"

"As a matter of fact, I did. It seems Blackwell used mesmerism on his clients."

"Mesmerism?"

"Yes, it's a technique where a practitioner puts someone into a state resembling sleep and then makes suggestions to them that they will still believe when they wake up."

"Are you telling me he was some kind of a magician?"

"No, mesmerism isn't magic, although it's sometimes used as a parlor trick. It's a valid technique for helping people overcome illness that is all in their minds, and many times illness *is* just in people's minds."

"Could he have mesmerized Mrs. Fitzgerald into giving him this house to live in?" That was the first theory that made the least bit of sense to him so far.

"No, but I do think he used his skill to make his patients relax and to convince them they felt better. His treatments no doubt helped relieve physical discomforts, but mental discomforts can be just as bad. Anyone who can figure out how to make people feel better mentally will be a guaranteed success."

Frank thought that was probably true. He wasn't going to tell Sarah Brandt that, however. She already had too high an opinion of her powers of observation. "So are the Fitzgeralds going to throw Mrs. Blackwell and her baby out into the street?"

She glanced around to make sure no servants were lingering near and lowered her voice. "I don't think Mrs. Fitzgerald has much use for the good doctor's wife. If I were of a suspicious nature, I'd say she was even a little bit jealous of Mrs. Blackwell. She was certainly overly fond of the doctor, although it's not uncommon for women to fall in love with physicians and ministers and other people who are kind or helpful to them."

"Nobody falls in love with policemen," Frank said sourly.

"I said *kind* and helpful, Malloy," she reminded him with one of her grins. "I've got to go check on Mrs. Blackwell, but then I'm going home. You can walk a ways with me and discuss the case if you've a mind to. I found out some other interesting tidbits of gossip this morning."

She knew perfectly well he would wait for her, Frank thought as he watched her mounting the stairs. How could he turn down an offer like that? Especially since she knew he lacked the necessary social position to mingle with the funeral guests to find out any gossip on his own.

He'd tried wandering from group to group, but they'd very neatly cut him dead each time, falling silent and staring at him until he moved on. He supposed they knew he was a policeman. People always did, even though he didn't wear a uniform or any other outward sign of his profession. Being who he was could be an advantage when dealing with certain elements of society, the ones who could be frightened or intimidated. It was a disadvantage when dealing with the privileged few, however. They knew he had no power over them and looked upon the police mostly as a nuisance.

Taking Potter up on his offer of a reward had probably been a mistake. Now he felt obligated to solve the crime, and not just by pinning it on an innocent boy, no matter how happy that would make Potter. Unfortunately, he didn't have the proper social credentials to find out what he really needed to know to solve the case.

But Sarah Brandt did.

The knowledge galled him, and he knew he shouldn't allow her to be involved, no matter how helpful she might be. He didn't need to solve the case that badly. Or at all, if the truth were known. Murders went unsolved every day in the city, and no one really cared, except perhaps a few grieving family members. If it wasn't for the reward, he certainly wouldn't be working so hard on *this* case. He didn't even need the reward that much—he had plenty of money put aside that he was saving to bribe his way to a promotion on the force—and he was starting to think that maybe Edmund Blackwell hadn't been such a great loss to the world anyway. Right now the only thing keeping him involved was the possibility that if he gave it up, Potter might get some other detective to arrest poor Calvin Brown for the crime.

He supposed he was actually fortunate that Sarah Brandt wasn't the kind of woman to care if he allowed her to do something or not, though. She'd help him with this case because she wanted to, no matter whether he approved or not. In fact, his disapproval would probably only encourage her, which saved him from having to humble himself and actually ask for her assistance.

"Are you still here?" Amos Potter inquired rudely from behind him.

Frank turned around to see the little man coming down the hallway from the dining room. "So it would appear," he replied mildly.

Potter sighed impatiently. "I can't believe you allowed that boy in here today."

"You mean Calvin?" Malloy asked just to annoy him.

"I mean the boy who killed Edmund," Potter sniffed. "Really, Mr. Malloy, you're wasting your time questioning Edmund's friends and supporters. They had no reason to wish him ill. Quite the contrary, most of them will suffer from his death. And it's especially troubling when you know exactly who killed Edmund and why."

"I told you, Calvin didn't kill his father."

"So you say, but I'm afraid you've been taken in, Mr. Malloy. Calvin was always fiendishly clever, even as a child. Edmund told me stories about the boy . . . Well, I'm not one to gossip, but suffice it to say that the child has been an accomplished liar his entire life. I'm not surprised he was able to deceive you, but you must be

careful not to let him escape without paying for his hei-
nous crime."

"If he's guilty, he won't escape," Frank assured him.

Potter didn't look convinced, but he didn't press the
issue. "I'll have Granger see you out," he said.

"I'm waiting for Mrs. Brandt," he replied, pointedly
sitting down on the bench in the hallway.

Potter seemed a bit disturbed by this, but he said, "I'll
be in the study if you need anything. Good day."

Potter closed the door behind him. Frank wondered
how he felt about working in the room in which his good
friend had been murdered. Maybe he enjoyed it. Potter
seemed to have been in Blackwell's shadow during the
doctor's life. Perhaps he felt he would come into his own
now. If he could achieve the same results as Blackwell
in healing people, he might gain respect and fame of his
own. Unfortunately, Frank didn't think he could. If half
of Blackwell's success had been due to his ability to
charm people into thinking they were healed, Potter
would never be able to duplicate his results.

Sᴀʀᴀʜ ᴅɪᴅɴ'ᴛ ᴋᴇᴇᴘ Malloy waiting long. He didn't
even look impatient when she found him sitting in the
hallway at the foot of the stairs.

"How is she?" he asked, rising to meet her.

"She's sleeping."

"Morphine?" he guessed.

"Yes." She sighed, and let him take her medical bag
to carry.

They didn't wait for the butler to show them out.

The street was quiet except for the muffled sounds of
the city all around it. She supposed the little park would
help with that. Traffic would avoid the square, and the
residents probably paid the beat patrolman to make sure
no riffraff lingered in the area. In fact, Sarah could see
him strolling along the street on the other side of the
park.

Malloy saw him, too. "Patrick!" he shouted, getting

the man's attention. "I need to talk to you!" He turned to her. "If you don't mind, I have to ask him some questions."

"Of course not," she said, more than eager to hear what Malloy would speak with him about.

The policeman hurried over to where they stood. He was middle-aged and overweight, his stomach bulging over his belt, and by the time he reached them, he was red-faced and out of breath. Unmistakably Irish, his large nose was blotched with broken veins from years of drinking. Malloy took him aside, not bothering to introduce him to Sarah, although he looked eager enough to make her acquaintance and kept glancing over at her curiously during his conversation with Malloy.

Sarah turned away, feigning interest in something in her purse while the two men talked, but she could hear every word.

"You were on duty the day this doctor fellow was killed, weren't you?" Malloy asked.

"Yes, sir, I was. Remember, I was guarding the door when you come in, and I told you what happened."

"Did you see anyone suspicious hanging around that day?"

"Suspicious? What do you mean by suspicious?"

"I mean anybody who didn't belong in the area, or somebody hurrying away, like they were scared or something," Malloy said. Sarah heard the edge of impatience in his voice, and turned her head so Officer Patrick wouldn't see her smile.

"I don't know if I can think of anything like that happening . . ."

"You'll not get anything from me but a cuff to the head, Patrick, so give up trying to get me to bribe you. Did you see a boy knocking on Blackwell's door that afternoon around two o'clock?"

"Well, now come to think of it, I did. Couldn't rightly say it was two o'clock, or even the same day, but I recall seeing a boy on somebody's porch in the last few days.

Banging on the door, he was. Looked like he belonged on a farm somewhere. From his clothes, I mean. Tried to tell me he had an appointment, but I knew he was just some bummer looking for a handout, so I sent him on his way. That's what I get paid to do, ain't it?"

"I suppose it is," Malloy agreed, not happy at all with this level of cooperation. "Did you see anybody else?"

"When?"

Even Sarah was starting to get annoyed with this Patrick. He might get his cuff on the head from *her* if he didn't give Malloy some better answers.

"The day the doctor got killed," Malloy said. He sounded as if he were gritting his teeth to keep from shouting.

"I thought he killed hisself," Officer Patrick said. "I saw him, and that's what it looked like to me. I was across the way there when I heard his wife screaming. She run out on the stoop and starts screaming like somebody's trying to kill *her,* so I come running with my nightstick ready. Wasn't nobody else in the house, though. I looked all around. Her servants come home about then, and they started carrying on, so I had someone telephone the station house. I waited outside until somebody come."

"When you saw Blackwell, did you touch anything in that room?"

"Sweet Mary, no! There was blood everywhere, and any fool could see he was dead. I didn't even go in the room except maybe a step or two. What makes you think somebody killed him?"

"There's some money missing from the house," Malloy told him. "If I find out you took it—"

"I didn't take no money from the house! What do you think I am?" Patrick asked, affronted.

"I just better not find out that you did. Thanks for your help, Patrick," Malloy said, disgust heavy in his voice. "You can go back about your duties now."

"Glad to be of help," he called after Malloy. Then, "Nice to see you, miss."

Sarah bit her lip to keep from smiling when Malloy muttered something under his breath. Malloy touched her arm and they started walking away. Sarah resisted an impulse to wave good-bye to Officer Patrick.

"Was it Calvin you were asking him about?" she asked when they were safely out of earshot.

"Yeah, the boy said he'd come to keep an appointment with Blackwell at two o'clock that day. Potter told me Blackwell had made the arrangements. Calvin said he heard the clock strike, so he knew it was the right time." Many people in the city couldn't afford timepieces of their own and kept track of the hour from the many clock towers in the city.

"And he said the patrolman saw him?"

"He said the patrolman run him off when nobody answered the door to let him in. That's how he can prove he never got into the house at all, so he couldn't have killed his father."

"Officer Patrick confirmed his story, then."

Malloy gave her a pitying look. "Officer Patrick is a stupid drunk who can't tell one day from another. He remembered seeing the boy, but he wasn't even sure whose porch he was on, much less if it was the same day Blackwell was killed. I believe it happened like Calvin said, but Patrick isn't going to be much help in proving it."

"Oh, dear."

"Yeah, oh, dear." Malloy sounded discouraged.

"You seem very interested in solving this case," she tried. She knew police detectives were ridiculously underpaid and had to rely on bribes and rewards to make their living. Consequently, they couldn't afford to waste a lot of time on cases that wouldn't supplement their meager incomes.

"Potter offered a reward," he told her reluctantly.

"Oh, my, I suppose that lets him out as a suspect,

then," she said with some disappointment. "I was rather hoping he was the killer."

"He's not one of my favorite people either, especially now that he's dead set on proving that the boy did it."

"It makes sense," Sarah pointed out, playing devil's advocate. "Blackwell had done a terrible thing to his family. The boy must have been very angry. Maybe he even hated his father."

"Maybe," Malloy allowed. "Potter said Blackwell told him the boy was an accomplished liar, too."

"Really? He looked awfully innocent to me, and he seemed genuinely upset today at the funeral. Why would he have had to be a liar?"

"That's an interesting question. I've seen lots of good liars in my time, but mostly they were raised on the streets, making a living any way they could, stealing and lying and cheating, sometimes even killing. But Calvin didn't grow up on the street."

"He would have had a difficult time of it, though," Sarah pointed out.

"He said he went to work very young. His mother took in washing. It was a hard life, but I just don't see him even stealing a loaf of bread, no matter how hungry he might've been."

"But what's this you were telling Officer Patrick about some missing money?" she asked. "Do you think Calvin stole money from his father?"

Plainly, he didn't want to discuss this, but he also knew she wouldn't give up until he told her. "According to Potter, Blackwell was going to give Calvin some money the day he was killed to buy the boy's silence. Calvin was supposed to take the money and go back home to Virginia. The money hasn't turned up, though."

"And if Calvin had gotten it, that probably means he's the killer," she guessed, "but if he *did* kill his father and get the money, it also doesn't seem likely he'd still be here in the city, does it?"

"That does seem reasonable," Malloy said just to keep

from admitting she was right. She knew he hated admitting she was right.

"But you don't think Calvin is the killer, at least."

"No, I don't. He's just too innocent."

"I'm impressed, Malloy. You hardly ever see good in anyone."

"There's hardly ever any good to see," he countered.

"With the people you deal with, that's probably true."

"With the people you deal with, too, if you'd admit it."

He was right. Sarah didn't like to think about it, but the father of the last baby she'd delivered *had* been murdered right in his own home. No one she'd met so far seemed completely innocent, either, except perhaps the baby himself.

"Did you find out anything else from the people at the funeral?" he asked.

"Just that all of Blackwell's female patients—"

"Clients," Malloy corrected her.

"Clients," she dutifully repeated, "were extremely fond of him. Apparently, his reputation as a ladies' man wasn't exaggerated."

"Do you think he actually seduced them?"

Sarah considered. "I believe there was some physical contact. Certainly, he had to touch his *clients* in order to perform his treatments, but there's different kinds of touching, if you catch my meaning."

"Wouldn't the women have objected if he took liberties with them?" Malloy asked with a frown.

Malloy was, Sarah remembered, something of a prude when it came to such things. "Not if they believed it was part of the treatment, and not if it felt very pleasant. And of course if they were under hypnosis . . ."

Malloy made a face to express his distaste. "If they were in some sort of trance, he could've done anything he wanted. So you're telling me that all the husbands of these women could've had a good reason to blow Blackwell's brains out."

"I'm telling you that Blackwell gave these women relief from their pain, and he may have even given them pleasure. Many women never experience physical pleasure from their marital relations, Malloy. Blackwell must have seemed like a miracle worker to them."

Malloy was glancing around anxiously to make sure no one had overheard her. "Do you have to talk about things like that?" he asked.

"We're talking about the case," she reminded him. "I'm just trying to help you understand the kind of man Blackwell was, and who might have had a reason to kill him and why."

"I guess you're ruling out all his female patients, then," Malloy said sarcastically.

"Unless one of them was the jealous type," Sarah said with some amusement.

"Could one of them have been jealous of his wife?"

"Mrs. Fitzgerald apparently was, but if that was the motive, then Letitia would be dead instead of her husband. Although . . ."

"Although what?" he prodded when she hesitated.

"Mrs. Fitzgerald was not aware that Letitia was with child. If Blackwell led his patients to believe he had a marriage in name only . . ."

"That's a little hard to believe," Malloy said. "These women are married, too. Why would they expect him to be faithful to them?"

"You're right. That's pretty farfetched. On the other hand, if Letitia was jealous of them . . ."

"I haven't met Mrs. Blackwell yet," he reminded her, "but you said she doesn't seem like the type."

Sarah sighed. "I'm afraid she's not."

They walked a block in silence. Finally Sarah said, "Why don't you just arrest Amos Potter? Neither of us likes him much."

"I don't like Maurice Symington, either. Why couldn't he be the killer instead?" Malloy countered.

"I like that idea. Do you know that he spoke at Blackwell's lectures when Letitia couldn't, and that the eulogy he gave today was the same speech he used for the lectures? He couldn't even be bothered to write a true eulogy for his son-in-law. But what would his motive be to kill Blackwell?"

"What would Potter's motive be?"

"Let's see, if either of them was upset about Edmund's bigamy, that would be a good reason to kill him. They're both devoted to Letitia and would be eager to protect her," Sarah said.

"Why should Potter care?"

"Because he's in love with Letitia."

"Then he wouldn't have to kill Blackwell. All he'd have to do was wait until her life was ruined by the scandal and be her sole remaining support. Then he could have her all to himself," Malloy pointed out.

"Only if she'd have him in return, and that doesn't seem likely. No, her father is a much more logical choice if Blackwell was killed because of his bigamy. Symington would want to save his daughter from the scandal and get revenge on Blackwell, too. Blackwell's death would ensure that the scandal never became public. He seems like the best suspect to me."

"Only if he *knew* about the Brown family, though," Malloy pointed out.

"You could ask him if he did," Sarah said.

"Yeah, if I want to be out of a job tomorrow."

He was right, of course. Having the audacity to question a man as powerful as Symington about whether he'd killed his son-in-law was a sure way to draw the wrong sort of attention to yourself if you were a police detective.

"Could Potter have told him?" Sarah asked. "Or even Calvin himself?"

"Calvin wouldn't even know who Letitia's father is, much less how to find him."

Sarah sighed. This was getting them nowhere.

Then Malloy said, "Wait, you said Symington spoke

at Blackwell's lectures. Calvin told me he went to one of those lectures. Someone had sent his mother one of the advertising posters so he would know where to find his father. That's what brought him to New York in the first place."

"Who sent him the poster?" Sarah asked eagerly. "That person would be a likely suspect."

"Calvin doesn't know. It was sent anonymously. Anyway, when Calvin went to the lecture, he heard Symington speak. The boy was upset because Symington said Blackwell was married to his daughter."

"So he did know who Symington was," Sarah said in triumph. "Could he have gone to see him, too?"

Malloy smiled grimly. "I think I'll pay young Calvin a visit and ask him that very thing."

7

MALLOY KNOCKED ON THE DOOR OF THE ROOMING house early Sunday morning. The landlady, a blowsy woman past her prime named Mrs. Zimmerman, opened the door.

" 'Morning to you, Mr. Malloy. How are you this fine day?" she inquired cheerfully. She'd been a good-looking woman once, Malloy judged, but the years were showing on her now. Her dark hair was streaked with gray, and the smile lines on her face had become permanent wrinkles.

"I'm well, thanks for asking. Is young Calvin in?"

"He's *always* in, Mr. Malloy. That boy hardly ever goes anyplace except for church, and he hasn't left yet, I don't think. I tell him he ought to see something of the city while he's here, but to tell you the truth, I think he's a bit scared by all the noise and such. He's awake, though. Up with the sun, our Calvin is, like he was still in the country. Come right on in."

Malloy knew the way to the boy's room on the second floor of the house. Mrs. Zimmerman wasn't much of a housekeeper, he noticed, seeing the dust on the edges of the stairs, but Calvin had said she was a good cook.

Frank found her pleasant enough, too, when he'd paid the boy's rent for a week in advance and asked her to send him word if Calvin didn't come back some evening. She was more than happy to be of service to the police, she assured him. As a business woman, she needed their goodwill.

Calvin's door stood open, and Frank surprised him whittling something at the small table in his room. He jumped up and gave the detective a welcoming smile.

"Mr. Malloy, do you have any news about who killed my father?"

He certainly didn't look like a killer, Frank noted again. Or a liar, either. His eyes were clear and met Frank's unflinchingly. And killers weren't usually so eager for him to find the guilty party.

"Sorry to disappoint you, Calvin," he said, "but I only came to ask you a few more questions."

"Come on in, then, and sit down. I'll tell you what I can, but I don't think I know anything besides what I already told you."

There was only one chair in the room, and Calvin had been sitting in it. He offered it to Frank now, however, after carefully brushing the sawdust off the seat. Frank glanced at what he'd been working on. It looked like a small, wooden face.

"It's a doll's head," Calvin explained, seeing Frank looking at it. "For one of my sisters. My ma makes the body out of rags."

"You're pretty good at it," Frank remarked.

Calvin shrugged self-consciously. "It keeps me busy. There's not much to do here."

Frank didn't point out that there were plenty of things to do in New York City if a person looked around.

Calvin sat down on the bed, which he had apparently made this morning. The covers were smooth and tightly tucked, just as the boy's extra clothes hung neatly on pegs along the wall. His mother had taught him well.

"What did you come to ask me?" Calvin asked, only

too happy to be of assistance, just the way an innocent man would be.

"Did you by any chance meet with anybody besides your father while you were in town? To talk about your problems with him, I mean?"

Calvin blinked. "I did go to see that Mr. Symington," he said guilelessly.

Only years of practice enabled Frank to remain expressionless. "Was this before or after you saw your father?"

"I guess you'd say before. I went to my father's house that first day, right after the lecture, and told that fellow who answers the door that I needed to see Dr. Blackwell, but he wouldn't let me in. He said I could knock on the kitchen door, and they'd give me some food scraps. I tried to tell him I didn't want any food scraps, but he just slammed the door in my face. I even tried at the kitchen, but they wouldn't let me in there either. I didn't know what to do, but when I told Mrs. Zimmerman, the landlady, all about it, she found out for me where Mr. Symington's office was."

"That was nice of her."

"She's been real helpful to me," Calvin said. "She's real nice."

"I could tell," Frank said. "Go on. When did you see Mr. Symington?"

"The next day. Mrs. Zimmerman said I should tell the fellow who'd be working at Mr. Symington's office that I had something important to tell Mr. Symington about his daughter. She said he'd probably at least let me talk to somebody, even if he wouldn't see me himself. They made me wait on the front stoop until they talked to Mr. Symington, but then they let me right in."

"You got to see Symington personally?" Frank asked in amazement. Surely, Symington's household staff would be better trained than Blackwell's. Why had Calvin been able to get past them?

"Yes, sir. I went right into the room where he was.

He was sitting behind this great big desk and he looked up when I come in. It was funny because he seemed real surprised, even though he knew I was coming in because they'd told him. He got over it real quick, though, and then he asked me what did I have to tell him about his daughter."

"What do you mean, he looked surprised?"

"I don't know. Just surprised. Like maybe I wasn't the person he was expecting to see or something. So I told him all about how Dr. Blackwell was my father and how he couldn't be married to his daughter because he was still married to my mother."

"I guess he was even more surprised then."

"I'd say he was more mad than anything. At first I was scared he'd hit me or something. At least throw me out of the house. He was that mad. But he didn't even shout. He just asked me what I wanted from him. I said I just wanted to see my father and make him take care of our family again."

"And what did he say to that?"

"He wanted to know why I come to him instead of going to my father, so I told him how they wouldn't let me in there. So he says he'll take care of everything, and he goes and telephones my father."

"What did he say to him?"

"I don't know. The telephone was in another room. When he comes back, he tells me to go right back to my father's house, and he'll see me for sure. He looked real strange."

"What do you mean?"

"I mean I never saw that kind of a look on anybody before. He looked like he could do murder . . . Oh!" he cried when he realized what he said. "I didn't mean . . ."

"I'm sure he was very angry to find out his daughter had been deceived like that. You wouldn't like it much if some man did that to one of your sisters, would you?"

"No, sir! I guess I'd want to kill anybody who did that."

Frank didn't reply, and after a moment Calvin asked, "Do you think that's what happened? Do you think Mr. Symington could've killed my father?"

"Why didn't you tell me you'd been to see Mr. Symington?" Frank asked, ignoring the boy's question.

"You didn't ask me," Calvin pointed out, "and in all the excitement, I . . . I guess I just forgot."

He seemed to be telling the truth. Frank looked for a sign, any sign at all, that he wasn't, and found none. Calvin's face was as open as a child's. "Is there anything else you forgot to tell me? Did Symington offer you any money?"

"No, sir. He didn't offer me anything."

"And have you seen him again?"

"Why should I?" Calvin asked quite reasonably.

Frank didn't bother to answer. "The day your father was killed, did you see anybody else around his house?"

"There was some people in the park, it seems like, and maybe somebody walking on the sidewalk."

"I mean anyone who looked like they were sneaking around or hurrying away from the house?"

Calvin considered. "I don't think so. Why . . . ? Oh, you mean the killer," he guessed after a moment. "No, I didn't see nobody like that. I wish I did. I'd sure like to help. The fellow Mr. Potter, he thinks I killed my father, so I want to help all I can to find the real killer."

"I know you do, Calvin," Malloy said wearily. He was more convinced than ever of the boy's innocence. And now he had another good suspect. Symington must have been furious when he found out the truth about his son-in-law. Could he have figured out a way to free his daughter from the scandal of Blackwell's secret family? The crime indicated that someone had carefully planned it, even down to establishing Calvin as a suspect if the suicide ruse failed. His daughter would be a respectable widow instead of a bigamist's wife.

But if Frank wanted to accuse a man like Symington of murder, he'd need a lot more than a suspicion.

"Does any of this help, Mr. Malloy?" the boy asked eagerly.

"Not enough," Frank replied with a sigh.

SARAH WASN'T SURE how often she could visit the Blackwell home before someone began to wonder what she was doing there. Sunday afternoon she once again arrived to check on Mrs. Blackwell's condition. Since no one in the house had any idea how often Mrs. Blackwell needed to be checked, she supposed the ploy would work for a while yet.

Mrs. Blackwell was sleeping when she arrived, so Sarah went to see how the baby was doing. He was being fed when the nurse bade her enter.

"Oh, Mrs. Brandt, I'm so glad to see you. Sit down and rest yourself," the nurse said from where she sat in the rocking chair. "I'll have some tea brought up. Would you pull the bell there? Someone will come."

The woman was so obviously desperate for company that Sarah couldn't refuse. She took a seat in a comfortable chair that had been provided for the nurse's use when she wasn't rocking the baby. She was glad to see the baby seemed to be suckling just fine and gaining some weight.

"He looks well," Sarah said.

"Oh, he's all right, I guess. Still sleeps a lot, but that's to be expected, I suppose. And sometimes I've got to tickle his feet to keep him awake while he nurses, but there's lots of babies what do that."

"Yes, there are," Sarah agreed.

"I was hoping you'd come," the nurse said after a moment. "I found out some things I thought you'd want to know."

"What kind of things?" Sarah asked politely.

"For instance, do you know how Mrs. Blackwell started using the morphine in the first place?"

"It's my understanding that she was injured very

badly in a riding accident," Sarah said. "She started tak-ing it for the pain."

"I suppose that's true as far as it goes," the nurse said, her homely face creasing into smugness. "But do you have any idea where she was riding off to, and with who, when she had that accident?"

Sarah hadn't given the matter any thought, but she was willing to play along. "No, I don't."

"Then you'll be surprised to hear that she was elop-ing."

Sarah's first thought was that she had been eloping with Dr. Blackwell, but that wasn't possible. She hadn't even known him then. "Who was she eloping with?" she asked.

"That's the scandal, don't you know," the nurse told her with satisfaction. "She was running off with the local schoolmaster!"

"Good heavens!"

"I got this from her maid what's been with her since she was in pigtails," the nurse informed her. "She said Mrs. Blackwell had been carrying on with this fellow behind her father's back. The father never would've ap-proved of a marriage between them, so the two of them were running away together. Except that Mrs. Black-well's horse stumbled in a ditch, and she was throwed."

"How awful," Sarah said, her mind trying to grasp this information and analyze its importance. She was sure Malloy would figure it out instantly, but for once she wanted to beat him to it.

"It was more than awful. Seems like it was night and her young man didn't want to leave her there and go for help, so he had to carry her back to her father's house. I guess there was quite a ruckus when he brought her in, with everybody thinking she was tucked up safe in her bed and all."

Sarah could well imagine how Mr. Symington would have greeted the man responsible for what he would consider abducting his daughter and causing a terrible accident. "What happened to the schoolmaster?"

"Oh, he was let go, as you can guess. Don't nobody know what become of him after that. And Mrs. Blackwell, she was confined to her bed for months and months. Her maid said sometimes she'd scream with the pain, and the only thing that'd help was the morphine. Poor thing, so young and pretty and not able to get up from her bed for all that time."

"It was quite fortunate that her father found Dr. Blackwell when he did," Sarah said, knowing she shouldn't encourage servants to gossip about their employers, but knowing the information could be important. One never knew which scrap of information might lead one to the killer. She was going to see Malloy tomorrow, and she'd love to have something interesting to report.

A maid's knock interrupted them, and the nurse instructed her to bring some tea for Sarah. When she had gone, Sarah said, "This makes it even more romantic that Dr. Blackwell and his wife fell in love after he treated her."

"Oh, it would, if that's what happened," the nurse confided. The baby was now fast asleep at her breast, but she hardly seemed aware of him.

"What *did* happen, then?" she asked, as the nurse was waiting for her to do.

The nurse looked around, as if she expected to find someone eavesdropping, but they were, of course, alone in the room except for the sleeping baby. "According to Daisy, Mrs. Blackwell's maid what's been with her since she was a girl, Dr. Blackwell somehow convinced her father to make her stand up at his lectures and tell how Dr. Blackwell cured her. She didn't want to do it, and who could blame her?"

Sarah nodded encouragingly, even though she already knew all of this.

"She did it for a while, but she wanted to stop. Her maid said she had to take morphine just to get her through it, but she didn't dare let her father or Dr. Blackwell know. They thought she'd stopped taking it after she got well. It seemed like the father was going to tell Dr. Blackwell his daughter was finished testifying for him, but then Dr. Blackwell, he starts paying court to the girl."

"Was her father pleased?" Sarah could hardly credit it.

"What do you think? The girl was damaged goods. If anybody found out she'd been carrying on with a school-teacher and tried to elope with him, she would've been ruined."

She was right, of course. If Letitia was no longer a virgin, or even if there was reason to believe she wasn't, then no respectable man of her own class would have her, particularly if she'd been having an affair with a penniless schoolteacher.

"Do you think she didn't love Dr. Blackwell?" Sarah asked.

"Oh, my, who can say? With a man like that . . . Well, you know what I mean."

"No, I don't," Sarah said. "I never met Dr. Black-well."

The nurse nodded knowingly. "Then you couldn't know. I only met him once, but I can see how he'd turn a girl's head," the nurse eagerly explained. "Right hand-some he was, tall and dark, and dressed real smart in his fine clothes. Good manners, too, and well-spoken. Had a way of looking right at you, like he knew what was going on inside your head. Made my heart flutter a bit, I don't mind saying, even though I knowed he wasn't interested in me *that* way."

Sarah could hardly comprehend it. A man who took the time to charm the woman who was going to be his child's wet nurse. He must have been a master at be-guiling women. Poor, tortured Letitia hadn't stood a chance.

"So Letitia fell in love with Dr. Blackwell," Sarah ventured.

"Or at least she thought she did. And only one person knows how he felt about her, but he's dead, now, ain't he?"

Sarah was fairly certain a man who could desert his first wife and family without a qualm would have no love to waste on anyone else, either.

"And after they were married, Mrs. Blackwell continued to speak at his lectures," Sarah said.

"Oh, yes, that she did. Didn't like it any better, but what could she do? He was her husband, and she didn't have any choice. And just between us"—she glanced around again and this time even leaned forward a bit, conspiratorially—"once they was married, he didn't have no more use for her except that, if you know what I mean."

"You mean he neglected her?"

"Something awful. Poor girl cried and cried many a night, according to her maid. If he cared for her at all, he'd forgot about it. Seemed like the only reason he'd married her was to make certain she'd keep speaking at his lectures. He was busy with his lady patients, keeping them happy and all, but he didn't have any time for her. Never even shared her bed, not hardly ever."

He must have managed it occasionally, Sarah thought, or she wouldn't have had his child. But all she said was, "How awful for her."

"Oh, my, yes. I guess it's no wonder she kept taking that awful morphine. She goes out every afternoon. Did you know? Tells everybody she's going to visit friends, but none of them ever returns the visits."

Sarah knew what this meant. Society demanded that formal visits be returned, and if they weren't, the visitor was put on notice she was being snubbed and would not be welcomed back again. But perhaps there was another explanation.

"I thought she was visiting the poor or the sick."

"Every day?" the nurse scoffed. The nurse obviously believed this was more charity than anyone could offer.

"I don't like to speak bad about someone who pays my wages, but her maid thinks she goes to one of them opium dens."

Since Sarah knew this was exactly where she went, she said nothing, managing to look shocked instead.

"You know what goes on in them places, don't you?" the nurse demanded.

"I'm afraid I don't know what you mean," Sarah said.

The nurse was only too happy to enlighten her. "I don't know myself, of course, not from experience, but I've heard awful things. Like white women and Chinese men together, if you can imagine a white woman doing such a thing."

Sarah was saved from answering by the maid's return with the tea things. She'd lost her interest in socializing with the nurse any longer. She really did think it would be a good idea for Mrs. Blackwell to find someone else for the job, but it wasn't her decision. Could she suggest a change on the grounds that the woman gossiped too much? Or because she had no respect for her employer? Somehow Sarah doubted Mrs. Blackwell would care about such things. As long as her baby was doing well, she most likely wouldn't want to make the effort required to replace her. A change like that would be difficult for the child, too, and heaven knew, he was having a hard enough time without it.

Somehow Sarah managed to be civil to the nurse and to chat about inconsequential things while they drank their tea, but as soon as she could, she made her escape. She had, she told herself, simply been trying to obtain information that might help Malloy solve the case. Why, then, did she feel so soiled?

FRANK HADN'T REALLY expected his mother to accompany him when he took Brian to see the surgeon that Sarah Brandt had found for him. She did not approve of meddling with God's will, or so she said. Frank suspected she was really just terrified over what would become of her if the surgeon could make Brian's foot right and Frank didn't need her to take care of the boy anymore. He didn't know what she thought the surgeon could do for Brian's deafness or for the fact that he was only three years old and would need care for many years to come even if he was completely normal, but Frank also knew that reasoning with his mother was a waste of time.

What Frank hadn't given any thought to was how he was going to manage his son without his mother on the long trip uptown to the surgeon's office. He'd spent precious little time with the boy, and had no idea how to amuse a healthy three-year-old child, much less one who couldn't hear or walk. Fortunately, the trip alone was amusement enough to keep the boy entranced.

The loud noises of the city didn't bother Brian at all, because he couldn't hear them. The many people didn't frighten him because he thought all of them were his friends. And since he'd never been more than a few blocks from their flat, everything was new and different to him. He couldn't look at it all hard enough.

Frank carried the boy on his shoulders as he walked through the streets, giving him a wonderful view of everyone and everything. Brian bounced with joy when they got on the elevated train and the buildings outside began whizzing past the windows. His little head wasn't still for more than a second as he tried to take in every detail of the big, wonderful world out every possible window.

Seeing his excitement was an unexpected thrill for Frank, but the best part was the way the boy clung to him through it all, as if he were the child's anchor of security. He'd expected to feel apprehensive and nervous and even uncertain about having sole charge of his son for the day, and he did feel all of those things. What he hadn't expected was to feel loved and trusted and important, and he felt all of those things, too. Something in his chest swelled into a sweet ache, and as he held his son on his lap while the train sped high above the city streets, he felt an absurd urge to weep.

The surgeon's office was on a quiet, tree-lined street in the more genteel part of the city. Plainly, only people with the means to pay a high fee for medical care would even bother coming to this neighborhood. The building where the office was located was identified only by a discreet bronze plaque bearing the doctor's name.

Frank was never one to be intimidated by the rich, but he knew a moment's hesitation before he could bring himself to open the door to the office and step inside, as if he had a right to be there. He found Sarah Brandt already there, waiting for him.

"Malloy," she said, jumping to her feet and coming to meet them. He felt the usual unreasonable pleasure at seeing her.

He hadn't expected her to be there. She'd known when the appointment was scheduled, of course, since she'd set it up, but he hadn't asked her to come, and she hadn't mentioned that she planned to be there. He hadn't wanted to impose any more on her generosity, but he couldn't deny that he felt relieved that she had come.

"Isn't your mother with you?" she asked, looking around. "How did you manage with Brian by yourself?"

"I knocked him unconscious and threw him over my shoulder," he said blandly. "He wasn't much trouble at all after that."

She just gave him one of her looks, then flashed Brian one of her brilliant smiles. "Hello, there, young fellow. How are you today?"

Brian couldn't understand a word she said, of course, but he understood her smile. Maybe he even remembered her from when they'd met before. She'd given him a present, after all. That must have made an impression. The boy returned her smile with one equally bright and reached out to touch one of the red flowers on her hat.

She quickly tipped her head away, saving the flower from certain destruction, but she held her arms out to him. "Would you like me to hold you for a while? Your papa must be getting tired," she said, just as if the boy could hear her.

But he didn't need to hear the words. He knew what extended arms meant. He threw himself forward so hard Frank almost dropped him, but she caught him with no trouble at all and drew him into her arms.

"Oh, my, you're such a big boy," she said, settling him comfortably on her hip and starting to walk around the room so he could examine the few furnishings of the modestly appointed waiting room. She looked very natural, holding the boy like that, as if she did it all the time. Frank found that thought disturbing. "I can't imagine your mother letting you take him away like this without her," she said to Frank over her shoulder.

"She didn't like it, but when I told her this doctor might be able to fix Brian's foot, what could she say?"

"Didn't she want to come along?"

"She doesn't like to meet people who might make her feel like she isn't as good as they are," he said, knowing that wasn't exactly an accurate description but unable to truly explain his mother. "She probably thought the doctor would make her feel ignorant or might blame her for Brian being crippled."

"David isn't like that at all," she said.

"David?" he echoed, feeling an uncomfortable twinge that might have been jealousy if he'd had any right to be jealous of Sarah Brandt.

"David and my husband, Tom, were good friends," she said with a small smile.

Frank couldn't help wondering if he was good friends with *her* now, and he hated it that he wondered.

The door leading to an inner office opened and a woman in a nurse's uniform appeared. "Well, now this must be Brian," she said in that voice people used when speaking to young children.

"Brian can't hear you," Mrs. Brandt explained in the most natural way Frank could imagine. "He's deaf."

"He certainly is friendly anyway," the nurse replied, returning Brian's delighted grin of greeting. She turned to Frank. "And you must be Mr. Malloy. You can bring Brian back now, if you will. The doctor is ready for him."

Mrs. Brandt handed the boy back to Frank. She must've seen the uncertainty he was feeling, because she said, "It'll be all right. David is an excellent surgeon."

"Are you going to come in with us?" he asked, hoping his desperation didn't sound in his voice.

"If you'd like for me to," she replied with a smile. Did she actually look pleased to be asked or was he imagining it?

"I might not understand the medical stuff," he said by way of excuse.

She nodded in acceptance and led the way, following the nurse down a short, narrow corridor. The nurse paused outside a door and indicated they should enter.

Sarah Brandt went in first.

Dr. David Newton was a man approaching forty, tall and somewhat stoop-shouldered, and wearing a tailored suit that fit him so badly it looked as if it had been tailored for someone else. His hair and close-cropped beard were threaded with gray, but his eyes shone brightly as he jumped to his feet and came around his desk to greet his visitor.

"Sarah, my dear, how wonderful to see you," he said, taking her hand in both of his and gazing at her affectionately. Frank might have said "adoringly," if he was of such a mind. Or if he really was jealous.

"It's wonderful to see you, too, David. How are Anne and the children?"

"Anne is as sassy as ever, and the children have grown a foot since you saw them last. Anne said I must make you promise to come to dinner soon. We've missed you terribly."

"And I've missed you, too. Tell Anne I'll call on her

next week, unless an onslaught of baby arrivals prevents me."

"I'll hold you to that," he said, then turned at last to where Frank had paused in the doorway.

"This is Frank Malloy and his son, Brian," she said. "Malloy, this is Dr. Newton."

Frank nodded, unable to shake hands because he was holding Brian, but the doctor didn't seem to be offended. "So glad you could come," he said, as if they'd been personally invited instead of making an appointment. "Please sit down and tell me all about young Brian here."

They took the chairs in front of Newton's desk while he resumed his place behind it, and Frank settled Brian on his lap.

"How old is Brian?" the doctor asked when they were all seated.

"A little over three," Frank replied.

"Has he had any medical treatment on his foot before now?"

"No," Frank said, feeling absurdly guilty. "When he was born, they said nothing could be done. A doctor told me that," he added defensively.

Dr. Newton didn't remark on this. He simply nodded his understanding. "Brian's mother isn't with you today?"

Frank ignored the pain he felt at the mention of Kathleen. "She . . . she died when he was born."

Dr. Newton nodded again. "I'm sorry to hear that. I hope you know that Brian's condition would have no relationship to your wife's death. By that I mean that Brian's foot would have been like this regardless of how your wife fared during the birth. We believe that clubfoot is caused by the way the child lies in the womb. We don't know for certain, of course, but that seems as good a reason as any for it to happen. The cause isn't quite as important, since we can't stop it from happening, but we do know some ways to treat it when it does, and to you that will be very important indeed."

"What can you do?" Frank asked, still not certain he believed Dr. Newton could do anything at all. "The other doctor said it was hopeless."

"Could I examine Brian's foot for a moment before I answer that question?" the doctor asked.

"Yeah, of course," Frank said.

"Let's take him into the examining room, shall we?"

The examining room was a small, sterile chamber containing a metal table and a couple of tall cabinets. Frank set Brian on the table and stood beside him, holding him so he wouldn't fall or try to get away. The boy sat quietly, as he always did, looking at Frank uncertainly but not at all frightened.

Dr. Newton poked and prodded Brian's leg and foot, then tapped his knees with a small hammer and made his legs jerk. Brian looked up in surprise when his leg moved as if of its own volition, and he grinned when the doctor made it move again. The doctor made the examination a game, tickling Brian and letting him hold the tiny hammer when he was finished with it.

After a few minutes he turned to Frank. "Your son is very fortunate, Mr. Malloy. I've seen feet much more severely disfigured than his. I believe that with surgery, we can repair most of the damage and that Brian will even be able to walk. He might have a slight limp or have to wear a special shoe on that foot, but he *will* walk."

Frank felt such a rush of emotion, he could hardly breathe. Relief and amazement and suspicion and a terrible rage. "Why did that other doctor tell me there was nothing he could do?" he demanded furiously.

Dr. Newton didn't look like he'd taken offense. "I'm afraid I can't speak for my colleague. Perhaps he was simply unaware of the advances that have been made or of the newer techniques."

This was, of course, the politic answer, the kind of answer Frank would have given if asked why one of *his* colleagues had failed to solve a case or had taken a bribe to make sure a case wasn't solved at all. It didn't make Frank feel any less angry, but at least he knew that Dr. Newton was an honorable man. And a modest one, too. He could have said he was just smarter than the quack Frank had consulted.

"What will you have to do to the boy's foot?" he asked.

Dr. Newton explained as simply as he could how he would cut and sew and rearrange the various parts of Brian's foot to make it whole, answering Frank's questions patiently.

Frank couldn't help wondering how patient the doctor would have been with the likes of Frank Malloy if Sarah Brandt hadn't brought him in herself, but he didn't let that stop him from making sure he understood everything as well as was possible.

Then he asked the doctor about his fees, and Dr. Newton replied straightforwardly, as if it never occurred to him that Frank wouldn't be able to pay them. Frank had been right, the reward in the Blackwell case would go a long way toward paying the good doctor.

"I'll bring you the money tomorrow," Frank said.

"There's no need to pay me until I do the surgery," the doctor assured him with a smile. "Shall we look at my schedule and see when we can fit Brian in?"

A few minutes later they were outside on the street, with the surgery scheduled toward the end of the month. Frank hoisted Brian onto his shoulder again, and he resumed looking at everything around him with the greatest fascination.

"Was he very upset when you took him away from your mother today?" Mrs. Brandt asked.

"I expected he'd throw a fit," Frank admitted, "but he just wrapped his arms around my neck so tight I thought I'd strangle and never even looked back."

"That's how much he loves you, Malloy," she said wisely. "He had no idea where you were taking him or why. He just wanted to go with you. He was willing to give up the only security he's ever known just for the chance to have your attention."

Frank felt a suspicious burning behind his eyes, but he blinked a couple of times until it went away. He had to clear his throat before he could say, "It was good of you to come today."

"Don't think I did it out of kindness, Malloy," she cautioned him. "I was as anxious as you to find out if David could do anything for Brian."

They walked a few steps in silence before Frank came up with the right combination of words. "I looked into your husband's file."

"His file?" she asked in confusion.

"The police file. To see what they found out when they investigated his murder, if they had any idea who might've done it."

Her fine eyes lit with interest. "What did you find out?"

"Not much," he said, resigning himself to her instant disappointment. "You were right. Without a reward being offered, there wasn't any reason to solve the case, so nobody tried very hard."

She sighed, and he thought she blinked a little harder than she usually did. "I suppose it's far too late to investigate now. After three years . . ."

Frank cleared his throat again. "I was wondering . . ."

"Yes . . . ?" she said when he hesitated, a small spark of hope lighting her eyes again.

"Maybe I could look through your husband's files. Of his patients, I mean. Maybe there's something there, a reason why somebody'd want him dead."

It was unlikely that he'd learn anything. Just as she'd said, after three years there was little chance of learning anything new. She must have known this, too, but still she smiled a little when she looked up at him.

"If you think it might help, you're certainly welcome

to look through all of his records," she said. "And Malloy . . . ?"

"Yeah?" he said.

"Thank you for caring."

8

MALLOY ARRIVED AT SARAH'S IN TIME FOR SUPPER. She'd felt obligated to cook for him since he was going to investigate Tom's murder. Also because she wasn't fond of eating alone, and Malloy was good company. Or at least interesting company. And they had a lot to discuss about the Blackwell case. Well, Sarah did, anyway, and she hadn't wanted to discuss it walking down a public street this afternoon when Malloy was wrestling with his restless son. So she'd invited him to supper.

"How's Brian doing after his exciting day?" she asked when she'd greeted him.

"He fell asleep on the train ride home," Malloy told her. "I guess all the excitement was too much for him."

"He certainly did seem to be enjoying himself."

Malloy frowned as he hung his hat on the coatrack in her hallway. "I never thought of it before, but his life is pretty boring. My mother takes him shopping with her, but he sees the same things all the time. And the same people, too."

"If he could walk, he could go more places," she suggested.

"Did you understand what all that doctor said he was

going to do to Brian's foot?" he asked with a frown.

Sarah bit back a smile. Malloy had behaved as if he'd understood perfectly when they were in the doctor's office. "Not all of it. The techniques he's going to use are pretty unusual, at least from my experiences with medicine. Basically, I think he's just going to fix the parts of Brian's foot that didn't form properly. And I know he's been very successful in the past. There's every reason to believe he can help Brian, too."

Malloy didn't look convinced, but he didn't look quite so worried, either. He'd probably question her some more later, but not now. He wouldn't want to belabor the issue and make her think he was ignorant.

The thought startled her, and she wondered how and when she'd become such an expert on Malloy's personality. Before she could decide, he said, "Something smells good."

"I hope it tastes good, too. Come on into the kitchen. Everything's ready," she said, leading the way.

She'd set the table carefully, not asking herself why she'd taken such pains. Malloy probably wouldn't even notice, and if he did, he might wonder himself.

"Sit down and make yourself comfortable," she said, indicating one of the chairs at the kitchen table. "Would you like a glass of beer?"

"Sure," he said, and she poured some from the pail that she'd gotten from her neighbor, who brewed it in his basement.

In a few moments she had the pot roast arranged on the plate with the potatoes and carrots around it. She placed it on the table with a sense of satisfaction.

Malloy raised his eyebrows and grinned a little, as if he were amazed that she had produced such a masterpiece. "You went to a lot of trouble," he said.

"Not really," she assured him. "I enjoy cooking when I've got someone to cook for. Would you do the honors?" She handed him the knife to cut the meat.

He didn't take it. "Better lay it down on the table,"

he suggested deadpan, indicating the knife.

"Are you afraid I'll stab you with it?" she asked in amusement, laying the knife down as instructed.

"No, but my mother wouldn't let anybody hand a knife directly to someone. Means you'll have an argument or something like that." He picked up the knife and, using his own fork, began to slice the meat.

"I'm sure Mrs. Ellsworth would say the same thing," she said. "She sent over a pie this afternoon. She must've known somehow that you were coming. Sometimes I think she has a crystal ball."

"Maybe she just bakes a lot of pies and can't eat them all," he said, slipping a slab of beef onto her plate.

When they had both been served and the bread passed, Sarah took her seat opposite him and began to eat. The beef was tender and moist, thank heaven. She was never sure how to tell when it was done but not too done. She'd guessed right this time.

"I have some interesting news for you," she said after a moment.

He stopped, his fork halfway to his mouth. "About Brian?"

"No, nothing like that," she assured him. "About the Blackwell case."

He gave her a look, but she ignored it. "Did you know that Letitia Blackwell had a lover before she met her husband?"

"A lover?" he echoed, and took a bite of potato, chewing thoughtfully. "She must've been pretty young. She isn't too old even now, is she?"

"No, she isn't. My guess is that she had a schoolgirl infatuation. The object of her affections was the local schoolmaster. Her father disapproved, of course, or would have if he'd even known about it, which I doubt he did. Then the two of them actually eloped, or tried to. That's when Letitia fell off her horse and was so badly injured. Apparently, the schoolmaster had to carry her home and face her father. It must have been an ugly scene, especially with Letitia hurt the way she was."

"What happened to the schoolmaster?"

"He was let go and no one saw him again. Mr. Symington probably had him fired and banished from the area, as any good father would do. In any case, he was long gone when Letitia finally met Dr. Blackwell."

"Any possibility he got more than banished?" Malloy asked.

Sarah blinked at him in surprise. "You mean killed?"

"You told me once that men like Symington aren't above doing something like that, and he did practically ruin Symington's daughter. Eloping with her was bad enough, but he nearly crippled her for life, too."

"I have no idea, but we could try to find out," she mused, then realized, "That would make Symington a definite suspect in Blackwell's death, wouldn't it? If he already had a history of killing men who harmed his daughter in some way."

"It's something to think about," Malloy allowed. "Anyway, so the schoolmaster, dead or alive, was out of the way when the good doctor shows up, and she turns her attentions to him instead."

"Not exactly," Sarah said. "From what I understand, Blackwell was quite a devil with the ladies, and Letitia certainly may have found him attractive. You know that she was speaking at his lectures, even though she was terrified of public speaking. That's why she started taking the morphine again. She injects it, did I tell you that?"

"Injects it? With what?"

"A syringe."

"She does that to herself?" he asked, horrified.

"People can do amazing things when the need is great enough," she said. "I understand that injecting it increases the drug's potency. She's very badly addicted."

Malloy grunted. Plainly, he had little sympathy for people who needed sedatives to cope with life. "All right, so she was speaking at the lectures and didn't want to. How did that lead to them getting married?"

"When Letitia said she didn't want to do the lectures anymore, Blackwell suddenly developed a passion for her. He began to pay her court."

"What did her father think about this? If he didn't want her running off with a schoolmaster, I can't believe he'd be any happier to have some quack doctor for a son-in-law either."

"Symington didn't think Blackwell was a quack," she reminded him. "He respected him and was grateful for all he'd done for Letitia. And Letitia wasn't an innocent young girl, either. If people found out about her elopement, she would've been ruined, and she wouldn't have had any chance to make a suitable marriage. If the schoolmaster had actually deflowered her, her chances were even worse."

"So her father was glad to get her safely married to anybody at all, even a poor quack doctor," Malloy said.

"I don't think it was quite that bad. He must have been genuinely impressed with Blackwell if he allowed his daughter to marry him—no matter what the circumstances. He also spoke at Blackwell's lectures, too, when Letitia couldn't because of her pregnancy, which proves he believed in the man. Or at least that he didn't disapprove."

Malloy took another bite of her pot roast. He seemed to be enjoying it, although he didn't say anything. "All right, so Letitia had a lover. What does he have to do with Blackwell's murder?"

"I haven't gotten to that part yet," she assured him. "I told you Blackwell courted Letitia. He must have been very charming, and Letitia would have been vulnerable. She'd had the broken romance with the schoolmaster, and she'd been an invalid for a long time, probably thinking she'd never marry at all. Then Blackwell apparently falls madly in love with her and begs for her hand in marriage."

"Sounds like a Sunday matinee," Malloy remarked, frowning with distaste.

"Exactly," she said. "She would have been flattered, but it appears that Blackwell's sudden affection for her was all a ploy. She wanted to stop doing his lectures, but he needed her. If they were married, he'd have her in his power, and she'd have to keep appearing at them whether she wanted to or not."

"Then you don't think Blackwell cared for her?"

"He wasn't in love with her, certainly," she said. "In fact, as soon as they were married, he stopped paying attention to her at all. According to her maid, Letitia was extremely unhappy because her husband neglected her so badly."

"If what Mrs. Ellsworth said about him was true, he was probably too busy with all his other lady friends," Malloy said.

"That's certainly possible, and if the grief expressed at his memorial service was any indication, it's true," she said.

Malloy mulled this over for a bit as he finished off his pot roast. "So Blackwell had an unhappy wife who used morphine. There's still one problem."

"What's that?"

"I already asked you if you thought she was the kind of woman who could put a bullet in her husband's brain, and you said no. Did you change your mind?"

"Well, no, but—"

"Now, if you told me that she had a lover *after* she got married, we might have something. They both would have a reason for getting rid of her husband, then, and the lover could've taken care of the nasty business of actually killing him. Any chance of that?"

It was Sarah's turn to consider. "An unhappy woman is easy prey to seduction," she mused. "Letitia had already been the victim of such a seduction twice, too, once with the schoolmaster and once with Blackwell.

And she did go out every afternoon, supposedly visiting."

"You think she was meeting a lover?" Malloy asked with interest.

Sarah frowned. "No, I think she went to an opium den."

"Good God," Malloy swore.

"Don't be so shocked. Upper-class women go to them all the time. It's the worst-kept secret in the city. Surely you already knew that."

"I never gave it much thought," he admitted. "I don't have a lot of dealings with upper-class women. Or at least I didn't used to."

He was referring, of course, to the recent crimes they had solved together that had given him more contact than he'd wanted with such women.

"Well, it's true," Sarah said. "They veil themselves so no one will recognize them, but their clothing gives them away. Only wealthy women can dress so well."

"All right, maybe Mrs. Blackwell met her lover at the opium den. Do you know which one she went to?"

"No, and I doubt she'd be willing to betray the place to me. She did mention a Mr. Fong, though. It sounded as if he was the one who sold her the morphine."

"A Chinese?" Malloy's interest was piqued again. "Does her baby look Chinese?"

"Malloy, really!"

"It's possible, isn't it? *Does* the baby look Chinese?"

"Not at all. He has red hair."

"I guess Mr. Fong is no longer a suspect, then. But if we can find a redheaded morphine user . . ."

"Now you're making fun of me," she accused.

"No, I'm just thinking that maybe Mrs. Blackwell was unhappy, but that doesn't prove she killed her husband. Find me her redheaded lover, though, either at the opium den or someplace else, and I might change my mind."

Sarah rolled her eyes. "I'll do my best, Malloy, but

probably the Symingtons just have a family history of red hair and there's no lover at all."

"Or maybe the Brown family does, for all we know," Malloy agreed. "I'll ask Calvin when I see him again."

When they'd finished their meal and Malloy had eaten two slices of Mrs. Ellsworth's pie, Sarah conducted him back into her office and sat him down at the battered desk that had been Tom's.

"The files are in alphabetical order, so there's no way to know which patients he'd been working with most recently without going through each one. I'm sorry," she said, laying a pile of folders in front of him.

He shrugged. "I figured it wouldn't be easy, and don't get your hopes up, either. It's still more likely he was killed by a common thief who chose him at random, and his death didn't have anything to do with him personally."

"If that's the case, we probably will never find out who killed him, then, will we?" she asked.

She knew she was right, but Malloy just said, "Never is a long time."

He started on the *A*s, and Sarah returned to the kitchen to do the dishes. When she'd finished, she checked on him, bringing him coffee and lighting a lamp because the sun was setting. Finally, she sat down by the front window and tried to knit, but she kept watching Malloy out of the corner of her eye, wondering if he'd found anything yet. Surely he'd say something if he had, but the only time he spoke was occasionally to ask her the meaning of a medical term.

After what seemed an age, she heard a clock outside striking nine. Malloy heard it, too. "Is it that late already?" he asked, stretching his shoulders wearily.

"I'm afraid so," she said, gratefully putting her knitting aside. She'd probably have to pull out all that she'd done tonight, since she'd been paying so little attention, she'd completely ruined the pattern. "Did you see anything interesting?"

"I saw a lot that was interesting, but nothing that somebody'd get killed over," he said, standing and arching his back to stretch out the kinks. "I'd better be going. The neighbors will talk if I stay too late."

"The neighbors will talk about you coming at all," she replied, rising to see him out. "Don't worry, though," she assured him when she saw his worried frown, "my reputation isn't in any danger. They'll just be speculating on how soon we're going to be married."

"Married?" Malloy looked horrified.

"Anytime a gentleman calls on a lady regularly, that is the expected outcome," she told him, amused by his reaction. "I'm sure our real relationship is beyond their ability to comprehend."

"That's because the police don't usually use midwives to solve murder cases," Malloy told her, "not even in Teddy Roosevelt's modern police department."

"Well, they should certainly consider using women of some kind in solving crimes," she replied in the same vein. "You see how successful you've been the times I've helped you solve a case."

"It's time I left," Malloy said diplomatically, "neighbors or no neighbors."

"You're right. If we continue this conversation, I'm sure we'll only argue. I'll get your hat."

He settled the bowler on his head and said, "Thanks for supper."

"Thank you for working on Tom's case," she replied. "I never thought anyone would care about it again."

"Like I said, don't get your hopes up. You know there's not much chance we'll find anything after all this time," he said.

"I do know that, but it means a lot to me that you're willing to try." To her chagrin, she felt tears welling in her eyes.

He was plainly uncomfortable with her gratitude and the remnants of her grief. "That's my job," he excused himself. "Keep an eye out for that redheaded lover," he said to lighten the mood.

"Don't worry," she replied with a forced smile. "I'm determined to be the one to solve this case."

"When you do, I'll put in a good word for you with Roosevelt. Maybe he'll make you the first female detective sergeant."

She was still laughing when she closed the front door behind him. Malloy had, of course, never even met Police Commissioner Theodore Roosevelt, while Sarah had known him all her life. And the thought of anyone, even Teddy, appointing a female police detective was too funny for words.

FRANK HAD NO desire ever to see Amos Potter again, but the man *had* offered him a generous reward for finding Edmund Blackwell/Eddie Brown's killer, so he felt a certain obligation to solve the case. If that meant asking Amos Potter a few more questions, then he'd overcome his personal prejudices just this once.

Only when he'd decided he should see Potter did he realize he had no idea where to find the man. He'd never needed to inquire before because Potter had so conveniently made himself available at Blackwell's house until now. But when Frank stopped by the next morning, Potter wasn't there. The butler, Granger, reluctantly gave him Potter's address. Frank thought Granger looked ill, so maybe that had weakened his resolve to be as unhelpful as possible to Frank's investigation. Whatever the circumstances, however, Frank finally located Amos Potter's residence in a shabby but respectable street between Greenwich Village and the infamous neighborhood known as the Tenderloin.

Potter lived on the fourth floor of a formerly grand home that had been converted into cheap flats. He opened the door in his shirtsleeves. He was unshaven, and his collarless shirt was open at the throat to reveal a few meager wisps of salt-and-pepper chest hair. His suspenders hung down at his hips, and his trousers were old and wrinkled.

"Malloy, what are you doing here?" he demanded, either annoyed or embarrassed by Frank's appearance at his door.

"I have a few questions to ask you, Mr. Potter," he said, exaggerating his tone of respect and making no intimidating moves. Potter wouldn't like being caught unawares and looking so disreputable, and he probably hated having Frank, of all people, find out where and how he really lived. He was, Frank had noted, a man who liked to maintain the image of genteel respectability.

"How did you find me?" Potter snapped.

"I asked at the Blackwell house," Frank said, still mild and unthreatening. "I won't keep you long, Mr. Potter. I just need to ask you a few more things about Dr. Blackwell. I know you want to help me find his killer, and I need a little more information from you to accomplish that."

"I already gave you all the information I had that would help find Edmund's killer, and in spite of that, you let your best suspect escape," Potter said impatiently. A door opened across the hall, and Potter glanced over uneasily. "Come inside," he snapped, having decided he didn't want to give his neighbors any more fodder for gossip.

Frank gladly obliged him.

Potter's flat was sparsely furnished with items that had probably been left by a previous tenant, judging from their condition. If Blackwell had been prospering in his career as a healer, he hadn't been sharing much of his newfound fortune with his assistant.

"What do you want to know?" Potter asked, making no effort at courtesy.

Frank chose to make himself comfortable anyway and took a seat in what appeared to be the best chair in the place. "Let's see," he said, pretending to try to recall why he had come. "I've been hearing lots of rumors about Dr. Blackwell and his relationship with his female patients," he tried.

"I have no idea what you're talking about," Potter said, grudgingly seating himself in another chair. He didn't lean back, though, giving Frank the silent message that he didn't intend to be sitting there very long. "I have no idea who would be spreading such scandalous rumors about poor Edmund."

Frank let him get by with the lie. "Some people seem to think that Dr. Blackwell laid more than just his hands on the women he treated."

"That's preposterous!" Potter sputtered. "Edmund was a healer. His treatments were revolutionary, but there was nothing improper about them or about him."

"Then if I question the husbands of some of these women, I won't find out that they had any reason to be jealous of Dr. Blackwell," Frank said.

"Certainly not! Of course," Potter added, backpedaling just a bit, "some men are just naturally jealous of any male who pays their wives attention. Dr. Blackwell's cures inspired a high level of gratitude and devotion from his clients, so naturally the ladies would be excessively fond of him. I'm sure you noticed how distraught they were at the memorial service."

"Yeah, like a real close friend had died," Frank agreed.

"And some men might feel a bit uncomfortable if their wives expressed such affection for another man."

"How do you think they expressed their affection?" Frank asked mildly.

Potter wasn't fooled. "Mr. Malloy, your questions are insulting. Although Edmund is beyond being hurt by your innuendos, the ladies in question are not."

"And speaking of the ladies in question, what do you know about this Mrs. Fitzgerald? The one you were talking to at the funeral."

Potter seemed surprised. "Why, nothing in particular.

Edmund treated her for a back ailment, I believe. He helped her tremendously."

"And she was so grateful she gave him a house to live in," Frank said, as if that were the most natural reaction in the world.

"I'm sure I don't know anything about that," Potter insisted.

"Have you met with Mr. Fitzgerald to discuss the matter?"

"Yes, but . . . Well, he's a reasonable man. He doesn't expect Mrs. Blackwell to move out under the circumstances. I managed to convince him to . . . Well, what gentleman could do such a thing?"

"Yeah, I was thinking the same thing," Frank said. "How long will he let her stay there? Or maybe you arranged for her to start paying rent."

"I . . ." For some reason, Potter's face grew red, and he seemed very uncomfortable. "That is, I haven't spoken to Letitia about this yet. I'm sure when she understands the situation—and when she's able, of course—she'll be only too happy to retire to her father's house. It's the only sensible course of action, under the circumstances."

"Why would she do that?" Frank asked. "She could just get another house if Fitzgerald doesn't want her in his. It would be hard to go home to live with her father again after being married and on her own."

Potter squeezed his mouth down to a bloodless line. Frank pretended not to notice his agitation. The man was, after all, taking great pains to appear reasonable. After a moment of intense self-control, he said, "I'm afraid Mrs. Blackwell would find it difficult to . . . to manage without her father's assistance."

Frank considered the possible meanings of this astonishing admission. "Are you saying that Mrs. Blackwell isn't able to manage a home on her own?"

"Oh, no, I'm sure . . . that is, she's been doing so for a while now, so . . . It's not that, not that at all."

"What is it, then?" Frank asked. It was, he had to admit, much easier to interrogate an intelligent man than a stupid one. He didn't have to bloody his knuckles.

"Well, it would seem that . . . I don't want to speak ill of the dead, you understand, but it would appear, from the records I have been able to find, that Edmund hadn't been . . . Well, what I mean is—"

"Spit it out, Potter," Frank ordered, unable to bear Potter's hedging another moment.

Potter's face blanched. "Edmund left no estate," he blurted.

"Did you think he would?"

Potter was obviously uncomfortable with this subject. "He was very successful. He led me to believe . . . I received a salary, of course, but I was also a partner in the practice. I handled the business aspects, scheduling the lectures and renting the halls, that sort of thing. In return, Edmund trained me in his techniques, and I was to get half of the profits of the practice as soon as I was proficient enough to become a healer myself. When Edmund bought the house on Gramercy Park, or rather, when he led me to believe he'd bought it, I believed I owned half of it, too. He had many wealthy clients who paid him well for his services, but now . . ."

"Now it looks like he managed to spend all of it before he died," Frank supplied. Too bad Potter had offered him a reward to find the killer *before* he found out there was no estate. If the man thought he'd inherit a prosperous business, he would have had an excellent motive for murder. But that would have been far too easy. Frank was going to have to work harder than that to earn this reward.

"Edmund was rather proud of his success," Potter was saying, making excuses for the dead man. "He'd never had any before. He felt it was important to maintain the trappings of affluence in order to win the confidence of the affluent clients he wished to attract. He kept a carriage and had a full complement of servants. That's very expensive."

"This must've been a shock to Mrs. Blackwell to find out she's penniless," Frank suggested.

"Oh, I haven't told her anything about this yet. She's . . . Well, she's not even receiving visitors yet, and this isn't something I could tell her in a note or through an intermediary, and certainly not until she's stronger."

"Of course not," Frank agreed. He wondered how Potter would break the news to the young widow and if he was hoping she would seek comfort from him. Or possibly even support. Potter may once have imagined he would be able to offer it, with half of Blackwell's estate at his disposal. Now, of course, he could only offer her space in his shabby flat. "Well, now, the reason I stopped by today is that I need a list of Blackwell's female clients, the ones who seemed most *devoted* to him."

"Whatever for?" Potter asked in alarm.

"So I can question them and find out if any of their husbands were jealous of the good doctor."

"You can't do that!"

"Sure I can. Don't worry, Potter. I'll find Blackwell's killer for you."

"Not from among his clients!" he insisted. "None of them would even consider . . . It isn't possible!"

"You think rich people don't commit murder?"

Plainly, he'd never given the matter a great deal of thought. "I'm sure I have no opinion on that, but you just can't question these ladies as if they were common criminals! They'll never allow me to—"

"Allow you to what?" Frank asked when Potter caught himself.

"Nothing, nothing at all."

Frank frowned thoughtfully. "Were you planning to take up Blackwell's practice where he'd left off?"

"Edmund performed a valuable service for people who are suffering," Potter insisted. "Someone must continue his work, for the good of humanity."

"And that would be you, I guess."

"I have been thoroughly trained," he reminded Frank indignantly. "I can perform the same adjustments Edmund performed, and I can relieve suffering just as well. There is no need for his work to end just because he is no longer with us."

"Not if you say so," Frank said. "So tell me, which do you want more? Do you want me to find Blackwell's killer or do you want me to avoid offending his clients so you can continue to treat them?"

Potter's face mottled with rage. "I want you to find Edmund's killer, but you had him in your grasp and you let him escape!"

Frank gave him a pitying look. "Are you still talking about Calvin Brown?"

"Of course I am! You know as well as I that he killed his father. He's the only one with any possible reason to want him dead. If you can't see that, then perhaps I should get another detective to investigate this case."

Now Frank was annoyed. "First of all, Calvin hasn't gone anywhere. He's still right there, in his rooming house on Essex. He's as anxious as you are to find out who killed his father."

"So you say. When was the last time you saw him?"

"Very recently," Frank hedged. "And his landlady will send me word if he tries to leave town. But he's not the killer, Mr. Potter. If he was, he'd be long gone, as you pointed out yourself."

"Unless he's more clever than you give him credit for, Mr. Malloy," Potter warned. "He's his father's son. He would know instinctively that running away would prove him guilty. That's why he's still here, continuing to deceive you with his innocent face and his country manners."

Frank didn't like Potter's opinion of his intelligence, but he managed not to mention it. "Could I have that list of names, Mr. Potter? Or maybe I could ask Mrs.

Blackwell for it," he added, knowing this was the one thing guaranteed to inspire Potter to action.

"You wouldn't dare! Besides, she won't see you. I told you, she's not receiving visitors yet."

"I could have Mrs. Brandt ask her," Frank said with a smile.

Potter practically swelled with impotent fury, and for a moment Frank entertained the fanciful notion that he might actually explode. Fortunately, Potter allowed his chivalry to override his anger. He wasn't going to permit Mrs. Blackwell to be involved in any unpleasantness if he could help it. "I will give you a list, but if you offend any of these people, I will have your job."

Frank managed not to grin in triumph.

SARAH KNEW SHE was wearing out her welcome at the Blackwell home, but until someone told her to stop visiting, she would certainly continue. Besides, this time she had a mission. She wanted to find out what had happened to the schoolmaster who'd been Letitia's first lover. If he had, indeed, died mysteriously on the orders of Letitia's father, as Malloy had suggested, Sarah would have a perfect suspect in the murder of Dr. Blackwell, too. Of course, proving Symington responsible for the schoolmaster's death would avail nothing. Symington would hardly have committed the crime himself, and even if he had, and had killed Blackwell, too, he would most certainly use his money and power to avoid prosecution. But at least if they could implicate him, they would have solved the case and exonerated young Calvin Brown.

A maid answered the door at the Blackwell home. She was a young girl whom Sarah had seen only in passing.

"Mrs. Brandt, I didn't expect you," she said in surprise, looking distressed. Probably she was afraid she had forgotten her instructions.

"Nobody expected me," Sarah reassured her. "I just stopped by to see how Mrs. Blackwell is doing."

"Oh, right this way, then," the girl said with relief, closing the front door behind her and leading her not up the stairs, as Sarah had expected, but down the hallway to the back parlor. This would be the room where the family would sit, as opposed to the front parlor, which would be reserved for guests. Probably Mrs. Blackwell was feeling well enough to get out of bed, although Sarah thought it was way too soon for that. The baby had been born less than a week ago, and Sarah encouraged her patients to stay in bed and avoid visitors for two weeks to recover. She'd have to caution the woman about exerting herself too soon, and especially about negotiating the stairs.

The maid didn't knock, as she should have, but threw the doors open and said, "Mrs. Brandt is here to see you, ma'am."

Sarah didn't know who was more startled, she or Mrs. Blackwell or the young man who had been sitting on the sofa with her. The two of them had been sitting very close, and if Sarah wasn't mistaken, he had been holding her hand. Now he was on his feet, his face scarlet with embarrassment, and Mrs. Blackwell was looking at Sarah in alarm, the color high in her face as well.

For her part, Sarah could only gape. The young man was tall and gangly and very ordinary in appearance except for one startling feature. He had red hair.

9

"MRS. BRANDT," MRS. BLACKWELL SAID WHEN SHE could find her tongue. "I . . . I . . . Peggy should have announced you." Her tone was unmistakably angry, and her glare was directed at her servant.

The poor maid paled. "I'm that sorry, Mrs. Blackwell," she said anxiously. "I didn't know . . . I guess I forgot. I never was trained about answering the door, I wasn't, and with Mr. Granger sick and all . . ."

"Hush, you stupid girl," Mrs. Blackwell snapped. "Never mind about that now. You may go."

The girl hastily withdrew and closed the doors behind her with an unseemly bang.

Mrs. Blackwell winced, then turned an obviously insincere smile on Sarah. "I didn't know you were coming today, Mrs. Brandt."

"I was in the neighborhood," Sarah lied brazenly, somehow managing to tear her interested gaze from the young man. "I thought I'd stop in and check on you. You must be feeling very well, however. I was sure I'd cautioned you about getting up too soon, so I'm a little surprised to see you up and entertaining visitors." She smiled expectantly at the young man, awaiting an introduction.

Had Mrs. Blackwell been more sophisticated, she would have known she could snub Sarah and send her on her way without that introduction. Sarah was, after all, just hired help and here without an invitation at that. But the young woman was either unfamiliar with the more subtle nuances of social etiquette, or she was simply too kind to snub someone who had been so helpful to her, no matter how annoying her presence might be at the moment.

Although she was plainly reluctant to do so, she said, "Mrs. Brandt, this is Mr. Dudley. He . . . he's an old friend of mine . . . from home. Mrs. Brandt is my midwife," she hastily added to Dudley.

"I'm very pleased to meet you, Mr. Dudley," Sarah said, giving him her best smile.

He didn't return it. He was still too flustered. If Mrs. Blackwell was unsophisticated, he was artless. He managed only to bob his head in acknowledgment. His face was still extremely red. Even redder than his hair.

"I'm sorry to have interrupted your reunion," Sarah said. "You must have a lot to catch up on." She should, of course, have offered to leave at this point, but instead, she sat down uninvited. Mrs. Blackwell apparently had no idea how to rid herself of an unwelcome guest, and Sarah was going to take shameless advantage of this to find out exactly who Mr. Dudley was and if he could possibly be responsible for the color of the Blackwell baby's hair. "How long will you be in town, Mr. Dudley?" she asked innocently.

Dudley sat down beside Letitia again, but this time he left a respectable distance between them. "I . . . well, that is . . ." He gave Letitia a desperate glance.

"Mr. Dudley actually lives in the city now," she replied for him, her voice brittle with strain. "We . . . that is, I . . . I mean . . ." This time she gave him a desperate glance.

"I saw the notice about Dr. Blackwell's death," he said too loudly, with the confidence of one who has, at just the right moment, invented the perfect excuse for something. "I thought it my duty to call on Letitia . . . uh, Mrs. Blackwell. To express my condolences, that is."

"How very kind of you," Sarah assured him, pretending to believe his every word. "I'm sure Mrs. Blackwell appreciates seeing a familiar face at this sad time."

"I know I shouldn't have gotten up," Letitia said anxiously, "but I felt I had to receive Mr. Dudley."

"Of course you did," Sarah said obligingly. "I know you'll be very careful not to exert yourself too much for at least another week."

"Is Mrs. Blackwell's health in danger?" Dudley asked with a worried frown. "Because you may be assured I would never do anything to harm her."

"I'm certain of that," Sarah said with false sincerity. "Mrs. Blackwell is the best judge of how well she feels, and I'm sure she will feel better for having seen you, since you were such close friends. Tell me, Mr. Dudley, what brought you to the city?"

"I . . . Well, I thought being here would be good for me," he said uncertainly, glancing at Letitia once more, as if for guidance.

Plainly, there was more to the story.

"I suppose your family has a business here and wanted you to take your place in it," she guessed, even though she'd already ascertained that he could not possibly be of the same social class as the Symingtons, unless he'd fallen on very hard times indeed. His clothes were cheap and ill-fitting, the crease in his pants betraying that they had been bought ready-made off a store shelf.

"Oh, no, I don't . . ." He glanced at Letitia again.

She finally took up the challenge. "Mr. Dudley is a very educated man, but the only suitable position he could find was as a schoolmaster until he came to the city," she explained, giving him a reassuring smile.

"Here he has a chance to better himself that he never had in a small country town."

"He certainly does," Sarah agreed, managing not to react to the word "schoolmaster." As she had suspected from the moment she saw him, Mr. Dudley was Letitia's former lover, and he was very clearly still involved with her. Sarah couldn't wait to inform Malloy that she'd already found the redheaded father of Letitia's child. And, of course, an excellent suspect in Dr. Blackwell's murder. On the other hand, Dudley's reappearance pretty well proved Mr. Symington hadn't had Letitia's lover killed, thereby eliminating a good reason to consider Letitia's father as a suspect. She had so wanted him to be the killer. "What kind of employment have you found here, Mr. Dudley?"

"Oh, I'm just . . . I'm a clerk at a bank at the moment," he said.

"But he has excellent prospects," Letitia quickly explained. The glance she gave him could only be called adoring.

Sarah tried to see what might have attracted her to Dudley in the first place. He was, as she had already noted, very ordinary looking. Unlike most redheads, he didn't have freckles, which was one thing in his favor. But his skin was pale, almost pasty, and his eyes were a washed-out blue. His hair was striking in color, but he wore it slicked down against his head in an unflattering style. His arms and legs were long and bony, and he seemed not to know exactly what to do with them. Perhaps he was utterly charming when he hadn't been caught by a stranger in his mistress's parlor, but Sarah couldn't imagine it. On the other hand, his very ingenuousness might have been what attracted Letitia, since most of the men of her class would have been overbearing and arrogant and probably overwhelming to a girl as retiring as she had probably been.

Sarah had been taught from birth how to conduct a meaningless and socially acceptable conversation, and she called upon those skills now. She chatted about the weather and the neighborhood and the city in general, asking Mr. Dudley what he thought about this or that, and of course he never had an opinion. Finally, she accomplished her mission, which was to make him understand that she wasn't leaving before he did.

"I . . . I suppose I should be going," he said in defeat after what seemed an age to Sarah. Letitia looked stricken.

She glanced at Sarah, probably wishing her in Hades, but her social skills had not included training in how to handle someone as rudely determined as Sarah. "I . . . I hope you'll be able to call again soon," she said to him at last, her eyes suspiciously moist.

"Oh, certainly," he quickly assured her. "I . . . I'll make a point of it."

She gave him her hand. "Thank you for coming. It was so very nice to see you. To see a familiar face, that is," she amended, remembering Sarah's presence.

He had to swallow before he could say, "It was very nice to see you, too. I hope I haven't hindered your recovery in any way."

"Oh, no! In fact, I'm sure you've helped it tremendously!"

Sarah somehow managed not to choke. "It was lovely meeting you, Mr. Dudley," she said in an effort to get him going. "Perhaps we'll encounter each other again."

"I . . . I'd like that," he said without conviction, releasing Letitia's hand with obvious reluctance.

"I'll ring for the maid to see you out," Letitia said. "Mrs. Brandt, will you be leaving, too?" she added almost hopefully.

Sarah smiled serenely. "I'd like to speak with you privately, if you don't mind. I need to find out how you're feeling."

Letitia frowned. She wasn't very adept at concealing her true emotions, and now she wanted Sarah even farther away than Hades. They sat in uncomfortable silence until the maid appeared in the doorway, and Dudley took his leave again.

It was painful to watch the two of them unable to say what they wanted to say because of Sarah's presence, but she steeled herself to the ordeal. When at last the door had closed behind him, she turned to Mrs. Blackwell.

"He seems like a very nice young man," Sarah ventured, and Mrs. Blackwell burst into tears.

Sarah hurried to her side. "I was afraid that entertaining a visitor might be too much of a strain for you," she said, searching for her handkerchief.

Before she could find it, Letitia pulled one from her sleeve and began to weep into it. "You don't understand!" she insisted.

"Oh, I believe I do," Sarah said. "You've known Mr. Dudley for several years, haven't you?"

Letitia cried harder.

"You obviously care deeply for one another. Anyone could see it in the way you look at each other, which makes me suspect that Mr. Dudley was the young man with whom you attempted to elope the night you were injured."

Letitia's head came up. Her lovely eyes were full of unshed tears, but she had been shocked into horrified silence. "Who told you that?" she whispered.

"You know how servants gossip," Sarah excused herself.

"They couldn't . . . He's never been to the house before! They've never even set eyes on him!"

Sarah didn't remind her that her maid had known him well. "But you have been seeing him elsewhere, haven't you?"

"No! Certainly not! That would be immoral. I'm a married woman. I mean I *was*! I *was* a married woman. Now, of course, I'm a widow, and it's perfectly proper for an old friend to call—"

"Mrs. Blackwell," Sarah said, out of patience, "you

don't have to make excuses to me. I have no wish to judge you. But it's obvious that you must have been seeing Mr. Dudley. He most certainly is the father of your child."

She gasped in feigned outrage. "How can you even suggest such a thing? He couldn't be. I haven't seen him in years! You heard him, he only saw the notice of Edmund's death in the paper and came to offer his condolences."

Her porcelain cheeks were splotched with red now, and her eyes were wild. She wasn't a pretty liar.

"I'm not the only one who will suspect that he's the baby's father," Sarah said. "One look at your child . . . I assume your father knows what Dudley looks like. He'll guess immediately."

This time Letitia practically wailed, sobbing uncontrollably into her now-soggy handkerchief.

Although she could not condone adultery, Sarah also couldn't bear to see such misery, and Letitia *was* her patient. She took the weeping woman into her arms. "There now, there's nothing you can do about the past. You can only do something about the future."

This made Letitia cry even harder, but Sarah patted and soothed, and after a few moments, with no encouragement at all, Letitia began to bare her soul.

"We never meant for it to happen," she insisted between sobs. "Peter left after the accident. My father had him discharged from his job, and he had no choice but to leave town. He found work here in the city, and we never saw each other again until . . . until I was already married to Edmund."

"That must have been a shock, seeing him again," Sarah suggested tentatively, worried about saying the wrong thing and stopping the flow of confidences.

"He came . . . he came to one of Edmund's lectures. He'd seen my name on the poster, and he came to see me. Just to find out how I was," Letitia added, and Sarah nodded her comprehension. "You have to understand, I was hurt when we . . . You see, Peter and I eloped one night. I knew my father would never allow us to marry, so what else could we do? But my horse stumbled in the darkness, and I was horribly hurt."

"So your father ran Peter out of town, and then Dr. Blackwell came to cure you," Sarah said, hurrying the story along. She already knew this part.

"But Peter saw my name on the poster, and he just wanted to make sure I was well. He still loved me, you see, and he hadn't been able to make any inquiries about me without drawing my father's attention to him. He only wanted to make sure I had recovered!"

Sarah nodded again. "Of course he did."

"When I saw him in the audience, I almost fainted. I could hardly finish my speech. He told me later that's when he knew I still loved him. I was desperate to see him privately, but I had no idea how to find him. But I didn't have to worry about that because he was able to find me."

"I'm sure that wasn't too difficult. Dr. Blackwell was famous."

Letitia ignored the mention of her dead husband. "Peter sent me a note and asked me to meet him somewhere. He just wanted to talk to me, to find out if I had forgiven him. He'd felt so guilty for leaving me and for having caused my accident. Or at least he always blamed himself, even though it wasn't really his fault."

"And so you met him. Weren't you worried about being seen?"

"Of course! That's why we . . ."

"Why you what?" Sarah asked when she hesitated.

"I couldn't risk Edmund finding out, and it was the only place we could meet without being seen," she said defensively.

"And where was that?"

"The . . . Mr. Fong's establishment," she admitted reluctantly.

"An opium den?" Sarah asked in surprise.

"They're very discreet," Letitia insisted.

"I'm sure they are," Sarah said.

"After that . . ." Letitia began, but her voice broke again.

"I know you must have been very lonely and unhappy," Sarah said, remembering what the nurse had told her. "I understand that Dr. Blackwell was very busy and was hardly ever at home."

"It wasn't that. He just never loved me," she informed Sarah indignantly. "Not at all! He only married me so that I would have to keep speaking at his lectures."

"He told you that?" Sarah asked in surprise.

"Not in so many words, but I'm not completely stupid. It was obvious. He never even . . . after the first few months he didn't . . . I had my own room, you see, and he didn't ever come to visit me . . ."

"I understand," Sarah said, trying to imagine how a man could neglect a wife as lovely as Letitia. And there was one other thing she didn't understand. "If that was the case, wasn't he the least bit suspicious when he found out you were with child?"

Her face twisted with a grief Sarah could only imagine. "That's what proves how little he cared for me! I was so frightened for him to find out. I was certain he would know the truth and that he would throw me out of the house in disgrace. But he didn't even suspect! He had no idea how long it had been since he'd shared my bed or that he couldn't possibly be the baby's father. He was only annoyed because my condition would make it impossible for me to appear at the lectures for several months. That was the worst part of all! He never even dreamed I'd been unfaithful to him!"

Sarah found herself sympathizing with Letitia a little, although she knew many women who had far more unhappy lives and who still didn't feel the need for either morphine or adultery to escape them. Sympathy would get her more information, however, so she allowed herself to feel it.

"Were you just going to allow Dr. Blackwell to believe the baby was his and go on as you had been, seeing Dudley secretly?" she asked doubtfully.

"I didn't know what else to do!" she wailed, dissolving in tears again. "I was afraid Edmund wouldn't divorce me. He still wanted me to speak at the lectures, and if he knew I wanted to leave him . . . Well, if we'd divorced, he could have kept the baby, even though he wasn't the father. Or at least he would have used that threat to keep me from leaving him. I know he would, just to punish me and force me to do what he wanted."

Sarah was very much afraid he might have. The law certainly allowed him to. A woman could be divorced and put out in the street, with nothing but the clothes on her back, and never allowed to see her children again. At the very least, Blackwell could have used the child as leverage to keep Letitia in line. He believed he needed her to promote his cures, and he wouldn't have let her go easily.

Letitia was sobbing again, and Sarah didn't have the heart to press her any further. She'd already learned what she needed to know anyway.

When the sobs died down to sniffles, Sarah asked, "Would you like me to call your maid?"

"No, I . . . Let me get myself under control first," she said, dabbing at the last vestiges of her tears. "Oh, Mrs. Brandt, what am I going to do now?"

"Well, as you pointed out, you are no longer a married woman. You are free to do whatever you wish, and if you wish to marry Dudley, there is nothing to stop you."

"But my father would never allow—"

"Your father really has no control over you anymore," Sarah reminded her.

"But Peter is practically penniless," she pointed out. "How could we live?"

Plainly, Letitia had grown more practical with the passage of time. She probably hadn't even considered this the first time she'd eloped with Dudley. "I'm sure Dr.

Blackwell must have left you some money," Sarah said, managing to conceal her disapproval. How could Letitia even think about money? But perhaps she was only being critical of Letitia because she herself had turned her back on wealth and social position to marry a "penniless" doctor.

Clearly, Letitia hadn't thought of having a possible legacy. "Of course! And there's this house, too. I never liked it, and Peter and I won't need anything so grand, in any case. I could sell it and buy something smaller."

Sarah bit her tongue. No one had yet told Letitia that the house had merely been a loan from a grateful patient, a patient whose husband wanted the widow to vacate the property immediately. "You don't need to make any decisions just yet," Sarah said. "I believe Mr. Potter has been taking care of your husband's business affairs. I'm sure he can tell you exactly what your situation is." Better he than I, she added silently.

"Oh, yes, Mr. Potter is very capable," Letitia recalled, and Sarah was glad Potter couldn't see the indifference in her eyes when she spoke of him. "He'll take care of everything, I'm sure. He always does."

And meanwhile, Sarah would make sure Malloy took care of questioning Peter Dudley to find out if he had an alibi for the afternoon when Dr. Blackwell was murdered.

WHEN SARAH TURNED down Bank Street, she could see Mrs. Ellsworth sweeping her front stoop. She called out a greeting when she was close enough, and Mrs. Ellsworth pretended to be surprised to see her.

"Hello, Mrs. Brandt! Have you been delivering a baby?"

"Not today," Sarah replied with a smile.

"That's good," she said as Sarah stopped beside her porch. "I dropped my scissors this morning, and they landed point down and stuck in the floor!"

"That's too bad," Sarah said. "I hope it didn't leave a bad mark."

"Oh, my, that's the least of it! Don't you know that when scissors stick in the floor, it's an omen of death? Dear me, the last time I had an omen like that, some poor girl you knew died."

Sarah remembered and shivered. "I'm sure it was just a coincidence," she said, as much to convince herself as to reassure Mrs. Ellsworth. "In a city this size, people die every day, you know."

"That's true, of course," Mrs. Ellsworth agreed. "And I'm always happy to be wrong about something like that. Are you and Mr. Malloy working on another case together? I saw him coming to visit you last night."

"Yes, and he enjoyed your pie very much," Sarah told her. "Actually, he's trying to find out who killed my husband."

"Is he?" she exclaimed, excitement lighting her wrinkled face. "Does he have new evidence?"

"I'm afraid not, but he's looking through Tom's old files to see if he can find someone who might have been angry with Tom or had a reason to want him out of the way."

"I'm sure he won't find anything like that," Mrs. Ellsworth said. "Dr. Brandt was such a fine man. How could anyone not wish him well?"

"That's nice of you to say," Sarah said, but she couldn't help thinking that while Tom truly had been a fine man, he was also dead, and someone had killed him. It might have been a random act of violence. Such things happened in the city frequently. But if it was, then there was little possibility anyone would ever be brought to account for the crime. Sarah didn't like to think herself vindictive, but she wanted someone to pay for having ended her husband's life.

"That reminds me, did you see that article in the Sunday magazine?" Mrs. Ellsworth asked. "The one about that new photography called X ray? It made me wonder what Dr. Tom would have thought of such a thing."

"Yes, I saw it. I've heard about it, too. I suppose it would be very helpful to be able to see inside someone's body." She thought about Brian Malloy's foot and wondered what an X-ray photograph of it would show.

"Although," Mrs. Ellsworth said, "I think some things are better off left a mystery. If there was something bad inside of me, I don't think I'd want to know about it."

"X-ray photography isn't likely to be able to do that anyway," Sarah said. "It's not very exact and the pictures aren't very clear. It may very well be just an experiment that has no practical purpose."

"I hope you're right," Mrs. Ellsworth said. "It seems kind of indecent to go looking inside of people like that."

Sarah bit back a smile.

"Will Mr. Malloy be coming back soon?" Mrs. Ellsworth said, catching her by surprise. "I'd be happy to donate another pie for his enjoyment."

"I'm sure he would appreciate that. He may stop by later, if he can. Like me, he can't always be sure when he'll be free."

"I guess crimes and babies make their own schedules, don't they?" Mrs. Ellsworth observed.

"That they do," Sarah said. "You have a lovely evening," she added as she made her way to her own front porch.

After eating her supper, Sarah was sitting by her front window, mentally composing a note to Malloy telling him she had some important information and needed to meet with him right away, when she saw him coming down the street.

Mrs. Ellsworth saw him, too, and he had to stop and make small talk with her for a few minutes. Ever since Mrs. Ellsworth had saved Sarah's life, she had taken a great interest in hearing about the crimes Malloy was working on. Unfortunately, Malloy studiously avoided telling her about any of them, which Mrs. Ellsworth found extremely frustrating.

As soon as he could, Malloy extricated himself from her and made his way to Sarah's door. She was waiting for him as he came up the steps. "Did she offer you some pie?" Sarah asked as he entered the house.

"No," he said, removing his hat. "She's probably going to bring it over later. She thinks I'm a saint for trying to solve your husband's murder. Did you have to tell her that?" He was pretending to be annoyed.

"It was either that or let her think you're courting me. Which would you prefer, Malloy?" she asked with some amusement.

He frowned as he pretended to consider his options. "If she thought I was courting you, she might not come over and bother us," he pointed out.

"I wouldn't count on it," Sarah replied. "Come in and have some coffee before you get started. I've got something very interesting to tell you."

He rolled his eyes, but he followed her into the kitchen and sat down obediently at the table.

"I found the redheaded lover," she told him smugly when she'd poured his coffee.

He almost dropped the cup. "You what?"

"That's what you told me to do," she reminded him. "The only problem is that he's the same fellow she eloped with before—Peter Dudley. They were running away together when her horse threw her, and she was injured."

"He's the schoolmaster, then?"

"That's right. It appears that Mr. Symington didn't have him killed, just discharged. I'm sure he figured Letitia would never encounter him again, so having him murdered was a needless expense."

Malloy ignored her sarcasm. "How *did* she encounter him again?"

"He went to one of Blackwell's lectures. He apparently saw Letitia's name on the poster and wanted to see how she was. He must have felt terribly guilty because she'd been hurt, and then he hadn't been able to find out if she'd ever recovered. He'd lost his position and come to the city, so he hadn't had any contact with her at all until then, according to Letitia. He works in a bank or something now."

"And he has red hair," Malloy said, sipping his coffee thoughtfully.

"Extremely red hair. But even if he didn't, Letitia admitted he was the baby's father."

"She just told you, right out?" Malloy marveled. "I know priests who can't get confessions like that!"

Sarah tried to look modest. "I think she just needed to confide in someone. Someone who wouldn't judge her, that is."

"She deserves to be judged," Malloy said flatly.

"Perhaps, but Blackwell wasn't without guilt either. He only married her because she wanted to stop doing the lectures. He pretended to be in love with her, and he used his considerable charms to convince her he was. But as soon as they were safely married, he didn't even bother to . . . uh . . . to share her bed."

Malloy choked on his coffee. She should have waited until he wasn't drinking to tell him that. She knew he didn't like discussing such things, especially with her.

"Are you all right?" she asked as he coughed.

He nodded and kept coughing for a few more minutes. Finally, he was able to speak again. "She told you that, too?" he asked incredulously.

"As I said, she needed to unburden herself. The strangest part is that when Letitia turned up with child, Dr. Blackwell didn't even realize he couldn't be the father. That's how little attention he paid to her. She must have been terribly lonely and unhappy."

"I guess committing adultery made her feel better," Malloy scoffed.

"I'm not excusing her, Malloy. I'm just explaining."

"All right, then explain why she didn't leave Black-

well for the schoolmaster after he found her again and
they discovered they were still in love."

"That's easy. Divorce is extremely difficult and expensive. Letitia's father was hardly likely to finance one
for her, and she and Dudley had no means of their own
to do so. Besides, if she did divorce Blackwell, he could
keep her child."

"Why would he want a baby that wasn't his?" Malloy
asked skeptically.

"He probably wouldn't, but he could legally keep the
child, and even the threat of that would be enough to
prevent Letitia from leaving him. Then he could make
her life even more miserable than it already was, and
she wouldn't dare complain. And Blackwell could force
her to continue appearing at his lectures."

Malloy needed no more than a moment to see the
significance of this information. "But if Blackwell was
dead, the lovers could be together with no other problems."

"I believe you already pointed that out to me," Sarah
reminded him, "which is why you assigned me the task
of finding the redheaded lover in the first place."

"I didn't really expect you to find one," he admitted.

"I didn't either," she admitted right back. "But now
that I have, you have another suspect in Blackwell's
death."

"Do you think this Dudley could have done it?"

Sarah considered. "He's certainly devoted to Letitia.
And he wasn't above bedding another man's wife. Did
I tell you they met at an opium den for their trysts?"

"Good God."

"He also eloped with an innocent young girl against
her family's wishes. I think he's extremely foolish,
maybe even foolish enough to commit murder and try
to make it look like suicide, especially if he thought it
was the only way to protect Letitia."

"A schoolmaster might be smart enough to think of
the suicide thing, too. A good way to avoid suspicion.

If there's no murder, nobody will be looking for a killer, and he can come courting the widow afterward with no one the wiser."

"Murder would solve another problem as well," Sarah said. "Letitia was concerned about living on a bank employee's salary until I reminded her she would inherit her husband's estate. She wouldn't have gotten anything at all if she divorced him."

"She won't get anything now, either," Malloy said.

"What do you mean?"

"I mean Blackwell didn't leave any estate."

Sarah frowned. "I know he didn't own the house, but surely he had something put aside."

"Not a penny, according to Mr. Potter, who seemed pretty upset about it himself. Turns out he was supposed to be a partner in the business and get half of everything. He even thought he owned half of the house."

"Oh, my," Sarah said, giving herself a moment to absorb this. "If Dudley and Letitia didn't know this, as they apparently didn't, then it wouldn't rule them out as suspects, but it also gives Potter another reason to murder Blackwell, besides being in love with Letitia. He thought he would inherit some money, too."

"Money that he'd use to pay me a reward for finding the killer," Malloy suggested mildly.

"Oh, yes, I keep forgetting about that. I guess I'm going to have to give up on making Mr. Potter the killer," Sarah said.

"I understand the temptation," Malloy said with a grin. "He's a hard man to like, especially when he keeps insisting poor Calvin Brown killed his father."

"That is tactless of him," Sarah agreed. "Oh, wait, I just thought of something else. If Letitia's marriage to Blackwell wasn't valid, then she wouldn't have needed a divorce to marry Dudley."

"She wouldn't have needed to kill her husband either, which would eliminate her and Dudley as suspects. Do you think she knew?"

"If she did, she's done a remarkable job of hiding it."

"She did a remarkable job of hiding the morphine, too," Malloy pointed out. "And she would have had to be an accomplished liar to keep her secret from her husband all that time."

He was right, of course. A woman as desperate and unhappy as Letitia might be guilty of anything, innocent face or not. "So if she knew her marriage was bigamous, then she and Dudley probably didn't kill Blackwell," she reasoned.

"Unless the money was just as important to them as being together. If she wasn't really married to Blackwell, she wasn't entitled to anything he owned, either. Killing him while she was still his recognized wife would ensure she'd get his estate. And there wouldn't be the messiness of a scandal, either."

"So either way they have a motive for killing him," Sarah realized.

A tap on the back door distracted them, and as Malloy had predicted, it was Mrs. Ellsworth bearing a pie.

"Mrs. Brandt said you enjoyed the one I sent over yesterday," she explained to Malloy when she stepped into the kitchen.

"I did," he admitted, doing his best to be gracious, even though Sarah could tell it was a strain.

"It's the least I can do. If you can find Dr. Brandt's killer, you will have done a great service."

"I told you not to get your hopes up," Malloy reminded her gently, for him. "There really isn't much chance after all this time."

"You can do it, if anyone can," she said confidently. "It's apple and raisin," she added, setting the pie on the table. "There aren't any good berries left this late in the year."

"I'm sure it's delicious," Sarah said.

After some more meaningless conversation, Mrs. Ellsworth reluctantly left, wishing Malloy success in his quest.

"I didn't realize that coming over here could be so dangerous," Malloy remarked, looking admiringly at the pie. "If I'm not careful, I'll be as big as a barn."

"You don't have to eat it," Sarah said with a grin.

"I didn't say I didn't want to eat it," he replied, grinning back.

SARAH BRANDT STILL needed some training in being a cop, Malloy mused the next morning as he made his way down Essex Street toward the rooming house where Calvin Brown was staying. She'd met Peter Dudley, but she had no idea where he lived or how to find him. He worked at a bank somewhere was all she could tell him. Letitia Blackwell was hardly likely to be forthcoming with the information he needed either, even if he could get her to see him, which seemed still more unlikely. Short of waiting on the Blackwells' front steps until Dudley showed up again, Frank had no other means of locating him. He was once again going to have to send Sarah Brandt on police business to obtain the necessary information.

Mrs. Zimmerman answered his knock at the rooming-house door. She patted her carelessly dressed hair, as if making sure she looked her best for her visitor. "Mr. Malloy, how nice to see you," she said with a smile so broad, it showed her missing molars. Frank thought she might be trying to flirt with him, so he played along.

"It's very nice to see you, too, Mrs. Zimmerman. How's young Calvin doing?" he asked, stepping into the house.

"The same as always. He's been quiet as a mouse this morning. Didn't even come down for breakfast."

"Is that like him?" Frank asked, a little disturbed by this news. She hadn't seen Calvin this morning and hadn't checked to see if he was still there. Maybe Potter was right, and the boy had finally fled. He didn't like the idea of explaining that to Potter.

"No, come to think of it, it isn't like him at all," she

admitted with a frown. "I just thought . . . He gets up real early. Maybe he was down and got something before I was up this morning. He does that sometimes . . ."

Frank didn't wait for her to show him upstairs. He took the steps two at a time, instinct telling him something was wrong. If the boy had escaped, Potter would be furious with him, and rightly so.

He knocked on the door. "Calvin?" he called, and received no answer.

The knob turned easily in his hand, and he threw the door open. To his great relief, he saw Calvin still curled up beneath his covers on the bed, fast asleep.

"Calvin, wake up!" Malloy called pleasantly, going over to shake him. But when he touched the boy's shoulder, he felt the chill and stiffness of his body.

Calvin Brown was dead.

10

"It's no mystery how he died," the coroner explained, having given Calvin's body only a cursory examination. "The arsenic is sitting in plain sight and see how yellow his face is? That's always a sure sign of arsenic poisoning."

Frank had to admit he was right. Calvin had left the box of rat poison out on the dresser. An empty bottle of sarsaparilla sat on the table and had apparently been mixed with the poison to kill the taste.

"There's the suicide note, too," the coroner pointed out. "That's usually enough to convince most people it's a suicide."

Frank ignored his sarcasm. He just didn't want to make a mistake. Or rather, he just didn't want to be wrong about Calvin Brown. He'd been so certain the boy was innocent, and truth to tell, he'd *wanted* the boy to be innocent. But here it was, a confession written with his own hand right before he'd taken his own life.

"Dear Mother," he'd written. "I can't live with this no more. I shot father and tried to make it look like he killed himself. He refused to help us or even to admit he was my father. I couldn't stand thinking that he was living so rich while you worked so hard to support us. I'm sorry I did this, and I don't want to bring more shame on the family by being arrested for it. I love you and the girls." He'd signed it, "Calvin."

Frank swore silently as he stuffed the note into his pocket. This didn't make sense. The boy hadn't acted a bit guilty, and Frank considered himself an expert in judging such matters. He also hadn't run away, which would have been the only sensible thing to do if he'd killed his father. And certainly far less drastic than killing himself. There was an irony here, he supposed. Calvin had tried to make his father's death look like a suicide, and now he'd committed suicide himself.

"He went awful quick," the coroner said, as if offering Frank comfort. "It's a mercy. Sometimes they suffer for days."

Frank had seen the results of such suffering, and he could only be glad Calvin had given himself a large enough dose so that he succumbed almost immediately. "Tell them they can take the body away," Frank said. "I'll get his things together to send back to his mother."

He could have left this for the landlady, but for some reason he felt he had to do it himself. It would be a penance of some sort, to help assuage the guilt he was feeling for his own mistakes. If he'd arrested Calvin, at least the boy would still be alive.

As he collected Calvin's meager belongings and laid them into the cheap suitcase he'd carried with him from Virginia, Frank couldn't help thinking how gratified Amos Potter would be to have been proved right. Collecting the reward for solving this case would give Frank no pleasure, though.

While he was putting away the last of Calvin's things, the orderlies came to fetch the body. They had a time of it, since Calvin was still stiff. When they'd gotten him on the stretcher, lying on his side because he was fixed in a fetal position, he looked small and vulnerable under the sheet, like a child curled up for warmth or safety. It didn't seem fair that a boy so young should have cut his life short because of a man like Edmund Blackwell. But then, as Frank had learned only too well, life was seldom fair.

When all trace of Calvin Brown had been removed from the room, Frank started down the steps after the orderlies, carrying the boy's suitcase. He should write Mrs. Brown a letter, explaining what had happened, he thought. That was when he realized he didn't know Mrs. Brown's address. Calvin had carelessly not written it on his note, either.

Frank stopped at the bottom of the stairs and saw Mrs. Zimmerman, the landlady, sitting in the parlor, weeping softly into her handkerchief.

"Excuse me, ma'am," he said.

She looked up, her red-rimmed eyes brimming. "Oh, Mr. Malloy, I'm so glad you was the one who found him. That sweet boy, I don't know if I could've stood it or not. I should've knowed something was wrong, though. I should've gone up to check when he didn't come down to breakfast. Maybe if I had—"

"The coroner said he died real quick," Malloy said by way of comfort. No use in the woman torturing herself. "There was nothing you could've done."

"I wish he'd come and talked to me if he was feeling poorly. Maybe I could've said something to stop him."

"I wish he'd come to me, too," Frank said, "but he didn't. Sometimes, you just can't help, Mrs. Zimmerman. If someone is determined to kill themselves, they'll do it. There is something I'd like to ask you, though."

"Oh," she said, as if remembering. "You'll be wanting a refund on the rent you paid for him. There's three days left, I think. I'll get—"

"No, it's not that," Frank said. "You keep the money, for your trouble. It's just . . . I packed his things to send them home, but I don't know his address. I was wondering if you had any idea—"

"Oh, my, yes! I'd almost forgot. He give me a letter

to mail to his dear mother just yesterday. Wait right here, I'll fetch it."

Calvin had written to his mother *yesterday*. He'd made his decision quickly, then. He wouldn't have bothered with a letter if he'd known he was going to be leaving a suicide note so soon. What could have caused him to decide to do something like that when he seemed to be getting away with the crime? Certainly, he had every reason to believe he'd fooled Frank, at least.

Before Frank could make any sense of it, Mrs. Zimmerman was back. She held out an envelope to him with one hand while she dabbed a damp handkerchief at her nose with the other.

The envelope was cheap, and the address had been printed in a bold, childish scrawl in pencil. Frank stared at the address for a long moment, trying to identify what was wrong. Finally, it all came together in his mind. He ripped open the envelope.

"What are you doing?" Mrs. Zimmerman cried. "That's the last thing he wrote to his dear mother! Don't you have any respect at all?"

Frank ignored her. He pulled the folded paper out of the envelope and scanned its contents. "Dear Ma," it began, and that's when Frank knew the truth.

"Did Calvin have any visitors yesterday?" he asked, interrupting the landlady, who was still expressing her outrage.

"Visitors?" she scoffed angrily. "He didn't know nobody in town but you! Nobody ever come to see him."

"Are you sure? Could someone else have let a visitor in without you knowing it? One of the other tenants, maybe?"

Mrs. Zimmerman stared at him for a long moment, trying to make sense of his question. "Why do you think he had a visitor?"

"Because Calvin didn't kill himself. He was murdered."

• • •

"CALVIN WAS *MURDERED*?" Sarah exclaimed in horror as she admitted Malloy to her house. She'd known the moment she saw him that something terrible had happened, and he'd been eager to unburden himself. "When? How?"

"The killer tried to make it look like a suicide again," he said, taking off his hat and hanging it on the stand by the door. It occurred to her that he was becoming very comfortable in her home, but for some reason, the knowledge didn't bother her as it should have.

"The boy was shot?" Sarah asked. "Didn't someone hear it?"

"No, he was poisoned. Arsenic."

"Oh, my." She felt sick to her stomach. "I hardly knew him, but he was so young. He seemed like such a nice boy. And his poor mother . . ."

"Yeah, this is going to be real hard on her. She'll probably blame herself for letting him come here in the first place."

"Of course, we're assuming she's the kind of woman who *would* blame herself," Sarah said.

"Calvin was pretty fond of her, so she must've been a good mother. Don't forget, she supported the family alone after her husband left her."

"You're right, of course. I guess I was just *hoping* that she'd be the kind of person who wouldn't take her son's death so hard. I know the pain she'll feel."

Malloy didn't say anything to that. He understood that pain, too, but he wasn't going to discuss the subject with her. She realized they were still standing by the front door.

"Come in and sit down. Can I get you some coffee?"

A few moments later they were sitting in her kitchen. She cut him a slice of the cake Mrs. Ellsworth had brought over that afternoon to have along with the coffee she was boiling. When she set the plate in front of him, she saw that he'd spread two pieces of paper out on the table for her to see.

"Look at these, and tell me what you think. This is the suicide note." He slid one over to her as she took her seat opposite him.

She winced as she read the words, and tears stung her eyes. She'd hardly known the boy, but he'd been far too young to die under any circumstances. "If you found this, why do you think he was murdered?" she asked when she'd finished.

He slid the other piece of paper over to her. It was the kind of letter a boy would write to his mother, telling her what he'd been doing and about the people he'd met. Malloy had made a big impression on the boy. He was a little afraid of the police detective, but Malloy had been very kind to him, even paying the rent so he could stay in his rooming house. Of course, Sarah knew this had been a ploy to make sure Calvin didn't disappear, but even so, it was a kind one. He could have locked the boy up instead. Locking him up would have ensured he didn't leave town, while leaving him in the rooming house was a gamble. The boy's homesickness was palpable through his simple words, as was his love for his mother and sisters. One other thing was also obvious.

"Calvin didn't write the suicide note," she realized.

"What makes you think so?" he asked.

"The handwriting, for one thing," she said, comparing the two letters. The letter to Mrs. Brown was written in a large childish hand, the letters formed carefully but awkwardly, as if by one to whom writing was an unwelcome chore. "Whoever wrote the suicide note was trying to make it look like a young person wrote it, but the printing is too small and neat to be Calvin's."

"How about what he wrote?"

Sarah compared the two letters more closely. "He calls his mother 'Ma' in the one and 'Mother' in the other. His grammar is much better in the suicide note, too."

"That's what I thought. I noticed the 'Ma' thing right away. And the handwriting. But if he hadn't written the letter to his mother the day before, I might never have figured it out."

"Or if he'd mailed it before you got to see it," Sarah added. "I'm surprised the killer didn't dispose of it."

"I'm sure he would have, if he was clever enough or if he'd seen it at all, but Calvin had given it to his landlady to mail."

"Thank heaven *she* hadn't mailed it yet," Sarah said with a sigh, laying the letters back down on the table. "Now you have two murders to solve. Do you have any idea who would have wanted to kill both Blackwell and his son?"

"We know it had to be someone who *knew* about Blackwell's first family. Out of those, just about anybody who wanted Blackwell dead, and probably all of them had a good reason to."

"That probably eliminates Letitia and Dudley," she guessed, "since they didn't know about Blackwell's other family."

"Not necessarily. We assumed Letitia didn't know about Calvin, but we could be wrong. As you pointed out, she wouldn't have needed a divorce to marry Dudley if her marriage to Blackwell was bigamous, but she would need to be a widow to inherit his imaginary fortune to support her and Dudley."

"And to escape any hint of scandal," Sarah pointed out. "Even if she was an innocent victim of the bigamy, her reputation would be tarnished. That would have been a motive for anyone who cared about Letitia, too."

"Do you mean her father?" Malloy asked with raised eyebrows.

"Her father or her lover," Sarah said. "Or even Amos Potter, if he hadn't already eliminated himself by offering a reward for Blackwell's killer."

"You're going to have to forgive him for that, Mrs. Brandt," Malloy said with just a ghost of a smile as he took a bite of Mrs. Ellsworth's cake.

"I'll try," Sarah promised. "Calvin's killer must have

gone to his room. Didn't anyone see him?"

"Not that I could find," he said. "One of the other tenants did remember someone out on the street asking if Calvin lived in the house, but that was earlier in the day, and the man didn't go inside."

"What did he look like?" Sarah asked eagerly. "That should tell us something."

Malloy just shook his head. "Mr. Snively doesn't remember. He's quite elderly, and his memory and his eyesight aren't too good anymore."

Sarah sighed in disappointment. "And nobody saw or heard the killer going in or coming out?"

"Not that they remember. He must have gotten in earlier in the evening, before the doors were locked, and he could have sneaked out later, after everyone was in bed. My guess is he brought Calvin a bottle of sarsaparilla that had been laced with arsenic. The boy drank it down, then started to feel sick. The killer probably helped him to bed and maybe even fussed over him a bit, to prevent him from calling for the landlady. The killer would have left the box of rat poison sitting in plain sight and put the suicide note out on the table, and then sneaked out. A pretty good plan, and I would've believed it if it wasn't for the letter the boy had just written to his mother."

"The killer is very clever," Sarah pointed out. "That's twice he's almost convinced you his victims killed themselves."

Sarah got up and poured him some of the freshly boiled coffee. He'd finished the cake and was rubbing his chin thoughtfully.

"A killer who thinks he's clever is usually pretty easy to catch," he remarked. "You just have to figure out how to let him outsmart himself."

"Are you suggesting we wait until he kills someone else and gives himself away?" she asked in alarm.

"Not exactly," he said. "I was thinking more about letting him think he got away with Calvin's murder. Nobody has to know just yet that it wasn't a suicide."

"But would you be able to continue with the investigation if everyone thought Calvin had killed his father?"

"I could pretend I didn't find the suicide note," he mused, obviously still working this out in his head.

"Then you could pretend you still didn't believe Calvin was the killer, or at least that you're not sure," she suggested.

"That's right. And only the killer would know about the note. He might give himself away if he thinks I didn't find it or was trying to conceal it."

"I suppose you'll have to speak with each of the suspects, then," she said.

"I'll certainly have to notify them of Calvin's death, just to see their reactions, if nothing else."

"Potter will be relieved, even though he's not the killer," Sarah said. "I'm sure Mr. Symington will be, too. You'll have to be careful with him, though. Men like Maurice Symington don't appreciate being visited by the police, and if he thinks you're considering him as a suspect, he can make your life very difficult."

"I know," he said with a frown. "I think I can get by with pretending I'm just notifying him personally in case there's anything he wants to do to hush things up and prevent a scandal over the boy's identity."

"That's a good idea. We already know he was aware of Blackwell's previous marriage and had met Calvin. Don't be surprised if he pretends he didn't, though. He may decide that denying the whole thing is the best course of action."

"I won't be surprised at anything Symington does," he assured her.

"At least now you can eliminate the Fitzgeralds as suspects, and all of Blackwell's other clients, too."

"And why is that?" he asked with amusement.

Sarah didn't like it when he found her amusing. "Because they would have no reason to kill Calvin," she pointed out quite logically.

"Unless it was to throw suspicion on him, which is the reason he was killed by *whoever* did it," he pointed out right back. "Of course, they'd have to *know* about Calvin and his relationship to Blackwell. That's not something Blackwell was likely to share with paying customers."

"Wait, the Fitzgeralds knew," Sarah remembered.

"You mean Blackwell told them?"

"No, remember they were talking to Calvin after the funeral. I heard Mrs. Fitzgerald asking him about his relationship with Blackwell. He looked very uncomfortable, so I told him you were looking for him, to give him an excuse to get away."

"That's right. You said they had his life story by the time you interrupted them."

"I was exaggerating a little. Oh, dear, what did I hear them saying? Something about how much he resembled Blackwell, I think, so they must have discovered the relationship. But even if they did find out he was Blackwell's son, why would they imagine Calvin would have a reason to kill his father unless they knew the whole story? Calvin didn't have time to tell them, even if he'd been willing to confide in total strangers, which I doubt. And we've already decided Blackwell wouldn't have told his patients."

"Clients," he corrected her absently. "The killer addressed the suicide note to his mother, too. Anyone finding out Calvin was Blackwell's son would naturally assume Calvin's mother was dead, since Blackwell had remarried, so whoever killed the boy had to have known the whole story. It doesn't seem likely the Fitzgeralds did."

"Unless—" Sarah began, stopping herself when she realized how silly this was.

"Unless what?"

"It's a little farfetched," she warned.

"Say it anyway."

"Remember that Potter was going to meet with Mr.

Fitzgerald the day after the funeral. What if he told Mr. Fitzgerald about Calvin?"

"Why would he?" he asked skeptically.

Sarah tried to reason the way Potter might have. She was amazed at how easy it was. "He's mentioned several times that Blackwell trained him in his techniques. If he wants to set himself up in practice, he'll need to win over Blackwell's patients."

"Clients," he corrected her again, this time with a wry glint.

She ignored him, still thinking. "Maybe he was afraid they'd be too loyal to Blackwell, and he wanted to ruin the good doctor's reputation so they'd turn to him."

"That's stupid. They're just as likely to turn on Potter for speaking ill of the dead," Malloy pointed out.

"Potter might not realize that. He doesn't strike me as very bright about dealing with people."

"He's not," Malloy agreed. "Of course, Fitzgerald would've had to have a reason to kill Blackwell in the first place."

"We decided he was jealous because of Blackwell's attentions to his wife," Sarah reminded him.

"No, *we* didn't," Malloy contradicted her. "Besides, Fitzgerald doesn't strike me as the jealous type. He seems more likely to be motivated by greed."

"Then he didn't like the fact that his wife was letting Blackwell live in her house for free."

"Then he could've had him evicted."

"Malloy, you're ruining my perfectly good theory," she complained, getting up to refill his coffee cup.

"Murder just seems pretty extreme if you're only unhappy about somebody's living arrangements," he said.

"I guess you're right," she grudgingly admitted. "Who else do you think could have done it, then?"

"I'm still favoring the young lovers."

"Then you have to prove they knew about Calvin and his family," she reminded him.

"Do you think there's any chance Potter might've told

Letitia? For the same reason he might've told Black-well's clients?"

"To turn her affections from Blackwell to him?" she asked skeptically. "It would never have worked!"

"You think that because you know Letitia already had a lover. But what if you didn't know about Dudley?" he challenged.

Now Sarah was beginning to understand. "And suppose you were Potter, who doesn't know too much about women in general. He might imagine that a distraught Letitia would turn to him for comfort and support."

"Instead she turns to Dudley, who kills her husband and tries to make it look like suicide," Malloy continued.

"Because he wanted to inherit Blackwell's money and preserve Letitia's reputation," Sarah concluded.

"Now, *that's* a perfectly good theory," Malloy said approvingly. "All we have to do is prove Letitia and Dudley knew about Calvin."

"They're certain to deny it, even if they did," Sarah guessed.

"Before we confront them about that, we should probably find out if they have an alibi for the day Blackwell was killed. According to the servants, Letitia was out."

"She'll probably say she was with Dudley, even if she wasn't," Sarah said. "In any case, I suspect she was at her opium den."

"They can't give each other an alibi, but if they *were* at the opium den, someone will probably remember. We could eliminate Dudley pretty easily if he was seen someplace else that day."

"Or not eliminate him if he wasn't," Sarah said.

"That's right, so now you have to arrange for me to finally meet with Mrs. Blackwell," he said.

"I could question her for you," Sarah pointed out.

He just gave her one of his looks.

"She'll claim she's not well enough," she tried.

"She was well enough to see Dudley. Remind her of that. And tell her if she doesn't get dressed and come downstairs, I'll be glad to visit her in her bedroom."

"You wouldn't dare!" Sarah scoffed.

Malloy smiled blandly. "She doesn't have to know that."

SARAH FOUND LETITIA Blackwell looking much better when she arrived the next morning. She was still in bed, but her color was good, and she greeted Sarah with a smile.

"The baby is doing well," she reported. "Nurse brings him in for a visit every day. She says he's growing, although he still looks very tiny to me."

"He does seem to be fine," Sarah agreed, not bothering to point out that he still needed morphine daily so he wouldn't die in agony.

"Will the morphine hurt him, do you think?" Letitia asked with a worried frown. "Could it do something to his mind?"

Sarah didn't want to offer false hope. "He won't be on it much longer," she hedged. "Now, let's see how *you're* doing."

When Sarah had completed her examination and was packing her things back into her medical bag, she said as casually as she could, "Detective Sergeant Malloy would like to speak with you this morning."

"Who?" Letitia asked in confusion.

"The policeman who is investigating your husband's murder," Sarah explained. "He needs to ask you a few questions."

"About what?" She was alarmed now, her hands nervously working the edge of the coverlet. "I don't know anything. I wasn't even here when it happened!"

"I'm sure he just wants to verify that with you. He'll probably also want to know if Dr. Blackwell had any enemies, or if you know of anyone who might have wished him harm. One of his patients, perhaps, or an acquaintance."

"Everyone loved Edmund," she insisted. "His clients were devoted to him!"

Sarah could have pointed out that his own wife didn't love him, but instead she said, "Someone killed him, Mrs. Blackwell, so at least one person didn't like him."

"Can't Mr. Potter take care of this? I don't want to speak with a policeman. I'm not well!"

"You were well enough to receive Mr. Dudley the other day," Sarah reminded her. "And Mr. Malloy knows it. He said to tell you he would be happy to interview you in your bedroom if you weren't well enough to come downstairs."

"Good heavens! He can't be serious!" she exclaimed, horrified. "My father would never allow it."

"I don't think your father could stop it," Sarah lied. "Mr. Malloy should be here in a few minutes, and I assure you, he will see you, one way or another. He's a very determined man."

Letitia's smooth cheeks were scarlet with either outrage or embarrassment, Sarah couldn't be sure which. But Sarah calmly stood her ground, just the way Malloy would have done, she told herself.

After a moment of strained silence, Sarah asked, "Should I ask your maid to come and help you dress?"

Letitia's china-blue eyes were blazing. "I suppose I have no other choice," she said in a strangled voice.

"I'll be happy to stay with you while he interviews you," Sarah offered. "If that would make you feel more comfortable."

Tears were flooding those lovely blue eyes now. "I'm sure nothing will make me feel *comfortable,* but I would appreciate your support, Mrs. Brandt. Thank you. You are very kind."

Sarah didn't feel kind at all. "It will be over before you know it," she said, hoping this was true. In any case, it would be over eventually. Sarah was pretty sure Letitia Blackwell was more than equal to the ordeal, in any case.

• • •

"You did tell her I'd come upstairs to see her if she wouldn't come down?" Malloy asked Sarah as he paced the front parlor restlessly. Mrs. Blackwell had kept him waiting over half an hour.

"I'm sure she just isn't ready yet. She'll want to look her best, and that takes time," Sarah said, concealing her amusement.

"Why would she want to look her best? She's not going to a ball," Malloy groused, checking his pocket watch again.

"A woman likes to have every possible advantage," she explained. "She doesn't have strength or power, so if she's attractive, she uses that. Letitia will want you to find her extremely attractive. Or at least vulnerable. Then you won't be so hard on her."

Malloy made a rude noise at such a ridiculous notion.

Before Sarah could say more, the parlor doors opened and Letitia Blackwell stepped into the room. She was a vision. Her golden hair had been brushed into a soft halo, and she wore it down, curling to her shoulders and tied off of her face with a ribbon, as if she were merely a child. Her gown was soft and pink and frilly, and she'd pinned a cameo at her throat. Not very appropriate attire for a widow, but an excellent choice for a woman who wanted to be treated gently by a man. Her face was pale, although Sarah suspected rice powder instead of genuine distress had leached the color from her cheeks.

Letitia turned her moist and lovely eyes to Malloy and lifted a trembling hand to her throat, and said, "Mr. Malloy?"

Malloy hurried to meet her and even took her elbow, as if he were afraid she might collapse without support. "I'm sorry to disturb you like this, Mrs. Blackwell, but I need to ask you a few questions," he said solicitously as he guided her to the nearest chair. "This won't take long, I promise."

Sarah had to cough into her hand. Malloy didn't even notice, and Letitia pretended not to.

When he was certain Letitia was comfortably settled, Malloy took a seat on the sofa beside Sarah.

"Would you like some refreshment?" Letitia asked, her voice breathy and weak, her hands fluttering uncertainly.

"No, we don't need anything at all," Frank assured her. "We'll be gone before you know it."

Sarah rolled her eyes, but Malloy wasn't looking at her.

"I already told Mrs. Brandt I don't think I can be of any assistance," Letitia said apologetically. "I have no idea who might have killed Edmund."

"Then you don't know of anyone who'd had an argument with your husband?" Malloy prodded. "Maybe one of his patients who couldn't pay his fees or who thought the doctor was a fraud or—"

"Edmund wasn't a fraud," she insisted indignantly. "How could anyone think he was?"

"Maybe somebody he wasn't able to help," Malloy suggested helpfully. Or perhaps hopefully.

"He helped everyone," she said, her eyes guileless.

Sarah had to cough into her hand again. This time Malloy glared at her, making her cough harder.

"Should I ask the maid to fetch you something to drink, Mrs. Brandt?" Letitia asked with a worried frown.

Before Sarah could shake her head, Malloy dismissed her with a, "She's fine."

Sarah felt compelled to cough again, just to prove him wrong, but Malloy was unmoved. "Mrs. Blackwell," he was saying, his voice amazingly patient, "I understand you were out the afternoon your husband died."

"That's right," she said, nodding. Her chin quivered a bit, as if she might weep at the slightest provocation.

"Could you tell me where you were and who you were with?"

For a second she looked uncertain, even frightened.

"I . . . I'm not sure I remember. The shock and everything . . ."

"I've already told Mr. Malloy about your visits to the opium den," Sarah said, gently so Malloy wouldn't glare at her again.

"If that's where you were, no one else need find out," Malloy assured her. "No one even needs to know except me."

But she still wasn't willing to confide her darkest secret. "What possible difference could it make where I was that afternoon, so long as I wasn't here? Do you think *I* killed my husband?"

"Certainly not," Sarah said quickly, earning a black look from Malloy, "but perhaps you could vouch for someone else, someone who might have had a good reason for wanting Dr. Blackwell out of the way."

Now Malloy was looking as if he wanted to strangle her, but she pretended not to notice as she watched the understanding dawn on Letitia's fragile face. As Sarah had known, she was no fool.

"I was with Peter that afternoon," she said almost eagerly. "We met every afternoon at Mr. Fong's establishment. Peter works in the morning and the evening, but he's free in the afternoon, so we . . ." Finally, she had the grace to blush, dropping her gaze to where her hands were folded in her lap.

"By Peter, do you mean Peter Dudley?" Malloy asked.

Letitia nodded, not looking up.

"I understand that the two of you were lovers," Malloy ventured. Sarah was gratified that he was finally getting to the point.

Letitia drew a deep breath and met Malloy's gaze bravely. "I'm not proud of what I've done, Mr. Malloy, but I can't allow you to believe that Peter could have been involved with Edmund's death. His only sin was in loving me."

"I'm afraid that gives him a very good reason for

wanting your husband out of the way," Malloy pointed out.

"We both did, but we never would have done anything about it!" she exclaimed. "How could you even think such a thing?"

"Men have been killed for much less, Mrs. Blackwell. But if you were at this Mr. Fong's place, he'll vouch for both of you. Can you give me the address?"

Now she really was frightened. "I can't send the police to Mr. Fong's!"

"Why not?" Malloy asked, his voice still gentle and kindly, as if he were speaking to a simple child. Sarah wanted to smack him.

"Because . . . I don't want to get him into trouble!"

"He won't be in any trouble. What he's doing isn't against the law, Mrs. Blackwell. Morphine and opium are sold openly in every drugstore in the city. The police would have no interest in this business."

"Because he probably pays his protection money regularly, too," Sarah murmured for Malloy's ears alone.

He pretended he didn't hear her. "If you give me the address, that's all I'll need. You can go back upstairs then and forget I was ever here."

Letitia still wasn't sure. She looked at Sarah beseechingly. "It's all right," Sarah heard herself say. "If you have nothing to hide, you don't have anything to be afraid of. And if Mr. Fong says you were both there, Mr. Dudley will no longer be a suspect either."

With obvious reluctance, Letitia gave him the address. Sarah saw his surprise. It mirrored her own. Mr. Fong must attract a very elite clientele, indeed.

"I'll need to speak to Mr. Dudley, too, to verify what you've told me," he said. "Where can I find him?"

Letitia made a small sound of distress. "I . . . I don't know where he lives. I can tell you where he works, but you mustn't call for him there. If the police come looking for him, he'll lose his job!"

"I'll make sure he doesn't lose his job," Malloy promised magnanimously.

Wiping a tear from her cheek, she gave him the name of the bank where Dudley was employed.

"Now, I need to ask you something even more difficult," Malloy said, his voice even kinder. Sarah was seeing a whole new side of him, and she was quite impressed, if a little disgusted.

Letitia lifted her chin and braced herself, as if for a blow.

"Can you tell me exactly what happened when you came home that day and found Dr. Blackwell?"

This time the color drained naturally from her face, and she shuddered slightly. "I came home, as usual," she said.

"How did you arrive?"

"I took a hansom cab," she said. "I always do."

"Who opened the front door for you?"

"No one. The servants were out. I opened it myself."

"Was it locked?"

"I . . ." She tried to remember. "I'm sure it was, but I can't remember. I have a key, so I probably used it."

"Go on," he urged.

"I came in, and the house was very quiet. I . . . I took off my gloves and my hat. Then I saw that . . . the study door was closed. It was only closed when Edmund was inside. I almost didn't . . ."

"You almost didn't what?" he prompted when she hesitated.

"I almost didn't open the door. He didn't really care where I was or when I came home, but I thought . . . I thought he *should* care, and so what if I interrupted him? He *should* pay attention to his wife. So I knocked on the door and called his name."

"But he didn't answer," Malloy guessed. "What did you think?"

"I thought perhaps he wasn't in there. Or that he hadn't heard me. I don't know what I thought. But I had the strangest feeling, as if something was wrong. At least I think I did. Maybe that was just afterward. But I opened the door. I was just going to tell him I was home and make him pay attention to me, just for that moment. And then I saw him—"

Her voice broke, and even Sarah wanted to spare her this gruesome memory, but Malloy pressed her.

"This is very important, Mrs. Blackwell," he said. "Did you see or hear anyone else in the house? Did someone run out or did you hear a door open or close? Anything like that, any noise at all?"

"I . . . I don't remember. I just remember I started screaming, and I ran outside and I saw the beat officer, and . . . and that's all I know." A lone tear slipped down her cheek, and she made no effort to wipe it away, silently reminding Malloy of her pain.

"Thank you, Mrs. Blackwell. That's all I'll need for now," he said. "I hope this hasn't caused you too much distress."

"Oh, no, not at all," Letitia said, pulling herself together bravely. "You've been very kind. I'm sorry I couldn't help you more, but I'm happy for the opportunity to remove any suspicion from Mr. Dudley."

Sarah couldn't help thinking that she would also be removing suspicion from herself if Fong gave them both an alibi, but she merely smiled and helped Letitia to the door, where her maid was waiting to escort her upstairs. As soon as she'd closed the parlor doors behind them, she turned to Malloy.

"Did you have to be so hard on her, Malloy?"

He didn't appreciate her sarcasm. "If she'd started bawling, we never would've gotten the address of the opium den," he said reasonably. "But did you have to tell her to give Dudley an alibi, too?"

"If they weren't together, this Mr. Fong will tell you," she pointed out just as reasonably. "And I don't think she would've given you Fong's address just to protect herself. She's too afraid of him. And as she said, everyone knows she wasn't here when Blackwell was killed, so it doesn't really matter where she really was."

"Actually, everyone *doesn't* know she wasn't here. They know she went out, and they know she discovered the body, but the servants weren't here during the murder, so how does anyone know she didn't come home earlier than she said?"

He had a point, but Sarah didn't think it would hold. "Can you really imagine her brazenly blowing her husband's brains out and then arranging everything very neatly to make it look like suicide?"

"Stranger things have happened," was all he'd say. "Now I have to go see this Mr. Fong."

"I've never been in an opium den," Sarah said hopefully.

"You're not going in one today, either," Malloy said.

II

FRANK WAS ACCOMPANYING SARAH BRANDT TO the Blackwells' front door when someone knocked on it. The butler, who had been waiting to see them out, seemed annoyed at the interruption. Probably he was afraid it might delay their departure. Granger looked as if he hadn't quite recovered from his recent illness and lacked the strength to deal with one more problem visitor.

He opened the door to Amos Potter. The man looked as surprised to see them as they were to see him.

"Is something wrong?" he asked, his gaze darting anxiously between the two, as if trying to decide what event might have summoned both of them.

"Not at all," Frank assured him. "And I'm glad you stopped by. I needed to speak with you anyway."

"I hope you have some good news," Potter said, handing his hat to the butler, who took it with a reluctance Potter didn't notice. "This has gone on far too long already. How much longer do you think Mrs. Blackwell can endure the strain after all she's been through?"

"She seems to be holding up very well," Frank remarked.

"And how would you know?" Potter sniffed.

"I spoke with her just a few moments ago," Frank told him, knowing how outraged Potter would be, since he himself had not seen the lovely widow since her husband's demise.

As he'd expected, Potter was furious. "How could you have allowed this, Mrs. Brandt?" he demanded.

For once, Sarah Brandt did exactly the right thing. She smiled sweetly—well, sweetly for her, at least—and said, "Mrs. Blackwell was only too happy to assist Mr. Malloy in his investigation."

Potter blinked a few times as he absorbed this information. "Is Mrs. Blackwell receiving visitors now?" he asked after a moment, his belligerence gone.

"Not regularly," she said, still looking like butter wouldn't melt in her mouth, "and I'm sure she's exhausted after meeting with Mr. Malloy today, but if you feel you must see her, perhaps she could receive you tomorrow . . ."

"Tomorrow, yes, of course," Potter agreed with the air of a boy hardly able to wait for Christmas morning. "There are so many things I need to discuss with her."

"I'm sure there are," she said politely. "I hope you'll excuse me now. I have other patients to see."

"Of course, of course. Would you like Granger to call you a cab?" Potter generously offered.

"I'd prefer to walk. Thank you anyway. Good day."

With a sly grin at Frank, she was gone. He managed not to sigh in relief. He only hoped she had the sense not to hightail it up to see Mr. Fong. Although, when he thought about it, he should hope that for Mr. Fong's sake, since he was fairly sure Sarah Brandt could take care of herself, even in an opium den.

"Why don't we go into the office," Potter suggested, and Frank readily agreed. He didn't want the snooty butler overhearing.

Frank noticed how naturally Potter took his place in the chair behind the desk where Edmund Blackwell had died. If he felt any discomfort at sitting in the very chair where his former partner had been murdered, he hid it well. He motioned for Frank to take the wingback chair in front of the desk.

"Now, what news did you have for me?" he asked, folding his hands expectantly.

Frank had no trouble at all looking grim. "Calvin Brown is dead."

"Dead?" Potter seemed more confused than anything else. "Calvin? You mean Edmund's son?"

"That's right. He died yesterday, very early. Probably during the night, actually." Frank waited for a reaction and for the questions that should naturally follow.

For a moment Potter seemed uncertain what to say next. "But what . . . ? Was he ill? This is very sudden."

"No, he wasn't ill. He died of arsenic poisoning."

"Arsenic? Good heavens, that's rat poison, isn't it? How on earth did he . . . ?" He paused, considering. "Did he take his own life?"

"Why would you think that?" Frank asked, fishing even though he knew he was probably wasting his time.

"Because that's what a killer is likely to do, isn't it?" he asked confidently. "Someone who cannot bear the weight of his guilt anymore might choose to end his own suffering. And poison—one hardly ever hears of a murder by poison. Do you think he killed himself, Mr. Malloy? Out of remorse?"

"It appears that he did take his own life," Frank admitted. "The box of rat poison was in his room, and he'd drunk it in a bottle of sarsaparilla. He didn't call for help when he became ill. All things considered, it looks like he died by his own hand."

"I don't suppose he left a note confessing to his father's murder, by any chance?" Potter asked hopefully. "That would be too neat."

"You're right," Frank said. "That would be too neat."

Potter studied Frank for a moment, as if trying to

judge him somehow. "You did look for a note, I hope. He may have hidden it."

"I went through everything in his room," Frank said quite truthfully.

Now Potter looked perplexed. "But it's obvious, isn't it? The boy took his life out of guilt. What other reason could he have had?"

"I don't know of any," Frank admitted. As far as he knew, Calvin had no reason at all to kill himself.

Potter looked extremely relieved. "As tragic as this is, it couldn't have worked out better. For Mrs. Blackwell, I mean. Consider the scandal if the boy had been put on trial. Everyone would have known that her marriage was bigamous and her child . . . Well, we can be thankful she will be spared all that. The boy did her a kindness by taking his life."

"Mrs. Blackwell seems to attract men willing to do her kindnesses," Frank observed, but Potter didn't seem to understand the reference.

"Now there is the matter of the reward," Potter said, all business again. "Although you didn't actually capture the killer, you have identified him and closed the case satisfactorily. That, I believe, entitles you to at least half of the reward. For your trouble, Mr. Malloy," he added with a condescending smile.

The offer was generous, since most people would have refused to pay anything at all under the circumstances. Frank remembered Brian's surgery and knew he could use the money. But still . . .

"I'm afraid I can't accept any reward for this," he said, even though the words wanted to lodge in his throat.

"What? Why not?" Potter asked in astonishment.

"Because I'm still not convinced Calvin is the killer."

"But if he confessed . . ." Potter gestured helplessly.

"He didn't confess," Frank said, wondering if Potter knew more about this than he should.

"His very suicide is a confession," Potter insisted, fingering his watch fob anxiously. "You said so yourself!"

Frank knew he hadn't, but he didn't want to argue. "I have a few more people to question before I can be sure."

"Honestly, Mr. Malloy, most police detectives are only too happy to solve a case! I can't believe any of them would want to keep investigating when the killer has already been discovered."

What he meant, of course, was that most detectives would grasp any solution to a case, correct or not, in order to collect a reward. Frank didn't like to think he'd ever done such a thing. His standards weren't high, but at least he'd never knowingly punished an innocent man. Still, he'd sometimes taken the wrong guilty man, a man who perhaps hadn't committed the crime he was investigating but had committed many others for which he was unpunished. At some point the truly guilty party would be punished for something else. Guilty men were punished, one way or another, and it all worked out in the end.

And once he might not even have looked quite so closely at a case like this. He might not have even noticed that Blackwell's death was a murder in the first place. No one wanted it to be, least of all those closest to him. Frank had changed a lot, and he knew perfectly well when and why.

Sarah Brandt was ruining him.

"It wouldn't be right to blame Calvin for his father's murder if he didn't do it," Frank pointed out. "Think of his mother."

"I don't know his mother, but I do know Mrs. Blackwell. She is the one whose welfare I must consider. I'm afraid if you insist on pursuing this matter, I must withdraw the reward entirely."

"You do what you think is right, Mr. Potter," Frank said without the slightest regret. Virtue might really be its own reward, but Frank was thinking more about Sarah Brandt's favor, which seemed an even greater reward. "Mrs. Blackwell is very lucky to have you looking out for her interests, Mr. Potter," he added without the slightest trace of irony. "Will you break the news to her that her husband's killer has been found?"

Plainly, Potter hadn't considered this possibility. "I . . . well, I suppose it's logical for me to be the one to do so."

"And does she know who Calvin Brown was?" Frank asked blandly.

Potter seemed confused again, but only for an instant. "Certainly not! Letitia has no idea that Edmund was married before, much less that he had a family."

"Then how will you explain that his son killed him?"

Potter started to bluster. Frank wasn't sure if he was angry or merely confounded. "You . . . I . . . It really isn't my place . . . I mean, perhaps it would be more appropriate for her father to . . ."

"Perhaps you're right," Frank agreed. "I was just going to inform Mr. Symington of Calvin's death as well. Should I mention to him that it's his fatherly duty to inform Mrs. Blackwell?"

"But Mr. Symington knows nothing of this either," he protested.

"I believe you're mistaken, Mr. Potter. You see, Calvin met with Mr. Symington when he was unable to get in to see his father. Mr. Symington knows everything."

Potter had apparently been struck speechless. After a few moments of moving his mouth in vain, he finally found his tongue. "Well, in that case, it seems only right that Mr. Symington . . . I mean, he is her father, after all. He would be the most sensitive and . . . perhaps he won't have to explain the relationship at all. We could just tell her that a young man killed Edmund. I could say he'd come to rob the house or something, and Edmund surprised him. That's really all she needs to know, after all. Yes, that's what I could do. And it really *is* my place to tell her, after all." He seemed very pleased at his decision.

"I'm sure you and Mr. Symington will do the right thing," Frank said, not sure at all. But at least Potter hadn't said anything to give Frank second thoughts about his being the killer. Potter was merely a fool, and a besotted one at that, but being a fool wasn't against the law. Yet.

FRANK HADN'T GIVEN any thought to how difficult it might be to locate Maurice Symington. He did, after all, have his main residence in Westchester County, but Frank was fairly certain he would be staying close to his daughter until her husband's killer was caught. At least that's what Frank would have done, in Symington's place. Potter had told him Symington was probably staying at his gentleman's club, one of many in the city that catered to the needs of wealthy businessmen, but he wasn't there when Frank went to the place. They suggested looking for him at one of the businesses that he owned. Finally, Frank realized he could telephone around and see if the man was anywhere about. He coerced the club steward into allowing him to use their telephone, and after half an hour of telephoning and waiting and shouting into the speaker to make himself heard, he discovered that Symington was at his home in the country but was expected back tomorrow.

That left Mr. Fong.

As he approached the house that Letitia Blackwell had identified as the opium den, Frank realized that even a respectable lady like Sarah Brandt would not have hesitated to enter such a place. It looked exactly like the rest of the respectable dwellings on the street, although Frank knew perfectly well that they, too, might not be dwellings at all, at least in the usual sense. The upper-class brothels prided themselves on their prime locations and elegant furnishings. The neighbors might not like the comings and goings at all hours, but if the business paid its protection money to the police, it could operate for years unmolested, even in the best neighborhoods.

Still, Frank was beginning to wonder if Letitia Black-well had misled him with a false address until the beau-tifully carved front door was opened by a burly man with slightly Oriental features.

He looked Frank over and judged him in an instant as unworthy of his notice. "Who are you?" he asked.

Frank noted that he was well dressed, if not well man-nered, in a hand-tailored suit with a diamond stud in his tie.

"Detective Sergeant Frank Malloy of the New York City police," Frank said pleasantly, showing his badge.

"You got no business here. We pay our protection to the captain every week. You got any complaints, you take them to him."

"How do you know I just don't want to make a pur-chase?" Frank asked, still pleasant.

The fellow looked him over and shook his head. "Not likely."

"Well, then, how about if I tell you I want to speak to Mr. Fong?"

"I'm Mr. Fong," the fellow said belligerently.

Frank shook his head, not fooled. "The Mr. Fong who owns the place."

"He ain't here."

"I'll wait, then. And maybe I'll take a look around while I'm waiting, see who's here and what they're do-ing."

"You can't come in unless I let you, and besides, no-body's doing nothing illegal," the fellow protested.

"Then they won't mind if I look around, will they?"

"Michael, what's going on?" an irritated voice called.

"Some copper says he needs to see you," the fellow who claimed to be Mr. Fong called back. He stepped aside so a much smaller man could take his place at the door.

This man was clearly Chinese. He wore a blue silk robe with dragons all over it, and he kept his arms crossed and his hands tucked into the voluminous sleeves. His raven-black hair was long and braided down his back. He looked Frank over shrewdly with his dark, narrow eyes.

"What can I do for you, sir?" he asked with far more courtesy than the first fellow had shown.

"Are you Mr. Fong, the one who owns this place?" he asked.

"Yes, I am, Mister . . . ?"

"Malloy," Frank said. "Detective Sergeant Malloy. I need to speak with you. Privately. About one of your customers."

"I am sure if you speak to the captain, he will explain to you that we pay our protection directly to him. If you have any problems—"

"This doesn't have anything to do with your arrangement with the captain," Frank said, growing impatient. "Look, a man's been murdered, and somebody we think might've done it is claiming to have been here when the man was killed. I'd like to come in peacefully and discuss this with you, unless you'd prefer that I come back with some other officers to help me force my way inside. Michael there looks like he'd welcome a fight."

Mr. Fong's eyes glinted as he smiled politely. "My son is very fond of fights, but I am not. Please come in."

As he did, Frank tried to see some resemblance between Mr. Fong and the younger Mr. Fong, who was standing nearby and looking sulky. Michael was nearly twice the size of his father, and he wore his jet-black hair cut short, Western style. His tailored clothes were distinctly American. Except for the sallowness of his complexion and the distinctive slant of his eyes, he might have passed for the proprietor of a prosperous Irish bar.

Frank noticed the sickly-sweet scent of the air inside the house. Incense or something else. The furnishings were rich and expensive, the rooms dark behind heavy draperies. Every detail spoke of opulence and excess.

"This way, please, Mr. Malloy," Fong said, and led Frank soundlessly into a room off the entrance hall that was furnished like a parlor. Another young man, even larger than Michael and with the same faintly Oriental features, stood just inside. "My other son," Fong explained, nodding at the man. "You will excuse us, Sean."

"We'll be right outside if you need anything, Father," Sean said.

Now Frank was very curious indeed. A Chinese man with sons named Michael and Sean?

"My wife, like you, is Irish," Fong explained, anticipating Frank's question.

"You're married to a white woman?" Frank asked in surprise.

Fong betrayed no hint of emotion, although he had every right to feel insulted. "Your country did not allow Chinese females to come here for many years," he pointed out. "We had no choice but to marry American women."

Frank had known that Chinese women weren't allowed into this country. The government didn't want the Chinese to settle here and had assumed that without their women, the men would soon return to China. Instead they had made do by marrying American women and stayed anyway. Frank tried to recall if he'd ever seen a Chinese woman. He didn't think he had. They must still be rare.

"I need to ask you about some of your customers."

"Then please sit down, and let me get you some tea."

Frank took a seat on the chair Fong indicated. "Thanks, but I don't need anything to drink. I won't be here that long."

Fong took a seat in the richly upholstered chair opposite him. "You said a man was murdered. Is this man someone I am supposed to know?"

"No, he's never been here, but his wife is apparently a regular customer. Letitia Blackwell."

"No one ever tells me their real name, Mr. Malloy,"

Fong explained kindly. "And even if they did, I would not remember it."

"You'll remember this lady, though. She's young and very pretty, with blond hair and blue eyes. She comes every day, in the afternoon, and meets her lover. The lover has red hair. And she was expecting a baby."

Fong didn't bat an eye. "Even if I did know of such people, what do you want of me?" he asked. Frank wondered if he ever showed any emotion.

"I need to know if they were here a week ago Wednesday, in the afternoon."

"And if they were?"

"Then they're innocent of murder."

Fong considered. "Mr. Malloy, you obviously do not understand how we do business here. People come and go. They do not tell us their names, and we do not ask. The women come veiled, and we may not even see their faces. They may meet someone here, and they may not. We take no notice. If they wish a private room and have the means to pay for it, we can provide one. In that case, we do not know who shares that room with them, when they come, or when they leave. One day is much like another here, and we keep no records or schedules. As much as I would like to help the police, I'm afraid that I cannot tell you if these people you described were here on that day or any other day because I make it my business not to know such things. I am sorry I cannot be of assistance to you."

He did look genuinely sorry, but Frank wasn't sorry at all. Letitia Blackwell and her lover had no alibi at all for the murder.

Frank would have preferred being at Sarah Brandt's house that evening, eating something her neighbor Mrs. Ellsworth had baked, instead of standing on a gaslit street corner waiting for Peter Dudley to come out of the bank where he worked. A discreet inquiry had told him that the clerks would be finished at nine o'clock.

The junior-level clerks in this establishment were scheduled to work in the mornings and then to return in late afternoon to count money and do the bookkeeping after closing. It was a schedule that left little time for amusements, Frank supposed, unless you spent your free afternoons in an opium den with someone else's wife.

A group of young men all dressed similarly in cheaply made suits and straw boaters came out of the building as the night watchman locked the doors behind them. They started off in the other direction, on their way someplace together, probably to have a few beers and some fun. Frank called Dudley's name, and one of the men stopped and turned.

"Who is it?" he asked in alarm. "Who's there?"

"I'd just like a word with you, Mr. Dudley. It's about Mrs. Blackwell," Frank said, knowing that would draw him.

"Who's Mrs. Blackwell?" someone asked with interest. "Some rich widow you're romancing?"

Others joined the teasing, hooting and making fun. Dudley didn't even acknowledge them.

"I'll see you fellows tomorrow," he said, leaving them and coming cautiously toward Frank.

"Give Mrs. Blackwell our love," one of them called, and the rest of them laughed uproariously as they went on their way.

Dudley approached cautiously, drawn by the mention of Letitia but still concerned for his own safety. When he was close enough for his features to be seen, Frank stared in amazement. He'd expected someone traditionally handsome, a man who could easily attract the attention of a romantic schoolgirl. Dudley was gangly and graceless, his face no more than ordinary. In the dim light, Frank couldn't even make out the notorious red hair, which was mostly hidden under the straw boater.

"Who are you?" Dudley demanded when he was close enough to speak quietly but still out of arm's reach. His fear was palpable.

"Detective Sergeant Frank Malloy," he said. "I want to ask you some questions about Edmund Blackwell's murder."

"I don't know anything about Edmund Blackwell," he said, not reassured. Policemen could be even more dangerous than crooks if they took a dislike to you. "I never even met the man. You've mistaken me for someone else."

He started to turn away, but Frank stopped him with a word. "You know his wife pretty well, though, don't you?"

Dudley stopped and half turned back. "I don't believe I do," he tried, forgetting that it had been her name that drew him in the first place.

"She'll be mighty surprised to hear that," Frank said. "What with her having that red-haired baby and all."

"Look, Mister . . ." He gestured helplessly.

"Malloy," Frank supplied.

"Malloy. I will admit that I know Mrs. Blackwell. We met years ago, when I was teaching school in her hometown."

"You more than know her, Dudley. She told me all about those visits to Mr. Fong's opium den."

Dudley gasped, his face a sickly color in the gaslight. "She *told* you about that? I don't believe it!"

"I know everything except exactly how you killed Blackwell," Malloy tried.

"I didn't kill him!" Dudley exclaimed. "Who told you I did? They're a liar!"

"No one had to tell me. You were the one with the most reason to want him out of the way. His wife, too. Did you plan it at the opium den? Tell me, did she talk you into it, or was it your own idea?"

"I didn't! I swear it!"

"Are you saying you didn't want him dead?" Frank asked in disbelief.

"Of course I did! We both did. But we couldn't kill

him, no matter how much we might've wanted to. That's a sin!"

"Adultery is a sin, too, last I heard," Frank said.

Dudley was visibly trembling. "We couldn't help ourselves. You don't know what it was like. We've loved each other for years, long before she even met Blackwell. And he was a terrible man. He treated her very badly."

"He beat her, do you mean?" Frank was enjoying this. He hadn't even had to lay hands on Dudley, and the man couldn't tell him enough.

"Well, no, not beat her," Dudley admitted reluctantly, "but he ignored her. He never took her anywhere or even spoke to her most of the time."

"Some women would appreciate that in a husband," Frank said wisely. "But not Mrs. Blackwell, I guess. It's sure easy to see how she could be unhappy, though. Blackwell just made her live in that big fancy house, with servants to wait on her hand and foot, and gave her anything she wanted. And the only time she got out was to visit her lover every afternoon at an opium den."

"It wasn't like that!" Dudley protested.

"What was it like, then? Is there something I don't know?" Malloy was more than willing to listen, although he doubted Dudley had anything of substance to add to his current knowledge.

"He drove her to use the morphine again! He forced her to appear at those lectures of his so he could lure people into taking his treatments. All he thought about was money. He didn't care that she was terrified of speaking in public. She begged him not to make her do it anymore, but he wouldn't listen. The only way she could bear it was to use the morphine."

"And how about you? Did you use the morphine with her? Was that why you met her at the opium den?"

"No! She wouldn't let me. She'd gone through hell trying to stop using it the first time, and she didn't want me to go through that, too. She made me swear I'd never touch that horrible stuff, and after seeing what it did to Letitia, I never wanted to."

"You expect me to believe that?" Frank scoffed. "You spend half your life in a place where you have to buy the stuff as the price of being there at all, and you never even try it?"

"Letitia bought the morphine. No one there cared who used it," Dudley explained frantically. He was sweating now, even though the evening was cool. "They never paid any attention to what we did at all!"

"I guess when you pay for a private room and close the door, you can do anything you want, no matter how depraved or immoral it is. Tell me, Dudley, does the morphine make a woman more willing? Is that why you helped her get it?"

"How dare you speak of Letitia that way!" he cried, outraged. "And I didn't help her! She was already going to that place when I found her here. She couldn't keep morphine at the house. Blackwell searched her rooms to make sure she wasn't hiding it anywhere. She lived in constant terror of being found out."

"And how tragic it would be for a woman's husband to insist that she stop using morphine. Blackwell must have been a monster to want his wife free of that poison."

"You can't possibly understand! Letitia isn't strong. She can't bear things the way the rest of us can."

"Is that why you picked her, Dudley? Because you thought she was weak?" Frank asked contemptuously.

"I didn't *pick* her," Dudley insisted. "I don't know what you mean."

"I mean when you decided that you'd like to marry a woman with money so you wouldn't have to work as a schoolmaster anymore. You saw pretty little Letitia Symington and figured if you seduced her, she'd have to marry you. Her father might not like it, but he'd come around once you were married and he didn't have any other choice."

"I love Letitia! I never thought . . . How could someone like you understand?" he asked, righteously indignant.

"You're right, I can't understand how a man could take advantage of a young woman's innocence to trick her into betraying her family and running away in the middle of the night like a criminal."

"She wanted to be with me! We were going to be married. That's what she wanted. It was all her idea!"

"Of course she wanted it, after you'd ruined her for any other man. How could she want anything else?"

Dudley covered his face with his hands. If Frank hadn't despised him so much, he might have felt sorry for him.

"What do you want from me?" Dudley asked brokenly, his voice muffled behind his fingers.

"I want you to tell me that you killed Edmund Blackwell so I can go back to investigating important crimes," Frank said wearily.

"But I didn't!" he cried, looking up again. "I'm not sorry that he's dead, but I certainly would never have murdered him. I could never do such a thing!"

"Where were you the afternoon he died?" Frank asked.

He thought for a moment. "I was with Letitia. We were at Mr. Fong's. He'll vouch for us!"

"I already asked him. He never heard of you. He never heard of any of his clients. That's how he stays in business."

"But we were there! If he knows we want him to tell you that, he will. He must!"

"No, he doesn't. In fact, he doesn't know if you were there or not. And even if you came in, he wouldn't know how long you stayed or when you left. You could have gone out, killed Blackwell, and then come back."

"But I didn't!"

"I probably wouldn't have been so annoyed with you

for killing Blackwell if you hadn't killed Calvin, too. That was stupid."

Something that might have been recognition flickered across his face, but Frank couldn't be sure. "Calvin? Calvin who?" he asked in apparent confusion.

"Calvin Brown," Frank said, watching Dudley's face closely in the lamplight for any more signs of recognition. "Eddie Brown's son."

"I don't know who you're talking about," he said, defensive now. "What does this Calvin have to do with Blackwell and Letitia?"

"A lot, but I don't think I have to tell you anything about it, do I?"

"Not unless you want me to know what it's all about. Who is Eddie Brown? Was he one of Blackwell's patients?"

Frank resisted the urge to remind him they were called "clients." He doubted Dudley would find it amusing. "Let's just say that he and Blackwell were very close, but I think you knew all about him, Dudley. I think that's why you tried to make it look like Calvin had killed Blackwell."

"I don't know what you're talking about!" he insisted again. "I've already told you everything I know. I have to go now. I have . . . an appointment. I'm sorry I couldn't be of more help to you, Mr. Malloy."

"So am I, Dudley," Frank said. "But that's all right. I'm sure I'll see you again real soon."

Dudley looked sickly again, but he didn't let that slow him down. His long legs carried him quickly away, into the shadows of the night. He'd gotten off lucky, and he knew it. Frank could have slapped him around at the very least. At worst, he could have taken him to the station house and locked him up and given him the third degree until he was willing to confess to anything. In the past, Frank would have thought nothing of doing either of those things. In fact, he would have felt justi-fied, whether he was convinced Dudley was the killer or not. But he no longer had the stomach for it. Now he was actually concerned about making a mistake and punishing an innocent person. If he'd been a little more certain that Dudley was the killer, he wouldn't have hesitated. But he wasn't, so he'd let Dudley walk away.

He was right. Sarah Brandt *was* ruining him.

12

Sarah was tired as she made her way down Bank Street back to her home the next afternoon. She'd had a difficult morning.

"Hello, Mrs. Brandt!" her neighbor Mrs. Ellsworth called as she came out onto her front porch. She was dressed for the street, in her bonnet and gloves, and carrying a shopping bag. "Looks like summer is trying to come back. How are you this fine day?"

"Better now that two little boys have made it safely into the world," Sarah replied with a smile.

"Twins?" Mrs. Ellsworth asked, her wrinkled face brightening.

"Yes," Sarah said. "One was breech. I was afraid for a while he wasn't going to make it."

"Oh, my, twins are so dangerous. I had a friend once who lost both of them. The cords got tangled or something."

Sarah nodded. She'd seen her share of tragedies. "These are fine now, though, and their mother, too."

"I'll wager she's hoping about now that these will be her last," Mrs. Ellsworth predicted with a smile.

Sarah thought she was probably right, although the

tragedy was that women couldn't make such a choice for themselves. The secrets of preventing pregnancy were passed around in guilty whispers, but anyone who tried to teach modern methods was subject to fines and even arrest.

"I did want to warn you," Mrs. Ellsworth said, distracting Sarah from her unpleasant thoughts. "I found some mouse droppings in the pantry this morning. And a mouse had been nibbling at my flour bag. You know what that means."

"That the mouse was hungry?" Sarah guessed good-naturedly.

Mrs. Ellsworth shook her head, despairing that she would ever teach Sarah anything at all about the mysteries of life. "It means something evil is going to happen. Nibbling the flour bag means that."

Sarah felt reasonably certain something evil was happening at any moment of the day in a city the size of New York, but she didn't want to be unkind to Mrs. Ellsworth by pointing that out.

"The mouse droppings just mean that we have mice, of course," Mrs. Ellsworth went on. "I set some traps, and you'd best do the same. They may go over to your place, too."

Mice were a continual problem in the city, where the waste from thousands of people was piled up in such a small area. Things were better since last year when the city had formed a street cleaning department that regularly attended to all the city streets. Until then, only wealthier neighborhoods that could hire private cleaners were regularly kept free of refuse and garbage. Some of the streets had been piled more than a foot deep with animal droppings and trash and the carcasses of dead animals. The street cleaners in their white uniforms and pith helmets looked like something out of an operetta, but they pushed their carts around the city at night and worked miracles with their brooms and shovels. So now the mice came inside, looking for richer territory to plunder.

"Thanks for the warning," Sarah said. "I'll do that. Where are you heading?"

"To the market," Mrs. Ellsworth said, referring to the Gansevoort Market several blocks away where farmers brought their produce and meat to sell to the city's residents. "Can I get anything for you?"

Sarah thought of Malloy and wondered if she would see him tonight. They did have a lot of things to discuss. Or rather she had a lot of things she wanted to find out from him, since he'd probably been to the opium den by now. "I'd like to have a chicken, if you see any nice ones," Sarah said.

Mrs. Ellsworth smiled knowingly. "I'll pick a nice plump one for Mr. Malloy. Do you need any potatoes to go with it?"

"I think I have enough," Sarah said, returning her smile.

"Will you be home this afternoon? In case someone calls for you," she added, lest Sarah think she was merely being nosy.

Sarah started to say she would, but thought better of it. "I might go out in a little while," she said. "To visit some friends, but I'll be back by suppertime."

WHEN SHE'D FRESHENED up from her labors of the morning, Sarah put on her gray serge suit and a hat that was reasonably fashionable, and made her way across town once again to Gramercy Park.

As always, she was struck by how lovely the square was. The houses surrounding it were a little ornate for her taste, but unquestionably comfortable and well tended. Edmund Blackwell must have felt that he'd finally achieved success when he moved his bride here. Never mind that he wasn't paying for the house and couldn't have dreamed of doing so. No one else knew that. As far as everyone was concerned, he was an equal to his wealthy and socially prominent neighbors.

A maid opened the door, the same one who had admitted her before. "Good afternoon, Mrs. Brandt," she said, dropping a small curtsy. "Were you wanting to see Mrs. Blackwell today?"

"If she isn't sleeping," Sarah said.

"Oh, no, she's receiving visitors in the parlor," the maid assured her. "I'll show you right in."

"Is Granger ill again?" Sarah asked with some concern. The butler hadn't seemed particularly grief-stricken over his employer's murder at the time, but perhaps the strain of the past days had taken a toll.

"He got better, but then he got worse again," the girl told her. "Mrs. Wilson says it's the dyspepsia."

"Does he get it often?" Sarah asked.

"Not that I ever heard," the girl said. "He never was sick a day that I knew of until poor Dr. Blackwell died."

Sarah had been right to suspect the strain was telling on the man to whom the responsibility of running the entire household would have fallen. "Do you know if he's seen a doctor?" she asked.

"No, ma'am. Mrs. Wilson, she's the housekeeper, she told him to, but she says he's too stubborn to go."

Sarah knew Mrs. Wilson would probably have a fit if she knew how freely the little maid was sharing the private business of the household with a stranger. Still . . . "I'd be happy to speak with Mr. Granger and see if perhaps I can't give him something to help his stomach."

"Can a midwife take care of a man?" the girl asked in confusion.

"I'm also a trained nurse," Sarah explained, managing not to smile. "And stomachs are pretty much the same, whether they belong to a man or a woman."

The girl's eyes widened at this fascinating observation. "I'll go ask Mrs. Wilson right now." She was halfway down the hall when she remembered her manners. "Oh, please have a seat while you're waiting!" she called back, then scurried away.

Sarah sat down on the bench in the hallway. She glanced at the closed parlor doors, wondering who Letitia might be entertaining in there. Well, she'd find out soon enough. And if it was Peter Dudley, as she suspected, they would appreciate not being interrupted for a while longer, she was sure.

Mrs. Wilson was a tall, skeletal woman of middle years. Her gray-streaked hair was pulled back in a severe bun, and her washed-out eyes stared at Sarah from dark hollows. "Peggy shouldn't have told you about Mr. Granger's condition," she said, giving the girl, who had followed at her heels, a reproving look.

Peggy dropped her gaze, suitably contrite.

"I'm sure she was only trying to help," Sarah said. "I *am* a nurse, and there's no need for him to suffer if I can help him. Probably it's just the unfortunate events of the past few days upsetting him. I'm sure I can prepare something that will help."

Mrs. Wilson still did not look pleased, but she said, "All we can do is ask him if he'd like to see you. If you'll come this way, to the servants' quarters."

Sarah followed her to the back stairs, which led up to a section of the house where visitors typically never went. The walls here were plain, the floors bare, and the furnishings utilitarian. Mrs. Wilson went to one of the doors along the hallway and knocked.

"Mr. Granger? It's Mrs. Wilson. I've got Mrs. Brandt here, and she's a nurse. She says she might be able to make you feel better. Can we come in?"

For a moment they heard nothing, and then a groan and a crash, as something fell and smashed on the floor.

Without waiting for permission, Mrs. Wilson pushed open the door and hurried in. Sarah was close behind her.

The room was sparsely furnished, and neat to the point of austerity, except for the unmade bed where Mr. Granger lay, wearing his trousers and an undershirt.

He'd tried to get up and knocked a tray of food onto the floor.

"Good heavens, Granger," Mrs. Wilson exclaimed. "Look at this mess. I'll get one of the girls up here to clean this up. And you haven't eaten a bite today, have you?" she added, examining the mess on the floor.

The food looked as if it had been sitting for several hours, and Granger's face was pale and his eyes held the unfocused look of someone in pain.

Mrs. Wilson summoned one of the maids to clean up the spilled food and continued to chasten him for not taking better care of himself. Mr. Granger's dignity was badly compromised in the process, but by the time everyone else had gone and the room restored to order, he seemed not even to care about that.

"I don't need a nurse," he told her crossly from the chair into which he'd moved during the commotion. He'd pulled on a shirt for the sake of decency, but hadn't had the energy to button it.

"Perhaps you don't," Sarah said, not pointing out how haggard he looked or how sick he'd obviously been. "But I'm probably a better judge of that than you."

Brooking no nonsense, she quickly examined him, asking a series of questions about his current condition.

"Were you here to see Mrs. Blackwell?" he asked with a worried frown when she was finished. "Is she ill?"

"I'm sure she's fine," Sarah said, not mentioning that the lady of the house was actually receiving visitors at this very moment. "I really came to check on the baby."

"This has been so hard on poor Mrs. Blackwell," he said. "Finding her husband like that must have been a shock." He put his hand to his head, as if the thought of Letitia's grief was more than he could bear.

"Women are frequently much stronger than men give them credit for being," Sarah said by way of comfort.

"Not Mrs. Blackwell," he protested. "She's one that needs protection. She tries to pretend she's strong. The way she visits the sick and gives so much of her time to looking out for others not as fortunate as she is, it's an inspiration. But she's really as delicate as a flower. She needs somebody to look after her. I can't tell you how many times she's thanked me, right out like that, for doing little things for her."

Sarah wanted to gag. What was it about Letitia Blackwell that made absolute fools of men? Even the butler was under her spell!

"It's nice to hear a servant praising his mistress," she said tactfully.

"Even that day her husband died, she thanked me for making sure all the servants left the house so he wouldn't be disturbed. She wouldn't leave herself until she was sure everyone else was gone, just like he wanted. She's always thinking about other people first, that's Mrs. Blackwell."

Sarah could have destroyed his image of his mistress by revealing that instead of visiting the sick, as he believed, Mrs. Blackwell had spent her afternoons with a lover, using the money her husband gave her for charity on morphine. But he probably wouldn't believe her. That was the nature of the spell women like Letitia cast.

"Mr. Granger," she said instead, changing the subject to more pressing matters, "I believe you aren't really seriously ill. I think you're just suffering from a nervous stomach, probably because you're under too much strain at the moment. This has been just as hard on you as it has on Mrs. Blackwell—"

"Oh, no!" he insisted. "It's not the same at all! She should never have seen her husband's body. I should have been here first. I should have found him. How will she ever recover from such a shock?"

"But she did find her husband's body. You can't change that," Sarah pointed out, "and there's no use blaming yourself either. You didn't know the doctor was going to be murdered that afternoon, and you didn't know Mrs. Blackwell would come home early either. If that's what's been causing you so much misery, you need to put it out of your mind, Mr. Granger. It's making you ill, and you won't get any better until you make up your mind about it."

"Are you saying I worried myself sick?" he asked doubtfully.

"I'm fairly certain that's true. The responsibilities of your position with the doctor dead have probably made things even more difficult, too. You can't do much about that, but you can stop worrying about Mrs. Blackwell. She'll recover and go on with her life. And if you're sick, you won't be any help to her, now will you? She shouldn't have to be concerned about how the house is being managed with everything else she has to deal with," she added, playing on his weakness.

"I hadn't thought of it that way," he said.

"You should," Sarah told him. "I'm going to give you some ideas to be kinder to your stomach, but the most important thing is to stop blaming yourself for things you couldn't help. Do you think you can do that? For Mrs. Blackwell's sake?" she tried when he looked unconvinced.

"I can do no less," he said finally.

Sarah managed not to roll her eyes. "You should watch what you eat for the next few days," she said, and gave him all the commonsense rules for someone with a bad stomach, along with a remedy to ease his digestive difficulties.

When she was satisfied that Granger had accepted her plan for his recovery, she went back downstairs, thinking she'd have to share this story with Malloy. If Letitia was able to inspire this sort of devotion in the hired help, it seemed very likely someone close to her would have happily murdered her husband to protect her. Perhaps that person was visiting her even now.

Just as Sarah reached the front hallway, eager to discover who Mrs. Blackwell's caller might be, the maid was opening the door to yet another visitor: Amos Potter.

"Good afternoon, Mr. Potter," Sarah said, setting her medical bag down on the floor near the parlor door.

"Mrs. Brandt, what brings you here?" he asked anxiously. "Nothing wrong with Mrs. Blackwell, I hope."

Sarah managed not to groan. "As a matter of fact, I understand that Mrs. Blackwell is well enough to receive visitors today. I was just going in to see her. I'm sure she'd be delighted to receive you, too," she lied without remorse.

As she had expected, Potter was thrilled at the prospect of meeting with Letitia at last. "I wonder if she would be up to speaking with me privately. There are matters of some delicacy I need to discuss with her as soon as possible."

He was fairly trembling with anticipation of such an audience.

"I'm sure she needs to consult with you as well," Sarah said shamelessly. "Shall we go in?"

"I should announce you, ma'am," the maid said, wringing her hands as she obviously remembered the last time when she'd failed to do so, with such disastrous results.

"Nonsense," Sarah said recklessly. "I don't need an introduction, and Mr. Potter is practically a member of the family."

Before the maid could protest again, Sarah pushed open the parlor doors.

It was difficult to say who was more surprised. Peter Dudley, who had been sitting on the sofa with Letitia, jumped to his feet. Letitia gasped aloud and nearly dropped her baby, whom she was holding gingerly. Amos Potter gasped, too, although Sarah wasn't quite sure what had surprised him more—the presence of a strange man in Letitia's parlor or the picturesque family tableau they made, with both father and son's coppery hair glowing in the afternoon sunshine.

Sarah felt a stab of guilt. She had merely intended to embarrass Letitia by allowing Potter to catch her with Dudley. She'd never expected them to have the baby there. Now, of course, Potter would figure out the whole sordid story in a moment, unless he was far less intelligent than Sarah had judged him to be.

"Amos," Letitia exclaimed, clutching awkwardly at the baby so he wouldn't fall to the floor. She had not developed much confidence in handling him yet, probably from lack of practice.

Sarah hurried to assist her, but Dudley beat her to it. He took the baby from her arms and cradled him awkwardly. Which was, unfortunately, the worst thing he could have done. If there was any chance Potter hadn't noticed the resemblance between them before, he couldn't miss it now. The two redheads were no more than a foot apart.

"Letitia," Potter said in a somewhat strangled voice. "I don't believe I've had the pleasure of meeting this gentleman. Is he a . . . a close relative of yours?"

Bless him, Potter was still clinging to a last shred of hope.

The baby, probably feeling insecure in Dudley's uncertain grasp, began to wail. Dudley tried bouncing him, which only made him cry louder.

"Amos, this is Peter Dudley. He . . . he's an old family friend," Letitia lied, raising her voice to be heard above the baby's squalling. "Mr. Potter is . . . *was* Edmund's business partner," she added to Dudley.

Sarah stood back for another moment, observing everyone's reactions. She told herself this was what Malloy would have done, if he were here, although she doubted he would have enjoyed the scene quite as much as she was. But then, he felt sorry for poor, sweet Letitia, too. *Men.*

Finally, she'd had her fill, and she stepped forward and took the baby from Dudley's arms. She crooned to him, and his cries quieted instantly. No one but she seemed to notice the child at all now. She was relieved to see that he seemed to be gaining weight. His little cheeks had filled out, and his arms were developing dimples.

"It . . . it's a pleasure to meet you, Mr. Potter," Dudley said without much enthusiasm, extending his right hand now that he was no longer encumbered with the baby.

Potter pretended not to notice his hand, or the rest of him either, for that matter. He turned all of his attention to Letitia. "You're looking well, Letitia," he said. His voice was strained, but he managed a smile for her.

She favored him with one in return. It was the kind of smile women like Letitia were trained from birth to offer in uncomfortable social situations. If a woman was pretty enough, she could get herself out of almost anything with that smile. This situation would certainly be a test of its effectiveness. "I'm feeling much better, thank you, Amos. It's kind of you to call. Won't you sit down?"

Potter hesitated a moment. He obviously wanted to take a seat beside Letitia on the sofa, but Dudley stood in the way. He'd have to shoulder him aside, and although he might want to do that, he decided to concede defeat and took the chair on her other side. Dudley sat back down on the sofa, although he was probably sitting a little farther away from Letitia now than he had been before Sarah and Amos came in.

No one paid the slightest attention to Sarah, so she sat down in the chair across from Letitia and Dudley, settling the baby in her arms. He seemed perfectly content, so she was able to devote herself to observing her other companions.

For a moment no one spoke. Dudley was plainly too socially inept to know how to handle an awkward situation, and Letitia's social instruction had apparently not included handling such an oddly mismatched assortment of visitors.

Finally, Potter said, "I would very much like to speak

with you privately, Letitia. There are some urgent business matters about Edmund's estate which I need to discuss with you immediately."

"Good heavens, I don't know what possible help I could be to you on business matters," Letitia said. "I don't know anything at all about them. I'm sure you should do whatever you think is best."

Potter gave Dudley a glance that said he wished him in Hades, and then he looked back at Letitia and spoke with the patience of one addressing a slow child. "I'm afraid it's not that simple," he said apologetically. "There are some things you need to know, things that will affect your future."

"Oh, yes," she said with sudden interest. "I've been giving the matter of my future some thought, and I've decided I want to sell this house, Amos."

Potter winced, and Sarah felt a measure of pity for him. The news he would have to break to her would be shocking. "Are you planning to move back to your father's house?" he asked hopefully.

Letitia's gaze drifted to Dudley, whose fair complexion showed every emotion. He turned bright red and dropped his gaze.

"I . . . I haven't really decided yet," Letitia said. "But in any case, I don't need such a grand house anymore."

"Yes, of course, well, that's something we'll need to discuss privately," he emphasized again. Although he was speaking to Letitia, this time he was watching Dudley. He seemed finally to be getting the entire picture, and he clearly didn't like it one bit. "Mr. Dudley, I don't recall ever hearing Mrs. Blackwell speak of you. How long have you known her?"

"I . . ." Dudley looked to Letitia for guidance, but she just frowned. She wasn't certain how much to tell Potter either. "I've known her for . . . for several years."

Potter fingered the Phi Beta Kappa key that hung from his watch chain. "When I was at Harvard, I knew a fellow named Dudley. From Providence. Would you by any chance be a relation?"

"No, I don't think so," Dudley admitted, visibly impressed by the mention of Harvard. "I mean, certainly not."

"Letitia said she knew you from her hometown. Is that where you still live?" Potter inquired.

"No, I . . ." Again he looked at Letitia, and again he got no assistance. "I live here in the city now. I . . . I saw the notice of Dr. Blackwell's death in the newspaper and came to pay my condolences."

Sarah hadn't believed that lie the last time he told it, and Potter seemed equally skeptical. He glanced at Sarah—or rather at the baby she still held—and back at Dudley. "I hope you've found a suitable position here. If not, I have many connections. Perhaps I can be of assistance in locating one for you."

"That's very kind of you, Amos," Letitia quickly replied, "but Mr. Dudley has an excellent position."

"Oh, really?" Potter asked skeptically. Dudley's clothes alone bespoke poverty, and his manner betrayed his lack of breeding. "And where are you situated?"

Dudley stammered the name of the bank where he worked. It was a small establishment, and he was understandably embarrassed to name it. Sarah supposed his position was far from excellent, too.

Potter frowned. "I don't believe I know where that bank is located."

Dudley gave him the address, looking even more ashamed.

"I see," Potter said, his tone telling Dudley that he saw everything about him. The young man had, in Potter's opinion, no right whatsoever to be sitting in Letitia Blackwell's parlor. If Potter had, indeed, figured out that Dudley had also fathered her child, Sarah couldn't even imagine what else he must be thinking.

Sarah imagined she saw hate radiating from Potter's dumpy frame, but perhaps she was being fanciful. Did he know that Letitia had been running away with a lover when she'd been injured? Had he been able to put the whole story together in his mind? Would that change his adoration of Letitia Blackwell? Such a response would be logical, of course, but for some reason, men never resorted to logic in their dealings with women.

"How long have you lived in our fair city, Mr. Dudley," Potter asked. He wasn't very good at feigning amiability, but Dudley wasn't very perceptive either.

"Almost two years, now, I guess it is. It's very different from the country, but I'm getting used to it."

"Does your family like the city or do they prefer living in Westchester?"

"I . . . I don't have any family," Dudley said, a little disconcerted.

"You're not married, then?" Potter said in apparent surprise. "What about your parents? Do they come down to the city to visit you?"

"I . . . No, I . . ."

"Mr. Dudley's parents are dead," Letitia quickly explained.

"I'm sorry to hear it," Potter said, still addressing Dudley. "No wonder you were so sensitive to Letitia's grief. You were very kind to visit her. Were you acquainted with Dr. Blackwell at all?"

"No, I . . . We never met." It was apparent that Dudley was growing increasingly uncomfortable with the endless questions. Sarah wasn't sure what Potter was trying to determine, but perhaps he wasn't either. Maybe he just wanted to find out whatever he could in an effort to identify some weakness in the man whom he instinctively recognized as a rival for Letitia's hand.

"It's a pity you never met Dr. Blackwell," Potter was saying. "He was very gifted. Letitia wouldn't be sitting here with us if he hadn't helped her after her terrible accident. Isn't that right, Letitia?"

"I . . . Yes," she admitted reluctantly. She was also uncomfortable. Sarah imagined that talking about your dead husband in front of the lover with whom you had betrayed him might be difficult. Add to this that Dudley had been involved in her accident, and she must be wishing the floor would open and swallow her up.

"We'll always be grateful for what he did to cure Letitia," Dudley said in an effort to be agreeable.

But Potter didn't miss the fact that Dudley had used her given name. He didn't like it, either. "Apparently someone wasn't grateful for something he did, or Edmund would still be alive," he noted.

"Do we have to speak of Edmund's death?" Letitia protested weakly.

"Does it upset you?" Potter asked in apparent concern.

"It was so . . . so unpleasant," Letitia said.

"Murder is always unpleasant," Sarah offered, and everyone looked at her in surprise. They had apparently forgotten she was there.

"But this one was particularly so," Potter said with an odd disregard for Letitia's sensibilities. "It must have been horrible for you, finding him that way."

Letitia had the grace to look pale, but perhaps she was just remembering all the blood. Heaven knew, she probably hadn't shed many tears over her husband's demise. "I shall never be able to get that image out of my head," she said faintly.

Instinctively, both men leaned forward to comfort her. Fearing they might collide, Sarah quickly spoke up. "Mr. Granger is quite upset that he didn't get home first to spare you that shock."

The men both caught themselves before actually touching Letitia, but Sarah wasn't sure if this was because of their own good sense or if her interruption had jolted them back to propriety.

Potter looked at her in confusion, probably having once again forgotten she was there. "Who is Mr. Granger?"

"The butler," Sarah said, smiling innocently. "He takes his responsibilities very seriously, and he's usually home before Mrs. Blackwell on Wednesdays. But he said she came home earlier than usual that day, which is why she was the one to, uh, to find Dr. Blackwell. He's actually made himself sick worrying over it."

"I didn't feel well that afternoon," Letitia remembered. "That's why I came home earlier than usual."

She glanced at Dudley, who was red again. Neither of them wished to discuss Letitia's activities of that afternoon, especially in front of Potter. Sarah wondered if there was a particular reason, other than the obvious one of Letitia's infidelity.

Why *had* Letitia come home early that day? Had the lovers quarreled? But if Dudley wasn't there—if he was off murdering Blackwell—they couldn't have. Perhaps they'd quarreled afterward, or even before. Or perhaps Letitia had grown too anxious waiting for Dudley to complete his task and had misjudged the time. Curiosity could have drawn her into the study even if she'd known her husband lay dead in there. She would have no idea how horrible the scene would be. She'd probably imagined Blackwell neatly laid out, in dignity and repose, like a corpse in a coffin.

Fortunately, the baby started fussing again, bringing an end to her fancies. Malloy would certainly find some flaw with her scenario, but Sarah thought it merited consideration, at least. She still liked the theory of the desperate lovers disposing of an unwanted husband, and neither of them had a dependable alibi for the afternoon of the murder. Besides, she liked them less and less each time she saw them, she decided as she tried to soothe the fretful child.

Letitia looked askance at the baby. "I should send for the nurse," she said. "He shouldn't be here anyway."

She was right, of course. No lady of her station would have brought her infant into the front parlor when she had a visitor. Unless, of course, her visitor was the baby's father and she'd wanted him to see the child.

"He's a . . . a handsome boy," Potter said without

much conviction. "What are you going to call him?"

"I haven't decided yet," she said with another glance at Dudley.

Potter frowned in disapproval. "You must name him after his father. Surely there is no other logical thing to do under the circumstances."

This time Letitia colored, but she lifted her chin defiantly. "I may do that," she said.

Dudley made a small sound, probably of surprise, and Potter's mouth thinned to a bloodless line.

Sarah was enjoying this thoroughly, but the baby was beginning to root, his hungry mouth searching her bodice in vain for sustenance. Although Letitia had said she should call for the nurse, she had made no move to do so. Sarah gathered the child up and carried him over to where the bell rope hung and managed to pull it to summon a maid. Letitia didn't even seem to notice.

Potter was still glaring at Letitia. "We must put an announcement in the papers about the birth," he said. "Edmund's clients will want to . . . to acknowledge the child." Trust Potter to be thinking about the practical aspects of the situation. Considering the condition of Blackwell's estate, a few monetary gifts would be well received.

"I don't want any of them to know. I don't need anything from those people," Letitia insisted.

"But they'll *want* to send gifts," Potter insisted. He sounded almost desperate. Sarah began to wonder if he needed the money even more than Letitia did. At least she had her father to fall back on. Sarah was sure Potter had no wealthy relatives in his family tree.

"I don't care if they do or not," Letitia said petulantly. "I don't *want* anything from those people. I had to let them gawk at me before, but I don't have to even see them now if I don't want to, and I *don't* want to."

"I've never known you to be so unreasonable, Letitia," Potter chided her. "It isn't very becoming."

She gaped at him. "And I've never known you to be

so imperious, Amos. What gives you the right to tell me what to do?"

"I'm only looking out for your best interests," he defended himself. "Someone must. Edmund left things in a terrible state."

"That doesn't give you any reason to be rude to me," Letitia reminded him. "I'm not responsible for what Edmund did or didn't do."

Potter was instantly contrite, probably because there was no advantage to being anything else. "I didn't intend . . . You have mistaken my meaning, Letitia. It's just that I'm so concerned for you . . ."

"If you were truly concerned, you would be a great deal kinder to me, Amos. I have been through a very difficult time, and my health is still precarious." She emphasized this by dabbing her nose with the handkerchief she pulled from her sleeve.

"Forgive me, Letitia. I forgot myself," he said, finally giving her the apology she was demanding. "It's just . . . You look so well, it's hard to remember you are so lately recovered from your confinement."

"I'm *not* recovered," Letitia informed him. "In fact, I'm surprised Mrs. Brandt isn't taking me to task for being up at all." She gave Sarah a challenging look, which Sarah returned with a smile. She was still standing by the parlor door, waiting for a maid to come and take the baby.

Sarah thought of several things she could say in reply, but all of them would have gotten her banned for life from the Blackwell home. "I'm sure you are the best judge of your ability to entertain visitors," she demurred.

This pleased Letitia for some reason. "Yes, you're right," she said, and turned back to Potter. "Thank you so much for coming to see me, Amos, but I'm afraid I'm growing quite tired and will have to bid you good afternoon."

Potter's face fell. "I . . . But I need to speak with you

privately," he reminded her almost desperately, "about matters of grave importance."

"Not today. I couldn't possibly deal with anything important. Could I, Mrs. Brandt?" she asked in challenge.

"Certainly not," Sarah replied obligingly. She still needed access to the Blackwell home if she was going to find the killer, and Letitia's favor was the only entrée she had.

"There, you see? I hope you will call again in a few days," Letitia said to Potter, who could no longer ignore the fact that he was being dismissed.

He got reluctantly to his feet, then looked suspiciously at Dudley. "Mr. Dudley, perhaps we can share a cab," he suggested.

"Please allow me to say my private farewells to my dear friend Mr. Dudley," Letitia said. "And he doesn't need a cab, in any case. He lives very close by."

"How convenient for you," Potter said coldly, then turned to Letitia and tried to muster up some charm. "I'm so glad to see you," he said, bowing over her and reaching out, expecting her to give him her hand.

She did so, but with little enthusiasm, and she let him hold it only for an instant. He was visibly disappointed.

"I'm afraid my business cannot wait much longer. I will call on you again tomorrow," he said, brooking no argument.

Letitia did not reply. Everyone knew she didn't have to receive him if she didn't want to, so he could call all he wanted. "Good afternoon, Amos."

His anger evident in every move, Potter nodded stiffly to Dudley, then turned and marched to the parlor door. Just as he reached it, it opened to admit the maid, who had finally come in response to the bell. She seemed a little breathless.

"Peggy, see Mr. Potter out," Letitia said. "Mrs. Brandt, would you take the baby back to his nurse?"

Sarah pretended not to hear the request. Instead, she handed the child to the unsuspecting maid, who was too startled to refuse him. "You may take him back to his nurse," she told the girl, then shooed both her and Potter out and closed the doors decisively behind them.

She turned to see Letitia's outraged expression. Dudley was simply looking confused.

"I'm afraid I must speak with both of you immediately," Sarah explained by way of excuse for her outrageous behavior, "and don't bother dismissing me. I'm not as easily intimidated as Mr. Potter, and besides, you need to hear what I have to say, whether you want to or not."

13

Frank found Maurice Symington in his well-appointed office in a building on upper Fifth Avenue. According to Frank's sources, Symington owned property all over the city and made his living by collecting rents and spending as little on maintaining his buildings as possible. Most of his property was located in the poorer sections of the city, so the tenants didn't complain much about their living conditions for fear of being evicted.

Anticipating the possibility that Symington would refuse to see him, Frank told the man's secretary that he had some news about Dr. Blackwell's death. Even so, Symington kept him cooling his heels for almost an hour, but finally the young man who handled the clerical work in the office invited him into the inner sanctum.

The office was large and meant to intimidate. The wall behind Symington's desk was a huge window providing a panoramic view of the city below and the sky above. Symington looked up impatiently from a stack of papers on his enormous mahogany desk.

"What is it?" he demanded. "And make it quick. I don't have time for any nonsense."

"Calvin Brown is dead," Frank said baldly, still standing because he hadn't been invited to sit.

Symington's gaze had returned to his papers, as if assuming Frank could have nothing interesting enough to say to distract him, but this time when he looked up, Frank had his undivided attention. "Who did you say?"

"Edmund Blackwell's son," Frank said politely. Symington knew perfectly well who he was talking about. "I know you were trying to be discreet when you pretended not to know who he was the other day with Potter, but Calvin told me he'd met with you. He said the only way he got in to see his father was because you intervened for him."

Symington was a careful man. He took a moment to weigh his options. He could, of course, have called Frank a liar and ordered him from the room. He could have feigned ignorance and demanded an explanation. But he was too wise to take any chances. He understood that a scandal like this, involving the betrayed daughter of a wealthy and powerful man, would sell a lot of newspapers. The respectable papers wouldn't publish it, of course, but there were many papers in the city that made no pretense to respectability. They would pay a large sum of money for the information Frank had, and Symington had no reason to trust Frank's discretion.

"Please sit down, Mr. Malloy," Symington said, instantly reasonable.

Frank did as he was told, noticing that the chair here was much more comfortable and expensive than the one in Blackwell's former office. This one was leather and as soft as butter. A real man's chair.

"How did the boy die?" Symington asked when Frank was settled.

"Arsenic. Somebody put it in a bottle of sarsaparilla."

"Somebody?" he asked, not missing the implication.

"It could have been a suicide."

Symington thought this over. "You don't believe it was," he guessed.

"I'm paid to be skeptical."

"Do you know the entire story?" Symington asked, folding his hands on the desktop. "About the boy, I mean."

Now it was Frank's turn to be cautious. He certainly didn't want to be the one telling Symington something he didn't know about his own daughter. "I know that Blackwell used to be Eddie Brown and that Eddie Brown had a wife he'd neglected to divorce and three children he'd deserted in Virginia. I know Calvin had traced his father here and that they'd met. Calvin said Blackwell had promised to give him some money and start supporting the Brown family again. I only have his word on that, since Blackwell wasn't around to confirm anything. Oh, and Amos Potter said Blackwell had gotten some money together and planned to meet with Calvin on the afternoon he was killed. The boy claimed nobody answered the door that day, so he never even saw his father, but nobody's seen the money since, either."

"Potter believes the boy killed Edmund. If he did, he could have killed himself out of remorse," Symington suggested.

"That would make everything neat and tidy," Frank pointed out. "But if he did kill Blackwell, why didn't he take the money and leave town? Why stay around and put himself in the way of being caught? If Calvin *didn't* kill his father—and that's a pretty unnatural thing to do, no matter what your old man did to you—then somebody's gotten away with murdering *two* men."

"Two men about whom I care little, Mr. Malloy," Symington pointed out without apology. "I do care very much about my daughter, however. Protecting her good name and that of her child must be my main concern."

"Any father would feel the same," Frank allowed. "Too bad Blackwell wasn't as concerned about his children. That Calvin, for instance; he seemed like a good boy, and he'd gotten a pretty rough deal from his old man. Had to go to work when he was just a kid to help support his mother and two little sisters. Now his mother's lost her husband *and* her only son. Don't hardly seem fair to mark the boy a killer if he's innocent."

"Many things in life aren't fair, Mr. Malloy, as I'm sure you are well aware. But I would be happy to compensate Mrs. Brown for her loss. It's not my responsibility, of course, but it's the right thing to do. The poor woman has suffered too much already. There's no reason she should be rendered destitute by the loss of her son, and I have the means to help her. I also feel some obligation because I allowed Edmund to marry my daughter in the first place."

He'd be responsible for blackening Calvin's name, too, which would be even worse, because he'd do it intentionally. Frank didn't think reminding him of this would help the situation any, though. He was already dangerously close to having Symington order him to declare Calvin as Blackwell's killer and close the case. A rich man had done this to him once before, and a word from Symington to Chief of Police Conlin was all it would take. Frank wasn't going to let that happen again if he could help it.

"But what if somebody else killed both of them?" he suggested to Symington. "Somebody you don't care about either. Somebody who'd be better off locked up. Somebody you'd also like to keep away from your daughter."

Symington's face hardened. "You seem to be speaking of someone in particular, Mr. Malloy. Is that the case?"

"I've learned a few things about your daughter's past that might give a man we both know a reason for wanting Blackwell out of the way," Frank said, not really answering the question.

Symington was angry, although he was trying not to show it. "My daughter's past is none of your concern, Malloy."

"What if her past has moved into the present?"

Symington was angrier still, but he was also afraid of how much Frank might know and of what he might do with that knowledge. "What are you talking about?"

"I'm talking about old friends suddenly showing up. Friends who might prefer it if your daughter wasn't married anymore. A friend who might even want to marry her himself the way he tried to once before."

"That's impossible," Symington insisted, but it sounded more like a frantic hope than a certainty.

"Peter Dudley visited your daughter just the other day," Frank said.

"That son of a bitch." Symington's rage was interesting. He looked as if he wanted to shout and pound on his desk and even throw something out that impressive window. Instead, he merely turned a deep shade of purple and stared murderously at a spot somewhere over Frank's left shoulder. Frank was afraid he might have apoplexy, and that wouldn't serve Frank's purpose at all.

"I also know the story of how Dudley tried to elope with your daughter," Frank said, saving Symington the trouble of making up any lies about their relationship and, with any luck, distracting him from his own rage.

"That bounder has no principles at all," Symington said with surprising restraint.

"So I gathered," Frank said agreeably. "I don't know what I'd do to a man who tried to steal my daughter and then left her an invalid."

"I know what I *wanted* to do," Symington admitted, this time surprising Frank with his candor. "He hardly seemed worth the effort, though. Have you seen him?"

Frank nodded.

"Then you know what I mean. How could I have imagined such a man was a threat to my daughter? If I'd ever dreamed a girl like Letitia would find a worthless creature like that appealing . . . But of course I had no idea. The next thing I know, he's pounding on my door in the middle of the night, holding my daughter's broken body in his arms."

"It must have taken a lot of courage to face you like that," Frank pointed out.

Symington snorted rudely. "I suppose you're right. He could have left her lying in the road and run for his life. If he'd done that, I most certainly would have hunted him down and made certain he got what he deserved."

"Instead you let him go," Frank guessed.

Symington sighed. "My only concern was for Letitia. If he simply left the area, she couldn't hate me for that, and I hoped she'd come to despise him for being a coward. He was terrified when he carried Letitia into the house that night, so it took only a hint to make him see the wisdom of vanishing from her life forever. Or so I thought," he added wearily.

"Maybe he really does love your daughter," Frank said, still playing devil's advocate.

"What possible difference could that make?" Symington asked disdainfully. "And if he *did* love her, he'd have the decency to leave her alone. Anyone can see he's completely unsuitable for her. You're obviously a romantic, Mr. Malloy, but don't be fooled. He's a fortune hunter and always has been. As soon as he found out Letitia was a widow, he came sniffing around to try his hand with her again. I won't have it, not this time. And this time I'll make sure he doesn't come back into her life." He had made his resolution, and Frank sensed he would dismiss him in another moment. He had to act fast if he wanted a chance to find Blackwell and Calvin's real killer.

"Mr. Symington, there may be more to this than you believe."

"More to what?" Symington asked absently, already mentally making his plans for disposing of Peter Dudley.

"Dudley didn't *just* come back into your daughter's life. They've been seeing each other secretly for over a year."

For once Symington was unable to control his emotions. This time he did strike his desk, with a force that sent a pen clattering from its holder.

"I know this is an unpleasant subject for you"—Frank hurried on before Symington could be distracted by his own fury again—"but I'm sure you'll agree that his involvement with her gives Dudley a very good reason for wanting to see your daughter a widow."

Symington took a moment to absorb what the detective had said. He needed only that moment. "You think *he* killed Edmund," he said baldly.

"It's possible. He had a motive, and he has no alibi."

"Then arrest him!" Symington exclaimed.

Frank had him where he wanted him now. "I'd like to, except that I'm afraid if I do, he might implicate your daughter."

"*What?* He wouldn't dare!"

"He very well might, if he thought it would keep him from being executed. Or if he thought the threat of a scandal would frighten you into protecting him."

Symington started to deny that he could possibly be influenced, but then he thought better of it. The threat was very real, and Symington did want to protect his daughter at all costs. Frank still wasn't convinced he hadn't killed Edmund Blackwell himself for that very purpose, either. "You're not going to let him go free, are you?" he asked.

"Not if he killed Blackwell," Frank said. "But I've got to be certain that he can be convicted of planning and carrying out the murder all on his own. I'll need a little more time for the investigation before I can be sure."

Symington nodded. He was sure that he and Frank understood each other, and that they both wanted the same thing. "Take all the time you need. I'll make sure no one interferes with you."

Frank was hard-pressed not to show his relief. "Thank

you, Mr. Symington. I'll do my best to get this matter settled as quickly as possible."

Frank rose, ready to leave now that he'd gotten exactly what he wanted from Symington and before the man could have second thoughts. He was almost to the door when Symington called out.

"Mr. Malloy."

Frank turned back warily. "Yes?"

"When Peter Dudley is convicted of murder, you will receive a one-thousand-dollar reward from me."

Frank almost winced. How easy it would be to make sure Dudley was convicted of the crime. Most detectives would gladly oblige for even a small portion of a reward like that. Unfortunately, Frank was no longer one of them. If Dudley turned out to be innocent, Sarah Brandt was going to have quite a bit to make up to him.

LETITIA BLACKWELL STARED at Sarah in astonishment, but only for a few heartbeats. Then she laid one small white hand on her bosom and said, "I believe I am going to faint. I must return to my rooms immediately."

Instantly, Dudley was supporting her, making sympathetic noises and offering to assist her.

"If you faint, I'll have to throw water in your face," Sarah said brutally.

Letitia's eyes grew wide. Apparently, no one had ever taken such a tone with her. Or failed to place her comfort above all other considerations. If she didn't want to discuss anything unpleasant—and plainly she didn't—she believed she should be excused from doing so. Sarah had no intention of letting her off that easily, however.

"Mrs. Brandt," Dudley chided. "How can you say such a thing? Can't you see how upset she is?"

"If you have so little concern for my health," Letitia said haughtily, without the slightest trace of faintness, "then I'm afraid I'm going to have to dismiss you."

"If you dismiss me, I won't be able to care for your child, either," Sarah reminded her. "But I'm sure you'll be able to find another nurse who will be willing to keep your child's illness a secret and treat it properly."

"Illness?" Dudley echoed. "What's wrong with him? He looked perfectly healthy to me. Letitia, what is it? If the child is ill, why didn't you tell me?"

Letitia had gone scarlet with fury. So much for her fainting spell. "There's nothing wrong with him at all. We'll discuss that later," she snapped at Dudley, then turned back to Sarah. "Say whatever you are so determined to say, and then leave us alone."

"Calvin Brown has been murdered," she said bluntly.

Their reactions were difficult to judge. Both looked surprised, and then they glanced at each other almost hesitantly, before turning back to her.

"Who—" Dudley began, but Letitia interrupted him.

"Who is Calvin Brown?" she demanded.

"Edmund Blackwell's son," Sarah said.

Neither of them looked particularly surprised, but perhaps they were simply confused.

"That's ridiculous," Letitia said after a moment. "Edmund didn't have a son. He didn't have any children at all."

"Are you aware that Dr. Blackwell was married before?"

Sarah thought she'd catch her there, but Letitia said, "Of course, but that was a long time ago. His first wife died very young."

A good story, and maybe even the one Blackwell had told her. "Did you know he had children by his first wife?" Sarah asked, playing along.

"I told you, he didn't have *any* children. Of that I am quite certain."

Sarah could have pointed out that even Letitia's child wasn't Blackwell's, but she restrained herself. "Dr. Blackwell had three children by his first wife, and one of them was Calvin Brown."

"Really, I won't sit here and listen to this nonsense a moment longer," Letitia insisted, rising to her feet.

"If you don't care about yourself, surely you're interested in protecting Mr. Dudley," Sarah suggested, stopping her when she would have started for the door.

"Protecting him from what?" she asked, outraged or at least pretending to be.

"From being charged with murder."

Dudley, who had risen along with Letitia, made a strangled noise in his throat and sank back down onto the sofa.

Letitia wasn't quite so fragile. She merely glared at Sarah. "This is insane. Are you implying that Peter killed this . . . this Calvin person? Why should he? He had no reason to do such a thing. We don't even know him!"

"I'm not implying anything. All I'm saying is that Mr. Dudley—and you, too, Mrs. Blackwell—both had a good reason for wanting to kill Dr. Blackwell. Anyone who sees your child will figure that out in an instant."

Letitia gasped, and Dudley paled. His eyes were so wide Sarah could see the whites around the blue irises.

"But Peter and I were together when Edmund was killed," Letitia reminded her. "We couldn't possibly have done it."

"The two illicit lovers swear they were together when the betrayed husband was murdered," Sarah said, trying the theory aloud. "I can't imagine a jury will believe you."

"I told you," Dudley said to Letitia. "That police detective said exactly the same thing,".

She ignored him. "It doesn't matter if they believe us or not. We didn't kill Edmund, and we certainly didn't kill this other fellow. Why should we?"

"Because he was going to cause a scandal," Sarah told her.

"What kind of scandal?" she asked skeptically.

"Letitia," Dudley tried, but she motioned him to silence.

"The scandal of bigamy," Sarah said, trying to watch

both of their faces at once. Dudley merely grimaced, but Letitia turned scarlet again.

"I haven't committed bigamy," Letitia insisted. "Peter and I only *tried* to elope. We were never actually married."

"Edmund Blackwell was," Sarah replied. "And his first wife, Calvin's mother, is still very much alive. He didn't bother with a divorce, either. He simply forgot about her and married you."

If Letitia was shocked, she gave no sign of it. "That's preposterous! No one would have believed a boy like that! No one would have even listened to him about such a thing. His name wasn't even the same as Edmund's!"

She seemed very sure of that for someone who had pretended not even to remember Calvin's name.

"Are you saying you knew nothing about Calvin Brown and Dr. Blackwell's other wife?" Sarah asked.

"I certainly am!" Letitia said with an air of triumph.

"That's a pity," Sarah said. "Because if you'd known, you would most certainly have been delighted to discover yourself a legally free woman. You and Mr. Dudley could have been married, and you would have been able to keep your child without fear of interference from Blackwell. Instead, you believed you were legally bound in a marriage with no escape unless your husband died."

"Letitia, please, you must sit down," Dudley said, hurrying to her and taking her arm solicitously. Indeed, she did look as if she really might faint this time. They both looked rather ill, in fact. She allowed him to lead her back to the sofa and seat her again.

"You have no right to upset her like this," he said to Sarah. "You should be ashamed of yourself. A nurse should have more respect for her condition."

"This gives me no pleasure, Mr. Dudley, I assure you. But the fact remains that someone killed Dr. Blackwell and his son. You and Mrs. Blackwell have more reason than anyone else to have wanted Dr. Blackwell dead."

"But we had no reason at all to want his *son* dead," Dudley reminded her.

Sarah bit her tongue. No one was to know that Calvin's killer had tried to implicate him in Blackwell's death. This was something only the real killer could know, and Malloy was using the information in hopes of tricking that person into betraying himself.

"I'm sorry our visit has been so uncomfortable to you," Sarah said, "but I thought you might want to know this information. I'll understand if you no longer want me treating the baby."

Letitia Blackwell didn't even look at her. She was staring off into space, her face creased into a frown of concentration. "Peter, do you know what this means?"

"No, my dear, I don't," he said, still worried. Perhaps he was afraid the shocks of the past few minutes had unhinged her mind.

"If my marriage to Edmund wasn't legal, then my child is illegitimate. My father should have no objections if I marry quickly to give my child a name."

"Letitia, dear," he began, his face reflecting his serious reservations, but she paid him no heed.

"I'll send for him at once. He can't stop us this time. I'm of age, and he doesn't control my life any longer. Besides, I have to think of my child's reputation. And my own," she added, still thinking out loud.

Dudley looked terrified. Most likely, he saw the flaws in this plan and realized that Symington could, and most certainly would, have many objections to it.

Sarah could have given them both some advice on how to handle the situation, but she doubted they would welcome it. Or that Letitia would even allow her to speak. She would have given a lot to witness the scene between father and daughter with the daughter's feckless lover cringing in a corner. Too bad she'd have to miss it.

"I'll be going now," she said, but neither of the lovers even glanced at her.

Dudley was too busy trying to get Letitia to pay attention to him and listen to reason, but she was having none of it. For the first time Sarah saw the side of Letitia Blackwell that had led her to risk her father's wrath and elope with a penniless schoolmaster. Stubborn to a fault, she was. Well, she wasn't Sarah's problem.

Without bothering to bid them farewell, Sarah let herself out. She certainly hoped Malloy planned to visit her tonight. She had a lot to tell him.

AT THE END of the day, Frank made his way to Sarah Brandt's house on Bank Street without even bothering to question himself. He could pretend he was going there to finish examining Tom Brandt's files in an effort to find someone who might have had a motive for killing him. He'd come to realize they were both pretending that now. Frank had long since realized he would find nothing in the files, and he suspected she knew it, too. It was just an excuse for him to go over there.

Really, he just needed to see her to talk about the Blackwell case.

The evenings were growing cooler. Winter was coming, lurking just out of sight. Soon the winds would start to prowl between the city's buildings, taking men's hats and catching ladies' skirts. Frank imagined a winter's evening sitting in Sarah Brandt's comfortable kitchen. Good thing the case would be solved long before then, and he'd have no more reason to meet with her. He could get very used to such comfort if he wasn't careful.

Mrs. Ellsworth came out onto the porch with her broom in hand, even though the light was far too dim now even to see to sweep. She just wanted a word with Frank, and he was growing more patient with her. He'd learned that nosy neighbors could be quite helpful now and then.

"Good evening, Mrs. Ellsworth," he called. "You're out late."

"It's not so very late," she said. "I just wanted to see

if the moon was up yet. If there's a halo around it, that means it will rain tomorrow. I was hoping to go shopping, but not if I'm going to get wet."

Frank looked around, but he couldn't see the moon. The tightly packed buildings permitted only a limited view of the sky, and that was more or less straight up. "The paper said it would be fair tomorrow, but if you're determined to find the moon, you're better off to look from an upstairs window," he advised. "Or even the roof."

"You're probably right," she said. "How was your day, Mr. Malloy?"

"Like all the rest of them," Frank said noncommittally.

"I imagine all your days are very interesting," she said with a smile that rearranged her wrinkles.

"Probably not as interesting as you think," Frank said, thinking of the drunks and derelicts and thieves and killers he usually dealt with. "Police work can be pretty boring."

"Oh, pshaw, Mr. Malloy. It's not nice to tease an old lady. But you get along now. Mrs. Brandt has a lovely chicken roasting, and I'm sure there's more than enough for you, if you haven't eaten yet."

A man didn't need police training to understand Mrs. Ellsworth's intentions. "I'll be sure to get my share of it," he said with a smile. "Good evening, and good luck with your weather predictions."

Sarah Brandt was waiting at the door when he arrived at her porch. Her knowing grin told him she'd witnessed the exchange with Mrs. Ellsworth.

"Is the chicken ready?" he asked as he mounted the front steps.

"It's started to get a little dried out. You're later than usual. I was afraid you weren't coming at all."

He felt a funny little spasm in his chest that might have been his heart, even though he knew perfectly well she was just teasing him. She had that cat-in-the-cream grin on her face, the way she always did when she was trying to get the best of him. "If I'd known you had a roast chicken for me, I would've been here earlier," he teased her right back.

"I'm going to have to speak to Mrs. Ellsworth about being more discreet," she said, closing the door after him. "She obviously led you to believe I got that chicken just for you."

"Didn't you?" he asked innocently, hanging his hat on the rack by the door.

"Of course. I needed a way to keep you occupied so you wouldn't interrupt me when I tell you all the things I learned this afternoon."

He didn't know how she always managed to best him in these little verbal matches they played. Probably because he liked the way she grinned when she won.

The chicken wasn't dry at all, and she'd fried potatoes just the way he liked them. She'd even gotten some beer from her neighbor for him.

"What have you been up to, Mrs. Brandt?" he asked suspiciously as she smiled smugly at his reaction to the meal.

"I visited Mrs. Blackwell today," she said.

"Do you go there *every* day?" he asked with a frown.

"Just about. I have to look after the baby, you know," she added when he would have scolded her. "Do you know she hasn't named him yet? He's more than a week old and doesn't even have a name."

"I'm sure she's had other things to worry about," he said to annoy her. "So you visited Mrs. Blackwell. What happened?"

"She had another visitor already when I arrived."

"Dudley?" he guessed hopefully.

"He'd apparently come to see the baby. The three of them were in the parlor together, alone."

"Very cozy," Frank noted.

"Especially because Amos Potter arrived right after I

did. He was so desperate to see Mrs. Blackwell that I decided he should finally get the chance."

"I'm surprised that butler didn't physically stop you from intruding on her," Frank said.

"Oh, I almost forgot: Granger is ill. He hasn't been well for several days. Turns out he was just sick with guilt for not getting home first the day Blackwell was killed so he could've discovered the body instead of Mrs. Blackwell. Even the butler adores her. What is it about that woman that turns men into idiots?"

"I don't know what you're talking about," Frank said.

She sniffed derisively, but she was too eager to tell her story to stop and argue. "Anyway, Granger was sick in bed with an upset stomach, so that little maid who let me in before was the only one guarding the door. It was easy enough to get past her with Potter."

"I guess Potter was surprised to see Dudley."

"Surprised? He was horrified. I told you the baby has red hair just like his. No one could miss the resemblance. Potter isn't a fool. I'm sure he figured it out as quickly as I did, and he obviously knew that Letitia had had a lover before Blackwell. He asked a few leading questions and quickly determined Dudley was the man."

"That must have been a blow. He thought Letitia would be his now that Blackwell is gone."

"What was I just saying about her turning men into idiots?" she asked. "Potter couldn't have Letitia if he were the last man alive on earth."

"You can't fault a man for dreaming."

She just rolled her eyes. "Needless to say, Letitia wasn't too happy to have Potter there—or me either, for that matter. She sent him on his way pretty quickly, and she tried to get rid of me, too, but I refused to leave."

"I don't doubt it for a moment. I know how stubborn you can be," Frank said, taking another bite of his chicken.

"I'm not stubborn, I'm determined," she insisted good-naturedly. "As soon as Potter was gone, I broke the news to them that Calvin Brown was dead."

"You did *what*?" Frank shouted, nearly choking on his chicken.

"Oh, dear, was that the wrong thing to do?" she asked.

"I told you, only the killer would know about the suicide note!" He couldn't believe she'd ruined his plan already.

"I didn't tell them about that!" she said indignantly. "I just said he was murdered. They pretended they didn't know who he was, but I could tell Dudley knew, at least."

"Of course he knew. I told him the other night."

"You did?" she asked, disappointed. "When did you see him? What did he say?"

"He said he didn't kill Blackwell or Calvin. What do you think he said?" Frank was remembering why he'd once vowed never to see Sarah Brandt again and certainly never to let her become involved in another of his cases.

"Well, I think Letitia knew about him, too," she said, still not showing any sign of understanding how she'd ruined the investigation. "She claimed that Blackwell had told her he'd been married before but his first wife had died young and that he didn't have any children. She's a good liar, so I wasn't sure if she was telling the truth or not."

Frank sighed. *He* would have known, but now he wouldn't have the chance. "What else did you tell them?" he asked wearily.

"I didn't tell them anything," she said defensively. "I just pointed out that if they didn't know about Calvin, they both had a very good reason for wanting her husband dead."

"And if they did, they had a good reason, too," he reminded her.

"So either way, they're still good suspects. Unless Mr. Fong gave them an alibi," she remembered.

"He didn't."

"He *didn't*?" she asked with delight.

"Mr. Fong is a good businessman. He doesn't know anything about his clients, including their real names. And he certainly doesn't make note of their comings and goings. That saves him the trouble of being involved in unpleasant things like murder investigations. You should follow his example," Frank pointed out.

She just gave him one of her looks. "There *was* one unfortunate result of my visit this afternoon," she admitted.

"I've already counted more than one."

She wasn't the least bit repentant. "When I pointed out that Letitia's marriage to Blackwell wasn't valid, Letitia decided to inform her father that she was going to marry Dudley immediately. I guess she doesn't feel the need to mourn a bigamous husband any longer, and she mentioned something about her child needing a father."

"*Her* father will be pleased to hear that. He offered me a thousand dollars to arrest Dudley as the killer."

"*What?*"

"It's a reward," he said a little defensively, "not a bribe."

"It's not a bribe unless Dudley is innocent. Does he really think he's guilty, or does he just want to get rid of Dudley? And when did you see Symington?"

He didn't feel he needed to explain his activities to her. "I think he wants to get rid of Dudley and hopes he's the killer."

She frowned thoughtfully. "A thousand dollars is a lot of money. Some detectives would make sure Dudley was found guilty whether he was or not."

"Do you think I'm one of them?" he asked, stung.

She was so surprised he knew she hadn't even thought of this. "Of course not! I know you better than that! But Symington doesn't. I was just thinking he must believe he's made sure he'll be rid of Dudley and have Blackwell's murder settled, too. What an evil man!"

Frank felt a pang of guilt. Sarah Brandt was sure he

wouldn't take a bribe to convict an innocent man, but
he knew his honesty was inspired only by the fear of
seeing disappointment in her eyes. In his own way, he
wasn't any better than Maurice Symington. "Maybe Symington thinks Dudley is really guilty. In any case, he's
just trying to protect his daughter."

"He's done a poor job of it so far. First he lets her
get involved with Dudley and nearly elope with him,
then he gives her to that charlatan Blackwell, and all the
time she's using morphine. Heaven help her if he'd been
neglecting her!"

She was right, of course. "Maybe Dudley really did
kill Blackwell, though. He's still a good prospect."

"And so is Symington," she reminded him. "Maybe
he's trying to make sure you don't look any farther than
Dudley. That way, he'd get rid of Dudley and save his
own neck in the process."

"Do you think a man like Symington would do his
own killing?"

She considered this for a moment. "Probably not. On
the other hand, maybe killing Blackwell was an accident
or a crime of passion. He hadn't planned it, and when
it happened, he had to cover it up. He couldn't trust
anyone else to keep his secret, so he had to kill Calvin
himself, too, and try to convince the police the boy was
Blackwell's killer."

"Blackwell's death wasn't an accident or a crime of
passion, either," Frank reminded her. "He was sitting at
his desk, calmly writing a letter, while his killer snuck
up behind him. He probably didn't even know his killer
was there until he got shot."

She frowned. She didn't like being wrong. That was
too bad. "So we're back to Dudley."

"Or Letitia," Frank said. "Wouldn't you like for her
to be the killer?"

"Oh, yes," she said, "but even if she was, she'd never
be convicted. Can you imagine a jury of men sentencing
her to death? They'd all fall in love with her and let her

go free in the hopes that she'd marry one of them out of gratitude."

Frank had to bite his lip to keep from smiling at that picture. "But she'd probably marry Dudley. Wouldn't that be punishment enough?"

"It would be for me, but for some reason she seems to love him. I wonder what she sees in him."

"Don't ask me. Maybe she likes having a man she can control."

She considered this. "I think you may be right, Malloy. She lived with a controlling father all her life, and she wanted someone who'd let her do what she wanted."

"Or someone who would do what *she* wanted."

"The only question now is did she want him to kill Blackwell."

Frank considered this. "Maybe I'll ask him just that."

14

Frank THOUGHT HE SHOULD JUST WAIT AT THE Blackwell house for Dudley to show up. The former schoolmaster was probably visiting Letitia daily now, but he didn't want to deal with the scheming widow. He went, instead, to the bank where Dudley worked. It was Saturday, so he'd only be working a half day.

Seeing no need for discretion, he went inside. He wanted Dudley to know he was waiting for him to get off. He'd be more cooperative if he worked himself into a state wondering what Frank wanted from him. But when Frank looked around, he didn't see Dudley behind the bars of any of the teller windows. He'd only been standing there a moment, looking in vain for Dudley, when the guard approached him.

"Something I can do for you?" the man asked, obviously recognizing him as a policeman and wanting to avoid any disturbance. Frank couldn't go anywhere without people knowing what he was.

"Is your manager here?" Frank asked in a tone that invited no questions.

The guard made his way hastily to a rear office, and in another moment a nattily-dressed man with a flower in his lapel anxiously approached Frank, the guard faithfully following at his heels.

"Could we handle this discreetly?" the manager asked, looking around nervously to see if anyone was disturbed by Frank's presence. No one wanted a cop snooping around at a bank. It gave customers the wrong idea.

"I was looking for Peter Dudley," Frank said.

"Dudley?" the man asked in surprise. "Whatever for?"

"Just send him out, will you?" Frank said impatiently.

The man glanced around again, making sure they weren't being overheard. "He isn't here."

"What do you mean? Doesn't he work here anymore?"

"Yes, of course he does, but . . . He didn't come in this morning."

"Is he sick?"

"I'm sure I don't know. He didn't send word."

"Does he do this a lot?"

"He wouldn't still work here if he did," the manager sniffed. "He's always been very reliable."

Frank felt the back of his neck prickle. Something was wrong. It could just be that Dudley had decided he didn't need this job anymore if he was going to marry Letitia. That was probably it. A man who'd seduce and elope with a young girl of good family probably wouldn't hesitate to walk out of a job like this without giving notice either.

"I'll just go check on him, then," Frank said. "Make sure he's all right. You know where he lives?" he added. Dudley was probably with Letitia, but just in case, he needed the man's address.

"I most certainly do not know where he lives!" the bank manager said.

"Then find somebody who does," Frank said with a friendly smile. "I'll wait right here until you do."

MOST ROOMING HOUSES were sad, smelling of cabbage and unwashed bodies, but the one where Peter Dudley lived was sadder than most. Paint was peeling off the front door and one of the shutters hung askew. The woman who owned the place was a slattern in a dirty apron, with a thin cigar dangling from her mouth. She even had a hint of a mustache.

"How should I know if he's here or not?" she demanded when Frank asked after Dudley. "Do I look like his mother?"

Frank was in no mood for this. He'd already been to the Blackwell home. The butler, who appeared to be recovered from whatever illness he'd been suffering, had informed him he hadn't seen Mr. Dudley that day. As usual, he hadn't been very friendly about it, either.

"Just take me up to his room," he told the landlady. "And bring a passkey. If he's not there, I'll still want to take a look around."

The woman grumbled, but she complied. Frank followed her laborious progress up the steep, narrow stairs, taking care not to slip on the debris that had accumulated since the last time the steps had been swept. Frank figured it had probably been a year or more since a broom had touched them. Ahead of him, the landlady's broad backside looked like two small boys fighting under a blanket. Frank tried his best not to watch the disturbing sight.

At last they reached one of the rear rooms, which lay down a stuffy, narrow corridor. The landlady knocked loudly. "Mr. Dudley, you in there?"

Frank nudged her out of the way and pounded even louder. "Dudley, it's the police. Open up!"

A door at the other end of the hall opened, and a curious face peered out, but Frank ignored the other lodger. He pounded once more and, still hearing nothing, said, "Open it."

Grumbling again, the landlady started searching through the keys on her large ring, looking for the correct one. After a couple of incorrect choices, she finally got the lock to turn and pushed the door open.

"I'll wait here to lock it back up when you're finished," she said, scowling at him.

Frank stepped into the room, and instantly the smell of death overwhelmed him. Dudley lay crumpled on the floor in a tangle of bloody bedclothes. Cursing, Frank hurried to him. In the doorway, the landlady started screaming and swearing, and Frank could hear footsteps running down the hallway. The curious face was coming to see what had happened.

Dudley was still in his nightshirt and had apparently been attacked while he was sleeping. The bedclothes were pulled half off the bed and had wrapped around his legs as he struggled. His nightshirt was torn and soaked in blood, front and back. Frank started to turn him over, and he moaned.

"Oh, Lord in heaven, is he still alive?" the landlady cried.

"Just barely," Frank said after a quick examination. "Send somebody for a doctor. *Right now!*" he shouted when nobody moved.

"Get Woomer!" the landlady said to the lodger. "You know where he lives. Tell him to hurry!"

Frank heard the pounding of feet going down the stairs, but he was too busy assessing Dudley's wounds to pay much attention.

"What happened to him?" the landlady asked, coming closer but not close enough to help.

"From the looks of it, somebody stabbed him," Frank said. "Hand me that towel over there," he added, pointing to a peg where a ragged towel hung.

"You're not getting my good towels all bloody!" the landlady told him indignantly.

Frank gave her his most evil glare. "Don't make me knock you down and take your petticoats," he warned.

She yelped in outrage, then stomped over to where the towel hung and snatched it from the wall. "I'll charge him for this, I will. I can't afford to be wasting towels on something like this."

"You can't afford to let one of your tenants die on the premises," Frank informed her, pressing the towel to the oozing hole in Dudley's chest. Out of spite, he jerked the sheet the rest of the way off the bed and used that, too.

She made a horrified sound, deep in her chest.

"Put this on his bill, too," Frank said. "And if he dies, good luck collecting."

Pushed beyond endurance, the landlady flounced out of the room, leaving the door standing open.

Frank was still trying to determine the extent of Dudley's injuries. He appeared to have been stabbed several times, both in his back and in his chest, but only one wound was very deep. Stabbing someone in the torso was risky at best, as Frank had learned from years of observation. There were all kinds of bones in the upper body. Unless you used a slender blade and knew just where to aim, you were more likely to hit one of them than not. The result would be a shallow gouge, painful but hardly fatal.

Sure enough, the wounds on Dudley's back were ugly but only bone-deep. His attacker must have come into the room and tried to kill him while he lay sleeping on his stomach. The pain would have awakened him, and he'd apparently struggled for his life. Now that Frank noticed, his left hand was bleeding from a gash across the inside of the fingers, as if he'd tried to grab the knife and gotten sliced instead. The attacker had landed three good blows on Dudley's chest; the first one slid along his collarbone and the second had gouged the center of his chest. Neither had been powerful enough to break through the bones and had, like the ones in his back, produced ugly but only superficial wounds.

The attacker must have been getting frantic by then. Dudley would have been struggling like a madman. Fear would have given both of them unusual strength. Finally, the attacker had struck a vulnerable spot and driven the knife between two ribs. Chest wounds like this one were serious stuff. Dudley wasn't dead yet, but he likely would be soon. Frank's only hope was to get him to name his killer before he died.

Dudley's body was cold, in spite of the relative warmth of the morning, so Frank pulled the blanket down from the bed and tucked it around him. Then he pulled down the lumpy pillow and stuffed it under the man's bloody head. The landlady would have a fit, but Frank was actually looking forward to her annoyance.

"Dudley, can you hear me?" Frank asked, patting his cheeks to rouse him. "Who did this? Did you see who did this?"

Dudley's eyes flickered, and his lips moved, but he only managed to groan very softly before going still. At first Frank feared he was already dead, but his regular, if shallow, breathing reassured him. He'd just passed out. Nothing to do now but wait and hope Dudley came to one more time before the doctor, whoever he was, managed to finish him off.

When he finally appeared, Dr. Woomer looked like he would do just that without half trying. An ancient, gin-soaked fellow in a shabby, stained suit, he looked like he'd been on an all-night bender, and smelled like it, too.

Frank's expression must have betrayed his opinion, because the doctor said, "Don't worry. I was doctoring before you were born, and I'm *better* when I'm drunk."

Maybe he just *thought* he was better, Frank thought, but he said, "Anything I can do to help?"

"Help me get him up on the bed. I'm too old to be crawling around on the floor."

The lodger who had fetched the doctor had followed him upstairs and stood outside the door, still staring curiously. He was a cadaverous man of indeterminate age who wore only a yellowed undershirt and trousers drooping because his suspenders dangled at his hips. Frank wondered that they hadn't fallen off during his trip to get the doctor.

"Get over here and give us a hand," Frank ordered him, and he came, however reluctantly.

Between the three of them, they managed to get Dudley back up on the bed. The landlady would be charging for a lot of ruined sheets.

"Now let's see what we have here," the doctor said.

Frank explained what he'd observed of Dudley's wounds. The doctor made his own assessment, turning Dudley with Frank's help. "Most of these'll just need a few stitches. This one here, though, that's the bitch."

"Did it hit his heart?"

"How should I know?" the doctor said sourly. "Think I can see through flesh and bone?"

Frank gave him a look.

"All right," the doctor relented. "Looks like it missed the heart. The lung, too, though God only knows how. He'd be dead by now if there was a hole in either one of those organs. Still, he's lost a lot of blood, and there's plenty of other stuff in there that could be sliced. All I can do is close him up and hope for the best."

"Just try to keep him alive until he can tell me who did this," Frank said.

"He a special friend of yours?" the doctor asked, opening his bag and rummaging for the tools he needed.

"No, but whoever did this killed two other men, and I did care about one of *them*. And I also don't like people getting away with murder."

The doctor gave him a funny look out of red-rimmed eyes. "There's a reward, I guess," he remarked to no one in particular.

Frank tried not to be insulted. The doctor couldn't be helped for his opinions of the police, which were, Frank had to admit, well justified. "If he lives to tell me who did this, I'll share it with you," Frank offered.

The doctor's eyes lighted. "I'll do my best."

As Woomer worked, Frank introduced himself. "You ever know a Dr. Tom Brandt?" he asked idly after the doctor had worked in silence for a bit.

Woomer looked up in surprise from drawing a stitch through Dudley's flesh. "Tom Brandt? Young fellow?"

"That's the one," Frank confirmed. "Got himself murdered about three years back."

"Has it been that long? God, I'm getting old."

"What kind of a man was he?"

"Tom? The best there was, I guess. Never heard anybody say a word against him."

"Somebody didn't like him," Frank pointed out. "Or he wouldn't be dead."

"He wasn't killed by somebody who knew him," Woomer said.

"You know that for a fact?"

"It's only common sense. Tom wasn't the kind of man who made enemies."

This wasn't exactly what Frank wanted to hear. Not only did it make it harder to figure out who'd killed him, he certainly didn't like the idea that Sarah Brandt had been married to a near saint. Not that he was trying to compete or anything, but still . . . How could any other man compare?

"What did people say? When he died, I mean."

"That it was a shame. Had a young wife, if I remember. He did a lot of good, too. Never turned anybody away just because they couldn't pay his fee. It's a wonder he didn't starve."

Just what he needed, more evidence of Tom Brandt's perfection. "I mean what did people say about how he died?"

Woomer was threading catgut into his needle for more stitches. He squinted and concentrated for a moment until he found the hole. When he'd gone back to stitching, he said, "I heard he got robbed. I figured somebody robbed him for whatever he was carrying and killed him, probably because he didn't have anything much. Happens often enough, you want to know the truth."

Frank knew it only too well. "You didn't hear any rumors? Maybe somebody had it in for him?"

"Tom? Not likely," Woomer scoffed. "How come you're so interested in a man got killed over three years ago?"

Frank didn't think it was any of his business, but he'd been friendly enough. "A friend of his asked me to look into it. See if I could find anything. The killer was never caught."

"Never will be, you ask me. You're wasting your time."

"It's my time," Frank pointed out.

Woomer looked up and studied Frank for a minute. "This friend of Tom's wouldn't be his widow by any chance?"

This really *wasn't* any of his business. "How's he doing?" He gestured toward Dudley.

Woomer chuckled to himself, not fooled by the sudden change of subject. "He's not complaining. And he's still breathing."

"Will he live?"

"For a while. After that, who knows?"

Frank would take what he could get. Woomer finished up the last of the stitches and wrapped a bandage around the worst of the wounds. Frank had to admit his work was neat and apparently competent.

"Should he go to the hospital?" he asked when the doctor was finished.

Woomer frowned as he started packing up his instruments. "Wouldn't do him any good. He's likely to catch something there and die from *that*. Besides, moving him at all right now might kill him. He's pretty weak."

"I can't leave him here alone," Frank complained.

"Does he have any family? Somebody who could nurse him?"

"What kind of care would he need?"

"Every kind," Woomer said. "He won't even be able to get up to relieve himself. That hole in his chest might bleed inside, too. Might be bleeding even now."

"So he needs a nurse," Frank said.

"That would be best. A mother would be second best."

"I don't have any idea where to find him a mother," Frank said. "But I do know where to get him a nurse."

SARAH DECIDED SHE was no longer going to be surprised at anything Frank Malloy did. This was the second time he'd summoned her to help him in this case, and she dearly longed to tease him about it. If she did, however, he might never call upon her again. Helping with his cases was far too interesting to take such a chance, no matter how much fun it would be.

The patrolman who had delivered Malloy's message had given her no other information beyond telling her Malloy needed a nurse and to come to this address. The lodging house was a step up from a flophouse, where men paid a nickel to sleep in a hammock or a cot or even on the floor for a night. This place at least provided a private room and probably a meal or two a day, but not much comfort beyond that.

Sarah judged that the landlady, who opened the door, was probably a retired prostitute who'd invested her money wisely in this house to support her in her old age. She looked Sarah up and down, withholding her approval.

"You the nurse?" she asked around the cheroot dangling from her lips. Ashes had spilled unnoticed down her ample bosom.

"Yes," Sarah said, offering no other information. "Is Mr. Malloy here?"

"Upstairs," the woman said, jerking her thumb over her shoulder toward the stairway. "End of the hall."

So much for the social amenities, Sarah thought in amusement. Malloy was waiting for her in the doorway of the room, looking grim.

"Who is it?" she asked. "And what happened?"

"It's Dudley. Somebody stabbed him," he said, admitting her to the room.

An older man sat in the one chair of the room, his head drooping to his chest, dozing. Sarah thought he looked vaguely familiar, but she went immediately to the bed where Dudley lay amid the bloodstained sheets. His face was pale, but he seemed to be breathing easily. "How bad is it?" she asked.

Malloy kicked the chair leg, jarring the older man awake. He shook his grizzled head and rubbed his hands over his face. He hadn't shaved in a day or two, and the stubble glistened silver on his cheeks. He blinked bloodshot eyes at her, and Sarah immediately recognized the signs of chronic alcoholism. She also recognized the man.

"Dr. Woomer," she said. "It's been a long time."

He gave her a sad smile and nodded. "Too long. You're looking well, Mrs. Brandt."

"I am well, thank you," she said, not returning the compliment. "How is Mr. Dudley doing?"

"He's alive," he said, rising stiffly from the chair. "No thanks to whoever attacked him."

He shuffled over to the bed and pulled down the top sheet so Sarah could see Dudley's chest. "Somebody took after him with a knife. Didn't know what they was doing, so most of the wounds hit bone and aren't deep. This one here is the worst. Don't look like it hit the heart or a lung, since he's still alive, but it's worrisome. He lost a lot of blood, too."

Sarah nodded. She gave Malloy a questioning look.

"Dr. Woomer here thinks Dudley needs a nurse to look after him for a few days," he said. "I was wondering if you'd take the job."

Would she? He knew perfectly well she was more than willing to remain involved with the case. Sitting beside an unconscious man who might well die hardly seemed like an ideal occupation for someone who wanted to find a killer, but she also knew Dudley had most likely been attacked by the same person who'd killed Blackwell and Calvin Brown. When Dudley regained consciousness—assuming he did—Malloy would want someone there he could trust to hear anything he might have to say. Sarah wanted to be that person.

"I'll be happy to assist in any way I can," she said, managing to sound merely cooperative. Malloy wasn't fooled, but probably Woomer was. "Unless I'm called out on a case, of course, but we'll worry about that if it happens. Just tell me what care he's going to need."

"That's good of you, Mrs. Brandt," Woomer said, scratching his chin. He quickly told her what Dudley's condition was and what he wanted her to do. Then he gathered his things and started to leave.

"Who's going to pay me for this?" he asked Malloy when he was ready to go.

"Mr. Dudley is," Malloy said, and he paid the doctor from a worn wallet he pulled from Dudley's suit coat. Woomer seemed relieved.

They both waited a few moments, until Dr. Woomer was on his way down the stairs, before speaking, lest they be overheard.

"I guess this means Dudley isn't the killer either," Sarah said.

"Unless he figured out some way to stab himself in the back," Malloy said in disgust.

"Was he able to give you any information at all?"

"No, although it looked like he was trying to say something before he passed out. The doc gave him some morphine, too, so it'll be a while before he's awake again."

"Morphine," Sarah said, thinking of all the trouble this drug had caused. She sighed. "Who could the killer be now? We shouldn't have too many suspects left."

"No, killing Dudley isn't something any of Black-well's clients would think of doing, even if they knew anything about him, which they wouldn't. They'd have been satisfied with casting suspicion on Calvin. And killing Dudley would eliminate him as a suspect, in any case."

"I guess it's a good thing you never got around to questioning the Fitzgeralds."

"That's right. I almost forgot all about them when Calvin was killed, but now it looks like they're eliminated completely. They didn't have anything against Dudley, and I think whoever tried to kill him did so for a very personal reason."

"Because Letitia was going to marry him," Sarah guessed. "It's too much of a coincidence to be anything else. That certainly gives Amos Potter a good motive," she added hopefully.

"But not for killing Blackwell and then Calvin. We know the person who killed Blackwell also killed Calvin and tried to make us believe the boy was the killer. We know the reason for Calvin's death was to end the investigation. We don't know why Blackwell was killed, but we do know why someone tried to kill Dudley."

"Yes, to prevent Letitia from marrying him. That was the only threat he posed."

"Which means only one person has a motive for all three murders," Malloy said.

"Amos Potter," Sarah tried again.

But Malloy shook his head. "He might've thought Blackwell was a bad husband—and we really don't even have proof of that—but he would hardly offer me a reward to find Blackwell's killer if *he* was the killer."

"And if he didn't kill Blackwell, he wouldn't have killed Calvin," Sarah said. "Then who's left?"

"The only person left who'd kill just to protect Letitia is Maurice Symington."

Sarah's heart sank. "Oh, dear."

"Yeah, oh, dear."

They both knew a man with Symington's wealth and influence would never even be charged with a crime like this, no matter how much proof they found against him. The worst part was that he might well have hired the killings done, which put him even further from being held responsible.

"What are you going to do?" Sarah asked.

He shrugged. "I'm not sure yet, but one thing I'm *not* going to do is tell Symington that Dudley is still alive. Or anybody else, for that matter."

"Why not . . . ? Oh, because if Dudley names his attacker—"

"I'll know who the real killer is," he finished for her. "If Dudley is still alive, the killer is liable to come back and try to finish the job, too."

"That's why you sent for me to take care of him, then. You want me to try to get him to tell me who did this."

"I just want you to keep him alive," Malloy corrected her.

Sarah smiled knowingly. "And guard him in case the killer returns."

"Absolutely not! I'm going to leave a patrolman here to guard you. I know you think you're practically a police detective now, but I doubt you're up to defending Dudley against the killer."

"Maybe you could get Mrs. Ellsworth to help me. Between the two of us, I'm sure we could—"

"That's not funny," Malloy informed her.

"Are you going to tell Letitia that Dudley's dead? She'll be very upset."

Malloy considered this. "I think I will. I'd like to see if she really *is* upset or if the whole thing with Dudley was a bluff. Maybe she was just trying to get her father's goat with talk of marrying him."

"You seem to have changed your opinion of the lovely Letitia," she noted.

"What do you mean?" he asked, a little affronted.

"Nothing," she said sweetly. "So you think the lovely widow might have been involved in the killings?"

"She's involved all right, but I'm pretty sure she's just the *reason* men are getting killed. I can't see her getting her hands dirty. Or sneaking around the city in the middle of night to stab her lover in his bed. And why would she want Dudley dead in the first place?"

"Maybe she was finished with him. If he'd served his purpose, he'd just be a hindrance, especially with that red hair. Everyone would know she was an adulteress, and if she threw him over, he might try to blackmail her or cause a scandal. With him out of the picture . . ."

"So maybe she hinted to her father that things would be easier with Dudley dead," Malloy admitted. "It still isn't likely she killed him herself. Anyway, it's not your job to solve this case. It's your job to keep our only surviving witness alive."

"All right, I'll do my best." She glanced at the figure on the bed. "I suppose it's too much to hope that Woomer disinfected the wounds before he stitched them up."

"Disinfected?" Malloy echoed.

"Cleaned them," she explained.

"He wiped off the blood."

Sarah rolled her eyes. "Would you tell the landlady that I'll need some clean sheets and lots of hot water and towels and some whiskey?"

"She won't be happy," Malloy warned her.

"And a broom, too. And a dustpan." She looked at the bloodstains on the floor. "I'll need a scrub brush, too. And some lye soap."

Malloy was chuckling when he made his way down the stairs.

FRANK HAD INTENDED to go straight to Maurice Symington, but Sarah Brandt had changed his mind. The quickest way to Symington was most likely through his daughter, in any case. Besides, Frank wanted to see her reaction to news of Dudley's supposed death before someone else had a chance to break it to her gently.

When he arrived, the butler reluctantly admitted him, but he said, "Mrs. Blackwell already has a visitor," in an apparent attempt to discourage Frank from staying.

Just then someone shouted, "Don't be a fool, Letitia!"

from the front parlor. It sounded like Maurice Symington.

Granger winced, most certainly a violation of the butler's code of conduct, Frank thought with amusement.

"Sounds like she could use a little protection from the police," he said to the butler. "Announce me."

Granger was torn, but his loyalty to Letitia won out. "Please wait here," he said, and went to the parlor doors.

He knocked perfunctorily before sliding the pocket doors open. "Mr. Malloy is here to see you, Mrs. Blackwell," he said, then stepped aside.

Frank wasn't certain what he had expected, but Letitia Blackwell didn't look the least bit upset that her father was shouting at her. Her delicate chin was raised and set in defiance. Symington's face was red and his neck swollen with rage. He turned on Frank with a murderous glare.

"What are you doing here?" he demanded, but didn't wait for a reply. "Oh, never mind. I want to report a crime to you."

"A crime?" Frank asked curiously as Granger closed the parlor doors behind him.

"Yes, Peter Dudley is blackmailing my daughter."

"Father!" she exclaimed in outrage. "How dare you?"

"What else do you call it?" Symington asked Frank. "The man is claiming to be the father of her child and demanding she marry him or he will ruin her reputation."

"That's a lie!" Letitia cried, jumping to her feet in her lover's defense. "Dudley loves me, and I love him!"

Her father ignored her. "I want him locked up. And this, of course, gives him a very good reason for having killed Edmund and that poor boy, doesn't it?"

Letitia made a strangled sound in her throat, but Frank ignored her, too.

"It would except for one thing," Frank said.

"And what's that?" Symington asked contemptuously.

"Someone has killed Dudley, too."

Symington looked appropriately shocked. *"What?"*

Letitia made a cry of distress. "Peter?" she asked

weakly, and sank back down onto the sofa.

At last she had their attention. Her father rushed to her. "There now, it's all right," he assured her, sitting beside her and taking her hand. Then he looked back up at Frank. "What's this about Dudley?"

"I'm sorry to have been so blunt," Frank lied, "but I'm afraid Peter Dudley has been murdered."

Letitia looked up at him with unfocused eyes. "But he was just here yesterday," she argued, as if that proved Frank was wrong. She looked stunned, but she wasn't crying, at least not yet.

"What happened?" Symington asked more practically. "When did he die?"

"Someone went to his rooms last night, it seems. I found him this morning when I went to ask him some questions."

Letitia's lovely face crumpled, and she finally began to weep quietly, pulling a lacy handkerchief from her sleeve. "Peter," she moaned.

Frank found her reaction a little too well-bred for his taste. Remembering how the patrolman had described her screaming when she found Blackwell's body, he would have expected a more violent reaction to losing the man she professed to actually love. Of course, she hadn't had to see any of Dudley's blood spilled on her carpet.

Symington was trying to comfort his daughter, but his mind was still working. He looked up at Frank again, this time with a silent challenge in his piercing gaze. "Maybe it was a suicide," he said. "He couldn't live with himself for trying to hurt Letitia, and he killed himself from the guilt. Maybe all three of the deaths were suicides, Mr. Malloy. Isn't that a possibility?"

He wasn't making a guess; he was giving Frank a solution. He'd already offered a reward to ensure that Dudley was charged as the killer in the case. He'd probably be even more grateful if Frank decreed all the deaths were suicides and closed the investigation completely. His daughter would be free of two fortune hunters, and no scandal would touch his family. What more could he ask?

Frank could have granted his unspoken request so easily, if only Sarah Brandt hadn't ruined him. "If Edmund Blackwell killed himself, then why would Calvin Brown have killed himself out of guilt for murdering his father?" he asked logically.

Symington was going to protest, but Frank didn't give him a chance. "And Peter Dudley hardly stabbed himself in the back, so who did that, if not the man who killed Blackwell and Calvin? Unless, of course, it was just someone who wanted to prevent Dudley from marrying your daughter," he added.

Symington needed only a moment to understand the implication. "There are many ways I could have prevented that, short of killing the man," he snapped.

Like having him arrested for murder, Frank thought, but he didn't dare say it aloud. Symington could have his job in an instant, and Frank had pushed him perilously close to doing just that already.

At the mention of killing Dudley, Letitia cried out again and began to sob. Her father instinctively put his arm around her, and she buried her head in his shoulder.

Symington looked as if he wished Frank in hell, but he also knew that he had to do something to help his daughter. Frank could almost see him considering and rejecting various options. Finally, he said, "What if that boy Calvin did kill Edmund and then himself? And what if Dudley was simply the victim of a robbery gone wrong? That must happen frequently in cheap lodging houses." He glanced down at the golden head resting on his shoulder, then back at Frank again. "I would still be willing to offer the same reward we discussed previously if you can find the person who robbed and murdered Mr. Dudley."

Frank nodded his understanding and breathed a sigh of relief. He knew perfectly well there was no robbery, but at least he was still on the case.

15

Dudley's landlady had grumbled and complained about every one of Sarah's requests. Sarah thought she should have been grateful someone was willing to clean one of her rooms for her, but no, she'd just been unhappy because Sarah was inconveniencing her with her demands for supplies. She'd been even less enthusiastic about providing supper for Sarah and the patrolman who was guarding Dudley's room, until Sarah had offered to pay her for her trouble. Sarah had regretted her offer as soon as the food had finally arrived, though. It was barely edible. She also wanted a rich beef broth for Dudley, if he regained consciousness, but she figured there was no use asking the landlady for it. Maybe she should send a message to Mrs. Ellsworth, who would be only too happy to prepare something if she asked.

It was getting rather late now, though. Perhaps she'd wait until morning. Dudley might not even make it through the night, although he seemed to be sleeping naturally now. Perhaps his wounds weren't as serious as they appeared. Perhaps they wouldn't fester and poison him either, although she considered that unlikely. But

Dudley was young and healthy. Maybe he could survive even that. She didn't think much of him as a man, but he hadn't done anything worthy of death, either, since it now seemed unlikely he'd killed Edmund Blackwell.

After a while she grew bored with conjecture and resumed her housekeeping duties. So far she'd changed the sheets and given the bloody ones to the landlady, and she'd scrubbed the blood off the floor. The rest of the room still needed to be swept, and if she was really bored, she could scrub that, too. Heaven knew when it had last been done.

Sarah started sweeping at the other end of the room, working her way over to the bed. She swept slowly, trying not to stir up too much dust, but the room was small, and she was at the bed in a matter of minutes. Being careful not to disturb Dudley, she slipped the broom under the bed and tried to gather up as much dirt as possible without accidentally striking the bed frame and startling him. She'd just dragged a pile of dust bunnies and debris out when Dudley groaned.

"Water," he croaked.

Sarah dropped the broom and quickly fetched him a glass of water. Blood loss created a mighty thirst, and if she quenched it, he might even be able to say a few words. She held the cup to his lips and let him drink as much as he wanted. At last he dropped back against the pillow, exhausted.

"Mr. Dudley, can you hear me?" she asked.

His eyes flickered and then opened. He stared at her with no sign of recognition. "Who . . . ?"

"I'm Sarah Brandt," she explained. "Letitia Blackwell's midwife. We met at her home the other day."

Dudley showed no sign of remembering. He seemed to be using all his energies trying to focus on her face.

"Mr. Dudley, do you know who attacked you?"

"Attacked?" he asked weakly, obviously puzzled.

"Someone broke in here and stabbed you while you were sleeping last night. Do you know who it was?"

He frowned, trying hard. "I don't . . ."

"You were asleep," she prodded him.

"I woke up," he recalled after a moment. "The pain . . ."

"Did you see who did it?"

"The pain . . . woke me . . . dark . . ."

"Someone tried to kill you, Mr. Dudley. Who was it?" she demanded, wanting to shake him but knowing that would only make things worse.

"I don't . . . too dark . . . couldn't see . . ." His eyes closed in a grimace of pain. He needed another dose of morphine. "Hurts," he murmured.

Sarah sighed with disappointment and began to prepare his dose. How ironic it would be, she mused, if he survived and became a morphine addict, too.

When Dudley was once again in a drug-induced sleep, Sarah remembered what she had been doing when he'd awakened. Picking up the broom, she had started to sweep the mess from under the bed into the dustpan when something shiny caught her eye. She reached down and picked it up, and that's when she knew who the killer was.

"Officer Moran!" she called, summoning her guard. "You must find Mr. Malloy right away!"

FRANK NEEDED TO tell one more person that Peter Dudley was dead, but he'd been having a difficult time locating Amos Potter. He wouldn't have been quite so determined if he'd gotten a better reaction from Maurice Symington. He'd fully expected Symington to act surprised at learning Dudley was dead, but he hadn't expected the act to be quite so convincing. Symington was behaving normally in first trying to get Dudley in trouble for supposedly blackmailing Letitia and then trying to bribe Frank to name Dudley as the killer, and finally by trying to convince Frank to rule all three deaths suicide. Why hadn't Frank been satisfied with calling Blackwell's death a suicide in the first place? Calvin Brown would still be alive, and Dudley wouldn't be dying. Frank could've saved himself a lot of trouble and the other two a lot of suffering if he'd just gone along with the killer's plan in the first place.

And who would thank him even when he *did* find the killer? Assuming he could, that is. Nobody but Sarah Brandt, that's who. Which was, Frank had to admit, quite enough, thank you very much. It had better be, too, because he was likely to make some powerful enemies if he wasn't careful. Or even if he was. Whoever said honesty was the best policy had never been a policeman.

The hour was growing late, and the city was growing dark when Frank climbed the stairs to Potter's flat once again. He was there earlier in the day, but Potter hadn't been home. He was going to try once more, having left the man a note saying he'd be back, before giving up for the evening and finding himself some supper.

The smells of cooking filled the stairwell, making Frank's stomach growl. He thought longingly of a meal eaten in Sarah Brandt's pleasant kitchen. Thank heaven that was out of the question tonight. She had other obligations, and Frank knew it was time to stop seeing her anyway. No good could come of it, as his mother would have pointed out to him if he'd allowed her to speak of Sarah Brandt at all. But tonight he wouldn't even need to make a decision about whether to go to her place or not.

Potter's door opened seconds after Frank knocked. He'd obviously been waiting for the policeman to arrive. He still wore his suit coat, and as usual, he was fiddling nervously with his watch chain. "Come in, Mr. Malloy," he said too jovially. "What can I do for you? Your note was very mysterious."

"I wasn't trying to be mysterious," Frank said, taking the chair Potter indicated. "I just had some news for you that I wanted to give you in person."

"Have you finally decided to close the investigation?"

he asked hopefully. "Although it pains me to think a boy could actually kill his own father, I don't really see any other solution to this unfortunate incident."

"I'm afraid there's been another murder, Mr. Potter," Frank said, watching the other man's face carefully.

And just as carefully, Potter betrayed no emotion except a mild curiosity. "I can't imagine who—" he began, then caught himself. "Good heavens, it can't be! Is Letitia all right?" he asked worriedly.

"She's fine," Malloy assured him, although he would have sworn Potter wasn't really worried about her.

"Then who . . . ?"

"Peter Dudley."

Potter frowned. "Peter . . . ? Oh, yes, that gentleman I met at Letitia's the other day. He's dead, you say? Whatever happened to him?" He didn't seem too upset, but then why should he be? Dudley was nothing to him, except perhaps a rival for Letitia's affections.

"Someone stabbed him."

"Good heavens! I don't know what the world is coming to. I never imagined I would know *three* men who died under unpleasant circumstances."

"Why not?" Frank asked. "Once a killer gets started, it's difficult to know when to stop."

"You can't imagine this Dudley's death is connected to Edmund's in any way," Potter protested. "They didn't even know one another. Why would the same person want to kill them both?"

"Why else would Dudley have been killed?" Frank asked in return. "He was just a simple bank clerk."

"I'm sure I don't know," Potter sniffed. "Besides, we both know that Edmund's killer is dead by his own hand. It's only your stubborn refusal to admit it that has kept us from putting this whole awful business to rest."

Frank saw no point in arguing the issue with Potter, who was determined to blame Calvin for the crime no matter what the evidence said. "Mrs. Blackwell was very upset to learn Dudley was dead," he tried.

He struck a nerve there. Potter's round, homely face reddened, but he said, "I believe they were good friends. And it's always upsetting to hear about a violent death. I'm upset myself, and I hardly knew the man."

He hadn't looked upset until Frank mentioned Letitia's reaction. Now he was fiddling with his watch chain again and looking as if he wanted to bolt. Probably he wanted to rush to comfort Letitia.

"Mrs. Blackwell was more than just good friends with Dudley," Frank said, still probing for a reaction. "She and Dudley were planning to be married."

"That's preposterous!" Potter exclaimed, jumping to his feet. "Her husband is hardly cold in his grave! Besides, she'd never marry a man like that. He's nothing but a bounder and a fortune hunter."

"I don't suppose she'll marry him now that he's dead, of course," Frank agreed mildly, "but she certainly intended to before. She'd even informed her father of her plans."

"Mr. Symington never would have allowed it," Potter insisted.

"I'm not sure he could have prevented it," Frank said. "Mrs. Blackwell is of age and no longer dependent on him."

"But . . . but . . ." Potter stammered. "I know he . . . He simply would have stopped it. Made her see reason or . . . or whatever it took."

"Such as killing Dudley?" Frank suggested.

Potter's small eyes grew as wide as they possibly could. Was it possible he hadn't considered this possibility? He sat down abruptly. "I . . . I can't believe . . . But surely, no one would blame him if he did," he added quickly, warming to the thought. "I mean, to protect his daughter from this man who had tried to ruin her life and almost gotten her killed before."

"Do you think I should accuse Mr. Symington of killing Dudley?" Frank asked curiously.

Potter gaped at him. "Certainly not! A man in Mr.

Symington's position would never stoop to such a thing! I was merely remarking that no one could blame him for *wishing* such a blackguard as Dudley out of his daughter's life for good and all."

"Death *is* pretty permanent," Frank agreed.

Potter was growing impatient with this conversation. "Is there some reason you came here tonight besides to inform me this Dudley person has been murdered?"

"You mean have I found out who killed Dr. Blackwell yet?" Frank asked.

"I already *know* who killed Edmund," Potter insisted. "For the love of God, when will you stop torturing poor Letitia and allow her to grieve in peace?"

Frank rose wearily to his feet to take his leave. "Very soon, I hope," he said. "Although now we won't be sure for whom she's actually grieving, will we?" he added meanly.

Potter frowned, but he had nothing more to say and made no move to detain him.

As Frank descended the stairs and emerged from the building into the darkened city, he tried to make sense of all his impressions. Amos Potter acted like a man guilty of something. Maybe it was just lusting after his neighbor's wife, but Frank's instincts said it was more than that. If only Potter hadn't offered him a reward for finding Blackwell's killer. Could he have been so confident of Frank's incompetence to believe Frank would never trace the crime back to him? Or had he made the offer to *ensure* that Frank wouldn't trace the crime back to him? It seemed a risky ploy. Or a masterful one. Frank had not allowed himself to consider Potter as the killer until now. Could he have been fooled so easily? Or was he letting his dislike of the man color his judgment?

What he needed was a square meal and some fresh air to clear his head. Maybe then he'd be able to put all the pieces together and figure out the truth of all of this.

• • •

OFFICER MORAN HAD been gone a long time in his quest to find Malloy. Sarah didn't know how long, because she hadn't noticed the time when she'd sent him off on his errand, and in the meantime her lapel watch had stopped. She knew from the sounds of the city that the hour was growing late, though. Decent people were asleep, their windows dark. Those on the streets at this hour were assumed to be up to no good. A woman walking out now would automatically be assumed to be a prostitute. A man alone would be fair game for robbery or worse.

Sarah watched from the small window of Dudley's room. She couldn't see the street from here. The view was of the back of the opposite buildings and the small patch of ground in between where outhouses squatted and clotheslines stretched, crisscrossing the open space like a massive cat's cradle. One by one, the lights of the other buildings blinked out, gradually obliterating even the poor view she had. The sounds of the house quieted, too, as the other tenants either went to bed or went out to prowl on this Saturday night.

Too bad she hadn't thought to bring a book to read, although reading by the light of the single candle in Dudley's room would have been difficult. About all she could hope was that she would somehow fall asleep sitting up in the straight chair as Dr. Woomer had done earlier.

Just when she was giving serious thought to waking the landlady to ask for bedding to make herself a pallet on the floor, Dudley groaned again. This time Sarah didn't wait for him to ask for water. She took it to him and helped him drink his fill. His color looked a little better, but he was still dangerously weak.

"Mr. Dudley, can you hear me?" she asked. He was probably ready for some more morphine.

"Where . . . am I?" he asked, blinking at her as if trying to focus on her face.

"You're in your rooms in your lodging house. Do you remember what happened?"

"No, I . . . I'm hurt," he said in surprise.

"Someone stabbed you while you were asleep."

"Someone *stabbed* me?" he asked in disbelief. "Who would want to do that?"

Sarah could think of several people who might want to dispose of him, in addition to the person who actually had tried to, and was surprised Dudley couldn't, but she said, "Don't think about it now. Is the pain very bad?"

He winced. "A little," he admitted.

She fixed him another dose of morphine. Fortunately, he didn't ask her what it was, so she didn't have to lie. Considering his experiences with Letitia's morphine addiction, he might not want to take it if he knew.

"There now, you'll feel better in a few minutes. Just try to get some rest. Could you eat something?"

"No, I . . . No." He closed his eyes, and Sarah thought the drug had started to work and he was asleep, but after a while he said, "Letitia."

Sarah thought he might be dreaming, but his eyes were open again, and he looked alarmed.

"What about Letitia?" she asked, wondering if he'd realized someone had wanted him dead because of her.

"Does she know? About me, I mean? She'll be worried."

Sarah couldn't help wondering just how worried Letitia would really be, considering Malloy was going to tell her he was dead. "Mr. Malloy went to see her," Sarah said. "I'm sure he'll tell her that I'm taking care of you."

That lie didn't seem to comfort him. "She'll be very upset. She isn't strong, you know," he confided. "And she's so afraid."

"What is she afraid of?" Sarah asked, wondering if she should encourage him to talk. As his nurse, she should let him rest. But if she didn't let him talk now, he might not get another chance, and the morphine would be taking effect soon.

"She's afraid of everything," he said. "And everyone."

"Her husband?" Sarah asked curiously. "Did he abuse her?"

Dudley shook his head impatiently. "He suspected she was taking morphine again. He wouldn't permit it."

"She told me he searched her rooms," Sarah remembered, "so she couldn't keep any in the house. That's why she had to go to the opium den."

"She was worried about the baby," he said.

"She had a right to be. Her baby could have died," Sarah said, feeling the outrage all over again.

"No, not that. Mr. Fong said the baby would be fine. She was afraid . . . when the baby came . . ." His voice trailed off, and he closed his eyes again. The morphine had begun its work.

Sarah stood there a moment, watching him to make sure he wouldn't awaken again while she tried to think of what else Letitia might have been afraid. When the baby came, he'd said. What more could she have feared? Dying in childbirth? It was an understandable fear. Or maybe she was afraid that Blackwell would realize he wasn't the baby's father.

Sarah heard footsteps in the hallway. Someone was moving quietly toward Dudley's room, but no one could move silently in this house because of the squeaky boards in the old flooring. It must be Malloy, at last, and she could show him what she'd found. She'd just set the bottle of morphine on the bureau as the door opened.

But her visitor wasn't Frank Malloy.

Amos Potter stared back at her, even more surprised than she.

"What the . . . ?" he began, and then he saw Dudley lying on the bed. "He's not dead!" he cried. He turned on Sarah, furious. "Malloy lied! He's still alive!"

"No thanks to you," Sarah said. "I found your key, the one from your watch fob. You must have lost it in the struggle." The one she'd seen him fiddling with time and again.

"Where is it? Give it to me!" He started looking around frantically, and Sarah instinctively felt her pocket where she'd put it for safekeeping.

Seeing the gesture, he lunged for her, but she was too quick for him, knocking over the chair as she dodged. He stumbled over it but managed to catch her arm.

"It's too late!" she cried, struggling to break free. "Malloy already knows!"

"No, he doesn't! He has no idea, or he never would've let me go tonight!" He caught her other wrist, and for a moment they grappled, Sarah scratching and clawing, Potter trying to reach the pocket of her skirt where she'd hidden the Phi Beta Kappa key.

Finally, it occurred to her to scream, so she did, as loudly as she could.

Potter started, but she'd only distracted him for a moment. He released one of her hands and grabbed for her pocket, but she drew back her free hand and boxed his ear. The pain, she knew from her medical training, was excruciating and could even cause deafness. Potter howled, flinching and releasing her other hand in reaction.

This time she lurched for the door, wondering vaguely why no one had yet come to her rescue. She'd taken only one step, however, when she came up short. Potter had grabbed her skirt. She heard the stitches at her waistband starting to pop. In another moment the fabric would give, but he might well overpower her before that. Then she saw the broom leaning against the wall where she'd left it. With one burst of strength, she threw herself at it. She felt her skirt giving at the waist and heard the rending of the fabric, and then her hands were on the broom.

Taking no time to think or to aim, she simply swung it as hard and as fast as she could. The wooden handle struck solid flesh, and Potter grunted, but he was on her again, too close for swinging. Almost without thinking, she drew the broom handle back and lunged toward Potter as he lunged toward her, meeting him with the handle aimed squarely at his midsection.

His gasp told her she had struck home. He went down in a heap, his face working furiously as he struggled, in vain, for breath. She only had a moment, she knew, so she gave him one more whack on the side of the head, just for good measure. If he was stunned, she'd have a bit of extra time.

As Potter lay poleaxed in a heap on the floor, Sarah snatched up her medical bag and dug down for a roll of bandages. In a matter of moments she'd tied Potter's hands behind his back, and by the time he finally succeeded in drawing a full breath, she was binding his ankles just as securely.

"You . . . tried . . . to kill . . . me!" he said breathlessly.

"That's funny coming from someone who's killed two men and tried to kill a third," Sarah said, using her considerable skill at bandaging to make sure Amos Potter wouldn't be able to work himself free before Malloy turned up. "I only knocked the wind out of you. There's a place right here," she said, giving him a playful punch that made him whimper. "It's called the solar plexus. It drives the breath right out of you. You think you're dying, but you aren't really hurt at all."

"I didn't kill . . . two men . . ." he gasped.

"You're wasting your time, Mr. Potter," Sarah told him cheerfully. "It's plain as day. You killed Dr. Blackwell for heaven only knows what reason, probably something to do with his wife, and then you tried to convince Mr. Malloy that young Calvin had done it and killed himself out of remorse. Except you botched the suicide note—"

"But Malloy didn't find the note!" he exclaimed.

Sarah smiled. "Malloy said only the killer would know about the note," she told him triumphantly.

Potter moaned, but whether from pain or despair, Sarah couldn't tell.

"And then you tried to kill poor Dudley because you didn't want Letitia marrying him after you'd gone to so much trouble to make sure she was free," Sarah concluded.

"You're wrong," Potter warned her. "About everything. You'll never prove a thing."

Sarah didn't bother to reply. She got to her feet and tried to examine the damage to her skirt. "I'm going to have to send you my dressmaker's bill, Mr. Potter," she said as she tucked the damaged garment up as best she could. "You've seriously damaged my gown."

This time he didn't reply, although his glare was rather eloquent.

She righted the chair and sat down to wait for Malloy. She knew they wouldn't *have* to prove Potter had committed the murders. By the time Malloy was finished with him, he would gratefully confess to everything. She almost felt sorry for him until she remembered poor Calvin Brown, who had died so needlessly for another man's stupid obsession.

Sarah listened to the silence in the house and realized that still no one had come to her aid. "Where is everyone?" she asked of no one in particular.

"They're either out or they're drunk," Potter said in disgust. "How do you think I got in here without anyone seeing me?"

And how else could he have attacked Dudley without drawing any attention? she realized.

"I'm very uncomfortable," Potter tried after a few minutes.

"It could be a lot worse. Just be glad you aren't dying of arsenic poisoning," she said sweetly.

After that, he didn't say a word until Malloy finally clumped up the stairs nearly an hour later. He actually swore when he saw Potter lying trussed on the floor of the tiny room. Then he looked around before finally settling on Sarah again.

"Where's Moran?"

"I sent him to find you."

He seemed relieved. "So he was the one who did this," he determined, indicating Potter lying on the floor.

"Oh, no," Sarah assured him. "I figured out Mr. Potter was the killer, and I sent Officer Moran to find you. Then Mr. Potter came back to find his key and—"

"At least tell me *Dudley* helped you," he begged.

"Mr. Dudley is hardly in any condition to exert himself," she pointed out. "Besides, I didn't need any help. Mr. Potter really doesn't have much imagination as an adversary, although he did tear my skirt," she added, remembering.

Malloy looked like he might tear something of Potter's. "He laid hands on you?" he demanded, outraged.

"He was trying to get this away from me," she said, reaching into her pocket and withdrawing the key she had found under Dudley's bed. "I found it when I was cleaning up. He must have lost it in the struggle with Dudley."

Malloy's face lit with understanding. "That's what was bothering me about him this evening. He kept fiddling with his watch chain, but the key was gone. He must have noticed it then." He turned back to Potter. "Is that what happened?"

Potter simply stared back, refusing to answer. Malloy had no patience for stubborn felons. He gave Potter's kneecap a gentle kick.

Potter howled in pain again.

"Is that what happened?" Malloy asked again. "You realized you'd lost the watch fob here and came back to get it? You must've figured the room would be empty by now. We wouldn't leave a dead body lying around very long, would we? How about a civil answer, Potter?" he added, preparing to issue another stroke of persuasion.

"Yes, yes," Potter said quickly, before Malloy could administer any more blows. "I noticed it was missing. I knew if you'd found it, you would have arrested me when you came to my flat tonight. All I had to do was come back here and retrieve it, and you'd never connect me with Dudley's death."

"Except Dudley isn't dead," Malloy pointed out. "And you attacked Mrs. Brandt and tore her dress. I don't have much respect for a man who'd do something like that."

"I didn't hurt her!" he exclaimed frantically. "I only tried to get the key from her. She was the one who attacked me!"

Malloy considered Potter's current condition for a long moment before turning back to Sarah. "You have to tell me how you did this."

She shrugged, it had been nothing at all. "A broom handle to the solar plexus."

"The what?"

"Solar plexus. Right here." She pointed. "One blow and the person is incapacitated for a short period of time."

Plainly, this came as no surprise to him except for one thing. "How would *you* know something like that?"

Sarah gave him a smug smile. "There are things I know about the human body that would astound you, Malloy."

"No doubt," he said, thumbing back his bowler hat in amazement. "Even still, you're lucky he didn't hurt you, and Dudley, too, for that matter. What were you thinking, sending Moran off like that?" He sounded exasperated, but not really mad.

"I never thought about Potter coming back here. Why should he, if he thought Dudley was dead? In any case, no harm done." She smiled again.

He didn't smile back. Plainly, he thought a lot of harm had been done, or at least could have been. "What about Dudley? How's he doing?"

"He's sleeping. Morphine," she added as an explanation.

"Good for him." He turned back to Potter, who had been listening avidly, probably hoping Malloy had forgotten about him. "I don't suppose you'd like to tell me about killing young Calvin, now would you?"

"I didn't kill anyone," he insisted.

Malloy glanced at Sarah, trying to determine how far he could go without incurring her displeasure or arousing her distaste. Probably not far enough, he judged, and turned back to Potter. "You know, I really liked that boy. He had a lot of guts coming to New York to find his old man. If you'd just stuck with Blackwell and Dudley, I wouldn't feel quite so strongly about this case, but the boy's death really bothers me. Lucky for you, Mrs. Brandt is here, so I can't ask the kind of questions I'd like to. But don't worry, I'll call for a wagon and take you down to the station, where we can talk in private about everything."

Malloy's mild tone didn't fool Potter. The mention of the station house made his eyes widen. Sarah knew she should disapprove of Malloy's methods, but she had also been fond of Calvin Brown. His killer deserved whatever Malloy saw fit to give him.

"Will you be all right here while I go find a call box?" Malloy asked her.

She gave him a pitying look, not bothering to remind him she'd been perfectly fine without him up until now.

He went out, muttering to himself.

16

As Frank had expected, by the time he got Amos Potter into the bowels of the Police Headquarters building, he was white with terror. The noises and the smells were horrible enough, but seeing the derelicts and bums being dragged in, bloody and broken from their earlier encounters with police on this busy Saturday night could turn a strong man's stomach. Amos Potter was not a strong man.

Frank had hauled him into one of the basement interrogation rooms, shoved him into one of the chairs, and closed the door behind them with a decisive slam. Potter sat there fairly trembling, his eyes stretched wide.

"Don't hurt me," he pleaded. "I'll tell you whatever you want to know."

"Do you still deny that you stabbed Peter Dudley?" he began pleasantly. "Bearing in mind that Mrs. Brandt found your watch fob under his bed and that Dudley will most likely identify you when he comes to."

"I . . . Yes, I must admit that, I suppose. I mean, I did, of course," he clarified at Frank's frown of disapproval.

"And exactly why did you think it was necessary to dispose of Mr. Dudley?" Frank asked.

Potter took a moment to consider his response. "A lady's reputation is at stake here, and—"

"I already know that Dudley is the father of Letitia Blackwell's baby, so you can forget protecting her," Frank informed him.

Potter's neck reddened, but he managed to maintain what little was left of his dignity. "I believe that he was trying to convince Mrs. Blackwell to marry him."

"A bit late, by my reckoning, but so what if she did?"

Potter seemed shocked. "Don't you understand? It would be scandal enough if she remarried anyone so quickly after Edmund's death, but as soon as people saw him and . . . and the child . . ."

"I understand the baby bears a striking resemblance to his father," Frank said.

Potter sighed. "Even if the red hair were merely a coincidence, it would be remarkable. People would assume the worst, regardless of the truth."

"And in this case, the truth *is* the worst," Frank reminded him.

Potter looked as if he'd like to defend Letitia's honor, but he refrained. "Letitia would be a laughingstock, her reputation ruined. She would be shunned in polite society."

Frank could think of worse fates, like being stabbed to death, but he said, "So you felt it was your obligation to murder Dudley and protect her from this fate worse than death."

Potter didn't appreciate his sarcasm, but he held his ground. "I can't expect you to understand, but this is the only life Letitia has ever known. She would be devastated if she were to be excluded from society."

"She would have had the man she loves to comfort her," Frank said.

Potter made a rude noise. "She didn't love Dudley. How could she? He was nothing and nobody."

"She tried to elope with him once," Frank tried.

"She was only an innocent girl then. Dudley beguiled

her. What kind of a man would steal a young woman away in the middle of the night against her family's wishes?"

Frank had wondered the same thing, and meeting Dudley for himself hadn't answered that question. The former schoolmaster still hardly seemed like the bounder and cad he would have had to be to seduce a young woman of good family into betraying everything she knew. Still, no one could deny that he'd done it, so he couldn't be the well-meaning clod he appeared to be.

"If she had married Dudley, she would have quickly regretted it," Potter was saying. "He had nothing to offer her except ruin. Someone had to protect her."

"Didn't you consider asking her father to do that?" Frank asked.

"Mr. Symington could hardly be expected to deal with a situation like this. He failed to protect her from Dudley before, and she almost died as a result. Besides, I didn't think he would . . ."

"He would what?" Frank prodded when he hesitated.

"I thought he might be squeamish about . . ." He made a helpless gesture with his hands.

"About doing away with Dudley permanently?" Frank suggested.

Potter nodded reluctantly. "Mr. Symington is a gentleman. How could he understand the determination of a man like Dudley? Even after nearly killing Letitia the first time, still he hunted her down and intruded on her life again. The man was relentless. I was afraid that if he didn't win Letitia this time, he might resort to blackmail or something worse in order to humiliate her. Nothing short of death would have stopped him from pursuing her."

Dudley hadn't struck Frank as relentless. Pigheaded, maybe, and foolish to a fault, but not relentless. Frank thought he just loved Letitia and wanted to be with her. But Potter didn't have the benefit of actually knowing Dudley, so he could be forgiven for making incorrect assumptions about him. But not for trying to murder him, of course.

"So you sneaked into Dudley's rooming house . . . How did you know where he lived?"

"I . . . I followed him home from his place of employment," Potter explained wearily.

"How did you know where he worked?"

"He told me, the day I met him at Letitia's home."

Frank nodded his understanding. Potter had showed some cunning but not enough to keep from being caught. "I guess killing a man with a knife was more difficult than you thought," Frank suggested.

Potter nodded gratefully. "Yes, it was! I thought I could stab him while he slept and he'd never even know what happened. But the knife wouldn't go in! And then he woke up and started to struggle. It was horrible!"

"I'm sure it was pretty horrible for Mr. Dudley, too," Frank reminded him.

Potter had the grace to flush. He lowered his gaze.

"All right, so I know why you tried to kill Dudley. It's no mystery why you killed Calvin, either. How did you get him to drink the arsenic?"

Potter raised his eyes. "I deeply regretted having to kill the boy. I know he never did any harm, but—"

"Potter, don't make me hit you," Frank warned. "And if you keep pretending you're sorry you killed that innocent boy, I might have to break your jaw. And a few ribs if I don't think you're repentant enough."

Potter swallowed nervously. "What do you want to know?"

"Just tell me how you did it," Frank said through gritted teeth. "And try not to say anything stupid enough to make me forget I want you in one piece until you've finished your confession."

"I brought him the sarsaparilla," he said quickly. "I told him it was a treat, to make up for how badly things had been going for him. He was very pleased."

"I'm sure he was." Frank restrained himself with difficulty.

"After he started getting sick, I helped him get to bed and offered to fetch a doctor. Then all I had to do was wait until he passed out. I'd already written the note, so I put it and the arsenic on the bureau. When everyone else in the house had gone to bed, I left."

Frank managed to hold his fury in a tight, white ball inside of him. He'd let it go in a minute, just as soon as he had the last of Potter's confession. "Now tell me why you killed Blackwell."

Now Potter looked really frightened. He swallowed again. "Could I have some water?"

"No, just start talking."

"Well, you know what Edmund had done. He'd involved Letitia in a bigamous marriage, and the scandal was going to break unless someone stopped Calvin Brown."

"I thought Blackwell was going to pay him off and send him away."

"Edmund thought that would be enough, but I knew that a blackmailer is never satisfied. The Browns would have wanted more and more from Edmund. You can't keep a secret like that for long, either. Edmund had enemies, doctors whose patients he'd been able to cure where they had failed. They would have been only too happy to expose him as a bigamist. They wouldn't care if they destroyed Letitia's life in the process."

"So you decided Blackwell had to die?" Frank asked incredulously.

"Don't you see? It was the only way! If he was dead, the Browns couldn't blackmail him. Letitia would be a respectable widow and . . ."

"And what?" Frank insisted.

Potter lifted his chin defiantly. "She would have had people who truly love her to look after her best interests."

"Like you?" Frank suggested.

"I will always be Letitia's devoted servant."

Frank managed not to choke. "I guess you knew Blackwell would be alone in the house that afternoon," he suggested.

"I knew he was going to meet with the boy. He'd asked me to help him get the money together, you see."

"That's right, you already told me that part. Did he also ask you to be with him when he met with Calvin?"

"No, I went there on my own, knowing he'd be alone. I tried to convince him once more not to allow himself to be blackmailed, but he wouldn't listen to me. We quarreled bitterly, but I still couldn't persuade him. I could see reasoning with him was hopeless, so I reached into the drawer where I knew he kept his pistol."

"How did you know that?"

"He'd shown it to me on several occasions. Having a gun for protection is only effective if people know you have it, Mr. Malloy."

"Did Blackwell think he needed protection from you?" Frank asked with interest.

"I don't believe he did," Potter replied stiffly.

"So you pulled out the gun. Wasn't Blackwell sitting right there at the desk? Didn't he try to stop you?"

"I don't suppose he thought I was any danger to him. In any case, he didn't do anything to stop me. He just sat there and . . . and stared at me. I knew what I had to do, so I pointed the gun at his head and fired." He looked at Frank expectantly, although Frank didn't know what he was expecting.

"Then what happened?" Frank asked.

"He . . . he slumped over the desk, just like you found him. And I left the house. No one saw me."

"What did you do with the gun?"

"The gun?"

"Yes, did you take it with you?"

"I . . . no, of course not, I . . . I must have dropped it. I really don't remember."

"Did you touch anything on the desk or in the room?" Frank prodded.

"I . . . I don't remember. It was so horrible. I think I just ran out."

"Didn't you take the money Blackwell had gotten to give Calvin?"

"Certainly not! I'm not a thief," Potter insisted, offended. Apparently, he felt he could commit murder but still maintain some integrity by not stealing from the dead man.

"Then what happened to the money?"

Potter looked genuinely baffled. "I have no idea. Probably one of your policemen took it. Or one of the servants. How should I know?"

Frank sighed. "All right, so you ran out. Where did you go?"

"Back to my flat. I . . . I waited awhile. Then I was going to go back to discover the body. I didn't want . . . Well, I certainly didn't want Letitia to find it."

"Of course not," Frank said. He'd proven he'd do almost anything to protect Letitia Blackwell from unpleasantness. Unfortunately, he'd also just proven he hadn't killed Edmund Blackwell.

SARAH HAD MANAGED a few catnaps during the night but nothing approaching real rest. Since the room was warm, she'd appropriated Dudley's blanket and made herself a crude pallet on the floor. She could have slept even in such uncomfortable conditions, but Dudley kept waking up from pain or thirst all night. She'd changed his bandages once when he'd opened one of his sutures, and just when she'd finally dozed off the last time, the landlady had come pounding on the door, demanding to know if Sarah wanted some breakfast brought up.

The next time Malloy needed a nurse, he could just hire one.

Dudley woke up moaning as the landlady delivered the breakfast tray.

"He ain't going to die, is he?" she asked Sarah. "I don't need nobody dying here. It's bad for business."

"I'll do my best to see that he doesn't," Sarah assured her. "I wouldn't want to inconvenience you in any way."

The sarcasm was wasted on the landlady, who just nodded her approval and left.

Sarah checked Dudley for fever. He seemed warm, but not too bad. No signs of serious infection yet, but it was still early. "You need to eat something," she told him when she'd examined his bandages. "Do you think you could manage it if I help you?"

"I don't . . . I'll try," he said. "It hurts, though."

"I don't want to give you any more medicine until you've tried to eat," she explained. "The medicine always makes you fall asleep too quickly."

He nodded and closed his eyes against the pain while she pulled the chair closer so she could feed him. Sarah had asked for soft foods, and that's what she'd gotten. Milk toast and something that might have been porridge.

He managed to swallow a few bites, and then he said, "Was I dreaming, or did you tell me that it was Mr. Potter who tried to kill me?"

"You weren't dreaming. He'd lost his watch fob in the struggle with you, and I found it last night, under your bed. Mr. Potter realized he'd lost it and came back looking for it. Since he thought you were dead—that's what Mr. Malloy told him—he thought it would be safe. Instead, he got caught."

She didn't see any point in telling him how she'd fought and overpowered Potter. She wasn't interested in impressing him, in any case.

"He was here?"

"Yes, you slept through the whole thing. Mr. Malloy took him away."

"And did you say that Potter had killed Dr. Blackwell and that poor boy, too?"

"I'm afraid so."

Dudley closed his eyes and shuddered slightly.

"If the pain is that bad, I can go ahead and—"

"No, no, I'm fine," he assured her, opening his eyes and managing a strained smile. He swallowed a few more bites before he said, "Don't let Letitia come here. I don't want her in this place."

Sarah couldn't tell him that Letitia still thought he was dead, so she was unlikely to try to visit him at all, but of course, Malloy would soon be informing her that her husband's killer had been caught and Dudley was, in fact, alive. Sarah couldn't help wondering if Letitia would then even *want* to visit Dudley. Sarah knew that if the man she loved had been lying grievously wounded, nothing could have kept her away, but she couldn't imagine that sort of devotion from Letitia Blackwell. But maybe she was doing the woman an injustice.

"I'm sure she'll want to arrange for a better place for you to stay when it's safe to move you," she said, hoping that, at least, was true.

"She will, but she probably won't think of it herself. She's really quite naive about things. That's why she needs someone to look after her. Blackwell never took proper care of her."

Which was, of course, why you felt obligated to commit adultery with her, Sarah thought, but of course she didn't say that. "Oh, yes," she said instead, not above a little shameless gossiping, even if it involved a dead man. "You started to say something last night about her being afraid of Dr. Blackwell. Was he abusive to her? Did he hurt her, I mean?"

"Not that I know of," Dudley said, taking another bite. When he'd swallowed, he added, "But there are other ways to hurt someone besides hitting them. He had forced her to give up the morphine. You can't imagine how horrible that was for her."

Sarah could well imagine it, having seen others going through the same agonizing process.

He swallowed another bite. "And then he made her

speak at the lectures, even knowing how terrified she was. She did it for him, because she was so grateful to him, but he never appreciated it. No wonder she turned to the morphine again."

"I suppose she was also concerned about her husband finding out about you and the baby," Sarah suggested.

Dudley frowned as he swallowed the next bite. "I don't think she was afraid of that so much. Blackwell paid hardly any attention to her at all, except that he . . ."

"That he what?" Sarah asked, trying to appear only mildly interested.

"Well, he disapproved of the morphine use. Actually, I don't think he cared about Letitia's health as much as he was worried that if she was taking the morphine again, it would reflect badly on his cure of her. He suspected that she was using it again, but of course he never found any proof because she was careful not to keep it in the house."

"Is that what she was so afraid of?" Sarah asked. "That he would find out and make her stop again?"

"It would have killed her," Dudley said, growing agitated. "You must understand, she just couldn't go through that again."

"I understand completely," Sarah assured him. Few people could endure such an ordeal even once.

"She tried to describe the pain to me, but I don't think I can even imagine what it was like. She was simply terrified he'd put her through that again. She was so terrified that I even thought . . ."

"What did you think?" Sarah prodded when he hesitated.

He smiled sheepishly. "You'll think I'm a cad."

Sarah already thought so, but she said, "You can't shock me, Mr. Dudley."

"I hate to admit it now, since I know it wasn't true, but I was actually afraid that Letitia might've killed Dr. Blackwell herself. That's how frightened she was that he would discover she was still using morphine."

"Oh, my, that is unchivalrous of you," she agreed, even as a chill stole up her spine at the very thought.

"If you could have seen her that day when she came to Mr. Fong's, you'd forgive me for believing it, though," he defended himself. "She was on the verge of hysteria. She'd quarreled with Blackwell, you see. He'd accused her of using morphine again. She'd denied it, of course, but it was an ugly scene. And she knew that when the baby came, she wouldn't be able to get out for several weeks. She'd have to keep the morphine in the house then, and if Blackwell found it . . ."

"I can certainly see why you were worried," Sarah agreed sympathetically. She couldn't help wondering how sympathetic Letitia would be if she were to learn of her lover's suspicions, however.

"I can't tell you how relieved I am to hear it was Mr. Potter all along," he was saying.

"I guess you forgot that Letitia was with you when Dr. Blackwell was killed, so she couldn't have done it."

"She was, of course, after their quarrel. But I couldn't help thinking . . . Well, no matter. None of it matters now, does it?"

Sarah supposed it didn't.

FRANK HAD BEEN looking forward to going to the Blackwell home to tell the widow her husband's murder had been solved so he could be finished with this case. Of course, he'd get no reward now. Potter was hardly likely to make good on his original offer, and Symington had only wanted to reward him if he proved Dudley was the killer. On top of all that, he'd have to tell Symington and Letitia that Dudley wasn't even dead. Not only would Symington be disappointed, they'd both be angry because he'd deceived them. Still, having the case over would be something to savor. He never wanted to see any of these people again.

Unfortunately, the case wasn't over.

No matter how much Frank wanted it to be true,

Amos Potter hadn't killed Edmund Blackwell, and his confession had proved it. First there was the problem of how Potter got the gun in the first place. Hard as he tried, he couldn't imagine anyone allowing another man, a man with whom he was supposedly quarreling, no less, to reach into the desk drawer at his very elbow to pull out a gun without trying to stop him. To make matters worse, Blackwell would hardly have just calmly kept on writing his letter while Potter raised the gun and pointed it to his head.

Potter had made no mention of trying to make the death look like a suicide afterward, either. He hadn't known Blackwell was writing a letter when he was shot, and he hadn't mentioned laying the pistol down beside him to make it appear Blackwell himself had used it. Most of all, he hadn't mentioned replacing the pen Blackwell had been writing with in its stand.

Probably he hadn't mentioned these things because he knew nothing about them, and he knew nothing about them because he wasn't even there when Edmund Blackwell was killed.

Which left Frank with the task of explaining why a man would confess to a murder he hadn't committed. And why he'd commit a murder to cover that one up if he wasn't guilty of it in the first place, because he'd apparently killed Calvin Brown. But most importantly, Frank would have to figure out who had really killed Edmund Blackwell in the first place.

That probably wouldn't be too difficult, though. Potter had only confessed to protect someone, and Frank knew there was only one person he'd die to protect: Letitia Blackwell.

Frank figured he shouldn't be surprised to realize he'd once again underestimated a female. Sarah Brandt was always accusing him of doing just that. But even she had been fooled this time. As difficult as it was to imagine, Letitia Blackwell had blown her husband's brains out and then calmly kept an assignation with her lover.

Now all he had to do was convince the chief of detectives, the police commission, and Maurice Symington that sweet Letitia Blackwell should be charged with murder.

Sᴀʀᴀʜ ᴡᴀs ʀᴇᴀᴅʏ to commit murder herself by the time she heard Malloy's familiar footstep in the hall. Dudley had been sleeping soundly for quite a while now, and she was tired and stiff and hungry and very annoyed with having to tuck and retuck her torn skirt back into its waistband.

She threw open the door before Malloy even had a chance to knock and said, "Thank heaven you're here! You've got to find someone else to look after Dudley for a while so I can . . . What on earth is wrong?"

He blinked in confusion. "I thought you were going to tell me," he said.

"No, I mean what's wrong with you? You look like someone died."

"It's worse than that. Is Dudley awake?"

She glanced over. He hadn't batted an eye at Malloy's arrival. "He's in the arms of Morpheus."

"Who?" Malloy leaned around the doorway to look himself, probably expecting to see someone sharing the bed with Dudley.

"Morphine-induced slumber," she explained. "Come in and tell me what's happened. Didn't Potter confess?"

"Oh, he confessed all right," Malloy said as he came in and allowed her to close the door behind him. "The problem is, he isn't guilty."

"I know he's the one who tried to kill Dudley," she insisted. "I found the key, remember?"

"Well, he's guilty of that, and he most likely killed Calvin, damn his soul, but he didn't kill Blackwell."

"Why would he have killed the others if he didn't kill Blackwell? Did he try to deny it?"

"Oh, no, he confessed to that, too, but he's not the

killer." He explained to her about Potter's failure to explain Blackwell's murder accurately.

"Maybe he just forgot he did those things," she tried.

"Would you forget if you'd gone to the trouble to make someone's death look like a suicide and the police didn't believe it?"

She supposed he was right. "Then who ... ?" She glanced at Dudley suspiciously. "Do you think ... ?"

"I think Letitia Blackwell did it," he said.

She was surprised, but only for a moment. Then everything fell into place. "Dudley just told me this morning that she was terrified Blackwell would find out she was using the morphine and make her quit again. You can't imagine how terrible an ordeal it is to wean yourself off of an opiate."

Malloy nodded. "That gives me a better motive, then. I was having a hard time trying to figure out why she would've been driven to blow her husband's brains out just because he was a bigamist."

"I don't think she even knew that," Sarah said. "But Dudley also said she and Blackwell had a terrible argument the day he was killed. Blackwell accused her of using morphine again, but he hadn't been able to find any in the house. She was very careful about that, but she knew when the baby came, she wouldn't be able to get out for weeks. She couldn't go without the drug, so she'd have to keep a supply in the house. Blackwell was sure to find it."

Malloy nodded. "She was desperate, and the only way to protect herself was to kill Blackwell."

Sarah shook her head. "I still can't imagine Letitia doing something so ... so messy."

"I guess you haven't seen the things morphine users do when they can't get their drugs. It turns them into animals. Besides, for who else would Potter confess to protect? He must know, or at least strongly suspect, that she was the killer. That's why he killed Calvin, too, to protect her again."

"And why he tried to kill Dudley, so Letitia wouldn't marry a man he considered unworthy of her."

"I think he just didn't want her to marry any man who wasn't him," Malloy said. "He'd somehow convinced himself that she'd turn to him if Blackwell wasn't around anymore."

"Maybe he even intended to tell her he'd killed Calvin to protect her," Sarah speculated. "He might have imagined she'd be so grateful to him that she'd fall into his arms. Of course, he didn't know about Dudley's prior claim."

Malloy sighed wearily. He looked as if he'd gotten as little sleep last night as she had, and that was probably true. He'd been questioning Potter for most of it. "So I guess now I have to go see Letitia Blackwell."

"What are you going to do?" Sarah asked in alarm. "You aren't going to try to arrest her, are you?"

"I've been trying to figure that out all the way over here this morning. I was hoping you'd have an idea."

He looked so forlorn Sarah had an irrational urge to hug him. Fortunately, she resisted it. Poor Malloy would have probably fainted from shock at such an inappropriate gesture.

"Oh, dear," she said, automatically tucking in her skirt as she moved to the chair and sat down. "Give me a minute to think. Obviously, you can't arrest her. Symington would have your head. And no jury would ever convict her. The men in the jury box would probably all confess to the crime themselves just to keep her from going to jail."

"So do we let her get away with killing her husband?" Malloy asked, frustration thick in his voice.

"Heaven forbid! I just can't think . . . What would be a punishment for her if she can't go to prison?"

"Being ruined socially?" Malloy suggested.

She looked at him in surprise. "What made you think of that?"

"Potter. He said that's why he killed Calvin, to protect

Letitia's reputation in society. He was afraid the bigamy scandal would ruin her. Would she really care if no one ever accepted her again?"

"I'm sure she'd be crushed, but she'd have her morphine to comfort her. She might not even remember she was being shunned."

"What else would be a punishment, then? Taking her morphine away?"

"Her father probably wouldn't allow it. If he thought she was suffering, he'd give her whatever she wanted. No, there must be something else. Maybe . . ."

"Maybe what?"

Sarah considered. "It's a risk, but if we can convince her father that she really killed Blackwell, he might take some sort of action to make sure she never harmed anyone else. There is her child to think of, you know."

"You mean he might keep her locked away or something?" Malloy asked.

"I have no idea, but he's the only hope we have. He's arrogant and unreasonable, but if he was convinced Letitia had killed her husband, he'd do something about it. He wouldn't want to risk her doing anything else so shocking. He must already be annoyed with her about Dudley and the baby. This could force his hand."

"He'd probably at least keep the lovers apart."

"Yes, and we could even suggest that. I'd hate to think of them living happily ever after with two men dead because of them."

"It isn't much punishment for murder," Malloy said.

"At least people will know she did it. Some killers never even get that much punishment," Sarah said.

"I guess I need to set up a meeting with Letitia and Symington, then."

"You'll need me there," she said.

"Why?" he asked with a frown of disapproval.

Sarah gave him a pitying look while her mind raced for a credible reason. Fortunately, she didn't have to think very long to find one. "What if Letitia decides to faint or even refuses to see you? Are you going to go barging into her bedroom and confront her? Besides, I'm a woman. I can probably keep one step ahead of her reasoning process. That's something you'll never be able to do."

Apparently, this was the right answer. "Can you leave Dudley alone for a while?"

"No, we'll have to find someone to watch him while I'm gone. And you've got to give me some time to go home and change. I can't go to the Blackwell house with my skirt half falling off."

"You need to do something to your hair, too," he said, making Sarah blink in surprise. Since when did Malloy notice her hair? "I'll go try to scare up Dr. Woomer. Won't hurt him to sit with Dudley a couple hours."

When he'd gone, Sarah realized with amazement that Malloy was willingly taking her with him to settle a murder case. Would wonders never cease?

17

SARAH HAD GONE OVER EVERY DETAIL OF THE CASE
with Malloy during the cab ride over to the Blackwell
house. They'd decided a hansom cab was better than
walking since they could talk without shocking any pas-
sersby.

"So you think the butler will say that Letitia was the
last one in the house that day," Malloy was saying as
the cab pulled up into Gramercy Park Square.

"I'm sure that's what he told me. She made certain
all the servants were out for the afternoon. She probably
didn't want her quarrel with Blackwell to be overheard."

"And we won't reveal that Dudley is still alive just
yet. I'll say he told me about the quarrel with Blackwell
when I questioned him several days ago," Malloy cautioned her.

"And don't forget to mention that Dudley thought she
killed Blackwell. That will shake her confidence."

Malloy looked as if his confidence had received some
shaking as he helped her out of the cab. This would be
a dangerous confrontation for him, she knew. Offending
a man as powerful as Maurice Symington could cost him
his job, and Symington could make certain he never

found another. For a moment she wondered why he had decided to take such a risk just on the chance that a killer might receive a slight punishment. And then she felt guilty. She would have done it, so why should she assume he would hold himself to a lower standard? Did she doubt his honor just because he happened to be an Irish cop? She knew better than that and felt the sting of guilt for doubting him, even momentarily.

Granger opened the door to admit them, his dignity severely taxed at having to be civil to them. "Mr. Symington and Mrs. Blackwell are waiting in the parlor," he said. Malloy had telephoned Symington that morning and arranged for the meeting.

Symington rose to his feet when they entered the room. Letitia looked up from where she sat on the sofa. She was dressed in something frothy and blue as a cloudless sky. Perhaps she'd decided to forgo widow's weeds since she now knew her marriage had been a sham. Or perhaps she just wanted to look lovely and vulnerable and found black did not suit her purpose this afternoon.

"This is very presumptuous of you, Malloy," Symington was saying as Granger closed the parlor doors behind them. "I trust you are as good as your word and that you've finally gotten this thing settled once and for all."

"Thank you for meeting with us on such short notice, Mr. Symington," Malloy said, not really answering the question or acknowledging the anger behind Symington's words. "Mrs. Blackwell," he added, nodding to her.

No one had asked them to sit, but Sarah took the chair opposite where Letitia sat in state on the sofa, her skirts spread artfully so no one could sit beside her. Malloy stood.

"Well, out with it," Symington said. "I haven't got all day."

"Amos Potter has confessed to killing Calvin Brown and stabbing Peter Dudley," Malloy said.

"Potter!" Symington echoed incredulously.

"Amos?" Letitia said. "That's ridiculous! Mr. Potter wouldn't hurt anyone! Besides, why should he want to harm Peter or that poor boy? He didn't even know them!"

"He wanted to harm Peter Dudley for the oldest reason in the world—he was jealous."

"Jealous of what?" Symington scoffed.

"Your daughter's affections," Malloy replied.

"What?" Symington cried. Letitia looked only mildly surprised. She was probably well aware of Potter's devotion.

"Mr. Potter fancied himself in love with Mrs. Blackwell," Malloy explained. "And he did not think Peter Dudley was worthy of her. He also wanted to protect her from the scandal that would have followed her marriage to Dudley. He believed people would at least suspect an adulterous relationship between them because of the baby's resemblance to Dudley."

Symington glared at Letitia. "I told you that's what would have happened," he said to her. "You're well rid of Dudley. He would've made you a laughingstock."

The color rose in her cheeks, but she kept her chin high. Sarah had to admire her for that, at least. Letitia turned to Malloy. "You said he also killed that boy, Edmund's son. Why would he do a thing like that?"

"Because he'd already tried to convince me that Calvin Brown killed Dr. Blackwell, so he poisoned the boy and left a suicide note confessing to the crime. He wanted to make me believe Calvin was the killer so I would close the investigation."

"Then he must have killed Edmund, too," Symington concluded. "Why else would he go to all the trouble to implicate the boy?"

"Because he was trying to protect someone," Malloy said.

"Who on earth would he have been trying to protect except himself?" Symington scoffed.

"Your daughter."

If Symington was stunned, Letitia was equally shocked.

"What was he trying to protect me from?" she asked with every appearance of innocence.

Sarah knew this was where her lighter touch was needed. Before Malloy could speak, she said, "I'm afraid that Mr. Potter believes that you killed your husband, Mrs. Blackwell."

Symington was blustering something about that being preposterous, but Letitia was just staring at Sarah in apparent fascination. "Why would he think a thing like that?" she asked with genuine interest.

This was where they were going to have to stretch the truth a bit. Sarah managed not to look at Malloy. They couldn't betray any sense of uncertainty.

"We know you quarreled with your husband the day he died, Mrs. Blackwell," Malloy said. "Peter Dudley told me that you were terrified he would find out you were still using morphine."

"Letitia," Symington said, outraged. "Tell him that's a lie!"

Letitia ignored him. "My husband and I often quarreled," she said. "If every woman who quarreled with her husband shot him in the head, there would be no married men left in the city."

"But you were afraid that if he discovered your secret, he would force you to quit taking the morphine again," Malloy continued. "You feared that more than anything in the world, from what Dudley said. He also said you were very upset when you met him that afternoon at the opium den."

"Opium den?" Symington nearly shouted. "What is this nonsense? I won't listen to another word of these lies about my daughter!"

"They aren't lies, Mr. Symington," Sarah told him.

"Mrs. Blackwell regularly met Dudley at an opium den uptown. She told me that herself, and the proprietor will attest to it," she added untruthfully, hoping Letitia wouldn't remember that Mr. Fong had already refused to vouch for their alibi and challenge her. "Letitia was forced to go there for her daily dose of morphine because Dr. Blackwell would not allow the drug in the house."

Symington looked to Letitia, expecting a denial, but all he got was silence. After a moment he sat down abruptly in the chair he had been occupying when Sarah and Malloy had come in. Sarah could see the understanding—and accompanying apprehension—coming to his face.

"Dudley even said that when he heard Blackwell had been killed, he believed you had done it," Sarah said to Letitia. "Because you were so upset that day when you met him at the opium den and because you were so afraid of your husband finding out about the morphine."

"And when your butler told Mrs. Brandt that you had personally sent the servants out of the house the afternoon Dr. Blackwell was killed, we knew that you were the last one to see him alive, and the one with the best opportunity—and most pressing reason—to have killed him," Malloy concluded.

Symington was blustering again, but with less enthusiasm this time. He was also watching his daughter with growing horror. Sarah was starting to feel uneasy as well. She wasn't sure what reaction she had expected, but it wasn't the secret, pleased smile now adorning Letitia Blackwell's lovely face.

"Are you saying that Mr. Potter and Peter Dudley both believe that I murdered Edmund?" she asked.

"I'm afraid so, Mrs. Blackwell," Malloy said, sounding genuinely apologetic. Either he was a better actor than Sarah had suspected or he really did regret accusing her of murder.

"And Amos Potter really killed that poor boy just to protect me?" she added.

"That's right," Malloy said.

Letitia stared up at the ceiling for a long moment, during which Sarah imagined she was contemplating her guilt and her chances for avoiding punishment. But when she lowered her gaze again, she said, "How diverting!"

"*Diverting?*" her father echoed in disbelief. "Is that all you can say?"

"Well, I suppose I could say that I didn't kill Edmund," she replied, still wearing that strange smile, "but surely you must know that's true, Father."

"Of course I know it's true! Malloy, is this the best you can do? Blaming a murder on an innocent girl? I'll have your job for this."

"Believe me, Mr. Symington, this gives me no pleasure, either," Malloy said, still truthfully. "I'd be more than happy to find out somebody else killed Dr. Blackwell, but it seems like all the other people who had a reason to didn't do it. And your daughter was the last one in the house with Dr. Blackwell before he died. She also had a very good reason for wanting him dead."

"But all you have is the word of the butler that she was the last one in the house." Symington sprang to his feet. "*Granger!*" he called, moving to the parlor doors and shoving them open. "Granger, get in here!"

In a moment the butler appeared, his dignity a bit ruffled by the unceremonious summons. "What can I do for you, sir?" he asked.

"On the day that Dr. Blackwell died, when did Mrs. Blackwell leave the house?"

"I . . . I can't be sure, sir, but I believe it was shortly after noon."

"Why can't you be sure?" Malloy asked. "Is it because you left before she did?"

"Uh, no, sir. I always wait until Mrs. Blackwell is gone before I leave for my afternoon off."

"But you told me Mrs. Blackwell made sure all the servants were gone before she left," Sarah reminded him.

"Well, she did," he said with a worried frown, "but I didn't actually leave until after she was gone."

"And why was that?" Malloy asked sharply.

He glanced at Letitia, as if asking silent permission. "I'm afraid I'm not at liberty to say."

"You'd better say, or I'll have to take you to Police Headquarters and ask you again," Malloy said impatiently.

Granger cast a pleading look at Letitia, who didn't seem to understand that he was silently asking her permission for something.

"Are you afraid of embarrassing Mrs. Blackwell?" Sarah asked him pointedly.

Granger straightened. "I would never do anything to harm Mrs. Blackwell," he said.

Finally, Letitia understood. "You may feel free to say whatever you wish, Granger," she assured him. "You see, Mr. Malloy is persuaded that I murdered my husband, so nothing you say can possibly hurt me worse than that."

"What?" Granger cried. "How could you believe Mrs. Blackwell capable of such a thing?"

"You would be amazed at what people are capable of when pushed beyond endurance," Sarah said. "And it seems that's what Dr. Blackwell had done to his wife."

"He was cruel to her, that's true," Granger admitted. "That's why I didn't leave the house that day. I knew he was angry about something, but she wouldn't go in to see him until she made sure the servants were out. She didn't want the servants to overhear, so I pretended to leave, too, but I stayed, in case she should need help."

"Why, Granger, how gallant of you," Letitia said with one of her glowing smiles.

Granger seemed to grow taller right before their eyes. "Dr. Blackwell was quite unpleasant and threatened Mrs.

Blackwell several times. She was very upset, but I assure you, he was still very much alive when she left the house. She couldn't possibly have killed him."

"How can you be so sure?" Malloy challenged him. "She may have known you were still there and pretended to leave so you'd say just that. How do you know she didn't come right back once you were gone and shoot him later?"

The blood seemed to drain from his face. "Because," Granger said, all his dignity still firmly in place, "I killed Dr. Blackwell."

SARAH FOUND MALLOY sitting alone on one of the benches in the hospital waiting area. Brian was being operated on today. He was surprised to see her.

"What are you doing here?" he asked, rising to his feet. He looked worried and like he hadn't slept well last night.

"Did you think I'd forget Brian's operation was today?" she scolded him, taking a seat on the bench beside him so he'd sit down again. "I would've been here sooner, but I had a delivery last night and wasn't able to get away until just now. Have you heard anything?"

"Nothing yet. He hasn't been in there long." He nodded in the direction of the operating room.

Sarah glanced around the sterile room with its worn benches and faded walls. "Isn't your mother here?"

Malloy gave her a pitying look. "She said if I wanted to butcher my son, she didn't have to go along to watch."

"Butcher?" Sarah echoed incredulously.

"She says she doesn't believe the operation will help him."

"Maybe she's afraid it will, and he won't need her so much anymore," Sarah suggested gently.

"He'll still be deaf," Frank reminded her.

There was no argument for that, so Sarah made none. "At least you can be sure Brian won't be butchered. I know Dr. Newton can help him. I wouldn't have told you about him if I wasn't sure of that."

Malloy nodded, plainly unwilling to speak about such a sensitive topic at the moment. He stared at the far wall for a moment, and then he said, "Have you seen Letitia Blackwell lately?"

"I visited her yesterday," she said, remembering with a smile. "I was afraid I might not be welcome after what happened, but she was actually happy to see me. Apparently, she's still very amused that you and I thought her a murderess."

"I'm glad she thought it was funny. Her father didn't."

"At least he wasn't angry," Sarah reminded him.

"Thanks to you," Malloy reminded her right back. "If you hadn't convinced him the whole thing was just a trick to make Granger confess, God knows what he might've done."

"I guess we're both lucky I thought of that," Sarah said. "So you're really convinced that Granger was the killer, then."

"He knew every detail of what happened. He'd asked Blackwell if he could take the pistol out and clean it, so Blackwell hadn't made any move to stop him. He just kept on writing his letter until Granger shot him. Then he carefully took the pen from Blackwell's fingers and set it back in its stand, laid the gun down, and left the house. Oh, and he took the money Blackwell was going to use to bribe Calvin with, too. Seems he's been using it to run the household since Blackwell died, because there wasn't any other money available in the household accounts. The only thing he regretted was that he hadn't gotten back to the house in time to discover the body himself."

"I suppose it was guilt over the murder that was making his stomach hurt instead of guilt over Letitia finding the body," she said.

"I don't know about that," Malloy said. "I don't think Granger feels guilty about the murder at all, and if he does, it's only because it caused Mrs. Blackwell an inconvenience."

Sarah sighed. "It's hard to believe that two men were willing to commit murder to protect Letitia Blackwell," Sarah mused.

"Are you jealous?" Malloy asked archly.

"Of what? That no man ever committed murder for me?" she asked in surprise. "Not likely."

Malloy looked like he didn't believe her, but she ignored the provocation. "What did Amos Potter say when you told him Granger had confessed to Blackwell's murder?" she asked instead.

"He was annoyed, I think. It seems we were wrong about why he killed Calvin, too."

"Wrong? How could we have been wrong?"

"Because Potter didn't kill Calvin to cover up Blackwell's murder. Well, at least that wasn't the main reason."

"What was the main reason?" Sarah asked, mystified.

"To keep me from questioning Blackwell's patients."

"Clients," Sarah corrected automatically. "Why on earth would he care about that?"

"Because he wanted to continue Blackwell's business. If I offended the *clients* by accusing them of murder, they wouldn't be likely to seek out Amos Potter's services."

"They wouldn't have been likely to do that anyway," Sarah reasoned, but Malloy just smiled sadly.

"Amos Potter didn't know that. He also didn't know who had killed Blackwell, but he wanted the case settled quietly and with no unpleasantness that would harm his future business."

"But surely he was also trying to protect Letitia," she argued.

"That's another thing we were wrong about," Malloy told her.

"Don't tell me he's not in love with Letitia!" she exclaimed.

"Oh, yes, very much so, but he wasn't concerned about a scandal ruining her. He lied about that. In fact, he was the one who sent Calvin's mother the poster of Blackwell's lecture and the train ticket so Calvin could come to New York and find his father. Potter was *hoping* for a scandal that would ruin Blackwell and drive his clients away and ruin Letitia's reputation. It seems he was more realistic than either of us realized. Potter knew she'd never be interested in him if she had any other choice, and he also knew Blackwell's patients would never come to him unless Blackwell was discredited. He hoped the bigamy scandal would bring him both things at once."

Sarah stared at him in amazement. "It does sound logical in a strange way," she admitted. "But then you were going to offend the clients with your investigation, so he had to put a quick end to it by killing Calvin. How awful."

"I'll never forgive myself for not sending him home when I had the chance."

"You couldn't have known," Sarah reminded him. "And you didn't hurt him, Potter did."

He didn't look convinced. Sarah knew the guilt of having needlessly caused another's death, so she didn't press him on the subject. "How's Dudley doing?" she asked instead to change the subject.

"Still alive, last I heard. You might want to stop in and see him while you're here. I doubt his lady love bothers to visit him in a place like this."

"I still can't believe they sent him to the hospital," Sarah said in disgust.

"Did you expect Letitia to take him into her house?" Malloy asked with a grin.

"No, but she could have made arrangements for a private nurse in a better lodging house or something. Anything would be better than lying in a charity ward."

"I figured Symington put him in the hospital hoping

he'd die. You saw how disappointed he was when I told him Dudley was still alive."

"Letitia wasn't exactly happy, either," Sarah said. "Apparently, her father had convinced her that protecting her reputation after Blackwell's murder was the most important thing she could do, and a dead Dudley could never embarrass her. Do you think she'll ever marry him now?"

"You're the one who understands female reasoning," he reminded her with a smirk. "You tell me."

"I don't understand this," she admitted, "but I have a feeling Mr. Dudley will be retiring to the country with a broken heart."

"He should be thankful it's still beating, at least. He got off a lot luckier than the other men who were involved with Letitia."

"I got a letter from Mrs. Brown," Sarah told him. "She appreciated the nice things I said about Calvin. Poor woman. What will she do now?"

"She'll make out somehow," Malloy said. "What other choice does she have?"

Sarah didn't feel like being philosophical today, so she let that pass as well. They sat in silence for a few minutes, waiting as people do when they have no other choice. Sarah thought about the sad things that had happened to so many people as a result of Edmund Blackwell's lies and wondered what kind of a life Letitia's baby would have without either of his fathers and a mother who was more interested in her morphine than in him.

Malloy interrupted her thoughts. "Doc Woomer knew your husband."

"Yes," she said, a little surprised by the change of subject. "Tom knew most of the other doctors in the city, I suppose."

"I asked him what Dr. Brandt was like," he said, and cleared his throat. "It sounds like he was a good man."

For a moment Sarah remembered Tom completely—

his deep voice, his laughing eyes, his big, gentle hands, but most of all his kindness to even the most unworthy or unlovable. The memory was so real it took her breath with the bittersweet shock of love and loss. Then, just as quickly, it was gone, and she was alone again with Frank Malloy.

And Malloy was even more real, solid with his strength and his determination and his unbreakable will. Different from Tom in so many ways she could hardly count them all, but still, somehow, the same.

She reached out and laid her hand on his. His skin was warm and alive beneath her palm. "You're a good man, too, Malloy."

AUTHOR'S NOTE

I hope you enjoyed *Murder on Gramercy Park*. The more I learn about the turn of the last century, the more I understand how little things have changed in the past hundred years. The wonders of technology have improved our quality of life, but they haven't changed the things people care about and are willing to live—and die—for. In spite of all the advances in medicine, people are still searching for something that works better through alternative, herbal, and holistic medicine and are still seeking to escape the problems of this world through the use of narcotic drugs.

Please let me know what you thought of this book and the others in the Gaslight Mystery Series, *Murder on Astor Place* and *Murder on St. Mark's Place*. Please write to me at the address below or send me e-mail through my Web page:

www.victoriathompson.com

Victoria Thompson
PO Box 638
Duncansville, PA 16635